Beryl Kingston was born and brought up in Tooting. After taking her degree at London University, she taught English and Drama at various London schools, as well as taking some time away from teaching to bring up her three children. She now lives in Sussex with her husband.

Beryl Kingston's five previous novels, HEARTS AND FARTHINGS, KISSES AND HA'PENNIES, A TIME TO LOVE, TUPPENNY TIMES and FOURPENNY FLYER, are also available from Futura.

D1324994

Also by Beryl Kingston in Futura:

BERYL KINGSTON

Sixpenny Stalls

Futura

A *Futura* Book

First published in Great Britain in 1990 by
Macdonald & Co (Publishers) Ltd
London & Sydney

This Futura edition published in 1990

ISBN 0 7088 4432 4

Reproduced, printed and bound in Great Britain by
BPCC Hazell Books
Aylesbury, Bucks, England
Member of BPCC Ltd.

Futura Publications
A Division of
Macdonald & Co (Publishers) Ltd
Orbit House
1 New Fetter Lane
London EC4A 1AR
A member of Maxwell Macmillan Pergamon Publishing Corporation

To Caroline

The Easter Family Tree

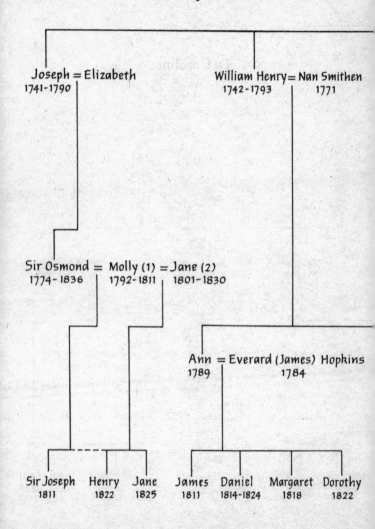

Joseph = Elizabeth
1741-1790

William Henry = Nan Smithen
1742-1793   1771

Sir Osmond = Molly (1) = Jane (2)
1774-1836   1792-1811   1801-1830

Ann = Everard (James) Hopkins
1789   1784

Sir Joseph   Henry   Jane   James   Daniel   Margaret   Dorothy
1811   1822   1825   1811   1814-1824   1818   1822

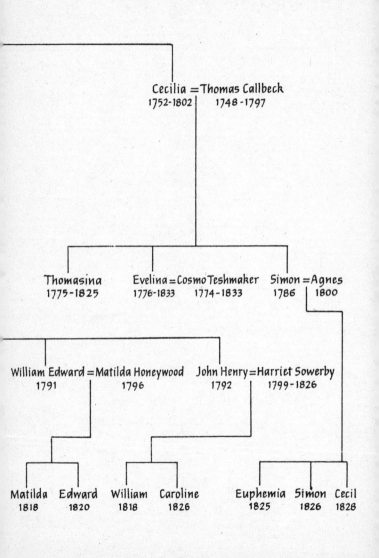

Cecilia = Thomas Callbeck
1752-1802 | 1748-1797

Thomasina
1775-1825

Evelina = Cosmo Teshmaker
1776-1833 | 1774-1833

Simon = Agnes
1786 | 1800

William Edward = Matilda Honeywood
1791 | 1796

John Henry = Harriet Sowerby
1792 | 1799-1826

Matilda
1818

Edward
1820

William
1818

Caroline
1826

Euphemia
1825

Simon
1826

Cecil
1828

Chapter 1

'Mr Burdock looks just like Humpty Dumpty, don't you think so, Papa?' Caroline Easter said, grinning across the breakfast table at her father. 'All your dinner guests are jolly funny, aren't they, but Mr Burdock is the funniest. He's such a pompous ass.'

It was just after eight o'clock on a dark December morning two days before Christmas and the dining room was miserably cold, for snow had been falling steadily since two in the morning, and although the fire had been lit at six it was hardly giving out any heat at all. Their breath was clearly visible in the chill air, steaming before them with every word, and poor Papa looked positively grey. A little joke about one of his awful dinner guests would cheer him up.

But this one didn't. He sucked in his breath in that sharp, snorting way that showed he was cross. 'Caroline!' he rebuked. 'That is no way for you to talk about a gentleman.'

'Why not?' she said, fighting back at once. 'It's true.'

'It's unseemly,' her father said, two deep frown lines scoring his forehead. He was shocked to hear such words coming from a child, but he remained calm, because he was always calm. It was important to him to be in total command of himself and his situation. He was renowned for it, Mr John Henry Easter, Managing Director of the great firm of A. Easter and Sons – Newsagents, the man in command. 'Come now, I cannot allow you to say unseemly things at my breakfast table. You are ten years old, miss, not a baby. Make some effort to behave yourself properly, if you please.'

9

'I *always* behave myself properly,' Caroline said, determined not to be put down by his stern tone, 'I am an Easter.' She was very proud of being a member of the great Easter family, and now, sitting opposite her father on the other side of his fine oak table, she certainly looked it, for her face was bold with defiance.

'Then pray try to act like one,' her father said. 'You should know by now that you cannot say whatever you please. As an Easter you should exercise a little more decorum.' If only she could have been more like her dear dead mother; if only she could listen to him patiently now and then and admit her faults instead of arguing back all the time. These constant battles were very wearing.

'I *do* exercise decorum,' Caroline said. 'I do too.' Her voice rang sharp as cut-glass in the chill of the room. Really, Papa was being quite ridiculous to make such a fuss over a little joke. Her grandmother would have laughed out loud at it.

'It is neither decorous nor kind to describe any gentleman as a pompous ass,' her father said, frowning at her, 'and certainly not this particular gentleman. Mr Burdock owns some of the most popular newspapers ever published in this city. He puts a deal of trade the way of Easter & Sons. He ain't a man to be mocked.' And yet he *was* pompous. The child was right. As she so often was, in that alarmingly forthright way of hers. It made correcting her extremely difficult.

'I don't mock him, Papa,' Caroline said, sticking her chin into the air. It was such an abrupt, determined movement it made her dark ringlets bounce against her cheeks. 'He doesn't know what I said about him. Nobody heard me except you. So how could I be mocking him?'

'That is not the point,' John Easter said, maintaining his calm with considerable effort, because her defiance was so provocative. 'Nobody should have heard you at all. It isn't the sort of thing a well-bred young lady would ever say.'

Her answer was immediate and infuriating. 'Nan says it.' Nan was her grandmother, who had brought her up ever since she'd been a tiny baby. Dear Nan, who took her to fairs and pleasure gardens and water sports, and played all sorts of marvellous games with her, when she wasn't in London overlooking the business, and treated her to pretty clothes, and a pony all of her own to ride about town, and two shelves full of books to read whenever she wanted. She adored her grandmother and missed her passionately whenever they were required to spend time apart. In Nan's nice warm dining room in Bury they both said all sorts of things about all sorts of people and nobody ever said they were rude or indecorous. They only laughed. Sometimes Nan would say, 'My heart alive, you *bad* crittur!' but always in tones of pure affection and approval. So why couldn't Papa be the same? After all, he *was* Nan's son, so he ought to resemble her, in one or two things at the very least.

'Yes,' her father sighed. 'I daresay she does.' The great Nan Easter was always saying things that would have been better left unsaid. Sometimes he wondered whether it had been altogether wise to allow her to bring up his two children after Harriet died. It had seemed the obvious solution at the time and Will had flourished in her care, but Caroline was becoming increasingly and infuriatingly independent, pitting her will against his on every single visit. 'I daresay she does.'

'Then I don't see why I shouldn't,' the child persisted.

'Because you are a young girl and she is a very old lady,' he explained, trying to be patient with her. 'Because she is your grandmother and the founder of the firm, and you are not. Because people make allowances for her, considering who she is, which they certainly wouldn't do for you. All of which you know perfectly well, so I wonder you argue about it.'

'I don't argue,' Caroline said defiantly, feeling rather put down by the weight of all this evidence. 'I made an observation, that's all. Miss Murphy says observation is the cornerstone of education.' Miss Murphy was her governess in Bury. 'Am I not to make an observation, Papa?' She looked straight at him across the table, grey eyes flashing, daring him to disagree with her.

'No, you are not,' he said, anger gathering in him despite his control. 'And especially in company.' When she defied him like this she looked like a goblin, indeed she did, dark and swart and glowering, despite her fashionable ringlets and that expensive woollen dress. That was his mother's doing too, he thought, scowling at it - rose pink and cream checks overprinted with scarlet flowers for a ten-year-old! No wonder she gets above herself sometimes. 'If that's the sort of observation you intend to make, you had better remain silent.'

'How long for?' she asked, and the question was a challenge.

'For as long as I say,' he told her, ruffled despite himself.

'All day?'

'All day if need be.'

'Am I to remain silent when I come down to meet your dinner guests tonight?' the child asked. 'They'll think that *very* odd. I always talk to your dinner guests.'

She is deliberately provoking me, John thought, looking at her bold face. Why must she do it? There is no need to drag this quarrel into the evening. Why can't she accept that she is wrong, apologize, and have done with it?

'If you wish me to,' he said coldly, 'I will explain to them that you are in disgrace for ill-mannered behaviour and not allowed to speak to anyone in consequence. How would you like that?'

She wouldn't like it at all, and they both knew it, but she had no intention of admitting it and allowing him the victory. 'As you please,' she said calmly. ''Tis all one to me. I'll come down and sit mum as a statue if that's what you really truly want. But they'll all think it jolly peculiar, I can tell you.'

'Well,' her father said, trying to rescue them both from their impasse, 'we will see about that when the time comes.' She might be more amenable by eight o'clock in the evening. 'Come now, eat up your breakfast and let us have no more of this.'

Caroline put a forkful of bacon into her mouth and grimaced. 'It's gone cold,' she said.

'And whose fault is that?' he asked, speaking mildly and trying to tease her a little, in the hope that this time she could admit error and grow more reasonable.

It was a vain hope. 'Not mine,' she said coolly, looking him straight in the eye, daring him again. '*I* didn't start all this.' She had joined battle with him and there was no backing down. If he was going to insist on silence when she was supposed to be talking and everybody would expect her to be talking, then she would fight him to the end.

He was suddenly annoyed beyond patience. 'Enough!' he said, and now there was no mistaking the authority in his voice, nor the anger. 'I cannot endure any more of your rudeness, Caroline. You have been rude to Mr Burdock and now you are being rude to me. You will go to your room, miss, and stay there until you are in a better frame of mind and ready to apologize.'

'Very well, Papa!' she said calmly. And she folded her napkin very very slowly and with the most aggravating precision, laid it neatly beside her plate, glared at him and flounced from the room, red skirt swinging.

She even takes her punishment with a flourish, he thought, admiring her despite himself. She behaves as though *she* is punishing *me*. Which in a convoluted way she was. For despite her bad behaviour, he was excessively fond of her, even though he knew he would never have been able to tolerate her presence in his house all the time, and even though he looked forward to her visits with a mixture of pleasure and dread. She lightened the routine of a life that had become undeniably dull and unvaried since Harriet's death. And besides, she was a living reminder of her mother.

In repose she was very like Harriet, for she had the same heart-shaped face and her hair grew in the same attractive widow's peak in the centre of her forehead, but where her mother had been pale-skinned and gentle, with blue eyes and hair so fair as to be almost silver, Caroline was dark-skinned and turbulent, with eyes the colour of storm clouds and thick curly hair so very dark brown as to be almost black, and unlike her mother, she was very rarely in repose. She was a springtime creature, that was the trouble, brightly coloured, strong tempered, quick and unpredictable, a creature of strong sunlight and sudden showers, and although the sunlight was warming, the showers could drench him with temper before he had a chance to prepare himself for them.

Sighing, he walked across to the fireplace to ring the bell for his man servant. She had taken away all his appetite, wretched child, he thought, as he positioned himself on the hearthrug with his back to the coals. Now he would have indigestion for the rest of the day. And the fire was giving out no heat at all. Even when he stood right in front of it with his heels on the fender and his coat-tails lifted high in the air, he could barely feel any warmth at all.

13

'Ah, Tom,' he said to his valet, when the young man opened the door, 'I shall be leaving for the Strand in ten minutes. Is my greatcoat ready?' He was pleased to notice that his calm was almost entirely restored.

'Yes, sir,' Tom Thistlethwaite said, 'and yer gloves and yer muffler, what I've took the liberty a' laying out. And two rugs fer the carriage today, sir. Snowing like billy-oh it is. Sky's full of it. Can't be too careful, eh sir?'

'There's no heat in this room at all, Tom.'

'Leave that ter me, sir,' Tom said at once. 'I'll 'ave that fire going a treat by the time you gets back. Was there anythin' else, sir?'

'Ask the housekeeper if she would be so kind as to see me for a moment,' John said. There were last-minute instructions for the dinner party to attend to before he could leave the house and set out for the comfort of his office in the Strand.

'She'll be with you in a jiffy, sir,' Tom promised, and went bustling out to make sure that she was.

Above his head, Caroline stood beside her bedroom window looking out at the falling snow and the white mound that was all that was left of the garden in the middle of Fitzroy Square. The bare trees were furred with whiteness and so were the railings, which looked coal-black through the curtain of falling flakes, and the cobbles below her were covered with such a thick layer of snow that they appeared quite smooth. She was shiveringly miserable at being treated so unfairly, and the cold air blowing in underneath the window and the depressing dowdiness of the bedroom were making her feel worse. I'm like a poor caged bird, she thought, a poor caged bird in a dirty cage.

There was nothing young and lively in the room except her and the fire. It had been a splendid room once, so people said, decorated in pink and gold and all ready for Will when he was born, but it hadn't been redecorated since, and Will was eighteen years old and up at Cambridge. Now the ceiling was ochre, and the once-pink fringes that edged the long curtains were an unpleasant dirty grey, and the wallpaper was faded to a dowdy monochrome, patterned here and there with a darker dirtier brown like old tobacco stains. It depressed her just to look at it.

Papa doesn't care about anything except his work, she

14

thought mutinously, watching him as he climbed into his carriage, stooping against the cold. He doesn't care about me or he wouldn't be so beastly. He doesn't understand how I feel and he doesn't care. Only Nan understood, and Nan was miles away in Bury St Edmunds.

The thought of her grandmother brought a wave of home-sickness so intense it was like nausea. No, she thought, why should I stay here in this dull house and be shamed because I've spoken the truth? It's not fair. I was only trying to cheer him up. I'll go to Bury, that's what I'll do. I'll go to Bury this very minute. The snow was falling quite heavily now, the flakes swirling in such profusion she couldn't see the square, but it was only snow. She wasn't afraid of snow. She'd put on her warmest clothes and her embroidered mantle and her nice new boots and her fur bonnet and her fur muff and she'd go to Bury.

She was dressed in ten minutes and out in the square in twelve, having crept down the stairs while the servants were busy cleaning the dining room, and let herself out of the house so quietly that the front door gave the merest click. I am like a caged bird, she thought, thrilled by what she was doing, escaping from captivity and flying home to my nest. It was exciting and romantic.

But bitterly cold, for a sharp north-east wind was blowing straight at her across the square and the snow was falling so thickly that her mantle was studded with it in seconds. There was nobody else about, although she could hear the muffled sound of horses' hoofs and a carriage creaking somewhere just out of sight.

She tucked both hands into her muff and began to run, slithering a little where the snow had been flattened by earlier feet, but moving as quickly as she could, partly to keep warm and partly to get away from the house before somebody saw her. It was the first time she'd ever been out on her own in the London streets and she knew it was improper to be walking abroad unchaperoned and that her father wouldn't approve, and the excitement and release of it filled her with energy.

But she had barely reached the corner of Fitzroy Square and Grafton Street when she heard somebody calling her name. 'Miss Caroline! Miss Caroline Easter!'

She turned her head at once, fearful but ready to defend herself, and found that a two-horse chaise was scuffling to a halt behind her and that she was looking up through the snow into the eccentric countenance of one of their next-door-neighbours, old Mr Fazackerly, who claimed to be 'an illustrator, me dear' but according to Cook had never been seen drawing anything in all the time he'd lived in the square. He was sitting above her in the driving seat, wrapped in a dilapidated rug from his armpits to his knees, and wearing an ancient topper brimmed with snow. He looked even odder than usual, for his wild grey hair was so wet it was sticking to his forehead and his long nose was the colour of port wine and his horsy face was a peculiar greyish-yellow. But he turned out to be a friend in need.

'No weather to be out walking, me dear,' he said, taking out a large pocket handkerchief and wiping the end of his nose with a brisk movement to and fro as though it were a bell he was trying to ring. 'And all on your own too. Where are you off to? I'm on me way to the city to see about a commission so I am. Can I give you a lift?'

'I'm going to Ludgate Hill, to the Belle Sauvage,' she told him, 'to catch a coach to Bury.'

'To meet your father, doubtless,' he said. 'Bury for Christmas, eh.' And when she didn't deny it, 'Hop aboard. I'll have you there in a jiffy.'

Which he did, or if not in a jiffy, at least in commendable time given the state of the roads and the age of his horses. 'What luck I was passing, eh?' he said as they creaked along Tottenham Court Road. 'Pull that rug right up under your chin, me dear.' And when they reached the entrance to the coach yard he helped her down most gallantly, as though she were a princess, and wished her 'Bon voyage!' before he creaked off into the snow again.

Now *that* was the proper way to treat an Easter, Caroline thought, as her boots touched the snow. Dear Mr Fazackerly. He's an omen, that's what he is, a good omen, a sign that this will be a great adventure. And she went trotting off to the booking office, which was full of bulky passengers and loud with argument. The clerk, who was small and sharp, stood his ground behind the counter like a terrier before a herd of buffaloes, barking to right and left that he couldn't make the coaches run, not nohow, not he, and that he only had one pair of hands *if* you please gent'men. And the buffaloes snorted and grumbled and shook the snow from their thick coats and stamped their feet in the puddles they were making.

Fortunately Caroline was used to dealing with irate gentlemen. She'd heard enough of them bellowing in her father's house at dinner time not to be afraid of their noise. She pushed herself through their greatcoats until she was standing in front of the counter. 'I want a seat on the next coach to Bury, if you please,' she said.

The clerk stopped barking and smiled at her. 'Well now, Miss Easter,' he said, 'that's something I *can* manage, Bury being a different matter altogether by reason of there being no proper hills thereabouts, you see, what *some* people don't seem capable of understanding. On your father's account was it, miss?'

'Yes please.'

'Leaves in eight minutes,' the clerk said as he wrote out her ticket. 'Just nice time.'

And sure enough the Bury coach was ready for the off, with ostlers at the horses' heads and most of the passengers already aboard. There were three people inside and two bundled in rugs aloft. But, as the coachman was explaining loudly to two gentlemen in green top-hats, there was no possibility of making a start while the Oxford coach was still blocking his way. 'He don't think a' the rest of us, not he, not that one. Stay here all day, we can, for all he cares.'

The Oxford coachman stood beside his bulky vehicle as though he were guarding a gate. 'I ain't a-taking no coach through the Chilterns today,' he said stoutly. 'I done it once, an' once is enough. You ain't seen the state a' them hills. It's a wonder we wasn't killed comin' through them hills.' He'd been complaining about it ever since he'd eased his snow-laden coach into the yard at a little after six o'clock that morning. 'Them roads is treacherous.'

Although there was less snow falling here in the shelter of the courtyard, it was foul underfoot, for the cobbles were awash with brown slush, horse dung and dirty straw. Caroline clambered up into the Bury coach at once, holding her mantle close to her knees to keep it as clean as she could. There was dry straw on the floor of the coach and one narrow seat still available squashed beside a very fat lady in a very damp cloak, and opposite two lugubrious gentlemen, one dressed entirely in brown and the other entirely in green, and both steaming like kettles.

'Just in time,' the brown gentleman said kindly, as the post-boys folded up the steps and shut the door.

'If they ever pluck up enough courage to make a start,' the fat lady said, 'which don't seem at all likely to me, I must say, Mr Grinder.'

'They are doing their best, my love,' Mr Grinder said. 'You must allow that, Mrs Grinder. They are doing their best.'

'Such a fuss about a little bit of snow,' the fat lady said. 'Such babies.'

'In all fairness, my love,' her husband murmured, 'it ought to be admitted that it is quite difficult to control a coach and four in bad weather, and this bids fair to be very bad weather.'

'Babies,' the fat lady said contemptuously. 'Blethering babies the lot of 'em. Give me the reins, that's what I say, and you wouldn't hear so much about snow.' She gave a splendidly derisive sniff and turned her attention to Caroline. 'Where do you hope to travel, my dear?' she said. 'Always allowing that they actually manage to get this coach out of the yard.'

'To Bury, ma'am, to my grandmother.'

'Who lives in Bury, I daresay?'

'Yes, ma'am. On Angel Hill. She is Mrs Easter, the news-agent.'

Mrs Grinder was impressed, as people always were when Nan's name was mentioned. 'I know the lady,' she said. 'By sight, of course. Mr Grinder and I live in Bury too, you know. A very great lady I believe.'

'Yes, ma'am,' Caroline agreed happily, 'she is.'

'Do you travel alone, my dear?'

'Yes, ma'am.'

'All alone?' Mrs Grinder said, swivelling her face towards the child and opening her eyes wide, like a plump barn owl.

'Yes, ma'am, all alone.' How thrilling to be able to say such a thing.

'There you are you see, Mr Grinder,' the fat lady said with

18

great satisfaction. 'You see how the world changes. It is 1836 now, my love, and not the Middle Ages. If Mrs Easter the newsagent, who is a very great lady, will allow her own grand-child to travel alone all the way from Ludgate Hill to Bury St Edmunds, why then anything is possible.'

There was a commotion in the yard.

'Now what?' the brown gentleman said.

Caroline took her hand out of her muff and cleaned a little porthole in the steamy window beside her. 'They're moving the Oxford coach,' she said.

'Are we off then?' the fat lady said.

And off they were, their great wheels lurching through the slush, echoing under the arch, crunching over fresh-fallen snow in the street outside, past Mr Sparrow's, the tea dealer, and Mr Parry's the shawl manufacturer and the Italian warehouse, off on the road at last.

Now, Caroline thought triumphantly, as the pole-chains clinked and the coach rocked from side to side, my adventure is beginning.

Chapter 2

It went on snowing all through the morning, with a steady, muffling, three-dimensional persistence. By one o'clock, when John Easter's housekeeper, old Mrs Toxteth, took a little light lunch up to Caroline's bedroom according to his instructions, the downfall was so heavy it was as dark as evening. She had to send a housemaid to light the lamps on the stairs and landings ahead of her so that she could see where she was going.

She was surprised to find that the room was dark and empty. 'Drat the child!' she said to herself. 'Where's she gone?'

The answer was on a card propped against the mantelpiece. 'I have gone to Bury to be with Nan, signed Caroline Easter.'

Mrs Toxteth went downstairs at once to consult Mr Wickham the butler.

'There's no point in telling Mr Easter,' that gentleman said. 'Not yet awhile. Not when she might turn up here again. I can't see many coaches getting out in all this. We'll send Joe out to see what's what.'

So Joe the boot-boy was sent on a tour of the coaching inns to make discreet inquiries. It took him nearly two hours and when he finally returned, his mouth was blue and his nose red and the front of his jacket was a solid mass of frozen snow. But he was bright with bad news.

Miss Caroline had caught the mailcoach to Bury, he said, as the scullery maid skinned him out of his frozen coat and bundled him into a chair before the kitchen fire. 'Left at a quarter to ten, so they say, though how they done it I can't think. All the roads out a' London are blocked off, bar one, so they say. Mails ain't in from Dover, nor nowhere else fer that matter. Them as went out from St Martin-le-grand this morning ain't been heard of since. One got stuck in a drift ten foot high, so they say. St Paul's is snow all over, an' there's hosses fallen everywhere yer look. They was a-shootin' one in the Strand. His legs was broke that bad you could see the bones all a-sticking out the flesh. An' they've 'ad a navalanche in the south some place. I can't remember the name, Lemming or Lewes or some such. 'T'anyrate it knocked down more'n a score of houses so they say. Ever so many dead.'

'If you can't say nothing more cheerful,' Cook reprimanded, 'you'd better hold your tongue.'

'I was only tellin' yer,' Joe said, spreading out his hands to the blaze of the fire.

'Well, don't.'

'What will Mr John say?' the housekeeper grieved. 'He'll be worried out of his wits. It's enough to send the poor man into a fit. Whatever possessed her to go wandering off in this weather? Where can she be, the foolish child?'

The foolish child supposed she was on the road out of Sudbury, for that was the town they had left about an hour ago, but she might as well have been at the north pole. The cold was so extreme that there were sharp little icicles growing all around the windows inside the coach. It was dark and there was a blizzard blowing, and what with fresh snow falling thickly out of the unseen sky in one direction and fallen snow being swirled thickly into the air in another, there was such a tumult all around them it was impossible to see more than a few feet in any direction. The wind screamed above their heads and beat the sides of the coach with thunderous blows and made progress almost impossible. The horses could only manage to haul them forward intermittently and then at a very slow pace. It was worse than any journey she could ever have imagined. She was sick with cold and stiff with travel and beginning to feel anxious.

Not that she allowed any of her fellow travellers to know how she felt. No, no, no, of course not. No Easter would ever admit to being anxious in front of strangers. That would have been infra dig. And Easters were never infra dig.

They seemed to have been travelling for ever. It had taken them nearly four hours to get to the Saracen's Head at Chelmsford and that was the shortest leg of the journey. By then the two outside passengers were so cold they decided enough was enough and booked in at the inn 'until the weather improves' which the landlord declared 'uncommon sensible'.

But as soon as they'd eaten their dinner, Mrs Grinder decided to press on. 'We are not the sort of people to be daunted by a little snow,' she said firmly, when her husband quailed that they might consider staying in Chelmsford themselves. 'What *is* snow, when all's said and done? Frozen water, that's all snow is. And where's the harm in that, I should like to know?'

They were to discover the harm in it during the next six terrible hours as the weather worsened and the day darkened and they grew steadily more and more chilled and uncomfortable in their icicled carriage. At Braintree they took on two extra horses because the coachman said four weren't sufficient, and several extra lanterns because by then the gale was blowing strongly and it was very dark indeed. But their team of six found the going as hard as four had done and fell into a walk whenever the coachman wasn't whipping them. And the gale became a howling blizzard. And now they seemed to be stopping again.

'Blethering fools,' Mrs Grinder was saying into the darkness, when there was a rushing, crunching sound so near and so loud that they could hear it above the wind. The horses screamed and the coachman swore and the coach gave a lurch to the left and fell over sideways, tossing them all down together against the icicled window.

Caroline found she was lying with her face pressed against the rough cloth of somebody's greatcoat and with somebody's hand clutching her about the neck. The darkness was total and terrifying and full of squirming flesh and frantic voices. 'Dear God!' 'Oh, stop! Stop!' 'What is it?' 'Are you all right?' 'Deuce take it all!' She realized that Mrs Grinder was squealing, on a high-pitched incessant note like a stuck pig, and she could just make out the shape of an open mouth and the gleam of broken teeth a matter of inches below her. She struggled free, bracing her spine, grabbing at the now-sloping edge of the seat, treading on the bodies underneath her, and stood up as well as she could, bent-backed and leaning forward to keep her balance.

The window below her was smashed, and snow was tumbling into the coach like white light to heap across the tilted seat and speckle the wriggling half-seen bodies of the two gentlemen and Mrs Grinder, who were writhing and heaving in the darkness like some terrible black-limbed octopus.

Caroline was filled with revulsion at the sight of them. I must get out, she thought, panic rising in her throat. I can't stay squashed in here with all these awful bodies or I shall suffocate. But how could she escape? One door was jammed tight against the ground and the other was tilted into the air. And Mrs Grinder was still squealing, which was making it very difficult to think.

Caroline pushed and scrambled to the upper end of the seat, where she clung to the strap with one hand while she struggled to open the door with the other. It was terribly heavy and when she finally managed to push it into the air it swung back on her almost at once, jarring her arms. But she held on grimly, pushing it open again, and with one last effort swung both legs out of the coach.

The snow drove against her face so strongly that for a few seconds she was blinded by it, seeing nothing but the sharp, black spikes of the flakes that were stuck to her eye-lashes. She brushed them away, on the back of her gloves so as to avoid getting her fingers wet, and peered into the murk again, aware that the lantern was still alight beside the door. But even so, her vision was obscured, for the light it gave was flickering and limited and the snow was swirling so violently around and below her that she seemed to be gazing down into a thick grey-white mist.

'Coachman!' she called into the howling air. 'Help! Help!'

There was a dark movement in the mist and a shape moved into the yellow light of the lantern, a stout, dependable shape, wearing the coachman's flat dependable hat and his nice broad-shouldered cape. 'Jump!' he yelled at her. 'I'll catch you, never fear.'

She jumped, at once and without thought, dropping into the mad air with her arms stretched towards him as though they were wings, as the wind screamed and the door crashed shut above her. And despite the force of her fall and the unsteadiness of the snow beneath his feet, the coachman caught her, just as he'd promised, and held her against his nice warm bulk for a few comfortable seconds until she'd found her feet and her balance.

'What happened?' she shouted, as he glanced up at the coach again.

'Drift,' he told her briefly. 'Come straight down from that there field above us. Watch yer step. There's more to fall.' And he looked rather apprehensively over his shoulder at the space in front of the coach where the horses should have been standing. There was no sign of them in the swirling snowfall, although Caroline could hear frantic whinnying and the guard's voice soothing, 'Whoa there my beauties. Whoa there.'

The coach door creaked open again and they both looked up and there was the dishevelled head of the gentleman in green sticking out into the void. His face shone silver behind the lantern as the snow veiled between them. 'Oh I say!' he said plaintively.

'Soon have you down Mr Johnson, sir,' the coachman called. 'Could you bring yourself to jump like the little girl, do you think?'

Mr Johnson mouthed words they couldn't hear and disappeared back inside the coach.

'Blamed fool,' the coachman said, narrowing his eyes against the snow and his annoyance. 'He'll have to jump come the finish. There's no way I can get up there.'

Caroline left him to it and began to edge her way round the coach to find out what had happened to the horses. The wind was blowing with such force that she had to lean forward to make any progress at all and the snow was so deep and untrodden that with every step she took she sank into it up to her knees. But at least she could see where she was going, for somebody had hung two lanterns on the topmost branches of a blackthorn bush that was still spiking up out of the snow, and in the pools of light they cast she could see the dark figure of the guard bent over the mounded snow, hard at work with a spade. She trudged towards him, brushing the snow from her eyes again and aware that her skirts were heavy with wetness and that her feet were so cold she'd lost all feeling in her toes, but what she saw next made her forget her own discomfort completely.

There had indeed been a snow-drift, and all six of their horses had been smothered by it. The guard was working feverishly to dig out the lead horse, who was buried up to his haunches and snorting with terror. He'd kicked his forelegs free and now he was putting up a desperate struggle to drag the rest of his body clear too, but the snow pressed and held and the more he fought it, the more he brought tumbling down upon him. His partner was in a worse state than he was, being buried up to his chest, and behind their heaving bodies, all that could be seen of the other four were straining necks, terror-strained eyes and flailing hooves. The weight of the fallen coach was plainly dragging them down and the pole had cracked in two. Caroline could see one broken end sticking up at a hideous angle among all those struggling limbs, just where it would be most likely to tear them. 'Quick!' she shouted to the guard. 'Have you got another spade?'

'By the lanterns,' he shouted back, without looking up or stopping his work.

Of course, she thought, pulling the heavy implement out of the snow. 'Where shall I dig?'

'Shift it back as I dig it out,' he said. 'We don't want to make another fall. Best keep clear of his feet. He's mortal feared.'

Even in the little light from the lanterns and with snow sticking to her lashes, she saw at once what was needed. For a few minutes the two of them worked together, he clearing snow in her direction, she flinging it as far behind her as she could. Despite the cold she was full of energy, charged with pity for the horses, fear of another snowdrift, and anger against that foolish Mrs Grinder, who was still in the coach, sobbing and wailing and making everybody feel afraid.

Presently Mr Johnson appeared beside her, dangling the third spade and red-nosed with cold, and the guard shouted instructions at him to clear a space alongside the wheeler. 'She's got her forelegs clear, d'ye see. Might jump if you could give her enough ground to take hold.' And the digging continued, endlessly, with occasional warnings yelled above the

25

wind, and falling snow filling the spaces up again even as they were shovelling them out. Caroline was beginning to think that they would never do any good no matter how hard they worked, when suddenly the lead horse was clear, struggling up out of his imprisonment, his sides heaving and scattering snow, as Mr Johnson held his head and the guard cut the traces.

Then all sorts of things happened. Mr Grinder and the coachman came puffing up to join them just as the second horse followed his companion out of the snow-pile. The poor creature was in a state of such terror that it took the combined strength of all four men to hold him, and the struggle went on for several very fraught moments, while he quivered and snorted and did his best to make a bolt for it. But at last he was still and the coachman went off to retrieve the two mail-sacks and to see if he could 'get that plaguey woman to stow her noise'.

'Follow the hedge below the high ground for as far as it goes,' he told the guard when he returned. 'It ain't much. Better'n nothing. Make for any light. There's bound to be beacons lit. Good luck!' The sacks were loaded onto the lead horse, and the guard wound his muffler tightly about his neck and across his nose, took a lantern, mounted and plodded off. They waved him goodbye, for he carried their hopes as well as the mail, and Caroline felt quite bleak as she watched the little swaying light move further and further away from them into the storm.

The coachman and the two gentlemen had taken up the spades again and returned to their digging and Caroline found herself with nothing to do. She was very very cold and very very tired and her back was aching as though it had been snapped in two, and even the fact that Mrs Grinder seemed to have stopped crying at last was very little comfort. I hope he's quick, she thought, shivering. But how could anyone be quick in such a storm?

After that, time and action were blurred by fatigue and snowfall. She watched the three men as they laboured to dig out the rest of the horses, and she got out of the way when the second pair were shivered out of the drift, and occasionally she stamped her feet to restore some feeling to them, and put her frozen hands into her muff or under her armpits, copying

26

the coachman, and now and then, when one of the gentlemen relinquished his spade, she was able to dig while he recovered his breath, which warmed her a little and took her mind off the storm for a few active minutes. But it was an endless, frozen time, and she felt cold to the innermost part of her body.

Presently the wind dropped and the snowfall eased a little and the lanterns gave more light, and now she could see the high field sloping above her. It was still thickly covered with snow despite the vast quantities that had fallen from it so treacherously, and she thought how beautiful it looked, so blue-white and smooth and mysterious, even though she knew it could have killed them all. But it hadn't killed them all, had it? They'd fought back. They'd outwitted it, and now there was only one more horse left in the drift, and sooner or later . . .

'Lights!' Mr Johnson shouted. 'Look there! Lights or I'm a Dutchman!'

And he was right. There *were* lights, a long wavering line of them, bouncing and swaying in the darkness, in an odd disjointed rhythm as though they were connected on a wire, at least twenty lights, a long way away, but clearly headed in their direction.

Mr Grinder went trudging off to tell his wife the good news. 'Mrs Grinder, my love, wake up. We are rescued.'

'Thought as much,' the coachman said with great satisfaction. 'A good lad is young Tranter. I knew he'd get through if anyone could. Meantime there's still this horse, Mr Johnson.'

Caroline climbed up onto the great upturned wheel of the fallen coach and watched the lights until they reached an invisible bend in their invisible road, where they bunched together and grew larger and larger until a great chattering company trudged into view, bright-eyed with lantern-light and exertion.

'What a mercy the snow's give over,' their leader said to the coachman. 'We've hung lanterns every quarter mile or so. You'll be safe as houses now, never fear. Name of Potterton, sir, landlord of the Bull Inn. We've brought a sledge for the ladies, and four strong boys to pull un.'

And strong they certainly were, for they managed to lift Mrs Grinder out of the coach, even though she was half asleep and complaining all the time.

Then there was so much bustle and movement that the shovelled snow was trodden quite flat for several yards all round the coach and the horses could be walked about to get them going again. Mr Johnson and Mr Grinder and the coachman packed up their spades and beat as much snow and ice from their clothes as they could, and Caroline was bundled into the sledge under several very smelly horse-blankets, crammed against the relative warmth of a grumbling Mrs Grinder with two carpet bags propped under her feet, and the procession began its homeward journey.

By now the wind was blowing from the east, or so the landlord said. 'There's another mercy, don't 'ee think, to have un blowin' with us.' His optimism was splendidly reassuring. 'We got a fine ol' fire waitin' for 'ee, don't 'ee fret.'

Caroline snuggled down under the blankets, eased her frozen gloves from her fingers and tucked her hands inside her muff, wincing a little because they were so cold and sore. There was no feeling in her feet at all and her wet skirts were chilling her legs, but the worst was over. She was on her way to that fine ol' fire, on her way to her dear dear Nan, on her way in a rocking soothing rhythm, on her way, on her way. She was fast asleep within minutes, and she didn't wake until the landlord peeled back the blankets ready to help her out of the sledge.

'Where are we?' she said, blinking up at him.

'Long Melford, miss,' the landlord said, 'and that ol' fire all a-waitin' for 'ee.'

It was marvellously warm in the Bull Inn, with the fire roaring and crackling in the hearth and hot soup steaming in a cauldron over the flames and pot-boys running to and fro with brandy and hot water. Mrs Grinder cheered up at once, and having despatched a boy to see to the disposal of her luggage, she kicked off her shoes, propped her stockinged feet on the fender where they were soon steaming most pungently, and embarked upon a long and highly imaginative account of their adventures, for the benefit of her busy and admiring audience.

'When that coach fell, I declare I quite gave myself up for gone,' she said between gulps of brandy and hot water. 'Quite gave myself up for gone. The torments I've suffered today simply beggar description. Beggar description. I'm bruised all over. Is there any more of this excellent brandy, Mr Landlord?'

'Lucky none of you was killed, mum,' the landlord said, replenishing her tankard. 'Never mind, you're safe and sound now, each an' every one. You can stay here the night and let the weather go hang. Beds is all aired.'

'It was the bull-dog spirit that pulled us through,' Mrs Grinder confided, as the soup was served. 'We may have been in mortal danger, Mr Landlord, but we never faltered. Never for a moment. We set to with our spades and dug out the horses with our own hands.'

The landlord murmured his admiration of her courage, but Caroline was fuming. 'The gentlemen dug out the horses, ma'am,' she said. 'I dug out the horses. You sat in the coach and screamed.'

Mrs Grinder waved her remarks away with one fat imperious hand, as though they were of no more consequence than the buzzing of a fly. The combination of extremely cold air followed by extremely hot brandy was mottling her fat cheeks with a sudden pattern of harsh purple. 'The bull-dog spirit,' she said, sighing with satisfaction at her remembered bravery. 'Were we not courageous, Mr Grinder? Did we not acquit ourselves with honour?'

He's going to agree with her, Caroline thought, watching the obsequious expression that was gathering on Mr Grinder's face. Oh, what a toady!

'Oh yes, my love,' Mr Toady agreed. 'The bull-dog spirit. Quite.'

'I'm off to bed,' Caroline said to the landlord. 'I can't stay here and listen to this. I shall eat my soup in my room. Is there a maid to lead the way and take my wet clothes? I got very wet *digging out the horses.*'

And she stomped up the stairs in high dudgeon.

It was warm in her little low-ceilinged room, for there was a fine fire burning in the grate and the maid got busy with a bed-warmer while Caroline ate her soup. But when her wet clothes had been stripped off and carried away to be dried overnight, the dirty dish had been removed, the lamps turned down to the merest bead, and she was finally tucked up warm beneath the covers, she couldn't sleep.

For the first time since she'd run out of Fitzroy Square she was thinking about the people she'd left behind. Poor Pa, she thought, he'll be wondering where I am in this storm. He'll be worried, not knowing. And although she'd left him that note to tell him where she was going, she wished there were some way she could send him a message now to tell him she was safe and warm and thinking of him. I wonder how long the storm will go on, she thought, listening to the wind howling outside the window. How will he get up to Bury if the coaches don't run? And as the fire crackled and spat, and the timbers of the old inn creaked and squeaked below her, she wished she hadn't run away. Poor old Pa, he'll be worried out of his wits. I'll write him a letter first thing tomorrow morning. Perhaps the mails will get through somehow. They always do.

But although she didn't know it, hers had been the last mail-coach out of London that day.

John Easter came home to Fitzroy Square late in the afternoon, squinting with worry. A. Easter and Sons had had a disastrous day. So few papers had been dispatched out of London that their losses would be severe, and as the weather showed no sign of improving, the newspaper proprietors had decided to cut down production, which would mean continuing loss of trade and profits in the days ahead. He had visited every coaching inn and railway station in the city, trying to find alternative routes out, but entirely without success. By mid afternoon even the new railways weren't running because the tracks were icy, and the coaches had packed up completely. He was so worried he barely noticed how cold he was, nor how slowly his carriage was travelling, nor what a hard time his bays were having struggling through the snow. And when Mr Fazackerly creaked up alongside him as he turned into Fitzroy Street, he did no more than nod him a vague acknowledgement.

'You didn't travel then, Mr Easter,' Mr Fazackerly shouted above the din of wheels and wind.

'Travel, Mr Fazackerly?'

'Aye. With the little girl. Your Caroline. I gave her a lift to the Belle Sauvage.'

'Caroline?' What was he saying? Caroline couldn't have gone to the Belle Sauvage.

'Yes indeed, sir. Your Caroline. I gave her a lift.' And then seeing how perplexed his neighbour looked, 'I trust that was in order?'

John Easter gathered his control and spoke courteously. 'Most grateful to you, sir. Uncommon kind.' But when the carriage reached his door he jumped down at once and took the area steps in one stride to find out what had happened.

He was so upset by what his housekeeper told him that he actually shouted at her. 'What were you thinking of to let her go? You should have stopped her. She was your responsibility.'

'I'm ever so sorry, Mr Easter,' Mrs Toxteth said, her face wrinkled with distress. 'We didn't know she'd gone, d'you see. She was that quiet.'

'In this snow!' he mourned. 'With every road out of London blocked. Every single one. She'll be stuck out in the country somewhere with no food and no money and no one to help her. Did she take any luggage?'

'Not that we could see, sir.'

'No luggage, no money, no food, all by herself,' John said. 'Whatever shall we do? Joe shall be sent out.' But he knew the boy would never be able to get out of London no matter where he was sent.

'Should we send out to cancel your dinner party?'

'What?'

'Your dinner party, Mr Easter sir. Tonight.'

In his anxiety he'd forgotten all about it. 'No,' he said, controlling himself with a visible effort. 'There is no need to inconvenience my guests. That would be impolite.' The dinner party would have to be endured. 'We cannot follow her tonight, not in this weather and with the roads blocked and icy. We are locked into the city. All of us. I've been trying to find a way out all afternoon and there isn't one. We are locked in and she is locked out. There is nothing we can do except wait.' And he sighed most miserably.

'Be better by morning pr'haps,' Mrs Toxteth hoped.

But daybreak brought no comfort at all. The heavy snowfall that had caused drifting on so many East Anglian roads the previous afternoon reached London at four o'clock in the morning and John woke to a blinding headache and a blinding snowstorm. The snow in the middle of the square was shoulder high, the steps and pavements thick with it, and the early traders slithering from door to door were awkward black shapes in the downpour, their street cries pitiful wails against the wind. There would be no possibility of travel that day.

That was the general opinion in Long Melford too.

'Best stay here till the weather clears,' the landlord said. 'We're well provisioned.'

Mr Grinder was finding the provisions uncomfortably expensive, but he knew they had no option but to stay, for as there'd been no snow falling when he got up he'd walked out to reconnoitre the village and had soon discovered that they were virtually cut off by snowdrifts.

'I must move on,' Caroline told her companions at breakfast. 'My grandmother will be wondering where I am. And my father will be travelling to Bury today. I can't stay here.'

'Nobody will be travelling anywhere today,' Mr Grinder said, buttering his toast. 'I can tell you that with absolute certainty, my dear. The roads are full of drifts, and there are no carts out and no horses either and very few people, if it comes to that. It will cost us a small fortune to stay here but I fear that is what we must do.'

'And more snow to fall if I'm any judge,' Mr Johnson said gloomily.

'And weak tea into the bargain,' Mrs Grinder complained, examining her cup. 'I do so hate weak tea.'

It began to snow again as they were finishing their meal, and it snowed steadily all day long, so Caroline didn't write to her father after all because there was no point in writing a letter if she couldn't send it. It was still snowing when they finally left the fireside at ten o'clock to yawn their way to bed.

But when day broke next morning the sky was clear. It was bitterly cold and the snow was mounded against every door and window, but the wind had dropped and the sky was clear.

Just before eight o'clock Tranter the guard came into the coffee room where they were all eating breakfast to tell the coachman that he'd hired the sledge and a nice good-tempered cob to pull it and that he was off to Bury St Edmunds. 'I'll get this ol' mail through, never you fear,' he promised. 'They've cleared a path out north and south, an' if no more falls I shall do well enough.'

Caroline made up her mind at once. 'I will come with you,' she said to him brightly.

That wasn't at all what he expected. 'Oh well now, Miss,' he said. 'I don't know about that.' Young ladies in embroidered mantles didn't go traipsing about the countryside with the mail.

'I'm strong,' she insisted. 'I helped you with the digging, didn't I? Very well then. I can help you drive the cob. Besides, I know the countryside. I was born and bred here.'

'My dear child,' Mr Grinder said, 'I admire your spirit, upon my life I do, but don't you think you are being a trifle foolhardy?'

'It's ridiculous!' Mrs Grinder said at once. 'You shan't go, child. It's unheard of.' She'd been impressed by Caroline's adventurous spirit when they set out from the Belle Sauvage, but since her outspokenness over the matter of bravery and digging out horses, she had quite taken against the child. Adventurousness was one thing. Insubordination was another. 'He won't take you.'

'Yes I will,' Tranter said, surprising everybody, including himself. He wasn't at all sure about the wisdom of allowing this child to travel with him, because she was only a young thing. But then he'd been walking long distances without harm ever since he was a child himself, so he knew how strong children could be. And besides he certainly wasn't going to take orders from the objectionable Mrs Grinder. 'Yes I will.'

'I'll be ready in two shakes,' Caroline said. And was.

Their departure was quite an event. Everybody in the inn turned out to wave them God speed, except for Mrs Grinder, and all along the high street people stared out of their windows and waved and nodded at them. And the little cob pulled his burden if not at a trot at least at a commendably brisk walk despite the snow, and Caroline was surprisingly warm under all those smelly horse blankets, with the mail bags tucked one on each side of her and the guard perched at her feet. Off on her adventures again!

They travelled due north for most of the morning, following

33

a pale sun and the easy undulations of the white landscape. They had no way of knowing whether they were using a road or not, but they were heading in the right direction and occasionally they crossed the tracks of earlier travellers, which reassured them both. But they didn't see another living soul until they reached a little smoky hamlet some time after midday. It lay on the east side of a frozen stream in a narrow valley between two gently sloping hills, its few dark cottages streaming smoke into the white sky and the higgledy-piggledy street at its centre completely empty. There were two mills signposting the western hill and a manor house sheltered in a white fold of the eastern hill like a lamb in a blanket, and close to the church, a small dishevelled inn, where they stopped to thaw themselves by the fire and eat a plateful of new bread and rather sweaty cheese washed down with ale.

Then feeling slightly warmer and rather less hungry they set off again, both on foot this time because the cob was too weary to pull them, following the valley between two more low hills and trying to remember the landlord's instructions. Five miles to Bury he'd said. Five miles, due north, keeping the woods to their left. That shouldn't take too long, not if the weather held. But as they reached the end of the valley their luck ran out and it began to snow again.

Nevertheless they continued doggedly onwards in what they judged to be the right direction, trudging slow and speechless through the thickening fall. But after several frozen hours there was no sign of Bury St Edmunds, and the afternoon was growing steadily darker and colder. They could see brown smoke rising into the snow-filled air from some hidden farmhouse a long way away, but that was all.

By now Tranter was wishing he'd never started this journey. 'I'm beginnin' to think we're lost,' he said. 'You ask me, we should make for that house, whatever it is. Least we'd be warmer there for the night than walkin' about out here.'

'We're not lost,' Caroline said with great determination. 'We just don't know where we are for the moment, that's all. If we go on a bit further we shall see the town.'

'I'm for goin' to the farm.'

'I'm not.'

It was ridiculous to be put down by a slip of a child, but there was no denying the force of this one. Even in a blizzard she blazed with determination, her face dark between ice-hung bonnet and snow-caked mantle. Now and a bit late Tranter remembered that she was one of the Easters, and that the Easters were formidable, everybody said so, rich and powerful and never took no for an answer. Was it any wonder she was answering back? It had been a great mistake to bring her along with him. A great mistake.

'It'ud be better a-goin' back, miss,' he tried, subservient before her, despite himself. 'It would truly.'

'No it wouldn't.'

'Just for a little while, eh?' he pleaded. 'A stop-over.'

'We're going on,' she said. And to his annoyance and alarm she set off on her own.

So they went on. And saw nothing, not even smoke.

By this time the cob was finding the going so hard that they had to walk beside his head and lead him.

'The next farm we sees, we stops,' Tranter said, brushing the snow out of his eyes. 'It's all very well you a-sayin' we ain't lost. I knows we are.'

'No we're not,' Caroline said stubbornly. He was making her feel afraid, and the more frightened she was the more stubborn she became. 'If we go on to the top of that hill ahead of us we shall see where we are.'

'We shan't see nothing, you ask my opinion,' Tranter said. 'I can barely see the hill, an' in any case tha's miles and miles away. And this 'ere animal is fit to drop. We're in a rare old pickle. Worse'n when we saw the farm.' Which was all true enough.

'Well, we can't stop now,' she said, trying to be reasonable, 'because there's absolutely nowhere to shelter here. So we might as well go on, mightn't we?'

'I can't feel my fingers nor my toes,' he complained.

'Neither can I.'

'We could die out here an' no one would know.'

It was true but she wouldn't even think about it. 'We shan't die,' she said stubbornly, because fear was gnawing her belly. 'We'll see the town, just the minute we've climbed to the top of that hill, you'll see.'

So he was persuaded again, and between them they coaxed

their poor weary cob into a walk again, dragging beside him through the heavy snow, slowly and painfully on their frozen feet. It seemed to take hours to reach the lower slopes of the hill, and by the time they'd climbed to the top, it was dark as night and they were completely exhausted.

But there below them, welcoming lights glimmered in the snow-swirled darkness. And the wind blew away the falling snow from before Caroline's eyes and with a spasm of relief so intense it was quite painful she knew she was looking down at Bury St Edmunds, set on its sloping hillside.

'We're home!' she said. 'Do you see? We're home at last. Didn't I tell you?'

Chapter 3

Nan Easter's house in Bury St Edmunds was modest compared to the grand establishment she kept in London's fashionable Bedford Square, but even so it was impressive among the lesser buildings of a market town, holding its own in the cobbled square of Angel Hill against the combined splendours of the famous Angel Inn and the classical balance of the Athenaeum Assembly Rooms. Like them, it was meticulously maintained, sumptuously furnished and brilliantly lit, for where other householders were content with a set of candles or a lamp or two, Nan Easter indulged herself with dazzling chandeliers ablaze with the new golden illumination of gas-light.

She might be sixty-five and grey haired, but she was still as full of energy as she'd always been, outspoken and outgoing, straight of spine and straight of purpose. And her home reflected her personality. When the nights were dark and the weather miserable she left her drawing-room curtains open so as to share her opulence with the passers-by.

'Tha's so bright there of an evenin',' the locals would say admiringly, 'you could read one of her ol' newspapers right out there on the pavement.'

At Christmas when her entire family usually joined her for presents and parties, fires were lit in every room and the whole house pulsed with light. It was a celebration she particularly enjoyed, so this year's blizzard was a nuisance and a disappointment, for it meant that both her sons would be stuck in London, her lover would stay where he was on his estate in Westmoreland, and even her daughter Annie, who lived a few miles away in the village of Rattlesden where her husband was rector, would certainly keep her family at home in the warm and defer travel until the roads cleared.

Nevertheless she did have company that Christmas, for her old friend and companion Bessie Thistlethwaite was with her as always, and Caroline's brother Will had ridden over from Cambridge two days before the snow began.

Nan was very fond of Will, partly because she'd brought him up since he was eight years old but more because he combined a protective affection towards his family with startling good looks. He was eighteen now and exceedingly handsome, tall and slender, with long limbs, elegant hands, a well-shaped head and an almost Grecian profile. His hair, which he wore in the romantic style brushed forward onto his forehead, was thick and curly and the colour of ripe corn, and his eyes were very large and very blue and fringed with thick dark lashes that gave his face an air of tenderness and vulnerability which was rather at odds with the rest of his dashing personality, and which Nan consequently found extremely touching.

It was always a pleasure to welcome him home, and feed his healthy appetite and sit about the fire afterwards, laughing and talking, which is what the three of them were doing that Christmas evening, gathered round the drawing-room fire with port and porter on the low tables beside them, enjoying the warmth and planning the party they would throw when the roads were clear.

The frantic knocking on their front door was a great surprise.

'Who in the world can that be?' Nan said. 'At this hour and in all this weather?'

Bessie went hobbling off onto the landing to find out. She was just in time to see Caroline's snow-caked figure totter into the hall.

'Caroline! Lovey!' she said as she eased her old legs down the stairs. 'However did you get here? Is yer Pa with you?'

'I w-w-walked from Long M-M-Melford,' Caroline shivered. 'Pa's still in London as f-f-far as I know.' After the cold and fear of her journey the hall was so warm and so full of bright colours it took away the little strength she had left.

'All the way?' Bessie said, still struggling down the stairs. 'You've never walked all the way from Long Melford! That's miles and miles. Mrs Easter, mum, she's walked all the way from Long Melford.'

But Nan's quick brown eyes had already taken in all the information she needed. She was busy taking command.

'Let's have you out of these wet clothes,' she said, untying the frozen ribbons of the poor child's bonnet and lifting it away from her head ice and all, handing her muff and gloves to the parlour maid, carefully removing that bedraggled mantle. 'I'll wager you en't eaten.' And when Caroline shook her wet head, 'Compliments to Cook, Bessie. Ask her to see what she can rustle up. There's goose a-plenty, and vegetables for bubble and squeak. Bring the kettle to the boil and we'll make a mustard bath. Two hot-water bottles. Blankets if you please, Will. Come along, my lovey. We'll soon have you to rights.'

Caroline followed her gratefully up the stairs, shivering all the way to the drawing room, where Nan sat her by the fire and removed her boots that were so wet they were dripping water, and her stockings that were so hideously dirty she felt ashamed of them, and her lovely red dress that was wet to the knee, and both her horrid damp petticoats. And then Will came into the room with his arms full of blankets and they bundled her up like a parcel and sat her in the chair again with her raw red hands in her lap and her raw red feet on the fender.

'There now,' Nan said, smiling at the child. 'That's a deal better, I know.'

And it was a deal better, so it was foolish to burst into tears. But that was what Caroline did. She couldn't help herself. 'Oh,' she sobbed. 'I'm so cold and so sorry. I wish I hadn't. I didn't know it was going to snow like this. Tranter said we'd die. It was an awful journey. Oh, poor Pa! He'll be worried out of his life and it's all my fault.'

At that moment Bessie limped into the room with a footbath, a dish of mustard and a jugful of hot water and she and Nan got busy at once preparing the mixture, so it was Will who cuddled his weeping sister and listened to her confession and dried her eyes and wiped her nose and told her not to be a goose. 'We'll get a letter to Pa, somehow or other,' he promised. 'Don't cry, Carrie.'

But her tears flowed freely, thawed into torrents by their warmth and affection.

'Now then, my lamb,' Bessie said, 'put your little toes in the water and tell me if it's too hot. We can't have our lamb taking a chill now can we? Both feet if you please.'

Caroline's feet were the colour of raw beef and they tingled and throbbed when she lowered them into the yellowing water, but the heat was blissful, warming the blood back into her toes, and rising over her ankles into her shivering calves like a spreading benediction. And finally drying her tears.

By the time Cook came upstairs with a tray full of good things to eat and a glass full of hot toddy to sip and a jug full of hot water to top up the mustard bath, she was red-nosed but almost herself again. She ate every last mouthful of her make-shift meal and drank the toddy as though she'd been downing intoxicating liquors all her life. And bit by bit she told them all about her adventure.

'My heart alive!' Nan said lovingly. 'You'll make an explorer before you're done.'

'No, she won't,' Bessie said. 'She'll find a nice young man to marry her, you'll see, and she'll settle down and be as happy as a sand-boy. Won't you, my lovey?'

Emboldened by safety and hot toddy, Caroline pondered the prospect, snug inside her blankets. 'Well I might,' she said, 'but I'd much rather work in the firm like Papa and Uncle Billy.'

'Good heavens!' Bessie said. And she looked disapproving.

'Well, why not?' Caroline asked. 'Nan worked in the firm. You did, didn't you Nan? So why shouldn't I?'

'No reason in the world as far as I can see,' Nan said, grinning at her. 'What would you do if you worked in the firm?'

'Well, for a start I think I'd sell other things besides news-papers and stationery.'

'Would you indeed, miss? What sort of things?'

'I don't know yet,' Caroline admitted. 'But I'd think of something.'

'Aye,' Nan laughed, 'I daresay you would.' What spirit the child had! It was just what the firm needed. Somebody with drive and passion and energy to push it forward into new directions. Her son Billy ran the warehouses with easy efficiency and John had made it his life's work to transfer the transport of goods from the coaches to the railways, but there was no one capable of inspiring the company except herself. And these days inspiration was often very hard work. She could do with a new young manager. 'I might give you a place yet.'

Will gave his sister a hug. 'She can have mine if she likes,' he said.

Now that was surprising, for they'd all assumed that he would follow his father into management almost as a matter of course. 'Why?' Nan quizzed him. 'Don't you want it?'

He reassured her at once, smiling at her. 'I'll go into the firm if you want me to,' he said. 'Of course I will. You know that. But I'd rather not.'

'What would you rather do?' Nan asked, intrigued.

'I would rather be a reporter and work for *The Times*. My friend Jeff Jefferson works for the *Cambridge Chronicle* and he says it's a wonderful life. Imagine it, Nan, travelling the world, meeting famous people, seeing great events as they happen, no two days ever the same.' His face was glowing with enthusiasm. 'I can't think of anything I'd rather do than that.'

'Such talk!' Bessie said, disapproving of it. 'High time this child was tucked up warm in bed, if you ask me, instead a' sitting here all night long a-talking nonsense.'

Will and Caroline grimaced at one another, half mocking their dear old Bessie, half admitting that they *were* ready for bed. So it wasn't long after that that they kissed their grandmother goodnight and retired, with Bessie in attendance to make sure that the beds were aired and the fires properly damped down. But Nan stayed where she was.

It had been an eventful evening and had given her plenty to think about. It amused her to imagine Caroline as a future member of the firm. She would certainly be a challenge to the old fuddy-duddies who managed the regions. I shall keep an eye on her, she decided, and on Will too, for he was uncommon serious about being a reporter. What a fine strong-willed pair they are! Children after my own heart. And the best of the grandchildren without a doubt, for although Annie's three were dear creatures, it was already plain that Jimmy would follow his father quietly into the priesthood and the two girls would marry and settle down in the most happily ordinary way and none of them would have the slightest interest in the firm. While as to Billy's pair, dear little Matty would marry Jimmy in a year or so, and Edward was so spoiled it was hard to tell what he would make of his life, which was a pity for he was an affectionate creature underneath all that cockiness.

No, no, she thought, walking across the room to her writing desk, these two are the best. And she sat down to write a letter to John to tell him they were both safe with her in Bury.

The terrible weather continued. It was seven fraught days before Nan's letter arrived in Fitzroy Square, sent by packet boat along the coast from Ipswich, and by then John Easter was suffering so much from sick headaches, indigestion and bad temper that his servants did their best to avoid him. And the odd thing was, as they told one another in the kitchen, that instead of bringing him relief, the letter seemed to make him worse.

'Safe and well with my mother,' he said to Tom bitterly. 'Safe and well and here I've been worried out of my wits.'

'Yes, sir,' Tom agreed. 'Don't need ter worry no more though, not now, do yer sir?'

'I shouldn't have been forced to worry in the first place,' John said. 'This sort of thing must never be allowed to happen again. I shall go to Bury on the first available coach and take some action.'

1837 was actually ten days old before the roads were clear enough for the mail coaches to venture out, and by then A. Easter and Sons had another problem to contend with.

As always after bad weather, there was an outbreak of serious illness in the capital, and this time it was influenza. The number of cases reported in the newspapers rose day by day, and although the coaches began to run again there were soon fewer and fewer drivers well enough to take them out. John carried his timetables about with him wherever he went, so that he could find other routes when particular services were cancelled, transferring papers from coach to coach, and sitting up into the small hours to keep his schedules up to date and ensure a smoother run the following day. Profits had been seriously affected by the snow and it was imperative to get his papers distributed now that it was clearing. But as the epidemic grew his task became more and more difficult.

By the end of January the contagion was so severe that there were a thousand funerals in London in one week; the undertakers were hard put to it to find space in the cemeteries and in St Pancras they had to arrange for navvies to dig and refill the graves. It was well into February and all the snow had long since melted before John felt able to write to his mother to tell her that he would be journeying to Bury in three days' time 'to attend to the matter of Caroline's misdemeanour'.

Caroline had been enjoying herself so much with her brother and Nan that she'd almost forgotten her 'misdemeanour'. She was quite cast down by his letter. 'Oh dear!' she said. 'Do you think he's still cross, Nan?'

'He sounds cross.'

'Oh dear!' Caroline said again. 'Then I'm for it!'

'We'll throw a party,' Nan said. Perhaps that would put him in a better humour. 'After all, we en't had Christmas yet.'

They had Christmas on the day John arrived, and Annie and James and their family came over from Rattlesden, so that the house was full of people and laughter and everybody talking at once. And less than half an hour after the London coach had brought John in to the Angel Inn, there was another great to-do as Aunt Tilda and Uncle Billy and Matty and Edward came skating across from their house in Chequer Square to join the party. Soon they were all sitting round Nan's great dining table eating their unexpected Christmas dinner. And after that Nan had presents for all of them. Caroline's was a length of soft woollen cloth printed with tiny yellow roses, and Will's a copy of the last two monthly parts of Mr Dickens' 'Pickwick Papers' which he and his friends had been enjoying ever since the first hilarious instalment came out nearly two years ago. And after that there were charades and bobbing for apples and hide and seek and carols round the pianoforte and so many riotous games that by the time Annie and Billy took their dishevelled families home, it was so late that Will and Caroline and their father only just had enough energy left to climb the stairs to bed.

Nemesis arrived at breakfast the next morning.

Nan Easter was in the habit of taking breakfast in the front parlour on the ground floor of her house in Bury, partly because it was nearer to the kitchen which meant that the food always arrived hot, and partly because in the winter months the sun slanted in low through the windows and added warmth to the little room.

It was a small, cosy room and it felt private after the expansive size of the dining room upstairs. So it was a suitable place for John Henry to pronounce judgement on his daughter. Which he did as soon as their meal was completed. The bell was rung and Tom Thistlethwaite sent for and instructed to have the chaise ready by half-past nine. Then when his servant had left the room, John gave his instructions to Caroline.

'You are to be dressed by twenty past nine,' he said, 'and ready to accompany me.'

'Where are we going, Papa?'

'To school.'

Her grey eyes widened in shock. 'To school, Papa?'

'Yes,' he said mildly. 'Your behaviour before Christmas was quite intolerable. But you know that, of course. I can't imagine what Miss Murphy thought she was teaching you. It certainly wasn't how to behave in correct society.'

'Miss Murphy is very kind,' Caroline said, springing to the defence of her governess. 'I learn all sorts of things . . . '

'Miss Murphy is dismissed,' her father said. 'I wrote to her last week. Now things have got to change. You are to go to school and learn how to behave. I have found an establishment here in Bury that promises to inculcate the proper attitudes, so that is where you are going. You may read the first page of their brochure, if you wish.'

Caroline took the paper he was holding out across the table and read the passage he had outlined in firm red ink.

'MRS FLOWERDEW,' it said, 'begs leave respectfully to acquaint her Friends and Public, that her Select Seminary for YOUNG LADIES in BURY ST EDMUNDS, will be opened on Monday the 13th inst.

'The charges for Board, exclusive of Washing, and for

44

Instruction in English, Reading, Spelling, Grammar and Composition, in Geography, and the Use of the Globes, and in Ancient and Modern History, are, Thirty Guineas per Annum, and Three Guineas for Entrance.

'The Terms for Instruction in the French Language, Music, Drawing, Dancing and Writing and Arithmetic, and for Washing, are inserted in a printed Paper, which will be delivered to any Persons who will do MRS FLOWERDEW the Honour to ask for it.

'To Day-Scholars the Annual Charges for the general course of Instruction, will be Eight Guineas.'

And then in large print at the foot of the page were the ominous words, 'The improvement of the mind is the primary object of all tuition. Learning in the usual sense of the word is by no means necessary. I will seek to impress upon the minds of the female pupil her duties in society and to inculcate the proper attitudes.'

Signed,

Amelia Flowerdew (Mrs)'

I shan't like her at all, Caroline thought. 'Duties in society' sounded as horrid as 'proper attitudes'. 'I know how to read and write, Papa,' she tried to argue, 'and I can read the globes well enough, Miss Murphy says so. Mrs Flowerdew won't teach me much, I can tell you. Do I really have to go there?' And she looked at her grandmother for support.

'Yes,' Nan said, 'you do.' And the expression on her face brooked no argument.

'You'll like it, Carrie,' Will tried to encourage. 'Schools are quite fun sometimes. You'll like it.'

'I shan't,' Caroline said with determination.

'I liked it.'

'It's all very well for you. You're a boy.'

'What has that got to do with it?'

'I'm a girl.'

'And a very naughty one,' her father said, adding with chilling firmness, 'You are not being asked your opinion of the place, miss, nor whether or not you are prepared to attend it. You are simply being required to obey.'

It was the moment when a lesser child would have capitulated. Caroline recognized the power before her and decided to

45

change tack. 'Very well,' she said, still defiant, 'I'll go, if that's what you want, but I shan't learn anything. You'll see. And I shan't like it.'

'Your school cloak and bonnet are in the hall,' her father replied calmly.

Nan took Caroline off at once to try them on before she could make matters worse by saying anything else. They were made very simply of plain brown wool and had no decoration at all. She didn't like them a bit.

'I look absolutely horrid,' she complained, scowling at her image in the hall glass.

'Well, of course you do,' Nan said, 'pulling such a face. What do you expect, you foolish crittur?'

'I hate school. And I hate uniforms,' Caroline said, scowling more ferociously than ever.

'Here's your father,' Nan warned. 'Now just go along like a good girl and do as you're told. At least it en't a boarding school and you can come home to me at the end of the day. You just think of that.'

So she went along and did as she was told, scowling all the way.

Mrs Flowerdew's Seminary stood just outside the west gate. It was a plain house behind a plain wall, and the parlour into which they were ushered by a sombre butler was a plain room, full of books. But Mrs Flowerdew was a surprise.

She didn't look a bit like a teacher. She looked like a bed that had been made in a hurry, and a very brightly coloured bed at that, for she wore a gown of bright rose pink, patterned in a trellis of green and gold and set off with a triple collar of elaborate blonde lace, and no stay-maker alive could do justice to the voluptuous curves of her figure. Everything about her was larger than life, from the fat mounds of thick chestnut-coloured hair piled above her forehead to the bulging curves of the odd chestnut-coloured shoes upon her feet. She wore a gentleman's signet ring on the middle finger of her right hand, and a gentleman's fob-watch on the grand slope of her left bosom and neither looked out of place on a lady of such proportions. She was plainly not a woman to tolerate disobedience.

'Mr Easter,' she said, holding out her plump hand. 'I am very pleased to meet you, sir.'

'Mrs Flowerdew,' John murmured. 'This is my daughter, as I explained to you in my letter.'

'That is all entirely understood,' Mrs Flowerdew said, smiling at Caroline. 'You may leave her with us, Mr Easter, with every confidence. Every confidence.'

'I believe I may, ma'am.'

'We understand one another I believe,' Mrs Flowerdew said. Then she turned her body, swaying it to one side so that she was facing her new pupil. 'Welcome to my seminary, Caroline,' she said. 'You may kiss your Papa goodbye, my dear, and then I will take you to the schoolroom.'

Caroline looked at her father in amazement. Was she supposed to start school this very morning? Surely not? He hadn't said anything about starting school straight away. Why, she'd hardly had time to get used to the idea! But he didn't say anything. He only gave her his distant smile and bent forward so that she could kiss his cheek. Oh, the treachery of it!

'That's the way,' Mrs Flowerdew approved, and she rang the bell, which was one of the new bell-pulls on a long velvet ribbon. 'Fenning will see you out, Mr Easter. So glad to have made your acquaintance.'

And that was that. The butler arrived, Papa gave a little bow and departed, and Mrs Flowerdew led her new pupil from the room.

I won't cry, Caroline thought, as she climbed the stairs, and I won't say anything, at least, not now, because that would be infra dig. But this is no way to treat an Easter.

Three minutes later her school-life began. It was all so quick that there was no time to protest or even think. Despite her bulk, Mrs Flowerdew moved at an extraordinary speed, rustling up the stairs like a clipper with the wind in her sails, and she fairly dashed along the gallery, calling as she went, 'Come out my dears. Come out. We have a new scholar. Out you come!'

Doors opened as she passed, as though she were flicking them aside with her skirts, and out came a tumble of girls in bright coloured gowns and brown holland pinafores, scampering after her, tossing their ringlets and all talking at once. Little girls no older than Caroline herself, and tall girls quite as old as her cousins, and so many of them all together that she couldn't count them or even distinguish one from the other, particularly as they were all on the move, their bright cottons swaying and fluttering like a great swarm of butterflies.

The clipper flung open a pair of double doors and sailed into the middle of a long panelled room where there were small chairs set in four rows facing the fireplace, and suddenly order was restored. The butterflies stopped fluttering and became demure young women, who walked quietly into the room and ranged themselves in front of the chairs each with her arms held neatly at her sides.

'Stand here beside me,' Mrs Flowerdew said to Caroline.

She's going to give me a public scolding, Caroline thought, with foreboding. But I won't cry. No, I won't.

But, as she was to discover later, Mrs Flowerdew rarely scolded anybody. 'This is Caroline Easter, my dears,' she said. 'You are to look after her and teach her what is to be done and what is not to be done, which I have perfect confidence that you will do because there are so many of you with a talent for caring. And now, Caroline my dear, we must see where to put you. Between Arabella and Betonia, I think. Make a space, my dears.'

Betonia was a rather superior-looking girl who wore her hair in tight braids. But her smile was friendly.

'Pray sit down,' Mrs Flowerdew said. And they all rustled into their chairs. 'The parable of the talents, Mary, if you please. The Gospel according to St Matthew, Chapter 25, verse 14, "For the kingdom of Heaven is as a man travelling in a far country".'

And the girl called Mary read the parable, in a quiet clear voice, in a room grown so still to listen to her that Caroline could hear the coals clicking in the grate.

'Talents you see, my dears,' Mrs Flowerdew said, when the reading was done. 'We all have a talent of some kind, every single one of us, you may be sure of that. The Good Lord would never send any of His creation into the world with no talents at all. No, no, no. So we can all be perfectly sure that we have at least one talent, and some of us will have more than one, and some will have a great great many. And what is the purpose of having a talent?' smiling round at her audience, 'Myfanwy?'

A girl in the second row stood up to answer her. All heads in the front row swivelled round. 'To use it, Mrs Flowerdew.'

'Quite right. And to what purpose? Helen?'

Another girl gave the answer. 'For the benefit of mankind, Mrs Flowerdew, and the greater glory of God.'

'Quite, quite right,' Mrs Flowerdew approved. 'For the benefit of mankind and the greater glory of God. What a splendid thing. Don't you think so, Caroline Easter?'

Well, of course she thought so. How could she think anything else? So she nodded, as that seemed to be expected of her, and was beamed upon, and felt vaguely aggrieved that everybody in the room seemed to be assuming that she would join in with them, and act as they did and believe the same things. Well, I won't, she thought. I didn't want to come here. I've no business being here. I won't.

'A splendid thing,' Mrs Flowerdew said, clapping her hands together and shifting all the bright colours in her unmade bed. 'And now let us return to our lessons and see how many talents we can discover today. First row to remain here with me for reading. Lead on Amy.'

The rest of the day was so full of movement and new faces that when she finally got home again in the evening Caroline could hardly remember any of it. She'd read from the Bible, eaten a stew that had turned out to be more appetizing than it looked, and begun to sew herself a holland pinafore, but the rest of her activities were mere confusion.

Bessie said it all sounded a fine thing and wouldn't she be a scholar by the time she'd finished, and Nan said her father had gone back to London on the afternoon stage, 'in fine good humour seein' the way you settled'.

Will had left her a most loving note before he caught the Cambridge coach, hoping that she'd write and tell him all about the seminary. 'The next time I come to Bury we will compare notes,' he suggested hopefully. But Caroline didn't even mention the school when she wrote back.

I shall never like it, and I shan't have any talents at all, she thought rebelliously, and if I have I shall take jolly good care

Mrs Flowerdew doesn't see them. *I* am an Easter. Not just any ordinary girl. And my mother was a saint.

But she had reckoned without Mrs Flowerdew's talents, which were considerable and subtle.

Mrs Flowerdew knew a headstrong girl when she saw one, and she'd seen one on that first morning, for Caroline's scowl when she was asked that very first question had revealed her feelings very clearly indeed. Accordingly her new teacher left her alone, watched her and waited. She was praised when she read well, and sewed neatly, and mastered the steps of the polonaise, but there were no more public questions. Time would provide the moment. It always did.

So Caroline lived out her first few weeks in the seminary under cover of its constant activity. She quite liked her new teachers. Miss Butts, who taught arithmetic, grammar and spelling, was dry and papery and predictable, but usually kind provided you did exactly what she asked, while Mr Pepperoni, who taught dancing and French and music, was so dark and quick and volatile you never knew what he was going to do or say next. 'No, no, no,' he would howl, when the dancers got into a muddle. 'Where-a you put-a your feet? I show you?' And he would leap behind the maladroit dancer and seizing her in his long bony arms pace out the entire measure with her, singing the tune at the top of his voice. It was just the sort of eccentric behaviour Caroline enjoyed.

But Mrs Flowerdew was quite another matter. Mrs Flowerdew was the person who was going to 'inculcate proper attitudes' whatever that might mean. So Mrs Flowerdew had to be resisted. Even though it was really rather difficult to resist Mrs Flowerdew. She was so large and overflowing and brightly coloured and full of praise. And her drawing lessons were the easiest times of the week.

The entire school would gather in the schoolroom as soon as their mid-day meal was over, to arrange the chairs and the rostrum, and set up easels, and hand out paper and paint and brushes and sketch books and pencils. The older girls stood at their easels anywhere in the room, but the younger ones always sat in a circle round Mrs Flowerdew's rocking chair. And by some peculiar magic, Mrs Flowerdew always arrived in the room at the very moment everything was in order, bringing with her the day's model, which was invariably either a box full of butterflies or a dish full of fruit or a vase full of flowers. But the subject matter was not important. What they were all waiting for was the reading and the conversation.

It was Mrs Flowerdew's custom on drawing afternoons to arrive with the day's newspapers or a book of historical or cautionary tales and read an uplifting article to her pupils as they worked. 'Art is always so much improved by agreeable circumstances, is it not?' she would say. 'Let us see what our dear little Princess Victoria is doing.' Or, 'Let us read a tale about our good Queen Bess.' For all the chosen readings were about famous women, so naturally enough, the conversation that followed was all about fame and heroism and the particular and undeniable talents of women. It was very enjoyable, particularly as Mrs Flowerdew's view of the world seemed very similar to Nan's. Caroline found it quite hard to sit mum and not join in.

But on the third drawing afternoon they were discussing whether or not it would be possible for a woman to own a factory.

'A woman could own one, I suppose,' Betonia said, 'if her father left it to her, or her husband or somebody, but she couldn't run it, could she?'

'Why not?' one of the older girls asked.

'She wouldn't know what to do.'

'Why not?'

'Well, for heaven's sake!' Betonia said. 'How could she? Women stay at home, don't they? They learn to run a household. They don't run factories.'

'If they can run a household then why can't they run a factory?' another girl wondered.

'Because it ain't natural,' Betonia said fiercely. 'That's why. Women are meant to stay at home and look after the children.'

'Oh, what a lot of nonsense!' Caroline said, her vow not to join in quite forgotten in the heat of the moment. 'My grandmother didn't stay at home and look after the children. She runs A. Easter and Sons, I'll have you know.'

Her fellow pupils were impressed. 'All by herself?' Helen asked, eyes wide.

'Of course,' she said, with great pride, forgetting the regional managers and her father and her uncle Billy. 'She founded it. Years and years ago when she was young. My grandfather died and she had no money so she sold newspapers from door to door.'

'Out on the streets?' Betonia asked. That was rather shocking, surely. No lady would sell things on the streets. Only costers did that. And costers were very low people.

'Of course,' Caroline said again. Now that she'd started her story she wasn't going to allow anybody to be shocked by it. 'If she hadn't gone out to work my father would have starved. I think she was very brave.'

'She was unnatural,' Betonia said. 'It ain't natural for women to run things.'

'They run households,' Caroline argued back at once, enraged to hear her dear Nan being abused. 'You said so yourself.'

'That's different.'

'It's not.'

'Anyway,' Betonia said haughtily, 'I'll wager your *mother* didn't sell newspapers on the street. Not if she was a saint, the way you keep telling us.'

'My mother,' Caroline said furiously, 'bandaged the wounded after a massacre. She tore up her petticoats to staunch the wounds. And after that she went from town to town all over the country making speeches so that people would look after them and not let them starve. And she *was* a saint. Everybody says so.'

It was an impressive story and her audience were obviously impressed.

'*My* mother,' Betonia said, annoyed to be losing the advantage, 'says it ain't natural for women to work. So there.'

'Well it is!'

'It ain't.'

'I know it is.'

'We can't both be right,' Betonia said smugly. 'Can we, Mrs Flowerdew?'

Every face in the class turned towards Mrs Flowerdew for judgement. Betonia's certain of endorsement, Caroline's suddenly anxious. Now she'd done it. Now she would be told she was wrong and made to look a fool. Oh, if only she'd kept quiet.

Mrs Flowerdew beamed at them all. 'Yes, you can,' she said easily. 'Oh indeed you can. There are as many different ways of being right as there are different ways of being wrong. And what is right for one girl and her family could be wrong for another and hers. It is a matter of attitude and the kind of talents you possess and how you make use of them. I will explain.' And she smoothed her skirt across her capacious knees and turned to look at Betonia.

'Betonia, as we all know, has a talent for order and dependability, which are both excellent things. Look how we benefit from her arrangement of this room at the start of our lessons, for instance. Her family have lived their lives in the same dependable way for centuries, as we also know, so naturally Betonia will do the same thing, and that is proper and commendable and an example to us all. The Easter family, on the other hand, are men and women of fire and imagination, the sort of people who change things, and take us forward into new ventures and over new horizons. Mrs Nan Easter owns shops all over the country, my dears, and all of them are run most successfully. They are renowned for being first with the news. Is that not so, Caroline?'

'Yes,' Caroline said, amazed to be receiving such support, 'we are. And we sell millions of papers every day.'

'Very true,' Mrs Flowerdew agreed. 'I bought this very paper from Easter's in the Buttermarket this morning. So you see, my dears, far from being unnatural, Caroline's grandmother is another example to us all. A lady who uses her talents to the uttermost, my dear, as we should all strive to do. Different talents, you see, different strengths, different attitudes, and all of them valuable.'

'But surely, Mrs Flowerdew,' Betonia said, struggling to recover her lost superiority, 'there is only one correct attitude.'

'No, my dear,' Mrs Flowerdew told her gently, 'there are as many attitudes as there are people, and why should one be more correct than any other?'

This was heady stuff and it emboldened Caroline to ask a question of her own. 'What does "inculcate" mean, Mrs Flowerdew?'

'Why do you ask, my dear?'

'My father said you were going to "inculcate" proper attitudes in me.'

'Ah!' Mrs Flowerdew said. 'To inculcate the proper attitudes, my dear, is to enable each and every one of you to discover for herself what attitudes are proper to her and her family and then to live by them. Do you see?'

Oh, indeed she did. How amazing! How absolutely amazing!

That night over dinner Caroline gave her grandmother a full report of the day's events. It was the first time she'd done such a thing since she joined the seminary, a fact not lost on the shrewd Nan Easter, who was highly amused to hear how her life had been the subject of conversation.

'Mrs Flowerdew says you are an example to us all,' Caroline said as she finished her account.

Nan Easter grinned at her granddaughter. 'A woman of sense,' she said. 'I take it you like her.' She could have added 'now' but forebore, being a woman of sense herself.

'Yes, I do. She's lovely.'

'So school might be useful?'

'Oh yes,' Caroline said. 'Very useful. I think I have a talent for working in Easter's, you see.'

54

Chapter 4

'Now,' Nan Easter said to her regional managers, 'let us turn our attention to enlarging our trade.'

It was March and their quarterly meeting in the Strand was nearly over. The last of their reports had been read and accepted. It was an ideal moment to test young Caroline's suggestion. 'Our trade is still in the doldrums, gentlemen. The price of newspapers is still too high, on account of that infernal stamp duty, and we can't sell the popular papers, cheap though they are, because they en't stamped and they en't legal. Now it's true we handle the bulk of the legal trade, and stationery sells handsome, but we en't expanding, and that's the truth of it. We got more than a dozen new railways to carry our merchandise to Swindon and Southampton and Rugby and such, but we en't expanding. How if we were to sell other articles besides newspapers and stationery?'

They were most upset by the suggestion, ruffling like pigeons in a breeze. 'What else *could* we sell?' they asked. 'Oh no, no. We *are* a newsagents after all, Mrs Easter.' And they begged her to think of the work it would mean, the trade it would lose, the customers it would upset. Profits might not be high, that was true, but they were steady. In their opinion, it would be most unwise. 'Oh no, no, no.'

How dull they all are, she thought, hard-working and thorough, certainly, but quite without imagination and with no sense of daring at all. If I could think of something sensible to sell, I'd sell it just to show 'em. She missed the old faces, dear old Alexander Thistlethwaite who'd run the East Anglian side

55

of the business until that awful winter when he'd died so suddenly and quietly, sitting in his chair by the fire with Bessie pottering about their parlour beside him. And Cosmo Teshmaker, who'd been such an ally in London, and had taken his wife off so happily for that awful tour of Italy, from which neither of them had returned. I'll ask John and Billy, she decided. See what they can suggest. And she dismissed her fuddy-duddies, as courteously as she could, thanking them for their endeavours.

John and Billy had been her lieutenants for so many years now that they knew one another's ways almost instinctively, which made the final part of their quarterly meeting relaxed and easy and enjoyable. They'd joined the firm when Billy was no more than fourteen, and his brother a year younger, young and slim and eager to do well. Now they were in their forties and looked what they were: men of business, knowledgeable and dependable, between them taking full responsibility for the day-to-day running of the firm, and yet still capable of enjoying a joke and teasing as they'd done when they were boys. If only the committee could be composed of such men.

But today her fat cheerful Billy was ill at ease.

'What is it?' she asked him when the managers had gone.

'I've got young Edward in my office,' he confessed. 'Tilda thinks he ought to see you.'

'What for?'

'To discuss his future, so she says.' His face was quite woebegone with embarrassment. 'If you ask me she's being premature, but you know Tilda.'

Yes, Nan thought, I do know Tilda. She's been nagging again. She makes a deal too much fuss of that Edward. But she didn't say so for that wouldn't have done at all. Billy was upset enough already. 'Then I'd best see him,' she said, 'if that's the size of it.' And she rang for her clerk to show him up.

Edward Easter was the most unprepossessing of her grandchildren, seventeen years old and all arrogance and pimples. Left to her own devices she wouldn't have entertained him for a minute. He and his sister Matty were as different as two siblings could possibly be, although they shared the same pale colouring, the same shape of head and the same baby-fine light brown hair. But where she lowered her beautiful big grey eyes

56

he raised his small bold blue ones; where she stooped to avoid notice, he, like the spoilt child he was, stood tall to attract it; and where she was quiet and unassuming, he grew louder and more demanding the more attention he was given. He was going up to Cambridge in the autumn, and he was very proud of his new status as an undergraduate and the fine new clothes his parents had provided to embellish it.

Now he came strutting into the boardroom as if he owned it and sat down at the table without being asked, which was a very bad start. 'Ma says I'm to ask you what my position is to be,' he announced. 'When I come down from Cambridge, you know.'

'You en't gone up yet awhile,' Nan said, rather taken aback by the effrontery of it.

'Ah yes,' he said, looking at her boldly, 'but it won't be long now, will it, and I need to know what the firm intends to do for me.'

'Do you indeed?' Nan said sternly. 'I'd ha' thought it more to the point to consider what *you* intend to do for the firm?'

'Why, I shall inherit it, Grandmama. After all, I *am* the heir apparent.'

'And how do you make that out, pray?'

'I'm the only son of the elder son.'

'We en't royalty,' she told him sharply, while his father winced. 'I got six other grandchildren besides you.'

'Ah, but they don't amount,' he said, and he proceeded to check them off on his fingers. 'Jimmy means to go into the priesthood, Will is to be a reporter, and you can't count the girls.'

'Why not?'

'Girls stay at home and get married. They don't work in newsagents.'

'I might remind you, young man, that I am female and I run the firm. Or en't you noticed?'

He wasn't a bit abashed by her sarcasm. 'But you ain't the same, Grandmama,' he said easily. 'You were born in the old days.'

'My heart alive!' Nan said to Billy. 'He's got an answer for everything, this boy of yours.'

'He's very like his mother,' Billy apologized.

'Very well then,' Nan said, returning her attention to Edward, 'if you join the firm, what will you do to increase trade?'

'Why, sell papers, I daresay.'

'Sales are static,' she told him. 'What would you do to increase them?'

'Pray for a war,' Edward said smoothly. 'Another Waterloo somewhere. That 'ud improve things no end.'

'Providing we won it,' John said, giving his brother a wry grin.

'No fear of that,' Edward said. 'The British always win.'

'No,' Nan said, 'that en't the way forward. Oh, I know bad news sells papers, and good news too if it's the right kind, but it en't the way forward. There's no virtue in waiting for events to increase trade for us. We ought to be a-taking action to do that for ourselves. What would you do?'

'Well, good heavens,' Edward said, 'if you can't think of something, Grandmama, I'm sure I can't.'

She was suddenly sick of him. 'You go to Cambridge, Edward,' she said, 'and see how you make out there. Then we'll consider your future. You've got a long way to go yet. And I suggest the first steps you take are out of that door. Your father and your uncle John and I have work to do.'

He went swaggering out, straight-spined and arrogant to the last.

'What a puppy he is!' his grandmother said. 'I hope he learns more sense at Cambridge, I tell 'ee straight, Billy.'

'Was he right about Will?' Billy asked his brother, helping them all to brandy and avoiding her criticism because it was too painful. 'Does he mean to be a reporter?'

'It's the first I've heard of it if he does,' John said. 'A whim, I daresay. He'll join the firm when he finally comes down of course, just like Edward. Perhaps he means to try something different in the meantime, which is no bad idea, when all's said and done. It would give him experience of another side of the business.' Then he too changed the subject, turning to his mother. 'Is Caroline well?'

'Settled at last, I do believe,' Nan said, and told him all about the drawing afternoon, because that at least was easy and pleasant and would soothe poor Billy's embarrassment.

58

John listened seriously, inclining his head towards her. 'Perhaps she will be a little better behaved now,' he hoped. Her lack of interest in the school had been rather a disappointment to him. This was more encouraging.

'She's a deal better behaved already,' Nan said, defending her. 'Give her another month and she'll be a child transformed.'

'Improvement I might believe,' he said, smiling at her, 'but transformation is another thing. If only she were more like her brother.'

'A good lad, your Will,' Billy said, finishing his brandy. 'I wish my Edward had half as much sense.'

'Yes he is,' John agreed. 'I shall be glad when he joins the firm.'

He would have been very surprised if he could have seen his son at that moment. For the sensible Will Easter was cheerfully drunk and planning a career outside the company.

Will and his two closest friends, Tubby Maltravers, who was short, stout and witty, and Dodo Overthorne, who was tall, sharp and lazy, had dined just a little too well that evening, and had consequently found themselves obliged to drink large quantities of British Hollands to ease the discomfort of their over-distended stomachs. Now they were hanging out of the window of his room in Pembroke College, blear-eyed with drink and waiting for the whores to arrive.

'Lissen!' Tubby commanded, holding up a fat hand. 'Ain't that the basket, dammit?'

They peered through the darkness of the quod and the fog of Hollands. Something was rattling over on the far corner and they could see two dark figures man-handling a ladder.

'Chains,' Dodo said. 'Tha's what it is. Chains.'

'They don't bring 'em up on chains, you duffer,' Will said, pushing his friend's head to one side so that he could see what was going on. 'Might hurt 'em.'

'Yesh they do,' Dodo insisted. 'Weight of the bashket don't ye know. Couldn't use rope.'

'Think of the noise,' Will said. His head was so muddled he couldn't even remember how the whores were lifted over the wall although he'd seen it done scores of times. They sat in a

59

basket, he remembered that. And everybody had to be very quiet in case the proctors heard, because of course it was all strictly against the rules.

White skirts bloomed like a rose on top of the wall, and now they could hear the scrape of the ladder and a scuffle of whispers.

'Tha's Molly!' Dodo said, flexing his long legs and stepping carefully away from the window, like a heron wading through weed. 'Bags I first.'

'How can you possibly see who it is?' Will said. 'In this dark?' But his friend was stalking out of the door, and now there were two white roses fluttering astride the wall, and somebody was giggling.

'Come on, Will,' Tubby said, pulling him by the arm. 'Lor' I'm squiffy. I hope old Shakespeare ain't right.'

'Shakespeare?' Will asked, staggering after him.

'Yes, you know. The porter in Macbeth. ''Drink is a provoker.'' You know. ''Provokes desire and takes away performance.'' 'That 'ud be a sell, eh?' ''Makes him and mars him. Makes him stand to, and not stand to.'' Eh?'

Personally and privately Will didn't really care what sort of sexual state he was in. But that was something he kept to himself. Being a gentleman of style, he always joined in with all the antics his friends proposed, but he was careful never to spend any time alone with any of the whores. This wasn't because he had no desire for them. He was young and easily roused and full of appetite. And it wasn't because he was afraid of catching one of their diseases. That was something that happened to other people. It was because he feared that if he ever made love to a woman he might become entangled, and this was something he was determined never to do. His father's terrible grief when his mother died had affected him so profoundly that he had vowed then and there, and young as he was, that he would never allow himself to be crushed in the same way. And as the only way to avoid the grief of loss was to avoid love and entanglement in the first place, he had decided to remain single and heartwhole. It was the most sensible course.

So although he went down to the wall to welcome their visitors and help them down the ladder, he had no intention of making use of their services. But it was a pleasure to lift them from the ladder, just the same, to breathe in their heady combination of strong perfume and musk, to see the swell of their white arms and the cloudy tangle of their loosened hair and their bright, bright eyes glinting at him in the lamplight. Drink or no drink, they roused him most painfully.

Fortunately for him the fourth head over the wall that evening was the tousled mop of their old friend Jeff Jefferson. Tubby and Dodo were none too pleased to see his horsy face grinning at them over the top of the basket.

'Dammit Jefferson,' Dodo hissed, 'can't you use the gate like any other Christian soul?'

'Not when you fellers'll haul me over the wall.'

'That's not cricket, old man.'

'Cave!' a voice warned. 'Bulldogs!'

The basket was dropped with a thud on the other side of the wall, and the quod was suddenly full of flying figures, suppressed giggles, swishing skirts, long legs silhouetted against the lamplight, the puff, pant and skid of frantic escape. Will seized Jeff by the hand and dragged him off to the stairway. 'Quick!' he whispered. 'If you're found you'll be for it.'

Within seconds the quod was cleared, doors shut, whores chosen and hidden, and Will and Jeff were safe in Will's room, pouring themselves two full glasses of Hollands while they caught their breath.

'Madness,' Will said admiringly. 'What possessed you to come in over the wall?'

'The hell of it,' Jeff said. 'Damned good Hollands, Will.'

'What if you're caught?'

'On an assignment.'

'Prove it.'

'Fight between town and gown in Petty Cury yesterday afternoon,' Jeff offered.

'True.'

'Interviews with protagonists?'

'Possible. Who?'

'Unable to reveal sources. Honour of the press and so forth.'

'Dammit Jeff, you could lie black was white.'

'Well now,' Jeff said, putting down his glass, 'what was it you wanted to see me about?'

'Matter of business,' Will said, trying to sound casual about it.

'Oh yes.'

'I want a job, Jeff. I've decided to be a reporter. How should I go about it?'

'Here or in London?'

'London preferably.'

'Try the *Morning Advertiser*,' Jeff advised. 'They're looking for reporters. Might take you on straightaway if that's what you want, particularly as you're a Pembroke man. It's as good a place as any and you can always move on if it don't suit. What's brought this about?'

'I sounded my grandmother.'

'Ah! And?'

'I think it's on.'

'She said "yes".'

'Well, she didn't exactly say "yes",' Will admitted, 'but then again she didn't exactly say "no" either.'

'And what about your father?'

'I shall speak to him later.'

'Make a name for yourself first, eh?'

'Something of that.'

'Very wise,' Jeff said, holding up his glass for more Hollands. 'Try a royal story for a start. They always sell. The old king's a-dying, so they say.'

'Is he?' Will said, refilling his own glass. 'Well, I can't say I'm surprised. And what's the rest of the gossip?'

Frederick Brougham, that other, more reliable gossip, was back in London. He had been Nan Easter's lover for more than twenty years, and although she saw rather less of him these days now that he had an estate in Westmoreland to care for, she was always glad of his company and warmed by his affection, for he was a gentle lover and a witty man, urbane and tolerant and wise in the ways of the world. Even now, after all these years, every homecoming was an event, and the time they spent together in her town house in Bedford Square or her country house in Bury or out in the wilds of his estate in Penrith were occasions to be cherished and savoured. As they drove to Holland House that Saturday evening, they were both bubbling with the pleasure of their reunion, and Frederick was primed with the latest unofficial news.

'The King is ill again,' he told her. 'Mallory heard it of the Queen's physician. A weakness of the lungs with high fever, so 'tis said.'

'There was no mention of it in *The Times*,' she said, as the carriage jolted over the uneven cobbles.

'Look for it tomorrow,' he said, putting out an arm to steady her.

'How so? Is it like to prove fatal?' If he died they would have a queen on the throne of England, and a young one at that, for the Princess Victoria was only seventeen. That would improve trade and no mistake.

'The physicians have taken up residence.'

'Then he's in a poor way, and Princess Victoria still under age. Who would be Regent, do 'ee think?'

'You would, I daresay,' he teased, 'if they gave you half a chance.'

'And make a better job of it than the Duchess of Kent,' she said, grinning at him.

'Old though you are,' he smiled at her, still teasing.

'You may admit to advanced years if you wish, Frederick Brougham,' she teased him back, 'but I don't. I've a deal too much spirit to sit in the chimney corner and wait to grow grey.'

'We grow grey together, my dear,' he said affectionately, 'and yet I love you more dearly than ever. I fear this must betoken a fundamental laziness in my disposition.'

'Long may it continue,' she said, kissing him, as the carriage wheeled into the avenue of limes that led to Holland House.

The London season progressed, and no news concerning the King's health appeared in the papers, but the rumours continued to circulate, and alarm and speculation increased together, so that the sales of newsprint were marginally improved. And in May, when the Princess Victoria celebrated her eighteenth birthday and so came officially of age and able to assume the throne in the event of her uncle's death, sales and speculation increased even further.

Mrs Flowerdew read the reports of the birthday celebrations to her pupils during their drawing afternoons.

'It was all done in great style, my dears,' she said, 'as you would expect when you consider that this young woman is heir to the throne of England. What a blessing it will be when this country is governed by a woman. Think of that. Oh, we shall see some changes then, I can tell you. Women will come into their own then.' And she read happily from *The Times*.

' "At 6 p.m. the Union Jack was hoisted on the Old Church at Kensington, and on the green opposite to the church a large white silk flag was unfurled with Victoria inscribed upon it in letters of ethereal blue." How perfectly charming. "At night a ball, seldom equalled in magnificence, was given in her honour in St James' Palace. The princess herself opened with the quadrille in which she was led by Lord Fitzalan, the eldest son of the Earl of Surrey, who is grandson to the Duke of Norfolk." Oh, entirely fitting, my dears. He would be an excellent match. "H.R.H. later danced with Prince Nicholas Esterhazy." But how splendid. The Esterhazy family own half of Europe, my dears. "There was great general regret at the absence of Their Majesties." Ah, you see. There is something amiss. There can be no doubt of it now. The poor man must be ill. He would never have slighted his little niece if that were not the case. We will say a special prayer for him tomorrow morning. Remind me, Helen.'

But although special prayers were said at the seminary for the next seven days the King took no benefit from them.

On 9 June his two physicians put out a statement from Windsor Castle, which *The Times* printed in full, admitting that the King was suffering from an infection of the chest, which had confined his majesty to his apartment, and produced considerable weakness. From then on they issued a bulletin every day.

Mrs Flowerdew read every single one to her assembled school, either first thing in the morning or during their drawing afternoons, which she increased to three a week in view of the gravity of the situation, and to the great delight of her pupils.

' "Crowds are gathered before the palace gates," ' she read. ' "The archbishops of York and Canterbury have said special prayers for him." Poor man!'

' "19 June. The King is in a very weak and feeble state and has received the sacrament from the hands of the archbishop of Canterbury, with attention and great apparent comfort." Then the end is coming!'

And the next day, dressed in really rather splendid half mourning of lavender and white, she called the school to assembly to read the final solemn words. ' "It has pleased God Almighty to release from his sufferings our most gracious sovereign King William the Fourth. His majesty expired this morning at twelve minutes past two o'clock, at his castle of Windsor, in the seventy-second year of his age, and the seventh year of his reign." So now we have a queen. Miss Butts will provide each of you with a black ribbon to wear upon your straw bonnet for the next two weeks as a token of respect. You will dismiss quietly, I know.'

But Caroline never got around to wearing her particular token of respect. That afternoon a letter arrived from Nan, telling her that she was to travel to London on the first coach out of Bury the next morning. 'The new Queen is to be proclaimed in St James' Palace in two days time,' she wrote, 'and that's a sight we shouldn't miss when reigning queens are such a rarity. Frederick has arranged seats for us all in the palace grounds. Be sure that Bessie travels with you. No escapades, mind. I will send Benson to meet you with the carriage and bring you straight to Bedford Square. Your brother will join us by dinner time, when I have a surprise for you both. Your loving Nan.'

Caroline needed no second bidding. She threw her straw bonnet into the cupboard, black ribbons and all, the minute she'd read the letter, and next morning she dressed herself in her prettiest gown and her new silk bonnet and her new blue mantle, and she and Bessie caught the coach with time to spare.

'Pussy cat pussy cat, where 'ave you been? Off to London to see the Queen,' Bessie said happily as she settled into the corner seat. 'What a lark!'

'And a surprise too,' Caroline said. 'What can it be, Bessie?'

'Could be anything knowing your Nan,' Bessie said. 'You'll know soon enough.'

But it was an intriguing puzzle to entertain them during the journey. And such an easy journey this time, with the horses in fine fettle and the roads just damp enough to lay the dust but not so wet as to make mud. 'One benefit of a showery spring,' as Bessie pointed out. So they made good time, and arrived in Bedford Square well before dinner.

Nan didn't say what the surprise was and when Will arrived he didn't know either. And when their father joined them he didn't mention it at all.

But then just before eight o'clock, when Caroline was beginning to wonder if they were ever going in to dinner, another carriage drew up outside the door, and Nan got up and announced her intention of going downstairs herself to attend to it.

'I shan't be long,' she said, grinning at them mischievously.

True to her word she was back within seconds. And following her into the room she brought three extraordinary strangers, an odd looking woman, an even odder looking man and a girl about the same age as Caroline.

All three of them were the most peculiar colour, a sort of brownish yellow, like faded curtains, and they wore the oddest clothes, most of them made of an off-white crinkled material that looked more like paper than cotton. The man had a jacket it was true but it was very old fashioned, being long, straight, unfitted and a very dull brown, like a servant's. His breeches were so crumpled he looked as though he'd slept in them and his cravat was patterned and very badly folded, falling lop-sidedly under a craggy chin, a broken nose and a very seamy forehead. Nevertheless, despite his unprepossessing appearance, or perhaps because of it, he strutted into the room like a fighting cock, jerking his head from side to side as though he were sizing up his enemies. And it was such a misshaped skull, revealed by hair cut so short that it was little more than stubble, and the oddest coloured stubble at that, part grey, part white and part ginger. Caroline disliked him at once.

The woman was very thin and she didn't seem to have very much hair either, for she wore a huge mob cap pulled low over her forehead. It was made of the same off-white material as her gown, which was high-waisted, straight-skirted, much turned and very old-fashioned. And her gloves were so ancient they were grey. She glided into the room after her husband, darting

66

anxious glances at the company and making a nervous whinny-ing noise, like a horse. Caroline didn't think much of her either.

But the girl was different. She too was very thin and dressed in the same kind of old fashioned gown made in the same grubby looking material, but she couldn't help that, poor thing, and at least she'd made an effort. She had a new blue ribbon tied about her waist and another in her hair, which was thick and curly and the colour of copper coins, and although she was probably as nervous as her mother, her yellow face was calm and her brown eyes serene as still water. I could like her, Caroline thought, trying to catch her eye.

'Come and meet my family,' Nan said to the gentleman. 'This is my son John and his son Will, and this gentleman, John my dear, is Mr Simon Callbeck, who is my nephew by marriage and your cousin. He's been in India for thirty-five years and is back in London for the season. En't that the most amazing thing? And this is Mrs Callbeck and their daughter Euphemia. And this is my granddaughter Caroline.'

It was a very difficult dinner party and not at all the sort of surprise that Caroline had hoped for. Mr and Mrs Callbeck were awful. Although they dressed like servants they talked about money and possessions all the time, and every possession they mentioned had to be bigger and better than anyone else's. Their house in Calcutta was 'a maharajah's summer retreat, priceless,' the quantity of jute they had sold over the years was 'the biggest in the country,' and they had a friend who had given his wife a ruby 'as big as a hen's egg, worth a king's ransom.'

'You will miss the life,' Will observed drily.

'No, no,' Mr Callbeck said. 'We're goin' straight back just as soon as the boys are settled. Ain't we, Agnes?'

Mrs Callbeck agreed that yes, they were, they were indeed. But John was interested to hear that there were boys in the family too.

'Oh yes,' Mr Callbeck said. 'Two fine boys, highly intelli-gent. Got them in to public school as easy as winkin'. Give 'em an education, that's what we say, don't we, Agnes?'

'Yes, yes, indeed.'

'We're sendin' Pheemy to boardin' school, in a week or

67

two,' Mr Callbeck said. 'We've rented a new house in St John's Wood, you know, just for the season, and we can't have nippers under our feet all the time, eh? Makin' a row and dirtyin' the place and all that sort of thing.'

Then they are rich after all, Will thought. St John's Wood was a prestigious address. Not quite up to the splendid style of Bedford Square, but certainly wealthy. And yet their clothes don't fit them. How weird. But perhaps Indian tailors aren't very good.

Caroline had been watching Euphemia all through this stupid conversation, annoyed by how totally the poor girl was being ignored. Neither of her parents bothered to include her in the conversation. They didn't even look at her. It was as if she wasn't there. And the poor girl went on dutifully eating her meal and keeping her eyes down and saying nothing.

So as soon as the cloth was removed and the meal completed and Nan had given the signal that the ladies were to withdraw, she rushed from her chair and took her new cousin by the hand. 'Come on,' she said. 'We will sit behind the piano. We can talk there. I know just the place.'

Euphemia allowed herself to be led but her yellow face looked anxious. 'Won't she mind?' she asked in a whisper. She pronounced the words rather carefully, with a slight hesitation before each one, as though she were speaking a foreign language.

'Who?'

'Your grandmother.'

'No, course not. Why should she mind? She likes her guests to enjoy themselves.'

'She is a very nice lady.'

'Yes, she is. Come on.'

So they hid themselves away behind the piano while Nan entertained her whinnying guest. And Caroline discovered something that was even more extraordinary than the peculiar cut of the Callbeck attire. Until that afternoon Euphemia had never dined at the same table as her parents.

'Never?' Caroline said, her grey eyes wide with amazement.

'No,' Euphemia said calmly. 'It is not done. Children are a nuisance. I stayed with my ayah most of the time.' Seeing Caroline's eyes widen further, Euphemia explained quickly, 'I liked that. She was very kind to me. When I had a pain she used to stroke it away.' And for the first time since her introduction her madonna face began to show emotion, yearning and sad, her brown eyes unfocussed, seeing that dear lost face such a long long way away. Oh ayah, dear ayah, how am I to live in this strange cold land without you? 'She was very kind.'

Her beautiful, brooding sadness triggered Caroline's sympathy into instant activity. 'Tomorrow morning we are all going to see the new Queen proclaimed,' she said. 'At St James' Palace, you know. Nan has seats for us. Shall you be there?'

The brown eyes misted back to the present. 'I don't think so,' Euphemia said. 'What a wonderful thing. You are lucky to be seeing such a thing.'

'Why don't you come with us?' Caroline offered at once.

'Could I?'

'I don't see why not. You could share my seat. You're not very big. I will arrange it.' The three men had finished their brandy and were walking into the drawing room, so there was a pause in the conversation. It was just the right moment. She jumped to her feet and was off at once to ask Nan.

'If her parents are agreeable,' Nan said, looking the question straight at them. She was delighted by the speed with which her impetuous granddaughter had taken Euphemia under her protection, for it was just what she had hoped for. With her connivance Mr Callbeck had already made arrangements for Euphemia's board and education, and if everything went according to plan she and Caroline would soon be school friends. But nothing was to be explained yet.

To Caroline's scorn and delight, the Callbecks hardly gave the matter any thought at all. They seemed pleased to be rid of their daughter. 'There are so many things that need our attention,' Mrs Callbeck said, 'and all of them so very much easier without a child perpetually about our ankles. It is very kind of you, Mrs Easter.'

Early the next morning the Easter chaise took Caroline and Euphemia chattering down the Mall towards St James' Palace.

It was a lovely summer's day, pearly with sunshine. The Mall was already thronged with excited crowds and the park of St James was a green bower, the waters of the lake shimmering sky-blue and leaf-green, and the massed trees whispering most lusciously in the morning air. Six field guns were drawn up on the grass ready for the salute and manned by a troup of the Royal Household Artillery, resplendent in busbies and gold-frogged uniforms. It was very exciting.

The palace grounds were full of carriages arriving, wheeling about and departing, and as the Easter party took their places facing the palace, their friends walked across to greet them and pass the time of day. Euphemia had never seen so many fine clothes, all so well cut and so beautifully fitted and in such clearly printed colours. Caroline was dressed in the most delectable spotted muslin, embroidered with pink rosebuds and little blue flowers that she said were called forget-me-nots, which seemed a quite charming name, and her bonnet was trimmed with magnificent blue ribbons that exactly matched the blue trim on her parasol.

'Pretty, ain't it?' she said to Euphemia, noticing her new friend's admiration, and twirling the little sunshade for her inspection.

'The fashion here is very fine,' Euphemia said. 'Your Nan looks grand enough to be the Queen.'

But at that moment the guns in the park began to fire the salute and a window opened in the middle of the first floor of the palace and there was the new Queen herself. Everybody stopped talking at once and looked upwards, straining their necks so as not to miss a thing.

'But she's tiny!' Caroline whispered to Euphemia. 'She's not much bigger than you and me!' And their new queen certainly looked very small, standing between the bulky figures of Lord Lansdowne and Lord Melbourne, the Prime Minister, both in full state dress with blue ribbands. Oh, very small and very pale. She was dressed in black except for a white tippet about her neck and white cuffs at her wrists and a border of white lace under her plain black bonnet. But she wore no veil and from where they sat they could see her little sad face quite clearly and the fair hair parted simply over her forehead. Oh, she was a dear little queen.

Then the Garter King at Arms rode into the courtyard on a splendid grey followed by heralds and pursuivants in their brightly quartered robes of office, and the cobbles were suddenly hidden by a blaze of red and gold and purple. There were eight officers of arms on horseback carrying massive silver maces, the Sergeant Trumpeter with his mace and collar, massed trumpeters and drummers, the Knights Marshal and his men, and last and most importantly the Duke of Norfolk whose function it was, as Earl Marshal of England, to read the proclamation.

The great crowd listened in a silence only broken by the snort of horses and the occasional rattle of accoutrements while the historic words echoed round and round the courtyard. But when the final phrase was spoken, they broke into such a cheer that they made the horses shift with alarm.

And the Queen smiled at them and waved her little white hand, and so the deed was done.

'Wasn't that thrilling!' Caroline said. 'Are you staying to lunch?'

'Of course,' Nan said, 'we can't send you home unfed, can we, Euphemia?'

In fact they didn't send her home until it was nearly time for bed. And by then she had taken lunch and dinner with them and Caroline had assumed full charge of her. During dinner Nan started them talking about schools. Will entertained them with tales of his life at King Edward's school, and Caroline had described her dear Mrs Flowerdew and the drawing afternoons.

'But then you are to go to school too, are you not?' she asked Euphemia. 'So you will see all this for yourself.'

'Yes,' Euphemia said, but she didn't sound at all enthusiastic.

'Don't you want to go to school?' Nan asked.

The answer was resigned. 'If my father wishes it.'

'Do *you* wish it?' Caroline said. 'Oh you must, surely. There is such a lot to do at school and so many people. Think how dull it would be at home all by yourself.' She'd quite forgotten how passionately she'd opposed her own schooling.

Euphemia was careful not to say anything that might appear critical of her father. 'If it is to be, it will be,' she said.

'If it is to be, then why shouldn't it be at Mrs Flowerdew's?' Caroline said, seeing the solution at once. 'If your father means to send you to a boarding school anyway, he might as well send you to Mrs Flowerdew's. You'd like *that*, I can tell you.'

Euphemia was so overwhelmed by the way she was being taken over by this energetic cousin of hers that she didn't know what to say. After the vivid colour of her life in Calcutta, and the muddled gentleness of it, all those dusty orange sunsets, and the river full of bobbing black heads and flowing arms religiously sluicing themselves with water, and the roads stained red with betel juice, and her dear ayah with her gap-toothed smile and her tender eyes, now here in this bustling, purposeful city she felt as though she was being dragged along behind a team of horses. It would be nice to go to school with Caroline, that was true, but everything was happening too quickly. In just twenty-four hours her life seemed to have changed entirely. 'I . . . that is . . . ' she said.

But Caroline was explaining her plan to her grandmother.

'Well now,' Nan said, grinning at them both. 'How would it be if I told you it was already arranged?' How well this was working out!

'Truly?' Caroline said, clapping her hands together.

'Truly. I gave Mrs Flowerdew's brochure to Euphemia's father some time ago. She is already entered there.'

Rapturous hugging and squeals of delight.

'And as she's to attend the same school, I daresay I could prevail upon Mr Callbeck to let her board with us, if you'd like that.'

Could there be any doubt?

So Euphemia came to stay with her cousin and was prepared for school. They had a marvellous time. First they went out with Bessie and bought material for a wardrobe of English clothes for Euphemia, and then they went to the pleasure gardens, and the theatre, and for a boat trip along the Thames as far as Richmond, and on the afternoon of the third day they discovered to their delight that they were both about to celebrate their birthdays, and that wonder of wonders,

Euphemia's twelfth birthday was on 27 June, the day before Caroline's eleventh.

'You are a year and a day older than me,' Caroline said. 'It's like the fair stories. It is always a year and a day in fairy stories. We must have two parties, mustn't we Bessie, one on each day.'

So they had two parties, and they went back to Mrs Flower-dew's Seminary together and by the end of that summer they were as close as sisters, and Euphemia said she'd never felt so happy in all her life. When her parents took ship for India in the autumn, she hardly noticed them go.

'Very satisfactory,' Nan said to John. 'A companion of her own age was just what your Caroline needed.'

Chapter 5

'Have you seen today's *Gazette*?' Jeff Jefferson called, striding through the Market Place in Cambridge towards Will Easter and Dodo Overthorne.

It was a bright spring day just before the start of the summer term in Queen Victoria's coronation year, and the town was suddenly a place of milk and honey, a place of generosity, a place anticipating the easy abundance of summer. The streets were strewn with fresh sand, a pleasant ochre after the grime of winter, the buildings glowed with that particular honey-coloured blue-shadowed patina that only early sunshine will bestow, and the canvas canopies of the stalls below them were long swathes of undulating cream and yellow. The market was busy that day, the stalls heaped with produce, earth-brown potatoes, cabbage and cauliflowers, mounds of yellow parsnips, green and white swedes, baskets of eggs in every shade from chocolate to cream. The poultry stalls were curtained with fur and feathers, ducks and chickens hung by the beak, and rabbits by the heels, their white bellies soft in the sunshine, and lying across one stall was a long line of plucked geese, their white-ruffed heads dangling a mere six dripping inches above the sand.

It was the first time Jeff had seen his two friends since the end of March. What a bit of luck they'd come up so early and dressed so stylishly. No one could miss them among all that buff and cream, for Dodo was flamboyant in his emerald green jacket, with a bright blue stock and a new waistcoat embroidered in sky-blue, orange and purple, and Will sported a new

74

jacket in burgundy red with a silk plush hat to match. They were lounging against the railings beside Hobson's conduit, watching as the market women filled their buckets and pails, and Dodo's monocle caught the sun like a jewel as he raised it elegantly to his eye.

'Never mind the *Gazette*,' Will said as his old friend came puffing up beside him. 'You ain't heard *my* news. I'm to start work with the *Morning Advertiser* this summer as ever is, providing I pass muster with my first commission. What do you think of that, eh?'

'They'll regret it,' Jeff said happily, punching Will on the arm to show how pleased he was. 'What's the commission?'

'He's to write about the coronation,' Dodo yawned, feigning boredom with the whole subject. 'Pretty damned original, eh?'

'Then you'd better read the *Gazette*,' Jeff said, thrusting the paper at Will. 'Remember that letter from Tubby?'

'Oh God!' Dodo groaned. 'Which letter? He's always writin' letters. Can't stop the fool.'

'The letter about the coronation,' Jeff said. 'You remember. "Let Cambridge feed the five thousand." Well, read that and see if he ain't started something.'

Will took the paper and read the article below his friend's urgent finger. 'My stars!' he said. 'They're going to do it. They're actually going to feed the poor to celebrate the coronation. "What better way could there be to mark our allegiance to the Queen than by a simple and public act of charity and goodwill towards the poorest of her people?"'

'Simple?' Dodo protested, swaying his long legs away from the splash of a passing pail. 'Feeding five thousand paupers?'

'Fourteen thousand,' Jeff corrected. 'Fourteen thousand from every single parish hereabouts. Ain't that the most amazing thing?'

'They are asking for volunteers to help in the organization,' Will said, still reading the paper. 'How about it, Dodo? I'm game if you are. It'll be a lark.' And it would give him the very thing to write about. A local piece, full of local colour. It couldn't be better.

'They don't need volunteers yet,' Dodo protested. 'It's only April, for heaven's sake. The coronation ain't for months.'

'Twenty-eighth of June,' Jeff told him. 'Nine weeks. No time at all.'

'It's my sister's birthday too,' Will said. 'I could invite her up to see this for a birthday treat. How's that for an idea? In fact I could invite all my cousins and you two and Tubby and we could have supper together at the Eagle, as a reward for our efforts. Come on, Dodo. Say the word.'

'Madness,' Dodo groaned, adjusting his monocle.

'I knew you'd agree,' Will said, grinning at him. 'Come on then. No time like the present.' And he went striding off through the covered stalls towards Petty Cury, walking at such speed that the six dangling geese swung their necks at his passing as though they were still alive.

John Easter was pleased to hear that his son had joined the organizing committee, and wrote off at once to pledge his support, 'which will be largely monetary, I fear, since I am unlikely to be in Cambridge for any length of time between now and the coronation.'

'It will be excellent experience for him,' he said to Nan when she came back to London at the beginning of May. 'Give him a taste for organization.'

'I thought he'd took a job with the *Advertiser*,' Nan said.

'If they'll have him,' John said. 'He has to earn it, so he tells me. And he might not like it, even if it is offered. No, no, I shall start him in the Stamping Office in July, you'll see. Unless Mr Brougham and his friends have repealed the Stamp Act by then.'

'Would that they could,' Nan sighed. The necessity to have all newspapers stamped was a daily chore she deeply resented. 'It'ud save us a deal of bother and earn us a deal of trade.'

'A pipe dream,' Billy said. 'The government are far more likely to increase the licence than abolish it, when it brings in such a steady revenue and keeps out undesirable news-sheets into the bargain.'

'Not all of them,' John said. 'There's a fiery publication new out, so I'm told, edited by a gentleman called Feargus O'Connor and advocating reform in no uncertain terms, and all stamped and legal and above board.'

'What's the price of it?' Nan asked, interested at once.

'Fourpence ha'penny.'

'Reasonable enough in all conscience. What's the circulation?'

'Thirty thousand, so they say.'

Her interest increased. 'Do we sell it?'

'No.'

'Then we shall.' It was one way out of the doldrums. 'I will negotiate with Mr O'Connor this afternoon.' And she brushed the palms of her hands against each other, swish, swish, the way she always did when she'd made an important decision.

'Your regional managers won't like it,' John warned. 'It's a very radical paper.'

'We'll persuade 'em.'

Billy laughed out loud. 'You mean you'll ride roughshod over 'em,' he said.

'Something a' that,' she agreed, grinning at him.

'And you wonder why your Caroline is so strong-willed,' Billy said to his brother.

'She's being saintly, just at present,' Nan said. 'When I left she was trimming her summer bonnet with white ribbon, ready for Will's coronation party.'

'What a blessing they are all going to Cambridge for the occasion,' John said wryly. 'London will be quite peaceful with only the ceremony and the procession to contend with.'

Will's coronation supper was all arranged. He had written to all his cousins, informing them that rooms had been booked for them to stay overnight at the Eagle in Benet Street where the party was being held, and urging them to meet him on Parker's Piece as soon after mid-day as they could.

'We are building a rotunda in the middle of the field,' he wrote. 'A sizeable construction which will make a first-rate landmark, so I suggest we meet there. I will walk around it until you are all arrived.'

He was right. Nobody could have missed the rotunda. It was set right in the middle of the field, topped by the royal standard, hung about with flowers, and big enough to contain the full string orchestra that had been hired to play throughout the proceedings. There was a circular promenade all around it, where the college hierarchy strolled in the deliberately careless splendour of their scarlet gowns, and the gentry gathered to admire their generosity. And radiating out from the promenade like the spokes of some enormous wheel were sixty very long tables, each one marked by a pennant on which was written the names of the parishes and Sunday schools that were to feed there.

When Caroline and Euphemia arrived, with Bessie in attendance, the feast had already begun and the Piece was swarming with people, the poor meekly following the bold colours of their parish banners into the field, walking in well-ordered columns and wearing their Sunday best and suitable grateful expressions, the rich driving their carriages through the throng and causing havoc among the horse-drawn wagons that were trying to deliver meat and pickles to the first arrivals. What with horses and marching columns, chattering crowds and squealing fiddles, the place was noisier than the Strand in high summer, and the stewards were having a hard time of it, trying to direct the new arrivals through loud-hailers which could barely be heard.

'What sport!' Caroline said. 'Let's find Will. He'll be in the middle somewhere, because he promised. Come on!' And she led them off between the tables.

'She don't stop to think,' Bessie grumbled, but she limped after her young mistress as quickly as she could because she didn't want to lose her in the throng. Not after what happened in that awful blizzard. 'Stick to 'er like glue, Euphemia,' she called, and was relieved to see that Euphemia was clinging onto Caroline's outflung hand.

And there was Will, looking very grand in his burgundy coat, with three of his friends leaping round him, all long legs and silly expressions, and her dear, sensible Jimmy behind them, talking to Edward, with his sisters clinging to his arms, and Matty sitting on a chair with her new parasol shading her pretty curls. Oh, thank heavens for that, they're all here safely. Being put in charge of them all was a heavy responsibility.

'Dear old Bessie,' Will greeted her, stooping from his lovely height to kiss her cheek. 'Ain't this just the style? All brought about by the power of the press. What do you think of that, eh?' And he turned to welcome Carrie and Euphemia.

He was bristling with excitement, thrilled by the enormity of their success, his thick hair bushing about his temples, his skin glowing with exertion and well-being, his eyes smiling and shining and the most startling blue, exactly the same colour as the sky behind his head and the forget-me-nots embroidered on his waistcoat. 'What do you think of that?' he repeated, beaming down at them.

'You're a clever old thing,' Caroline said, flinging her arms about his neck to be kissed and swung about.

But Euphemia, who had received the full force of his triumphant masculinity, Euphemia couldn't say a word. She suddenly found she was suffering from a most peculiar paralysis. Her throat was dry and her limbs were incapable of movement, but her senses felt as though they were being stretched, she was experiencing so much and so acutely: the starchy swirl of Caroline's white skirt and Will's hands holding her strongly about the waist; violins on the rotunda singing shrill as robins; the clatter of carriages and the reek of horses; the smell of warm new wool from Will's beautiful burgundy jacket wafting out upon her as he turned; the hissing rustle of a passing petticoat somewhere behind her; voices and laughter and people munching; Will's kiss, smacked against Caroline's cheek, once, twice, three times. Oh, what rapture to be kissed by Mr William Easter!

And then Jimmy and Matty were beside her, greeting her, and there was an onrush of Easters as they all set off to stroll around the promenade, and she found she could walk after all, and the moment was pushed aside by the activity of the afternoon.

By three o'clock, Caroline declared she was 'just about ready to faint with hunger with all these people making pigs of themselves everywhere,' so they all trouped off to the nearest inn for potted trout and veal cutlets washed down with ale or lemonade. And after that they followed the crowds to Midsummer Common for the rustic sports.

Although Euphemia had been to the theatre and the opera and lots of parties during the past year, because Will and Caroline treated her like a sister and took her with them everywhere they went, she had never seen an English summer fair before and was quite amazed by it. She was intrigued to watch grown men playing like children, bolting biscuits until they were apoplectic, or permitting their hands to be tied behind their backs and then struggling to eat apples suspended on a bobbing string, or pulling their faces into the most grotesque expressions they could manage while the crowd roared and shrieked encouragement. But when Will took his stand for the Town versus Gown tug-of-war she cheered with the best and was quite cast down when the locals finally hauled the students over the line.

They watched wheelbarrow races, that were fast and rough, and donkey races, that were haphazard and reluctant, and boys rooting in tubs of bran for the prize of a penny loaf and a tin of treacle. They tossed quoits over sticks and hurled wooden balls at coconuts and Jimmy won a little doll carved out of a clothes peg and gave it to Matty. And as the evening began to draw in, with a flourish of orange cloud under the darkening trees, they all ran over to the far side of the common to watch the renowned Mr Green of Vauxhall actually ascend into the air in a wicker basket suspended under a huge red and yellow balloon.

By the time the fair was over they were all hoarse with laughter and wonderfully dishevelled, their hair tangled, their gloves grimed and their shoes grey with dust. And there was still the supper to come.

So Bessie discharged her last duty of the day, ensuring that Caroline and Euphemia were washed and groomed and dressed for the occasion and sent them down to the meal, glad of the chance to put her feet up. And the Eagle did them proud, with boiled fowl and oysters, a very tasty sirloin, fresh pickles, walnuts and gherkins, wines both dry and sweet, and an excellent strawberry tart heaped with cream.

'Not half bad,' Dodo approved, holding up his plate for a second helping of tart. 'Well, we've celebrated the coronation in high old style, wouldn't you say?'

'Couldn't have been bettered,' Jeff said, propping his feet on the edge of the table. 'Is there any more claret?'

'By Jimmy's elbow,' Will said, beaming. 'Fill your glasses, all of you. I've a toast to make.'

Glasses were filled and faces lifted towards him, expecting to hear the name of the Queen. But he surprised them. 'Here's to my sister, Carrie,' he said, 'who is twelve today. Happy birthday Carrie!' And he walked round the table, glass in hand, to kiss her.

They drank and grinned at her and wished her many happy returns. 'Did the Queen ask your permission to be crowned on your birthday?' Tubby teased.

'Course,' Caroline said, saucing him. 'We great ones have to stick together. Am I allowed to offer a toast too?'

'Offer away, birthday queen!' Tubby said, spreading his arms wide.

'A toast!' Caroline said. 'A toast to our cousin, Euphemia Callbeck, who celebrated *her* birthday yesterday.'

'Euphemia!' they said, drinking her health. 'Happy birthday!' And Will carried his glass round the table once again and bent to kiss her too, briefly, on a cheek grown rose-pink with expectation. And the kiss made her blush so violently that she had to duck her head in a vain attempt to hide her feelings. She had spent her birthday quietly with Caroline because that was only right and proper, and now here she was being given the most public congratulations. Oh, dear dear Will, dear handsome Will. I shall remember this moment for ever.

'We should drink to the Queen now, shouldn't we?' Jimmy said, rescuing her.

'The Queen, God bless her,' Jeff said, raising his glass. 'Long may she reign over us.'

'She's young enough, in all conscience,' Dodo observed when he'd drunk the toast.

'Mrs Flowerdew says she will start a reign of youth,' Caroline told him. 'Youth will come into its own, she says.'

'And about time too,' Edward said, smoothing his hair. 'Youth at the helm, eh? Why should the greybeards run the world?'

'Because they have more experience of it?' Will said. He was annoyed with Edward because he'd done nothing at all to help the organizing committee. Lazy toad.

'Experience, pooh,' Edward said. 'What the country needs now is vision, let me tell you, and only young men have vision.'

'What about young women?' Caroline asked, ruffled by the superiority of his tone. 'Don't they have vision too?'

'Course not,' Edward said disparagingly. 'How could they? They're women.'

'There's a woman on the throne of England.'

'That's different,' he said, rather miffed at being opposed.

'I don't see how.'

'She doesn't have to do anything.'

'Oh, how can you talk such rubbish? Of course she has to do things. All sorts of things. And if she can do them so can other women. I mean to do all sorts of things myself.'

'Like get married and have children,' Edward said, sneering at her. 'You may talk of women and their visions if you like, but the only thing that interests you is weddings.'

Caroline rounded on him at once. 'Well, that's where you're wrong, Edward Easter,' she said fiercely. 'You ask me what I mean to do and you'll see.'

'Very well then,' Edward said, crossly. 'What do you mean to do?'

'She means to work in Easter's,' Will said, smiling at her. 'Don't you Carrie?'

'No,' she said, smiling back. 'I mean to be the managing director.'

In the cheering amazement that followed none of them noticed that Edward was looking sour.

Later that evening when his guests were finally in bed, Will started his first newspaper article, 'Picnic at Parker's Piece', sitting alone in his room with two candles at his elbow and their reflected images flickering like stars in all the dark panes of the window beside him. He had used up so much energy in observation during the day that now he was exhausted, but he wrote at speed, his pen scratching the paper and his hair falling into his eyes, afraid he would forget half the things he wanted to say before he could commit them to paper. The rich helping the poor, gown serving town, commoner and Queen rejoicing together.

He was still writing when the dawn chorus began and the sky lightened to a dark dusty blue, then to blue streaked grey, then to grey streaked green. And he wasn't satisfied with what he'd written until the sun was up, the candles snuffed and another summer's day was blowing warmth upon him through his newly opened window. He took the article to the post before breakfast, tremulous with hope and fatigue. Then he went to Benet Street to wake his sister.

Whatever came of it, he had taken his first step towards the career he wanted. Now it was just a matter of waiting and keeping quiet. He told no one what he'd written, not even Carrie, just in case he was rejected, and he determined to fill the waiting days with study for much the same reason.

He didn't have to wait long. His article was published by the *Morning Advertiser* the following day and that afternoon a letter arrived with a sizeable fee and the offer of a job, 'six months as a reporter exclusive to this Paper'. When he rode over to Bury on Saturday morning, Caroline and Euphemia greeted him like a hero.

'My brother, the journalist!' Caroline said, hugging him. 'We've started a scrap book, ain't we, Pheemy. Come and see. We're going to keep every single one of your articles and you're to sign them with loving messages for us so that we can show our friends. Here's a pen.'

Her admiration was like sunshine. 'Where's Nan?' he said, basking.

'Gone to London to see Pa. She said it was good too, didn't she, Pheemy?'

'I must go to London tomorrow,' he said. 'The editor wants to see me on Monday morning.' How marvellous to be able to say such a thing. But he knew he would have to speak to his father first and that was going to be difficult. Perhaps Nan would help him. What a blessing she was in London too.

Chapter 6

'I can't say I'm not disappointed,' John Easter said. 'No, no. You know I can't say that. You know how much the company means to me.'

'Yes,' Will said. He was torn by the pain he was causing his father but he was still resolved, buoyed up by success and an odd boiling excitement that was putting fight into him whether he would or no. 'I do know father.'

'Yes,' John echoed, giving Will his wry smile. 'I can see that you do. So what is to be done?'

'I would like to accept their offer.'

'For six months?'

The true answer should have been 'For ever', but the warning flicker of Nan's glance and his own compassion suppressed it. 'For six months, yes.'

'I had hoped you would start work with me this summer,' John said. But then he felt alarmed to be showing his feelings so clearly. 'However . . . '

The cloth had been removed but they were still at table. Outside in Bedford Square a blackbird was piping its sad, sweet, full-throated song into the opal colours of the sunset. Nan stood up and walked across to the window, looking out into the deepening green of the gardens.

'You could spend a part of your time with the firm, I daresay, Will,' she said quietly, 'even if you did take up with this reporting. That en't beyond the bounds of possibility. Two or three mornings a week, perhaps, some afternoons. To learn the trade.'

It seemed a pointless exercise to Will but seeing the hope on his father's face he agreed that he could. 'After finals, of course.'

That was understood. 'It would be sensible to get to know the business,' John said. 'Just in case . . .'

'Yes.'

'I would prefer you not to undertake to work abroad.'

Work abroad was forsworn, 'for the time being'. It was a sacrifice, but a possible one considering what was being gained.

'Then I think we have found a workable solution,' John said. And they shook hands upon it.

Like all compromises it didn't satisfy either of them, but they were pleased with it nevertheless. All was not lost. There was still hope.

'That's settled then,' Nan said, dusting the palms of her hands against each other. 'That's what we'll do.'

'Phoo-eep phoo-eep tirralirraloo!' the blackbird sang. What a sad, sweet, compromised world we live in!

Nobody in the family was surprised by the decision. It was just what they expected.

'Will's a sensible lad,' Billy said to his wife.

'He always has been,' she agreed. 'He is very like his father.' Actually his good sense and his good looks were a private aggravation to her. 'Of course he hasn't got the same brilliance as our Edward, but you can't have everything.'

'I would like it better if our Edward had a little of Will's ability to compromise,' Billy said gruffly.

'That ain't his nature,' Matilda admitted.

And it never had been. For Edward was a child apart, a creature of extremes, confident to the point of arrogance when he was in command and things were going his way, but withdrawing into a silence that was disquietingly like a melancholy when things were going wrong. Life would have been a great deal easier for all of them if he could have been effortlessly agreeable like his sister Matty or his cousin Will. But that had never been the way of it. It would be a good thing when he'd finished his education and could take his rightful place in the firm and be in command all the time.

When the results of Will's final examinations were announced, Matilda was rather put out to hear that he had taken a first, but she comforted herself that her son would do just as well when he settled down to serious study. At the moment of course he was still enjoying himself with all his new friends, as she knew very well because she and Billy bore the expense of it, but with his brilliant understanding of mathematics he could afford to waste a little time.

Nevertheless he was still gadding in October when his sister married the Reverend Jimmy Hopkins. That was another family event that caused no surprise. Everyone had always known they would marry. They'd been constant companions from childhood, ever since that awful season when they'd both caught the smallpox that had left them so horribly scarred. And now they were married and had gone to live and work in Clerkenwell because they wanted to help the poor. Edward didn't think that was at all sensible.

'If you ask me,' he said to Will at the wedding breakfast, 'the poor should learn to help themselves. There's no need for poverty. Most of it is mere laziness.'

'Or lack of political power,' Will suggested. 'There is a new charter being written to petition for universal suffrage. Did you know that?'

Edward neither knew nor cared.

'Nan's friend Mr Place is organizing it. I'm to interview him on Monday. If the poor had the vote, they would be able to help themselves, don't you think?'

'Nonsense!' Edward said. 'They don't need the vote. That would be casting pearls before swine. They wouldn't know what to do with it if we gave it to them. No, no, cousin Will, all they need is determination and a bit of hard work. That's all. I shouldn't bother with Mr Place if I were you.'

Will paid no attention to such advice. He'd been looking forward to this particular assignment ever since it was first suggested. Having described the trivialities of a May Ball, an opening night at the theatre, Henley Regatta and Derby Day, it was pleasant to be given something more important to write about. And besides he'd heard a great deal about the renowned Mr Place from Nan, who had known him since they were both young.

'He's a good man,' she told her grandson. 'He's been a-worriting for the vote these thirty years, to my certain knowledge, but he don't weary and he don't give up. He knew your mother of course. She spoke at several of his meetings after Peterloo. A good man.'

But a very dusty one, standing in the gloom of his untidy bookshop among piles of pamphlets and tables heaped with papers and shelves collapsing under books, blinking in the sudden shaft of sunlight that had entered the door with his visitor; a pale, dusty man with a shock of grey hair bristling above his forehead and a face seamed with worry lines and sharp, bright, shrewd eyes.

'Come in, come in,' he said, holding out his hand to Will. 'You are your mother's son, Mr Easter. I can see that, even in this poor light.'

It was a good start. And the interview that followed was friendly and informative. A copy of the charter was produced and explained. 'Six points, as you see, all deemed to be of equal importance, so we may take them in any order you wish. Full adult suffrage, of course, salaries for members of parliament, otherwise a poor man could not stand, voting by secret ballot to avoid corruption, parliaments elected annually to encourage accountability, equal electoral districts for the sake of fairness, and no property qualification for members of parliament, for obvious reasons.'

Will thought it all manifestly just and honourable.

'And so it is,' Mr Place said, 'as any just and honourable man may see. Now as to the means by which it is to be achieved, we intend to gather a million signatures upon a massive national petition, which will be presented to parliament some time next spring. I trust you will report upon that, too?'

'So do I, Mr Place, sir. So do I.' A petition of such a size sounded most impressive.

'You may not come of a poor family as your mother did,' Mr

Place observed, 'but I see that you share her sympathies notwithstanding. It is a great credit to you. I am glad to have made your acquaintance, Mr Easter.'

'And I yours.'

'Howsomever, if you truly wish to understand this movement and the despair that inspires it, might I suggest that you take your notebook for a stroll through one of the slums of this metropolis. There are plenty of them. Seven Dials for instance, or Spitalfields, or Saffron Hill.'

'My cousin is rector of the New Church in Saffron Hill.'

'Then visit with your cousin, sir, with all speed, and preferably before you write this article. Nothing speaks more clearly than first-hand experience. Depend upon it.'

This advice seemed eminently sensible, so Will took it, writing to Jimmy that very evening 'in hopes of an invitation', which was instantly given.

He was a most rewarding guest, praising Matty's housewifery and admiring the furnishings of their home on Clerkenwell Green, and listening at length to Jimmy's tales of life in Saffron Hill.

'When I read Mr Dickens' new novel, you know,' Jimmy told him, as their meal came to an end, 'his *Oliver Twist*, I thought he must surely be exaggerating, but now I know better. It is every bit as bad as he says. Every bit. He wrote the book about this very place, you see, which was one of the reasons why I wanted to work here. The 'Three Cripples' is a stone's throw from my church, and I really do mean a stone's throw. In fact we are lucky if it is only a stone. The children here will throw anything they can lay their hands upon. But no wonder. No wonder. I cannot blame them, for they know no better. Who is there to teach them better in this dreadful place? That terrible man Fagin lived in Saffron Hill and lives there still as far as I can see.'

Will looked round their dining room, at the bright fire in the hearth and the lamps glowing against the wall, at the neatly flowered wallpaper and the fine red damask of the curtains, at the table set with good china and well-polished silver and crystal glasses winking in the firelight, and he understood the concern of this tender-hearted cousin of his. 'You are here now,' he said. 'You will teach them better, I am sure of it.'

'Indeed yes,' Jimmy said. 'I have started a Sunday school already, which is always crowded, I'm very glad to say.'

'Well of course it's crowded,' Matty said, loving him with her eyes, 'when we feed them soup before we send them home.'

'What are good words without good works?' Jimmy said. 'The soup may tempt them in through the doors in the first place, but it is the word of God that will change their lives. And oh how much these lives need change, Will. I will take you to Field Lane presently, and you will see what it is we have to oppose. It is a mighty task.'

So when Will had been persuaded to remove the diamond pin from his cravat and the cash from his pocket, and to leave his handkerchief and scarf behind, because they could so easily be stolen, the two young men took a lantern and set off on a tour of the parish.

They walked south towards the City, up Little Saffron Hill, where children swarmed like flies outside every beer-shop, tousle-headed, bare-footed and rank-smelling in rags so thin and tatty they gave no warmth and precious little cover, then into Saffron Hill and past Jimmy's candlelit church, and from there to Field Lane, where a solitary street lamp cast just enough light for a circle of street arabs to play dabs, their grey hands scrabbling in the dirt. It was a very dark alley and so narrow that in some places it would have been possible to stand in the middle of the street and touch the rotting houses on either side. Possible that is, but not likely, for the place was teeming with people and commerce.

There was a barber's shop, full of tatty customers being shaved by candlelight, a very sour beer-shop doing a raucous trade, and a fish shop offering dollops of fried fish bloated with batter, but every other house was selling scarves. They hung from poles on either side of the alley, lit by lamps hung above the doors and windows, dangling just above the level of the tallest top hat, pegged out like washing. And very expensive washing, for these were silk scarves and paisleys, embroidered and fringed and inappropriately beautiful in such a setting.

Will raised his eyebrows in enquiry.

'Stolen,' Jimmy explained succinctly.

'But who would buy such articles, here in this poverty?'

'Merchants,' Jimmy said, 'small shopkeepers, all manner

of people, but mostly those who have had their scarves stolen. They come from miles around to buy them back. Look about you. It's a recognized trade.' And sure enough there were plenty of well-dressed customers among the jostling poor.

'It's a scandal,' Will said. 'Why, that is tantamount to giving thieves a licence to steal.'

'Now you see what it is I face,' Jimmy said, watching as two gentlemen carefully examined a row of silk scarves, pulling them towards the nearest light. 'Most of my parishioners live outside the law, outside society. They do not belong, either to the church or the city. They are pariahs. Matty and I have rescued four of them by training them up as housemaids and giving them somewhere decent to live. I realize it could be said that they are only four among so many, but at least we have made a start. And great oaks from little acorns, you know.'

That night Will wrote his article, describing the charter and advertising the petition. 'Each signature will be an acorn dropping upon the ground of parliamentary indifference,' he wrote. 'What oaks will grow of them we cannot tell. But any man who walks in Field Lane after dusk must surely recognize the need for the changes they request.'

The article was edited, as he expected, but enough of it survived in Wednesday morning's paper to make Nan pat him on the back on his way in to the stamping. 'A fine piece,' she said. 'Your mother would be proud of you.'

'I do my best to spread the word,' he told her cheerfully.

'You and Mr O'Connor both,' she said.

All through that winter and the following spring, Mr Feargus O'Connor's powerful newspaper, the *Northern Star*, kept his readers informed about the progress of the petition, which had a million signatures before Christmas, and was supported by torchlit processions and passionate meetings up and down the country, some of which Will reported. And the great firm of A. Easter and Sons sold the *Northern Star* in all their shops, to the considerable agitation of the regional managers. Or to be more accurate, to the considerable agitation of Mr Hugh Jernegan and his new ally Mr Joshua Maycock, who was manager of the region of Middlesex.

'I do question,' Mr Jernegan said towards the end of the March meeting, 'I do question whether we are altogether wise to be seen as the purveyors of such debasing opinions as those expressed in the *Northern Star*, especially at a time like this, with the likelihood of violence in the streets when this wretched petition is presented.'

'T'en't for us to question the politics of what we sell,' Nan said briskly. 'We'd be here all night if we started that sort of caper. The *Northern Star* is a legal newspaper, stamped by the Post Office and selling better every week. Forty thousand copies en't to be sniffed at, gentlemen. That's all need concern us.'

'I feel I should point out,' Mr Maycock smoothed, 'that the sale of such violently radical opinions might well have an adverse effect upon trade, given the government's feelings upon the matter.'

'If the government have feelings upon the matter,' Nan said coolly, 'then I daresay the government will take action, that being their business. Our business is to sell newspapers.'

'But what if our sales were affected?' Mr Maycock said. 'I only ask out of concern for the firm. That is my one and only concern, Mrs Easter, as I'm sure you appreciate.'

'This month's figures are uncommon healthy,' Nan said. 'I don't see many signs of adverse influence there. Meantime there's the matter of the Bradford shop. Is that roof mended yet?'

'She thinks revolutionaries may be dealt with in the same way as roof-tiles,' Mr Maycock muttered to his friend.

'She will learn better when they present that foolish petition of theirs,' Mr Jernegan muttered back, smoothing his mutton-chop whiskers with the back of his hand. 'There'll be bloodshed on that day, I can tell you, and then where shall we be?'

'A black-hearted lot!' Mr Maybury agreed. 'And it will be a black-hearted day, you mark my words.'

The black-hearted day began with a symphony of church bells and birdsong. The chorus in Bedford Square was so loud that it woke the household. Nan smiled at it, and turned on her side to sleep again. But Will got out of bed and walked to the window

91

to see as well as hear, excited now that the great day had arrived, and particularly as Jeff Jefferson was being sent to London to report the event too and they planned to watch the procession together as soon as his morning's work was done.

The stamping that morning took for ever. It wasn't until eleven o'clock that his father said he could cut off if he wanted to, and by then Jeff had been waiting in the coffee house for 'more than half an hour, old thing'. He was twitching with impatience and the minute he saw Will he rushed out into the Strand to call a cab and take them to Regent Street.

They found the new avenue packed with people waiting for the procession. Will paid their cabbie his exorbitant sixpence and he and Jeff eased themselves into the throng, standing right on the edge of the pavement despite the complaints of two rather seedy gentlemen who were now behind them. They were determined to get the best possible view. And their determination was rewarded.

After thirty minutes or so, they heard the bray of a brass band above the noise of the crowd and the outriders turned into Regent Street from Langham Place with the marchers close behind them.

'That's Mr Feargus O'Connor on the grey,' Jeff said, squinting up the road at them, 'and the fat fellow on the mare is Bronterre O'Brien.'

Not very imposing, Will thought, glancing at Mr O'Brien, whose face looked too babyish for the leader of such a demonstration, but Mr O'Connor was a man with an air, tall, grey haired and handsome on his bold white horse. I'll interview him when they get to the House. No wonder Nan speaks well of him. And the marchers were equally impressive, all immaculately dressed in their Sunday best, their jackets in suitably sober colours, dark blue, brown, magenta, bottle green, their hats black, their trousers fawn or grey or dark brown tweed, their expressions serious. They marched like soldiers, keeping firm step across the column, but as each man followed the drumbeat a fraction of a second later than the man in front of him, the march had acquired a rhythmically rippling effect that made the approaching column look like some huge pale-legged centipede.

Even if the marchers' clothes were sombre, they were spotlessly clean, and the banners that streamed above their heads were dazzling, huge sheets of scarlet, orange, purple and sky-blue with the words 'Liberty' and 'Reform' written on them in bold black letters.

And then suddenly the petition itself was upon them, its vast bulk neatly folded and cloud-white above the dark hats of the marchers. It was carried in a wooden cage like an enormous orange box mounted on two long stout poles that were supported shoulder high by twenty-four bearers, twelve before and twelve behind. And as it passed the crowd grew silent and some bowed their heads or removed their caps and even children who had been noisily bowling hoops and playing tag were stilled and overawed.

'Over two million signatures,' Will said, 'and three miles long! It's a wondrous thing, Jeff. The government must accept these reforms now, surely.'

The petition was passing, the crowd beginning to murmur again. And behind the bearers was a wide red banner bearing the inscription 'Murder demands justice: 16 August 1819'.

'16th of August 1819?' Jeff wondered.

'The battle of Peterloo,' Will explained. 'In Manchester. When the local militia attacked a peaceful demonstration and massacred eleven people. That was for universal suffrage too. You must have heard of it. My mother was there.'

'At a massacre?' Jeff asked.

'Yes,' Will said proudly. 'She helped tend the wounded. She and a weaver called Caleb Rawson. I think that's one of the reasons why everyone says she was a saint.'

'Well, good for her,' Jeff said, much impressed. 'So that's the reason you're reporting all this now. Following in mother's footsteps and all that sort of thing, eh?'

But Will was already looking for another cab to take them to Parliament Square. He wanted to see the petition arrive, and to find out when it would be presented to the House, and to interview Mr O'Connor.

Their second cab was speedy because the driver was eager for dinner and had no time to waste in detours or conversation, so the two young men arrived in Westminster long before the procession. Neither of them had realized what a long time such a march would take to walk from the West End, nor what a business it would be to accommodate so many people in a small square crowded with builders' carts and gangs of navvies and all the paraphernalia that was required to clear the ground for the building of the new Houses of Parliament.

It was late afternoon before the petition finally arrived at the portals of Westminster Hall only to discover that its container was too big to be carried through the door. There was a passionate argument, which Will duly noted, while the crowds milled about inside the enclosed space, craning their necks to see what was going on, and at last reason prevailed and the petition was taken out of its box and divided into sections small enough to be carried into the House.

'Now what?' Jeff said, as the last pile of paper disappeared.

'We wait,' Will said. 'I will interview Mr O'Connor as soon as he comes out again, and then we'll wait.'

The interview was short and lively, the wait was very long and very boring. The marchers gradually drifted away, more and more reporters arrived, lounged about with diminishing patience, took themselves off for food and sustenance, and returned to lounge again. From time to time members of the House emerged to announce that various debates were being conducted, but that no date had been set for the presentation of the petition. Lights were lit inside the building; Will and Jeff took it in turns to cut off for a bit of dinner; the debates continued; it was nine o'clock, ten, half past eleven.

Finally just before midnight, there was an eruption of excited MPs striding out into the square bellowing for carriages, and all of them hot with the latest news. Instead of receiving the petition and promising to present it, the Prime Minister had resigned.

Will made rapid notes, scanning the crowd for Frederick Brougham, and darting off to collar him the moment he saw him strolling out of the door.

'A poor business, Will,' he said, easing on his gloves.

'Has he truly resigned?'

'I fear so.'

'What will happen now?'

'We shall have a new government.'

'And the petition?'

'The petition will be delayed, I fear. It is the reform crisis all over again.'

'That won't please the Chartists,' Jeff observed.

'Indeed,' Mr Brougham said. 'To dash their hopes at the very moment of their great success is ill-judged, to say the very least. No good will come of it. We shall see heads broken for this.'

But the Chartists maintained their patience for a very long time, waiting for Mr Peel to form his new government, which took until the middle of June, and debating what further steps should be taken if that government too refused to consider the petition. Their disappointment was acute when the date set for the debate of the petition was not until mid July, but there were no riots and no hint of any until the beginning of that month, when the Chartist Convention suddenly decided that London was no longer a fit place for their assemblies and decided to reconvene in Birmingham.

'Follow them there,' the editor of the *Morning Advertiser* instructed Will Easter. 'This peace can't last. Not when feelings are running so high.'

'How long do you want me to stay?' Will asked.

'Until something happens.'

'What if it doesn't?'

'It will.'

Papa won't like this, Will thought, as he made his way homeward. An indefinite leave of absence always annoyed his father.

But this time he got an easy reception. For a start Caroline and Euphemia were in Fitzroy Square when he arrived, come up to London to buy materials for their new summer dresses and consequently full of excitement. And far from raising objections his father said he thought a visit to Birmingham was a capital idea.

'It's high time you saw the Birmingham end of the business,' he said. 'We dispatch papers from our warehouses there to every city on the north-west, you know. I daresay you could fit in a visit to the warehouse now and then, could you not? When do you want to go?'

'Well, as soon as possible really.'

'Tomorrow?'

'Yes.'

'Travel by railway train,' John said. 'They're not exactly comfortable, but they're a deal more dependable than the roads, especially in wet weather. Tom shall go with you. He knows the place. Stay at the Golden Lion in Deritend.'

'Well, you're a pretty beastly sort of brother!' Caroline pretended to complain. 'Rushing off to Birmingham the minute we get here. Pheemy thinks you're beastly too, don't you Pheemy?'

'No,' Euphemia said in some confusion, 'you know I don't, Caroline. Oh dear! You shouldn't say such things.'

'You can both come to Euston to see me off, if you like,' Will promised, rescuing her, 'and the minute I get home we'll all go to the theatre. How will that be?'

'A partial redemption,' Caroline allowed. 'What is Euston like?'

Chapter 7

It seemed peculiar to Will Easter to begin his journey in a high, echoing barn chilled in the middle of a meadow instead of a crowded inn-yard snug and low in the middle of the City. Euston station was a bleak place, even at three o'clock on a summer's afternoon. It had been built in the fields just north of Euston Square, with long bare platforms where the passengers waited to board their train, a disconcertingly high glass roof supported by narrow steel pillars, designed to accommodate the steam from the locomotives, and one end of the building left completely open to the wind and rain.

Will wasn't sure whether he liked the place or not, but Caroline was thrilled with it, declaring that the locomotives were 'splendid', and so they were, chuffing along their impossibly narrow rails towards him, belching steam like dragons through their long stove-pipe chimneys.

When Will and the two girls arrived, with Bessie and Tom Thistlethwaite in attendance, the train to Birmingham was waiting by the platform. It consisted of a long line of open carts like empty farm wagons smartly painted in magenta with gold trim, and behind them, at a good distance from the smoke and smuts of the engine, two first class carriages, each one built exactly like three stage-coaches stuck together.

'There y'are, Mr Will sir,' Tom said, opening the door of the second one. 'Seat number 4, by the winder. I shall be in the next coach back should yer want me for anything.'

'May we get in too?' Caroline asked, one foot already on the step.

'I suppose so,' Will said, helping her up, 'or I shall never hear the last of it. What do you think of it?'

'It's much better than a stage-coach,' Caroline said, bouncing up and down on the upholstery. 'Sit there, Pheemy, and you can see out of the window. Do those curtains pull?'

Euphemia was just settling into the corner seat when there was a commotion at the far end of the platform, a tramp of marching feet and a harsh voice shouting commands. The two girls had their heads out of the window at once to see what it was, and Will looked back too, from his vantage point on the step.

There was a company of Bobbies marching down the platform, about sixty of them in all, and as formidable as an army in their dark blue uniforms.

'Are they policemen?' Caroline said, hanging out of the window to stare at them as they climbed into two of the open carts labelled '3rd Class'.

'Yes,' Will told her. 'They are.'

'What are policemen doing on a train?' Euphemia wondered rather anxiously.

'Never you mind about policemen,' Bessie scolded. 'And put your heads back in the carriage, do, or you'll fall out.'

'I don't know,' Will said, stepping back onto the platform again, 'but I'll soon find out.' And he was off at once, notebook in hand to find their sergeant.

'Yes, sir,' that gentleman said stolidly. 'Off ter Birmingham we are, sir. We been sent for on account a' the Chartists. They're a-meeting in the Bull Ring you see, sir, an' the magistrate sez that ain't allowed.'

'Much obliged to you, sir,' Will said, writing rapidly. He realized that he was excited by the information. It roused a sense of impending danger that was alarming, but invigorating too, so that he was suddenly full of energy, trembling with a recklessness he could neither control nor deny. It was as if he'd lost all sense of balance and self-preservation.

He ran back to his carriage, eyes shining.

Bessie was urging the two girls out of the train. 'It'll go with you on it, and then where will you be?'

'Is there going to be a fight?' Caroline asked, alerted by his excitement.

'I shouldn't wonder.'

She threw her arms about his neck and kissed him. 'How thrilling!' she said. 'I wish I could go with you.'

'Well, you can't,' Bessie said. 'And thank the Lord fer that. You just come on home and be a good girl.'

'What a lot we shall have to tell Papa,' Caroline said, unabashed. 'Won't we, Pheemy?'

The arrival of the police, Will's heroic departure, and the forbidding appearance of Euston station were all discussed at length over dinner that night.

'It's a horrid place,' Caroline told her father, annoyed with it now that it had taken her brother away from her, 'so cold and bleak and empty. There isn't even a coffee shop. Only a windy old platform for people to stand on. Ain't that right, Pheemy?'

'It *was* very draughty,' Euphemia said.

'I gather you weren't impressed,' John said, rather pleased by their lack of enthusiasm, for he'd always preferred the old stage-coaches to the new railways.

'I'll tell you what though,' Caroline went on. 'I think Easter's ought to sell papers there. We would do a roaring trade.'

'I doubt it,' her father said. 'Not in all that noise. Not in a place like that.'

'But we could alter it,' she urged. 'Don't you think so, Papa? If there were a newsagent's there and a coffee shop and somewhere to shelter think how different it would be.'

The suggestion annoyed him. She had no sense of decorum at all. Couldn't she see what presumption it was for a child of her age to be telling him how to run the firm? 'We have more than enough to do these days selling papers in the shops,' he said. And the expression on his face brooked no further discussion.

Caroline grimaced at Euphemia when her father wasn't looking, but she changed the subject. 'I wonder what Will is doing now,' she said.

On Birmingham station the policemen were mustering two by

two with a military swagger. In the half-light of the early evening, they looked more like an army than ever. An army come to do battle in a foreign city, Will thought, as he climbed stiffly out of his carriage, for Birmingham was certainly a very different town from any other he had visited.

The air smelt of smoke and sulphur, the brickwork was a harsh, coarse red like raw meat, and the station bristled with steam hissing and whistles screaming, nasal voices shouting and metallic echoes clanging up into the high ceiling. He noticed that his fellow passengers were rushing out of the building, as if they too were excited and fearful, just as he was. Something is going to happen, he thought, and he led Tom through the massive Doric columns at the entrance to the station and set off into the dark streets to find Deritend and the Golden Lion.

Deritend was no distance away and the Golden Lion was easy to find, being an old half-timbered building standing very noticeably at one end of the High Street, not far from the church. It was very dark inside despite a plentiful use of candles, and the bar was awash with spilt ale, but the landlord was friendly and told Will at once that the Chartists were meeting at the Bull Ring that very evening. 'They been banned by the magistrates, sir, so 'tis said, but they don't take no notice.'

Will decided to go to the Bull Ring at once. 'My man will deal with the luggage,' he instructed, feeling rather grand. 'I shall need a cold supper when I return.'

'Beggin' yer pardon, Mr Will sir,' Tom said, following as his master walked away from the counter, and speaking quietly so as not to embarrass him, 'only Mr John gave me strict instructions I was ter stay by yer.'

'Oh did he?' Will said, annoyed that his father was treating him like a baby, but touched by Tom's tact, and really quite glad of his company. 'Well, in that case you'd better come too, I suppose. I will wait ten minutes while you see to the luggage. Only ten mind.'

'An' besides,' Tom grinned, 'it'ud be a bit of a lark ter see them Chartists mesself, seein' I've read all about 'em in the *Northern Star*.'

So to the Bull Ring it was, charged with impatience and a

churning, mounting excitement, following the landlord's directions and Tom's knowledge of the place, down Deritend High Street into the Digbeth, which was loud with smithies and garish with fires and sparks, and so on towards a dark bulk looming across the skyline that Tom said was St Martin's church.

'The Bull Ring's a sort a' square, slopes up in front a' the church yard, sort 'a triangular like,' he explained. 'They use it fer horse fairs an' cattle markets an' meetings an' such, bein' it's the only square of any consequence hereabouts. There ain't another the length and breadth a' the city.'

Even if he'd had no directions at all Will could have found the meeting, for the roar of voices could be heard even above the clang of the smithies, urging him onwards most powerfully. They walked round the side of the church and found themselves facing such a close-packed crowd it was almost impossible to push their way into it. Men were herded into the triangular space like penned beasts, shoulder to shoulder and haunch to haunch. Many of them had brought rush-torches with them and the darkness was restless with moving lights, and hot with flame and sweat and excitement. An army, Will thought, looking at the angry faces all round him, seamed and dark-eyed and gilded by sweat and lamplight, an army waiting for battle.

'Over 'ere, sir,' Tom was calling, elbowing his way through the mass, towards the low wall that surrounded the churchyard. 'There's a man a-speechifyin' in the Shambles, look.'

Will glanced at the line of low buildings on the left-hand side of the ring, and saw that a man was standing above the crowd, his head on a level with the guttering. He was a stocky man with a thick set of whiskers, and he was dressed like a sea captain, in a sailor's blue jacket and a dark hat with a badge of some kind on the rim.

'Never you mind "man",' a dark face corrected Tom from the other side of the wall. 'That there is Doctor Taylor.'

'Stow your noise,' another face said. 'I wants to hear un.'

But Doctor Taylor had no intention of being unheard. His voice was stentorian, booming across the ring, the captain addressing his crew.

'Comrades!' he shouted. 'Citizens! True-born Englishmen!

101

We demonstrate our right as true-born Englishmen to meet here in the Bull Ring as our fathers and forefathers have done before us. The magistrates had the presumption to declare this meeting illegal, the gall to impose a ban upon our activities. Upon our activities as true-born Englishmen. So much for their ban! So much for their authority! We have gathered here, as we have every right to do. By our presence here tonight we prove their ban illegal, immoral and unworkable.'

The crowd gave him a deep-throated cheer. 'We'll show 'em, lad!' they called. 'They'll not ban us! Tha's right! We've a right to our meetings!'

Dr Taylor waved his arms at them, as though he were conducting their cheers. 'I urge you, comrades,' he called. 'Mr Peel's new government may reject our demands, just though they most certainly are, they may reject them and they may reject us, in the same high-handed manner as the old government would have done. If that is to be the case, I say we should stand up to them. We should never take it tamely. Never, never! We must fight like true-born Englishmen, that's what I say to you.'

'Aye!' the crowd growled. 'Aye! We should. He's right an' all. That's the way.'

'If we cannot obtain justice by any other means,' Dr Taylor went on, 'we must take up arms to defend our rights. Yes, comrades, we must take up arms, as the people of Paris did before us, as the people of the American colonies did before us, as all good men and true have done throughout the ages. We must take up arms.'

And this time the roar of approval was a battle cry. Hats were tossed and torches brandished and there were gilded fists punching the air. 'Huzzah ! Huzzah!' And the church clocks began to strike the hour, seven, eight, nine, as if they too were giving tongue to some universal determination.

They mean it, Will thought, thrilled by the orator and full of admiration for the crowd, as the sounds echoed and rolled in the enclosed space of the ring. Oh, I wouldn't have missed this for worlds.

But the clocks were silent now and the cheering had changed, its note deepening alarmingly with muddled yelps of warning and instruction. 'Give way! Look out! Stand firm there!'

'It's the Bobbies!' Tom said, climbing onto the wall for a better view.

In the excitement of Dr Taylor's speech Will had forgotten the policemen. 'Where?' he said, leaping up onto the wall, foreboding knotting in his chest like a hard clenched fist.

It was hard to see anything in the crush, but at the top of the incline the rushlights were parting to right and left and there was a solid, moving mass of darkness in between them. As he watched, a dark uniform climbed onto the hidden rostrum and standing above the crowds began to read from a white paper.

'Our sovereign lady, the Queen Victoria, charges and commands all persons being assembled immediately to disperse themselves and peaceably depart to their habitation or to their lawful business . . . '

He was reading the Riot Act. If the crowd didn't disperse at once, everyone in it could be arrested.

'He can't do this,' Will called to Tom. 'There's no riot.'

'There will be now,' a man shouted back to him.

'Aye!' another man called. 'Build a barricade, boys!'

There was a confusion of movement around the rostrum and in the massed light of the torches Will could see that someone was being arrested and that the Bobbies were striding into the crowd, truncheons thwacking. There was no sign of Doctor Taylor, but another man was clambering above the crowd, yelling at the top of his voice, 'Treachery! Teachery! Stand firm! We have every right to meet here. This is an outrage!' before gloved hands pulled him down. And as he disappeared, Will was knocked from his perch too, caught off-balance by a sudden rush of dark bodies, running pell-mell into the church-yard. Then there was a frantic scramble of bent backs and grabbing hands, pulling at the stones of the wall, loosening them, lifting them, piling the large ones into a barricade, hurling the small ones into heaps behind them.

Will was jammed among the boots and bodies, and drunk with recklessness. To be part of this, he thought, piling stones like everyone else. Part of it. In the middle of a battle, part of this great army, fighting for freedom, for the right to meet in the Bull Ring, the right to petition and protect, the right to vote. Men were hurtling across the broken walls, leaping the stones, shouting defiance, and in the Bull Ring itself they were punching like prize fighters.

Dr Taylor arrived behind the wall, panting with his exertions, his whiskers powdered with brick dust, and seconds later, a man they called MacDouall tumbled over the barricade head first, yelling that the police were close behind him. Their arrival was the signal for the fusillade to begin. It seemed to Will that the air was instantly full of flying stones and jagged bits of brick, and that within seconds the missiles were being thrown back at them and twice as hard.

He had no idea how long the battle raged. He stayed behind the barricade, gathering stones, too busy even to wonder where Tom had got to, too thrilled to be afraid, while the warm night air ricocheted with roars and thuds, and his nostrils filled with the stink and heat of conflict. The clocks struck the hour, but the hour had no meaning. There was no time, only passionate anger and an overwhelming excitement.

And then without any warning, a sharp blow caught him on the temple and he went down like a felled ox, as darkness yawned in upon him, swallowed him, held him, and spat him out in a confusion of feet and stinking trousers. There was a pale hand being trodden on close to his face, and somebody was hauling him up by the collar of his jacket. He croaked for breath as the cloth tightened, slithering to his feet, grabbing the air for balance.

Dr Taylor was striding about among the bricks and stones calling, 'Don't throw, comrades. I beg you. The penalty for riot . . . ' But his voice came and went like the sound of sea in a shell. Throw? Will thought, still bemused, and then his legs began to shake and he sat down on a pile of stones and put his head in his hands.

'My stars!' Tom's voice said above him. 'That was a close call an' no mistake. You all right, Mr Will sir?'

'Right as rain,' Will said at once, but there was blood dripping through his fingers onto the stone.

'We'll cut back ter the Golden Lion,' Tom said. 'Needs a plaster does that.'

'No,' Will said, staunching the blood with his handkerchief. 'Can't desert the field, Tom.'

But the field was deserting him. There were truncheons

rapidly approaching through the mêlée in the Bull Ring, and taut faces running before them shouting, 'Run! Run! They've called out the military! Run! For God's sake!' Lights were flickering out all over the square with an acrid smell of snuffed wick and burnt straw; bodies were scattering to left and right in the noisy darkness. Most of the fighters in the churchyard were already scrabbling away over the stones, and somebody was shouting 'You're under arrest!'

'Run!' Tom hissed. 'This way.'

So although running was out of the question, they limped away from the battle, along a street full of retiring warriors still hot with fury.

'What a thing to have seen!' Will said as he recovered. 'What a thing!' Now he knew what his mother must have felt on the field of Peterloo. 'To call out the soldiers, Tom. It's a disgrace!'

'White of egg that wants,' Tom said, 'ter stop the bleedin'. We'll get it bound up the minute we're back.'

That was the opinion of the landlord's wife, who came up to Will's room with hot water and clean lint and a little white of egg in a flat dish and grumbled all the time she was cleaning the wound. 'What a way for people to go on, Mr Easter. I'm sure I don't know what the world's a-coming to. If a nice young man like you, sir, can't come to Birmingham without having his poor head broke for him, then I really don't know.'

But Will was hardly aware of his injury. He was burning with eagerness to write his report. It took him until nearly four in the morning to get all his impressions onto paper, and as there didn't seem to be much point in going to bed at such an hour, he wrote out a careful copy of the finished article and walked down to the Post Office to send it to London on the early morning mail.

Then he decided that he would have breakfast at the nearest inn and spend the morning in the Easter warehouse, just to show willing.

The nearest inn was a place called the Hen and Chicks and to his great delight it turned out to be full of Chartists and bristling with rumour.

There had been twenty-seven arrests and scores of injuries. Mr Feargus O'Connor was in town, staying with Mr Smith the pawnbroker, and the two of them had gone to Warwick Goal to stand surety for Dr Taylor. And a new pamphlet had been printed early that morning, entitled 'Resolutions unamimously agreed to by the General Convention'. Several of the men gathered in the back parlour already had a copy and were happy to let Will read it. It was inflammatory stuff.

'This convention,' it said, 'is of the opinion that a wanton, flagrant, and unjust outrage has been made upon the people of Birmingham, by a bloodthirsty and unconstitutional force from London, who seek to keep the people in social and political degradation. That the people of Birmingham are the best judges of their own right to meet in the Bull Ring or elsewhere, have their own feelings to consult respecting the outrage given, and are the best judges of their own power and resources to obtain justice. And that the summary and despotic arrest of Dr Taylor, our respected colleague, affords another convincing proof of the absence of all justice in England, and clearly shows that there is no security for life, liberty and property, till people have some control over the laws they are forced to obey.'

'My hat!' Will said. 'This'll put the cat among the pigeons.'

'Aye,' the nearest man growled. 'It needs to.'

'What will you do now?' Will asked.

'We shall be back in the Bull Ring at seven this evening,' the man said grimly.

'You intend to meet there again?'

'Aye, we do.'

And they did. For the next four nights there were angry gatherings between the High Cross and the Shambles, although the Riot Act was read and the police called every time, and around midnight the military showed a presence too. Will soon learned to live on very little sleep, for he stayed with the demonstrators every night until they finally dispersed and he was in the warehouse at seven o'clock every morning. It was a peculiarly disjointed way to live and the oddest thing about it was that the Easter warehouse was the most peaceful place in the city.

It was built behind the railway station and although it covered several acres of land and was extremely busy, particularly first thing in the morning when all the London papers arrived, it was also extremely well organized.

Despite his present lack of interest in the affairs of the firm

Will had to admire his uncle's system for distributing the news by rail. Teams of porters delivered the papers to the backs of their allotted shelves while at the same time the newsboys gathered their carefully up-dated local orders from the front, pushing their trolleys along the lines until they reached the packing tables and a second team of porters who were to rush the completed bundles back to the railway. The operation was presided over by a small, briskly efficient gentleman called Mr Warner, who said he was more than happy to explain it all to Mr Will Easter, and volunteered the information that all the shops in the city were doing a brisk trade, particularly in sales of the *Northern Star*.

But Will's heart was with the Chartists, and when the *Morning Chronicle* arrived on Saturday with his article fully and prominently printed, he was so proud he didn't know what to say.

The Times' reporter arrived that afternoon, followed by six or seven others, and soon they had set up a journalists' club in the Hen and Chicks where they met every evening to drink brandy and talk over the day's events.

It was a great disappointment to Will when the Chartist meetings were finally disbanded. He'd been in Birmingham for more than a week; he'd made new friends; he'd been accepted as a fully fledged member of his chosen profession; his wound was healed, his enthusiasm fired, his mind made up.

'I've seen history being made,' he said to Tom rapturously, as they waited for the London train to start. 'I've been right in the thick of it. I've seen the best and the worst this job can offer and I know it's what I want to do. I can't work in Easter's now. I should stifle. I must be a full-time reporter.'

'Quite right, sir,' Tom agreed.

'I shall tell my father as soon as I get home.'

'Yes, sir.'

'The first thing.' It would have to be the first thing while his courage and determination were high.

But, as so often happens when we try to plan our lives, things didn't work out that way.

When he arrived in Fitzroy Square that afternoon, the house was empty. Miss Caroline was with her grandmother in

Bedford Square, the housekeeper said, and Mr John was visiting Mr Billy.

It wasn't until he was back in the hansom cab and well on his way to Bedford Square that her form of words struck him as odd. Why should his father be 'visiting' Uncle Billy? They saw one another nearly every day in the Strand.

Nan's parlour maid was more communicative. 'They've all gone over to Torrington Square, Mr Will,' she said. 'Miss Caroline and Miss Euphemia are still here, but Mrs Easter she went out like a rocket so she did. Something's up, you ask me, sir. I never seen her go out like that afore, I tell yer straight.'

By now Will was beginning to feel alarmed. He ran up the stairs two at a time to find out what was the matter. The sun had gone behind a cloud since his arrival and the landing was dark and surprisingly chill. Caroline and Euphemia were in the parlour, sitting side by side in the window seat, their heads bent over their sewing, and their voices so subdued that they alarmed him even more than the parlour maid had done.

'Oh, Will!' Caroline said, putting down her sewing and walking across the room to him. 'I *am* glad you're home. It's perfectly beastly here. Uncle Billy's took an apoplexy.'

An apoplexy? How dreadful. 'Is he . . . ?'

'No,' Euphemia said, understanding at once. 'He's not dead. But he's very ill. The surgeons have been called. We're to stay here until Mrs Easter returns.'

'What have you done to your head?' Caroline said, looking at the scab on her brother's temple.

'Nothing,' he said. 'Got in the way of a stone, that's all. Tell me what happened to Uncle Billy.'

'There was a frightful row,' Caroline said, her grey eyes earnest. 'Edward came down from Oxford with his creditors after him three days ago, and Papa said his debts were a scandal and Uncle Billy said he was to leave Oxford and start work in the firm that very day or he wouldn't pay a penny to bail him out and Aunt Tilda cried and cried and Edward shouted and then Uncle Billy took an apoplexy and fell right down. Isn't it dreadful!'

'I'll go straight over,' Will said.

Billy was propped up in his high bed against a mound of pillows, his usually jolly face sagging and grey and his eyes tightly closed. But he stirred himself when Will came in and tried to mumble that he was glad to see him.

'He's been bled three times since,' Nan whispered, as he seemed to sleep again, 'so he ought to be seeing the benefit soon.'

'My poor Billy!' Tilda sniffed, from her seat beside the bed. Her eyes were red-rimmed from all the tears she'd shed in the past two days.

Nan led them both out of the room. 'He's on the mend, Tilda,' she said. 'Try to look on the bright side. It don't do to pity the sick. Leastways not in their hearing.'

'Where's Papa?' Will asked.

He was in Billy's study, examining his brother's warehouse book. 'Thank heavens you're back, Will,' he said. 'We're in a proper pickle. The doctors say he won't be well enough to work for months.'

'I am sorry.'

'Yes, well . . . Did you get to see how the Birmingham trade was handled?'

'Yes, Papa. It works very smoothly.'

'That's one blessing, I suppose.'

'It's a simple system, Papa. Mr Warner has it all under control.'

'You understood it?' John asked, giving his son a quick, almost calculating glance.

'Yes,' Will said, giving a truthful answer even though the glance had made him feel anxious about where the question could be leading.

'Could you handle the London warehouse, do you think, Will? It's a lot to ask, I know that, but you can see how we're placed.'

Oh, how much Will wanted to say no, I can't. I'm a reporter. But his father's face was peaked with worry, his forehead ridged and his eyes squinting, and the sight of such distress aroused a protective affection in his son that was so strong it overthrew ambition and hope in one taut second. 'Yes,' he said. 'I think I could.' Perhaps it would only have to be for a month or two, until Uncle Billy was well again.

109

'Could you start this afternoon?'

'Yes.' So soon! He'd hardly got back!

'We will train Edward up to it, in time,' John said. 'When your uncle recovers, which he will do eventually, according to the doctors. You should do more than simply handle the warehouse. I know that. And so you shall, I promise you, once this present – um – difficulty is over.' Then he turned to Nan. 'What a relief to have our Will home to help us,' he said.

'You're a good lad, Will,' Nan said, reaching up to kiss him. 'I don't know what we'd do without you.'

'You'd better take the warehouse book for the time being,' John said, handing it across. 'I'm going back to the Strand myself in a minute or two. We will travel together, eh. You can tell me about Birmingham on the way.'

There is nothing I want to tell you now, Will thought, taking the heavy book into his hands. I have lost my chance. I am committed to this firm for ever now. I shall never escape. And resentment filled his brain despite the knowledge that he was doing the right thing by his family, the right and only thing.

And he resented every shop they passed on their way to the Strand, until the smart green and gold sign seemed to be mocking him.

Billy was kept to his bed for the next fortnight and when he was finally allowed up he was so weak that when Will went sick-visiting, he could see at once that his uncle wouldn't be back at work for a very long time.

He called in at the offices of the *Morning Advertiser* the same afternoon on his way back to the Strand, and told the editor as politely and unemotionally as he could that he was not in a position to accept any further commissions, 'for the foreseeable future'.

'A pity,' the editor said. 'I like your work, Mr Easter. There's a permanent job here for you should you want one, you know.'

It was bitter-sweet to hear it.

'I'm beholden to you for the offer, sir,' Will said, polite to the end, 'but I must refuse I fear. I have accepted a position in the family firm.'

'A pity,' the editor said again.

However, the warehouse was simple enough to run, providing he planned ahead, and the men who worked there were friendly and cheerful, so it wasn't long before he'd settled in to the new routine, despite his disappointment, which he never mentioned to anyone, not even Carrie. Fate had decided this for him and it was no good kicking against the pricks.

But he kicked against Edward whenever he got the chance, giving him the dirtiest and heaviest jobs to do and shouting orders as though he were the lowest and most objectionable of his workmen.

It was a surprise to him that his cousin never fought back. Edward accepted his new life dumbly, saying very little, simply doing as he was told, with an uncharacteristic meekness that was downright aggravating. Whatever else happened now he had no intention of entering into an argument. That would only make matters worse and he had enough to cope with as it was.

'Deuce take it, Edward,' Will shouted on one particularly busy morning. 'Why ain't you unloaded those boxes? We shall miss delivery.'

Edward unpacked the offending boxes. He didn't feel in the least bit apologetic but he apologized at once and meekly. 'I'm sorry, Will.'

'And so you should be,' Will said, resentment towards him spilling over into accusation at last, 'when it's all your fault. If it hadn't been for your damned extravagance we should neither of us be working here.'

'It wasn't intended,' Edwards said, as mildly as he could. 'I didn't mean Pa to take it so hard. I didn't mean to make him ill.' This was the truth, and a painful one.

'But you did.'

'Yes,' still unpacking with his face averted.

'And you cost me a good job as a reporter. Do you realize that?'

'Yes. I'm sorry.'

'So you damned well should be,' Will said, walking away. He wasn't mollified by the apology, because too much damage had been done, but at least Edward had the grace to admit responsibility for it, and that was something.

But then Jeff Jefferson wrote to tell him the latest news about the Chartists who had been arrested in Birmingham, and he read accounts of their trials in the London newspapers and knew that he could have written about them far more sympathetically and knowledgeably, and he was cast down despite his determination to appear cheerful. And a week later there was worse to endure.

He had gone down to Printing House Square to negotiate new terms for the sale of *The Times* with Mr Walters, the proprietor, and when the business had been satisfactorily concluded, he had accepted Mr Walters' invitation to 'cut across to Periwinkles for a spot of lunch'.

It was a pleasant meal and they finished it with brandy and cigars and gossip, which Will recognized and accepted as something of an accolade. To be treated as a full working member of the newspaper fraternity was decidedly flattering, especially as Mr Walters had been a friend of Nan's for many many years, and had known him since he was a small child trailing through the newspaper office at his father's coat tails. But just as he was feeling most at ease and comfortable, Mr Walters suddenly said something that made his heart lurch as if he'd been punched.

'That was a fine piece you wrote on the Bull Ring riot,' he said. 'I had half a mind to offer you a position on my staff on the strength of it. You write well, Mr Will Easter. But I daresay you know that.'

It was all Will could do to say thank you, and then the words emerged as a husky growl. A position on the staff of *The Times*. That was even more tantalizing than the offer of a job with the *Morning Advertiser*. Oh, if only he could take it! If only it wasn't being talked of now!

'Not that I would embarrass you by asking you to choose between *The Times* and Easter's,' Mr Walters went on. 'Easter's couldn't function without you these days, I hear.'

'That *is* the rumour,' Will admitted wryly.

'Aye,' Mr Walters said, finishing his brandy. 'Still, if you ever need a job, you know where to find me, eh?'

It was offered in a jocular tone, and although Will answered in the same style, he meant what he said, 'I will bear that in mind, Mr Walters.'

That night as he drove home along the Strand on his way to Fitzroy Square his grandmother's green and gold signs mocked him most cruelly. 'A. Easter and Sons.' Caught. Caught. Caught.

Chapter 8

In Caroline's and Euphemia's bedroom in Nan's house in Bedford Square sunlight poured in through the window in a visible column. The motes bounced and gyrated in springtime abandon, gleaming with rainbow colour like little swirling diamonds. It was nearly seven o'clock on a bright May evening, and the room was sultry with accumulated warmth and dusted with golden light, the long cream curtains folded into tawny shadow, the starched sheets and pillow cases glistening, the looking glass above the mantelpiece a dazzle of little gold suns.

Caroline sat before the dressing table in her chemise and petticoats admiring her sun-misted face in the mirror. Now that she was eighteen she was really quite womanly, everybody said so, and very much like her mother, whose quiet portrait she admired every time she visited her father's house. She and Euphemia never stayed there nowadays because Papa was always too busy to entertain them, and that was an arrangement that suited her very well, for the portrait was far more welcoming than the house. There was something peculiarly attractive about its air of gentle sanctity, something at once poised and tender and calming. Every time she saw it she wished she could emulate it.

'Do I look saintly, Euphemia?' she asked, speaking slowly and dreamily so as not to disturb the expression she was cultivating. She had propped her elbows on two fat lavender bags because the table was much too hard for comfort, and now she cupped her chin in her hands and gazed soulfully at her reflection, at grey eyes suitably wide apart and innocently round, at the warm flush of her skin, at her nose, which wasn't really so very big, was it, especially when you looked at it from the front, at the salmon-pink rosebud of her mouth, held carefully so as to appear as small and well formed as she could make it, at the thick dark ringlets bobbing so artlessly beside her cheeks. The hairdresser had arranged them quite well, all things considered. 'I do look saintly, don't I?'

'You look very beautiful,' Euphemia said truthfully. 'You will be the belle of the ball.'

'So will you,' Caroline said, returning the compliment and smiling at her cousin in the mirror.

And it was true. There was no sign now of the skinny sallow child who had come to Bedford Square so timorously seven years ago. At nineteen, Euphemia was langorously beautiful, with a creamy complexion beneath her splendid auburn hair, pale arms deliciously rounded, white neck most tender, the prettiest tip-tilted bosom and the face of a dreamy madonna. Now she lay on the chaise longue in her cream chemise and a froth of petticoats, with white satin slippers on her feet and one pale arm draped across the back of the chaise like a milky goddess in a painting. But where Caroline was striving for the effect she wanted, Euphemia was simply being herself, gentle and quiet and calm as always, resting before the very first ball of her very first season.

The season was all Aunt Matilda's doing. Ever since Uncle Billy's apoplexy, which was nearly six years ago now, she'd been the driving force behind her entire family, ensuring that Billy's return to work was very, very gradual, organizing the household to suit the new slow pace of his life, advising Matty when her two little boys were born, and once her dear Edward had settled into the firm, joining the London season so as to find him a suitable wife. So far, it had to be admitted, without success.

But now that the two girls would be joining the festivities, she had hopes of a better outcome. Caroline could be difficult but she was a lively little thing and her presence at the opening ball would certainly add spice to the occasion.

John had been rather sticky about it to start with, protesting that he saw no reason why Caroline and Euphemia should be

115

involved in a 'man-hunt'. But she had talked him round.

'No, no,' she told him firmly. 'The time has come for us to make a concerted effort on behalf of all our sons and daughters.'

'I would have thought we had made excellent provision for them,' John observed. 'Will and Edward are both settled into the firm. Your Matty is happily married and has made you a grandmother twice over. Even Caroline is improved by her years at Mrs Flowerdew's seminary. Why gild the lily?'

'Why, in order to find them suitable partners to be sure,' Tilda said, widening her fine grey eyes at his simplicity. 'That is what all responsible parents do nowadays. They must be properly launched.'

'You make them sound like ships!' John protested.

She ignored such flippancy. 'Edward will be twenty-five this year,' she said, 'and your Will twenty-seven and both of them still unwed. And Caroline will be nineteen, which is quite old enough for a girl. More than high time I should say.'

'Let us hope she agrees with you,' her father said wryly.

'Of course she'll agree with me,' Matilda said with some exasperation. 'I'm offering her balls and parties and young men to dance attendance on her. What more could she possibly want? It is any young girl's dream.'

'However,' her father pointed out, 'Caroline is not any young girl. She might take it kindly and join in with the best. On the other hand she might walk off into the snow.'

'There is no snow in May,' Matilda said. 'What are you talking about?'

And so the season was planned and the clothes made and despite John's misgivings the two girls were delighted to be part of it, although they both declared they had no intention of catching a husband, for such an idea was really too shameful, indeed it was. Which was one reason why Caroline was concerned about her appearance, for a saintly expression would show that she had no desire to enter the marriage stakes.

'I do so want to look saintly,' she said, returning to her reflection in the dressing table mirror. 'There is something so beautiful about saintliness, don't you think so, Pheemy?'

'There are many kinds of beauty,' Euphemia said seriously. 'The beauty of youth and beginnings, the beauty of age and experience, beauty of action, beauty of sleep, oh so many.'

'Who told you all that?' Caroline asked, forgetting her expression because she was so impressed.

'My ayah,' Euphemia said, her face softening at the memory of her.

'Ah!' Caroline said. 'Indian philosophy again.' Mrs Flowerdew had once said that there was nothing so profound as Indian philosophy and she had stood in awe of it ever since. 'What about the beauty of women? Brides are always beautiful, aren't they?'

'Yes,' Euphemia agreed, and she remembered dreamily. 'The beauty of women, the beauty of men, beautiful clothed, more beautiful naked.'

Caroline was rather shocked by this. She'd never seen a naked man, of course, and even the idea was scandalous. But scandalously appealing. She often wondered what people looked like without their clothes, and at even more daring moments, whether married people saw one another naked. In the 'Eve of St Agnes' Keats had described a young woman undressing, and he'd done it so beautifully it had made her breathless simply to read it, so he must have seen it at some time or another. But perhaps poets were different. Perhaps the rules didn't apply to poets. 'Men aren't beautiful,' she said. 'Comical perhaps, pleasant enough sometimes in a well-cut coat, but not beautiful.'

'Your brother is, I think.'

She admitted that, languidly – 'Oh, he looks well enough.' Do married people? she wondered. But she couldn't ask. There was so much about marriage she didn't know and couldn't ask. It was all a very great mystery, and never more so than on a wedding day, when the air was full of unfamiliar emotions, the married women sighing and worldly-wise, the unmarried bright and brittle, and a sort of excited expectation pervading everything, as though something tremendous was going to happen that nobody would talk about. 'I don't think I would like to see a man with no clothes on, would you Euphemia?'

But Euphemia was still in India on another golden day, oh years and years ago, standing with her ayah in the Temple of the Sun in Konarak, lost in wonder at the beauty of the carvings, life-sized couples amorously entwined, their stone hands rapturously fondling, their stone faces seraphic with

117

satisfaction. The undeniable, overwhelming, holy beauty of love, accepted so openly in India, but taboo here in England.

That had always seemed most extraordinary, although she accepted the taboo, of course, for she would never willingly have done anything to upset anyone and particularly when they'd been so kind to her. Nan Easter had accepted her into her family as if she belonged there, allowing her to spend every single holiday with Caroline, as though they were sisters, furnishing this room to suit them both, permitting her to stay on as a member of the family when she really ought to have followed her brothers back to India, meeting all the expenses of this season. It would have been unthinkable to do anything to upset such a dear kind lady.

'Euphemia?' Caroline said.

But the dear kind lady herself was at the door, leaning on her ebony stick and already dressed in a ball gown of deep blue silk and black lace, her grey hair beautifully arranged beneath a head-dress made entirely of blue feathers. 'My dear heart alive,' she said, brown eyes teasing, 'en't you dressed yet, you bad critturs? Shame on 'ee both. We shall have the carriages here presently.'

Euphemia got up at once and picked up her gown from the bed, but Caroline went on admiring her reflection.

'Do I look saintly, Nan?' she asked.

'Angelic,' her grandmother said shortly. 'Now get your stays on, or the carriage will be here and you won't be ready. I shall send Bessie up to chivvy you along.'

Caroline had been putting off the moment when those stays had to be put on, because she knew it was going to be difficult and painful. When her gown was being made, she had decided that if she couldn't be the prettiest girl at Aunt Matilda's opening ball then she would at least have the smallest waist. So she had laced herself as tightly as she could and had instructed her dressmaker to cut the gown to fit a waist of eighteen inches. Now she would have to face the consequences of her vanity. She picked up the tape-measure and took it across to the bed, where the dreaded corset was waiting, smoothed her chemise as close to her skin as she could and arranged the stays very carefully about her waist, for the slightest fold of cloth beneath the whalebone would nip her flesh most painfully. Then she stood beside the bed-post to be laced.

'Are you ready?' Euphemia asked, standing poised behind her with the drawstrings in her hand.

Caroline took a deep breath, pulled in her waist as hard as she could, grabbed the bed-post and nodded. Speech was impossible, of course, but speech wasn't needed.

The strings were pulled tight, tighter and tighter still, until both girls were panting with the effort they were making.

'Eighteen and a half inches,' Euphemia said, examining the tape-measure.

'Ooof!' Caroline panted, catching her breath as well as she could with her lungs so constricted. 'It feels like twelve. Pull again.'

But she had to admit that the gown looked extremely fine once her waist was the right size for it. The new fashion was so pretty with straight-cut simple sleeves and a lovely neat bodice above the widest skirts you could imagine. Of course you had to wear at least four petticoats if it was to look really well, and one of them had to be made of horse hair, which could be scratchy if you weren't careful, but the resulting image was well worth it, especially when you were wearing dove-grey silk embroidered with white and pink flowers and flounced with yards and yards of pink lace.

'Yes,' Nan said, 'you'll do. Now lace Euphemia. You have a quarter of an hour. No more dreaming, Carrie.'

Caroline's stays began to nip her on the way to Uncle Billy's house and during the reception, when she stood in line with Aunt Matilda and Uncle Billy and Edward and Will and Euphemia greeting their guests, she found it quite hard to breathe. But to be here, at her very first ball, in a ball room dizzy with the scent of flowers and the glitter of jewels and a positive blaze of gaslight, and all her friends around her so grand and self-conscious in their new fashionable clothes, and the band tuning up ready to play, and that odd excitement swelling and pulsing in her chest, why it was all so pleasant that any discomfort was easily ignored. Whatever she might think of Aunt Matilda and that dratted Edward of hers she had to admit that they knew how to organize a ball.

That dratted Edward had actually been responsible for most

of the arrangements for this one. For the past six years he had gradually taken over responsibility for the warehouses, using his talent for mathematics to order the stock, and his organizational skills to ensure that delivery and despatch were both handled methodically. But he felt that he was above such menial tasks and worth far more than the pittance his grandmother paid him, so it was soothing to be the centre of the family during the season. And this year when it was agreed that the opening ball was to be given in his house and in his name, he took an interest in every single detail, supervising the delivery of chairs and trestle tables, advising on the hiring of pastry cooks and wine waiters and the quality and quantity of the food, even querying the number of players in the string band his mother had hired. After ten days of it even Matilda's doting patience wore thin and Billy took to drifting in and out of the resulting chaos like an amiable ghost.

But from the first notes of the opening quadrille Edward turned his energies elsewhere, being all charm to his dancing partners, particularly when they were well-born and wealthy. For he was on the look-out for a rich wife. He had accepted that he was unlikely to obtain the power and influence he desired from his present position in the firm, so with unthinking arrogance he had decided to get it by marriage. By the end of this first season he had marked down five possibilities and by the middle of the second, when the three younger and prettier ones had made it clear that they did not like him – and the more fools they! – he had decided to offer for the other two, both older than he was and both undeniably plain, but both the possessors of considerable fortunes. The first indicated that her interest was not strong enough to warrant courtship, so now he was about to pay court to the second, a certain Miss Mirabelle Artenshaw, who had a cast in one eye, a flat bosom, no surviving parents and a twelve thousand pound inheritance.

Caroline was intrigued when she saw them dancing together. 'Whoever is that?' she asked Bessie, when she and Euphemia returned to their chaperone at the end of the waltz.

'Miss Mirabelle Artenshaw,' Bessie sniffed. 'And he'll marry her I shouldn't wonder.'

'But she's old!'

'Old and rich,' Bessie said, sucking her teeth with disapproval.

'Pheemy!' Caroline said. 'How could he do such a thing?'

'He might love her,' Euphemia suggested generously.

'But she's hideous!'

'Beauty in the eye of the beholder?' Euphemia suggested.

'Humph!' Bessie snorted. 'All that young man can see is pounds, shillings and pence.'

'I wonder what Nan thinks of it,' Caroline said. And she made up her mind to ask her as soon as she got the chance.

But to her surprise Nan seemed to be supporting the match.

'I've invited the lady to dine with us a' Thursday,' she said, 'and join us at the opera afterwards, so you'll have the chance to see her for yourself, won't 'ee my dear?'

It turned out to be a very interesting dinner party, for despite her peculiar figure, which would have been perfectly straight all the way down if it hadn't been for her stays, and that odd clouded eye, which was most disconcerting because you could never be sure whether it was looking at you or not, Miss Artenshaw was good company. She knew so many of the new poets and pretty well all the novelists, and what was more, she'd read all their books, even the ones that had just been printed and weren't even in the lending libraries yet.

'Miss Barrett has a new book of poetry out this very week,' she told John and Nan.

'I saw the advertisement of it,' John said. 'Is it as good as they claim?'

'I cannot speak for others,' Miss Artenshaw said, 'for all art is a matter of taste, is it not? I enjoyed it beyond measure and think it quite her best.'

She'd read Mr Dickens' *Martin Chuzzlewit* and *Nicholas Nickleby* and *The Christmas Carol* and Mr Tennyson's *Idylls of the King* and Mr Disraeli's new novel, *Sybil*, which she seemed to have understood.

Even Nan was impressed to hear that. 'I used to dine with poets when I was young,' she said, 'and powerful good company they were.'

Miss Artenshaw was very interested. 'I should love to hear of it, Mrs Easter,' she said, 'and to know who they were.'

'William Blake was one,' Nan said. 'But he's gone out of fashion long since, I fear.'

'A great man,' Miss Artenshaw said warmly. 'I have a copy of his *Songs of Innocence and Experience*. Profundity and simplicity combined.'

'You have the man to a T,' Nan said.

Caroline lost interest in this literary talk because the strawberry syllabub was being served, so there were other, more delicious things to occupy her, but she noticed that Edward was looking most put out by the conversation, as if he didn't understand it either, and that pleased her, especially when Will noticed too and winked across the table at her in that nice conspiratorial way of his.

Nan and Papa and Miss Artenshaw talked all through dinner, and would have gone on talking all through the opera too if Edward hadn't insisted that she sit by him in the corner of the box, 'for I declare I must hear your opinion of the production, my dear Miss Artenshaw, there being no other lady whose opinion I value more highly.'

'He didn't mean a word of it,' Caroline said to Nan and Will and Euphemia when they were in their carriage and on the way home. 'You only had to look at his face. He was putting on a show.'

'What happened to Christian charity, Miss Easter?' Will teased.

'I daresay he wanted a little of her company to himself,' Euphemia said, 'which is only to be expected if he means to marry her.'

'He don't mean to marry her,' Caroline said. 'He couldn't.'

'Why not?' Nan laughed. 'She's rich enough in all conscience, and 'tis my opinion she'd be more than a match for him. A crittur of sense, our Miss Artenshaw. She could be the making of our Edward.'

Caroline didn't think much of that for an answer. 'But she's over thirty,' she said. 'I think it's scandalous, I do indeed.'

'To be over thirty or to marry for money?' Nan asked, laughing again.

'Both.'

122

'What do you think, Will?'

'Nothing may come of it,' Will said diplomatically. 'It's a long way to the altar rail.'

'But most of us reach it in the end, eh?'

'So they say, grandmama.'

In fact, Will Easter still had no intention of arriving at that particular place, whatever his cousin might be planning to do. But he kept his thoughts on the subject to himself, for there was no need to provoke trouble. He simply made private plans in order to protect his independence.

By now he was resigned to the fact that he would have to work in the firm for as long as he could foresee. Billy's gradual return to the warehouse had made it impossible for him to find the right moment to extricate himself. There had never been a day when things changed, that was the trouble. Billy took over part of his old job in a piecemeal fashion, a day at a time, with Edward in virtual command but supposedly assisting him, and day by day Will was inched into another and even more demanding one. During the last six years more than thirty new railways had been built and countless new sections of track opened on the existing ones, and every new piece of railway meant a negotiation for the transfer of the transportation of the Easter papers from stage-coach to rail. It was very demanding work and in an odd kind of way he quite enjoyed it, although he resented the way it had been wished upon him.

But that was all the more reason why he should avoid the complication of being wished into marriage too. So he resolved to dance with any young woman his aunt manoeuvred towards him, which would please her, but never to dance more than once with any one of them, which would keep him safe from gossip and matrimonial ambitions. The only trouble was that in order to plead a full dance card to Aunt Matilda, he had to book all the other dances with somebody else and somebody safe, and the only young women who were really safe were his sister Caroline and Euphemia, who was as good as a sister nowadays.

They were very helpful about it. In fact Euphemia was an absolute brick, allowing him to fill in all the spaces with her name, whenever he needed to. It was a real pleasure to dance with her, to talk about everything and anything without feeling anxious.

'It's such a burden,' he confessed at their third ball. 'Sometimes I can feel the pressure Aunt Matilda puts upon me as though it were a weight around my neck. I'm sure I never asked her to find me a wife. Now she says I've danced three waltzes with you and the next one is to go to that awul Cholmondley woman. What do you think of that?'

'Shall you do as she says?' Euphemia asked, from within the supporting circle of his arm.

'We will walk in the garden instead,' he said, 'if you are agreeable.'

And she was, very agreeable, strolling beside him in the moonlight with her fingers resting lightly on his arm and her lovely calm face listening attentively to every word he said. So he told her how much he wished he could work as a reporter again, and travel the world, and write for *The Times*.

'But then you know what a fine thing it is to travel the world, do you not?' he said.

'I have travelled, yes,' she agreed. But she didn't sound enthusiastic.

'Did you not enjoy it?' he asked, surprised by her reaction.

'I was sick for a great deal of the time, I fear. I do not travel well. And I missed my ayah of course. We had never been parted for more than a day before then.'

'But you were with your parents, surely?'

'Yes,' she said. And she spoke the word with such a touching mixture of sadness and resignation that he knew in that instant that the Callbecks had ignored her on the voyage just as they ignored her in England.

'You were lonely,' he said, remembering his own loneliness when his mother died.

'Yes,' she admitted. And then feeling she had to explain, 'My father had a great deal of business to attend to. I could not expect him to spend time with me. It is not the custom for parents to spend time with their children in India, you see.' There wasn't a hint of criticism in her voice, only this gentle, rather weary resignation.

'Do you miss them, Euphemia?' he asked, knowing the

answer before she gave it, but wanting to hear it just the same.

'No,' she said. 'I'm afraid I don't. I daresay I should when you consider who they are, but I haven't seen them for so long, you see, and I am so happy here with you and Carrie and Nan. I write to them twice a year of course.'

'Do they reply?'

'Oh yes,' she said, grimacing at the thought of their letters. 'They tell me all about their business ventures and what a lot of money they are making and how successful my brothers are. I cannot say I know any more about them than that, for they never write of other things, and they never answer any of my questions. In fact, horrid though it is to say it, I really don't think they read my letters at all.'

This was no surprise to Will. How patient she is, he thought, admiring her resignation and yet irritated by it too. She is too good, too meek, she complains too little, and that is the surest way to be put upon. If that were Caroline she'd fight back and let them know how unfair they were being. 'That is how I remember them,' he said, smiling at her. 'They are rather like my other grandparents, I think.'

'Your other grandparents?' Euphemia asked. This was the first time she'd ever heard of such people.

'My mother's parents,' he explained. 'They were a terrible pair, hard cruel people. They didn't love my poor mother at all. I can remember it very well. In the end Nan sent them packing and none of us have ever heard a word from them since. Which in my opinion is just as well, for they certainly wouldn't have fitted into the family.'

'Do you not feel the lack of them?'

'Not a bit,' he said cheerfully. 'Nan is grandmother enough for me.'

'And for me,' she said. 'I never knew anyone with so much love in her.'

'It is a riddle to me,' he confessed, 'why some people find love so easy while others are hardly capable of it at all.'

But as he spoke them, the words sounded altogether too daring, so he decided to change the subject, in case the intimacy of this conversation was overstepping the mark. 'Shall you ride in the Park tomorrow?'

'If the weather holds.'

'I wish I could join you,' he said, and meant it. 'But Papa and I are both off at first light.'

'Where do you go this time?'

'He is off to Edinburgh. I only have to go to Rugby.' But even Rugby was too far when he would rather be riding with these two sisters of his. 'I hope you enjoy your outing.'

'I would enjoy it more if you were with us,' Euphemia said. 'It will be dull without you.'

But as it happened, she was wrong.

Chapter 9

The bridle path that ambled through an avenue of lime trees in London's Hyde Park, linking the great houses of Belgravia with the greater ones of Grosvenor Square, was a most exclusive place, reserved for the gentry and those nouveaux riches who had enough wealth to run a string of good horses and enough daring to dress in the latest fashion and brave the disparagement of the elite. It was always crowded on summer afternoons during the season, particularly when the weather was fine and all the young bloods were out to dazzle one another.

Caroline and Euphemia rode every afternoon whatever the weather. They were both good horsewomen and they both had excellent mounts, and very pretty riding habits too, which they wore with green top hats trimmed with yards of green veiling floating out behind them. It was fun to canter past the amblers with their full skirts ballooning and their veils streaming, and even better to outstrip the young men who had been saying foolish things to them the previous evening. And all without the need for a chaperone, impropriety being deemed impossible on horseback. Tom Thistlethwaite was required to wait at the park gates with the carriage so that he could drive them home, and there were two grooms in attendance to lead the horses, but that was all.

'I could ride for ever and ever,' Caroline shouted as she and Euphemia thundered down the ride. 'No chaperones! No silly men grimacing!'

'Oh Carrie, be fair! They don't all grimace,' Euphemia called back, thinking of Will.

'They do too,' Caroline shouted. 'I haven't seen *one* worth looking at.'

And saw one at that very moment.

He was trotting towards them, sitting very straight on a splendid palamino, and dressed in the very height of fashion, in a brand-new pair of snow-white breeches, blue riding boots and a superbly cut mustard coloured jacket. But although his clothes were splendid, it was his face that made her notice him. He had dark curly hair and dark brooding eyes, and a long pale face, dominated by a long pale nose, very straight and aristocratic and accentuated by the peculiar cut of his sideburns which were little more than a fringe of dark hair but had been grown so low that they curved about his jaw. He wore his beard and moustache in the Spanish style, with two comma-shaped wings of hair above a well-formed upper lip and the neatest triangle of beard below a voluptuous lower one. And he held his head high, his chin up like a guardsman, looking neither to right nor left, so that he seemed to have his eyes fixed upon some distant horizon unseen by anybody else. It gave his face an expression at once romantic, haughtily aristocratic and distant. It was as if he had set himself apart from the ordinary run of mankind.

Caroline reined in her horse abruptly. 'Who is that?' she said.

'Who is who?' Euphemia panted as she passed, reining in her horse more gently.

'Why, the gentleman in the . . . ' Caroline began. But the palamino suddenly kicked up his hind legs, like a trooper's horse, snorting and tossing his white mane until it flew like feathers. His beautiful rider was thrown from side to side and finally unseated, slipping sideways out of the saddle and landing with a crunch just out of range of his horse's hooves.

Euphemia hung back, because the path was full of riders, but Caroline bullied her way through them and was beside him in an instant.

'Are you hurt, sir?' she asked, looking down at him where he sat on the path, collecting his senses and dusting his breeches. 'Do you need assistance?'

'Devil take that damned animal,' the young man said

128

furiously beating his trousers. 'No, no I ain't hurt, devil take him.'

The palamino was grazing between the trees a few yards away, as meek as a lamb.

But Caroline was more interested in the young man's left foot, which still lay twisted beneath him in an ominously awkward position. 'Can you stand, sir?' she said.

'Devil take it,' he swore again. 'Of course I can stand. Do you take me for a fool, ma'am?'

'You may not be a fool, sir, but you are horribly ill-mannered.'

He ignored her rebuke, put his hands on the ground to steady himself and started to stand up, saying crossly, 'Of course I can stand.' But his left foot had no sooner touched the ground than it gave way beneath him. 'Hell fire and damnation!'

'Quite,' Caroline said, with some satisfaction. 'You will need a carriage to take you home. Do you have one?'

'No I do not.'

'A groom then?'

'No, devil take it.'

'My carriage is at the park gates,' she said. 'I will send my man to collect you and a groom to lead your horse, since you are in no fit state to lead him yourself. I would advise you to call a surgeon when you get home, if you can persuade one to attend upon you when you are so ill-mannered, which I very much doubt. Good afternoon to you, sir.'

He sat on the path looking up at her again and suddenly gave her a smile of quite melting sweetness. 'I am a wretch,' he said. 'A foul-tempered wretch and I don't deserve your kindness and that's the truth.'

She was mollified but she didn't show it. Instead she turned her horse's head ready to walk away and give Tom his instructions. 'Where shall he take you?' she asked.

'South Audley Street,' he said, cradling his foot in both hands. 'I'm uncommon grateful to you, Miss . . . ?'

'Easter,' she told him. 'Miss Caroline Easter.'

'You jest!' he said. 'You cannot possibly be called Easter.'

'Indeed I can, since that is my name.'

'Extraordinary!' he said, smiling at her again. 'Then if that is truly the case you must allow me to present myself. I am

129

Henry Osmond Easter, of Ippark, in the county of Sussex, and pleased to make your acquaintance.'

'Good heavens!' she said as Euphemia picked her way across the now empty path to join them. 'Euphemia, this gentleman is called Easter. Henry Osmond Easter. What do you think of that? My cousin, Miss Euphemia Callbeck.'

'Your servant,' Henry Osmond said pleasantly. 'My father had cousins by the name of Callbeck. One of them called upon us once, I remember. A Mr Simon Callbeck from Calcutta. Do you know of him?'

'My father, sir,' Euphemia explained.

'Then that accounts,' Henry Osmond said. 'We must all be related.'

'So it would appear,' Caroline said, 'but this ain't the time to talk of it. You should be at home and having that foot attended to. I will call upon you tomorrow to see how you are, which you don't deserve, but I shall do it, notwithstanding, because I am a woman of principle. Stay where you are. My man will collect you.'

'He could hardly do anything else,' Euphemia said as they rode back to the gates, 'with his ankle swelling up before our eyes, poor man.'

'He ain't a poor man,' Caroline said. 'He's the rudest creature I ever met in all my born days.' But quite the most handsome. Quite the most thrillingly handsome. 'Oh Euphemia, dear, dear Euphemia, we are like warrior maidens, rescuing an injured knight-at-arms. What a tale we shall have to tell when we get home!'

Bessie's forehead crinkled into instant concern when she heard they'd arrived at Bedford Square on horseback. 'Whatever were you a-doing of,' she asked, bustling them up the stairs, 'riding through the streets when you had a carriage to fetch you? Anyone would think you were gypsies.' But when the story of their daring rescue was told, instead of being impressed and pleased, she scowled more darkly than ever. 'Well, I don't know what your Pa will say, I'm sure,' she grumbled. 'Easters from Ippark! I don't know!'

'She's getting old and cantankerous,' Caroline said, when Bessie had taken away their boots and riding habits and gone grumbling off downstairs. 'Wait till we tell Nan.'

And Nan was certainly a better audience, although she already knew who the young man was, which was rather a disappointment. 'Henry Osmond,' she said. 'That would be Sir Osmond's second son.'

'I couldn't say.'

'What did he look like?'

'I could invite him here to our next ball on Thursday, if he's able to stand,' Caroline suggested hopefully, 'and then you could see.'

'Aye, I daresay you could,' Nan said, 'and I suppose you will.' But although the words apparently gave permission, they were said too grudgingly for Caroline's liking.

'What is the matter with them all?' she asked Euphemia, when dinner was over and the two of them were waiting for the carriage to take them to the theatre. 'You'd think they'd be glad we'd found another relation. But no, they all start huffing and puffing as if we'd done something dubious. I don't understand it. Do you?'

Euphemia admitted her lack of understanding too.

'And another thing,' Caroline went on. 'It's curious that I've never heard a word about these Ippark Easters until today, don't you think so?'

'Yes,' Euphemia said. 'It is. Very curious.'

'Perhaps we have uncovered a mystery,' Caroline said. 'A family mystery. Now that would be truly romantic, would it not?'

'Will might be able to tell us,' Euphemia suggested, intrigued by the thought. But Will was still on his travels.

'We will ask him the minute he gets back,' Caroline said, putting on her gloves. 'But tomorrow I shall visit Mr Easter, no matter what. We will see what he has to say about it.'

'You won't ask him anything directly will you, Carrie?' Euphemia said rather anxiously, for you never knew with Caroline.

'Oh come!' Caroline said. 'I've more tact than that. No, no, I shall winkle it out of him. You'll see.'

So the two of them set off for South Audley Street with Bessie as chaperone as soon as they'd finished their ride the following afternoon. It was a first-rate house, which was only to be expected of the son of a person called Sir Osmond Easter, but the furniture was old-fashioned and the decor dull, and even though a manservant brought them cakes and tea on a silver stand, there was a general air of discomfort about the place which Euphemia found disquieting and Caroline noticed with disapproval.

But their host was charming.

'Can't rise to greet you, I'm afraid,' he said, when his servant ushered them into the room. 'I've to sit here for the next four days with my foot on this wretched stool and not move an inch, so the surgeon says.' But although he kept his heel on the stool the rest of his body was remarkably active, twisting and turning to offer cakes and pour tea, or to give his entire attention first to one and then the other, making sure that Bessie was comfortably seated and urging tea upon her too, his whiskers very glossy and handsome in the muted light of the room.

They learnt quite a lot about him too, for he was very forthcoming and not a bit bad-tempered.

'Quite right,' he said cheerfully, when Caroline told him what Nan had said of him. 'Second son of the late Sir Osmond Easter, that's who I am. Married twice did my old man. Brother Joseph belonged to his first wife, and don't we all know *that*. Jane and I were his second brood, heaven help us.'

'You have a sister?' Euphemia said, ignoring the bitterness in his account and trying to steer their conversation into something more pleasant.

'Jane?' he said. 'A dear girl, Jane. Married last year though, that's the pity of it. Married and went off to Cumberland.'

'You must miss her,' Euphemia commiserated.

'Yes,' he admitted, 'I do rather. Being orphans and all that sort of thing you know.'

'Are both your parents . . . ?'

'Yes,' he admitted, shrugging his shoulders as though it was of no importance. 'The old man died in '36. Took a fall out hunting. Broke his neck. It seems we are rather prone to fall from our horses, we Easters.' He gave them a deprecating smile. 'My mother died in the cholera epidemic when I was seven.' And his long face was suddenly drawn with such a brooding sadness that both girls felt a rush of sympathy for him.

132

'I am an orphan too,' Caroline said, to show him he wasn't alone in his sadness. 'My mother died when I was born.'

'It's a hard world,' he said, smiling his sweet smile straight into her eyes. 'Pray have some more cake.'

So they ate cake while the girls tried to think of something positive to say, and Bessie tried to signal to them that the visit had gone on quite long enough, and despite himself, Henry remembered the days when his mother had still been alive.

He and Jane had been loved and petted then, and taught to read and write and cipher, and encouraged to fish the trout streams and ride to hounds. And after her death they'd done well enough, left in the care of a series of rough-handed nannies and generally allowed to run wild. But when their father broke his neck and their half-brother Joseph inherited the estate and the title, their lives had been horribly changed. Oh, horribly changed. What a long time ago it all seemed.

'I daresay you went to school, did you not?' Euphemia said gently.

He shuddered. 'Did I not! I should just say I did.'

So he told them about Harrow and Mr Oxenham, 'a terrible man, flog you as soon as look at you. He used to drop off to sleep in our lessons. Sound asleep. Snoring. We used to put curl papers in his hair and he never noticed.'

'Weren't you afraid he'd wake up and flog you?' Caroline asked.

'He'd wake up and flog us no matter what we were doing,' Henry explained. 'I think he enjoyed it. Oh no, there was no use worrying about being flogged. People were flogged all the time. When we were fags the seniors used to beat us with thorn sticks they'd pulled out of the hedges.'

'Whatever for?' Euphemia said.

'Oh anything,' Henry said airily. 'If we couldn't keep up at football. If we were late back with their beer. That sort of thing. The blood fairly poured down our jerseys. It was the very devil to get clean.'

'But that's barbarous!' Caroline said, quite horrified at such a story. 'It oughtn't to be allowed.'

'It's the way of the world,' he said. 'All schools are like that.'

'Ours wasn't,' Caroline said firmly, and she was just about to tell him about Mrs Flowerdew, when his man soft-footed

133

into the room to announce that the Fortescues had arrived. So to Bessie's relief, the visit had to be cut short.

'I brought you an invitation to our ball on Thursday,' Caroline said casually as they stood to go.

'Honoured, Miss Easter,' he said, taking the little card. 'I shall be there, depend upon it, whether I may dance or no. If I can't dance, then I will shuffle, I promise you.'

'Goodbye Mr Easter,' Euphemia said, holding out her hand.

He took it and kissed it. 'You are very kind to visit the sick as you do,' he said.

'We could hardly have left you lying on the ground,' Caroline said tartly because it irritated her to see Euphemia being kissed like that.

He swivelled in his seat and gave her his full attention, taking her hand and holding it tightly so that she was forced to step towards him. 'Indebted for ever!' he said. 'When I am a world famous poet I shall let it be known that it was Miss Caroline Easter who rescued me in my hour of need.'

'A poet?' she asked, thrilled by the information. 'Are you really?'

'Of course,' he said, still holding her hand. 'What else could I be?'

'A published poet?' Well, well, so Miss Artenshaw wasn't the only one with a poet for a friend.

'Well, not exactly published yet,' he admitted. 'I haven't quite gathered enough poems for a full volume.' Actually he'd only written three short lyrics so far, but there was no need to tell her that, especially when she was gazing at him with such flattering admiration.

'How thrilling!' she said. 'Do you write every day?'

'Oh no,' he said, shocked at the idea. 'You have to wait for inspiration, you know. It ain't the sort of thing you can do to order.'

'Perhaps you would let us read one of your poems some day,' she hoped.

'I might,' he said. 'I might indeed.' And he kissed her fingers, gazing straight into her eyes all the time.

The touch of his lips gave her the oddest sensation, as though her heart were turning a somersault in her chest, so perhaps it was just as well that at that moment Mr and Mrs Fortescue and their son and daughter were shown into the room. At least it gave her a chance to recover her composure. They exchanged pleasantries and said how much they were all looking forward to the Easter ball on Thursday and the Fortescue ball the following Monday, and Henry Osmond said goodbye to the two girls all over again, only this time without kisses.

Oh, it was a most successful visit.

'Do you think he will come to the ball?' Euphemia wondered, as Tom Thistlethwaite drove them back to Bedford Square.

'No,' Bessie said firmly, 'he won't.'

'It's of no consequence to me whether he does or not,' Caroline said with splendid aplomb.

But he did. So that was all right. And Nan seemed quite pleased to meet her new relation and asked after his brother and sister as though they were old friends. So *that* was all right. And despite his bandaged ankle he managed two waltzes, one with each of them. And that was the best thing of all, and quite the most romantic, for his gloved hand held her so firmly in the small of her back and their faces were so close together that she could see her own candle-lit reflection in the pupils of his eyes. I am dancing with a poet, she thought. It's a wonder I don't swoon away.

The next Monday he was at the Fortescue Ball and his ankle was so much better he'd removed the bandage. This time he danced three times with each of them and Caroline was sure he would have asked her a fourth time if such a thing had been acceptable, and if she hadn't already filled her dance card to help her brother.

'You become a pest, Will Easter,' she scolded him while they were dancing the quadrille. 'I can't spend all my time partnering my own brother, I would have you know.'

'So it would appear,' he teased, noticing the direction in which her eyes were continually straying, and the answering glances that were being sent her way. 'Very well, miss. I will release you from the next waltz, out of the kindness of my

135

heart, but you'd better not let Aunt Matilda see you if you dance with Mr Easter again, or she will have you married off before you can say knife.'

'Humph!' Caroline snorted. 'That just goes to show what a lot of nonsense conventions are. Mr Easter is a poet and above such things.' And she went straight off to find the gentleman, her pretty pink skirt swinging with determination.

'I do believe Aunt Matilda will have another match before long,' Will said to Euphemia as he led her onto the floor for the following dance.

'Caroline and Henry Osmond?' Euphemia said. 'Do you think so?'

'They spend a deal of time in one another's company.'

As we do, Euphemia thought, lifting her arms as they took the first two steps together. Oh, if only we could make a match! 'What would her father say?'

'He should be pleased,' Will said, as she turned beneath his forearm, her white skirt belling. 'He comes of a good family, when all's said and done.'

'Bessie doesn't approve,' Euphemia ventured as she completed the turn. 'We thought there might be – well – bad blood perhaps – between the two branches of the family.' And then the dance took her away from him to set and turn single with her opposing partner.

'I haven't heard of any,' he said when she returned to him.

'But you were not on visiting terms.'

'No,' he admitted, as she rested her hand on his arm to be led.

'And you were told nothing about them?'

'No,' he said again. And thinking he ought to find some explanation for this peculiar state of affairs, 'Perhaps we lost contact because we are in trade and they are county. There was a time when landed gentry and trade used not to mix.'

'They are mixing now,' Euphemia said, glancing over her shoulder to where Henry and Caroline were sitting with the Fortescues. They were so close to one another they were head to head, and his arm, flung along the back of the two-seater, looked as though it was holding her about the shoulders. Poor old Bessie, hovering in the background, was chewing her lips with anxiety.

'Yes,' he said, smiling at them all fondly. 'I think we must either hope that Papa will consent or that Aunt Matilda will not notice.'

But his father was still on his travels and that evening Aunt Matilda heard that she was to have a wedding in her own immediate family that would keep her more than occupied for the rest of the season.

Edward Easter's engagement to Miss Mirabelle Artenshaw was announced in *The Times* on the first day of June, immediately before the grand ball which was to be held in Holland House and was to be a most prestigious occasion, and on the very day John returned from Edinburgh. The timing was perfect, according to Matilda.

'They are to marry at the end of July,' she said to Nan and John. 'In St George's, of course. It will be a splendid affair. Of course our dear Mirabelle is not so young as she might be, that I'll grant you, nor so well-favoured, but she has a shrewd head on her shoulders for all that, and of course Edward is madly in love with her.'

'Of course,' Nan said, so smoothly that her sarcasm was lost to everybody except John, who gave her his lop-sided smile of recognition when Matilda was looking the other way.

'I shall wait with great interest to see how *this* turns out,' she said to John when Billy and Matilda had gone home.

'I can't imagine that even twelve thousand pounds will keep our Edward content for long,' John said. 'He has expensive tastes.'

'And will doubtless acquire more, when he has his hands on his wife's fortune, poor woman.'

'Well, well,' John said. 'At least our Will don't hunt fortunes.'

'Our Will,' his grandmother said sagely, 'has the best of wives right under his nose, if only he could see her.'

But John was more interested to know how Caroline had been behaving.

'I kept the dance cards for you like you said, Mr John dear,' Bessie said, laying them out before him on his mother's desk. 'An' I kept a good eye on her all the time.'

'I'm sure you did, Bessie,' John said, reading the names on the little cards. John Fortescue, that daft boy Montmorency, Will, Jerry Hollands, Henry Easter . . . 'Henry Easter? Who is that?'

'He's one of those dratted Easters from Ippark,' Bessie confessed miserably. 'I did try to warn her, Mr John dear. I knew you wouldn't like it. But you know what she's like.'

'Twice here,' John said, still examining the cards. 'Twice there. Once at the Montmorency's. I don't think there's any harm in it. He doesn't seem to signify.' But he would speak to her just the same, nip it in the bud, just to be on the safe side. He would call in tomorrow morning, after the stamping.

Caroline was rather surprised to see her father at the breakfast table and even more surprised when he asked her to remain behind when all the others had left the room. She tried to catch Nan's eye to find out what was up, but Nan was deep in conversation with Will, and Bessie had Euphemia out of the room almost before she'd put down her coffee cup. It was rather alarming.

She sat where she was at table, while her father stood up and walked across to the window and stood beside the long curtains looking down at the square. Yes, something was very certainly up. He was drumming against the window sill with the tips of his fingers.

'I understand that you have been visiting a young man called Henry Easter,' he said, and he was pleased to notice that his speech was commendably calm, given the passion that was shaking him.

'Yes, Papa,' she said, turning in her chair to face him. 'I have. He fell from his horse in the Park and sprained his ankle. Pheemy and I went visiting the sick.'

'So Bessie tells me.'

'And he's a cousin of ours. Ain't that the most amazing thing?'

'I would not call it amazing, Caroline,' he said, straightening the curtains. 'I would call it unfortunate.'

She chose to misunderstand him. 'He soon recovered, Papa. He was dancing again within the week.'

'Aye. So I've heard. And with you I believe.'

'Yes, Papa,' she said, smiling brightly at him. 'He dances very well.'

It was necessary to speak out plainly. He could see that she would not understand a hint. 'I must tell you, Caroline, that I do not approve of this young man. He belongs to a branch of this family with whom your grandmother and I have had no contact for more than forty years. A branch which I might say once behaved extremely badly towards this family.'

Ah, she thought, then that's the meaning of the mystery. They had a quarrel. 'Nan invited him to our ball,' she said, facing him boldly.

'I daresay she did,' he conceded. 'She has a more forgiving nature than I have. If it had been up to me no invitation would ever have been offered.'

'But it was, Papa. And he accepted it. I think he's a very nice young man and I'm sure you will too, once you meet him.'

'I have absolutely no intention of meeting him,' John said, recoiling from her and the idea. 'Nor have I any intention of fostering any possibility of any kind of alliance between our two houses. From now on, Caroline, you are to avoid this young man. We shall not invite him to any more functions of ours, of course, so there is no necessity for you to spend any further time with him.'

'We are bound to meet one another, Papa,' Caroline said, trying to be reasonable, 'since we both move in the same society. He will think it very rude if I ignore him.'

'There is no need for you to ignore him,' John said with exasperated patience. 'On the rare occasions when you might meet socially you must do your best simply to greet him politely and seek out some other company immediately.'

'But I don't want to seek out other company,' Caroline protested. 'I like him, Papa. He's a very nice young man.'

'I do not ask your opinion of him,' John said sternly. 'Nor whether or not you would wish to seek out other company. I have given you my instructions in this matter, and I expect you to obey them.' And he rang the bell.

Caroline left the table without another word, inwardly seething at the injustice of it.

'If he thinks I'm going to cut poor Henry Easter just because of some stupid old family quarrel,' she said to Euphemia when she'd told her cousin everything that had been said, 'then he may think again. It's positively barbaric. Besides being ill-mannered.'

'But you'll obey your father, surely?' Euphemia asked.

'More or less,' Caroline said, grinning at her. 'I won't talk to him when there's anyone there to see, and I won't dance with him more than twice, because Bessie's got eyes like a hawk, but I ain't cutting him dead and that's flat. If we happen to meet one another, in the Park say, or at some ball or other, then I shall talk to him. I don't care what Pa says.'

But although she rode up and down the ride that morning, several times and keeping the sharpest look-out, there was no sign of Henry Easter. So she couldn't put her threat into action after all. Which was very annoying.

Chapter 10

Henry Osmond Easter was driving down to Ippark to see his brother Joseph. The visit had been rather delayed because ever since that extraordinary young woman had met him in the park he'd led a busy social life attending one function after another, and sometimes two or three in an evening until he reached the one that she was attending too. For if he was honest with himself, and apart from his carefully acquired poetic sensibilities, he *was* honest with himself, he had to admit that he was very taken with her. He'd never met another young lady quite like her. She didn't seem to mind what she said or what she did, so he never really knew quite what to expect of her. And that trailed gunpowder into every meeting. To say nothing of the mystery that had kept all knowledge of this branch of the family from him and his sister, and Joseph too presumably. As soon as he got to Ippark he would ask Joseph what he knew about it.

The Easter country seat was set in the Sussex fields six miles south of Petersfield. It was a fine square red-brick house, built in the time of Queen Anne, with a suite of spacious high-ceilinged state rooms that were impressive but the very devil to keep warm in winter. There were two curved wings on either side of the main building, which housed the stables and the kennels, the game room and the dairies, and before the south front the stone steps of the drawing room gave out onto a prospect worthy of Mr Capability Brown, with a wide lawned terrace and a rose garden where guests could promenade in summer and beyond that, rolling green fields, thick woods and copses, and the long lush acres of the estate, dotted with grazing cattle and distant sheep like balls of cotton wool. Henry loved it, even in cold weather, and would have given anything to have been the owner of it. But sadly being the second son that wasn't possible.

When their father died Joseph had explained the situation in words that still stuck in his brother's mind like burrs to sheep. 'I'm the owner now,' he'd said, with the splendidly careless arrogance of a newly ennobled twenty-five-year-old. 'You've got an allowance. Quite handsome, I'd say. And Jane has a dowry so she can get herself a good husband when the time comes. We're all taken care of.'

'What am I to do?' Henry asked, caught in the bewilderment of sudden loss.

'Whatever you like,' his brother said. 'That's the beauty of it.'

'Am I to continue at Harrow?'

'Of course you are. Why ever not?'

'And go to Cambridge?'

'If you want to. I did, so I don't see why you shouldn't.'

'But where shall I live in the hols?'

'Here if you like,' Joseph said. 'Or in Grosvenor Street. Or both places. It's up to you now. You may come and go as you please. I'm off to see to the dogs.'

But Henry didn't want to come and go. He wanted to belong. To be the master of his own house. To be an important person like his father and his brother. And at a mere fourteen years of age he knew he had no importance whatsoever. No rank, no status, no importance, and as far as he could see no chance of any. It was horribly demoralizing, worse than his grief.

He was demoralized for the next three years until he went up to Trinity. But almost as soon as he got there, he found the solution to his problems. He would become a poet, that most admired member of the literary fraternity. He would make his name, acquire fame and fortune and the admiration of women, be his own man. From then on he worked towards that happy goal.

He grew a beard and moustache. In fact he grew several beards and moustaches until he found the one that suited his new image of himself. He dressed with bohemian stylishness,

142

in bold coloured coats and extravagant boots and the most elaborate cravats. He bought a gold-topped cane and learned to drive a four-in-hand. And he sat up into the small hours drinking claret and discussing Poetry and Life and Art with his poetic friends. The fact that he never actually got around to writing any verse didn't worry him unduly. There was time enough for that later. That was the easy part.

When he left Cambridge and went to London to apply himself to his chosen career, he was annoyed to discover that his poems didn't emerge onto paper in quite the same brilliant style in which he imagined them in his head. But he felt certain he would achieve the brilliance he wanted sooner or later and in the meantime he had acquired the cachet of poet, which was enough to be going on with. It had made him the centre of attention at his brother's wedding.

And it had certainly impressed Caroline Easter, which was very gratifying because she wasn't the sort of young woman who was easily impressed. There had been times during the last few dizzy weeks when he'd wondered whether she might not be the sort of woman who could be a poet's muse and inspiration. Until then his image of such a lady had been rather hazy. He'd felt she would be beautiful, of course, in an ethereal sort of way, vague and drifting and detached from mundane affairs, but passionately attached to her particular poet. Now he was beginning to imagine quite another style of inspiration, forthright and bold and exciting. To say nothing of romantic, for it was highly romantic to be the centre of a mystery. I'll ask old Joseph, he promised himself as his carriage rumbled him along the dusty road to Petersfield.

Unfortunately old Joseph was surrounded by guests when his brother arrived and it wasn't until after dinner the following day that they found themselves with the time and privacy to talk to one another and even then it wasn't for very long. Henry had gone into the red drawing room to get away from a garrulous dowager who wanted to discuss Shelley, and to his delight, his brother and sister-in-law were there before him, sitting on either side of the fire with the dogs at their feet and brandy glasses in their hands.

'Join us,' Emmeline said, indicating the decanter. 'Who are you hiding from, my dear?'

'Mrs Mullins,' he said, helping himself to brandy.

She grimaced, her little round face full of mischief between her long swaying curls. 'She'll not think to look here. She likes company. And the louder the better, I fear.'

'Is Jane to join us?'

'No,' Joseph said. 'Prefers her husband's company these days.' And he grinned his agreement of such good sense. 'Can't think what the world's coming to.'

But Henry sighed and the sigh wasn't lost on his sister-in-law.

'You miss her, my dear,' she said sympathetically.

'I do rather.'

'You should get yourself a wife,' Joseph said. 'That's my advice.'

'I can't do that until I'm an established poet.'

'And when will that be?'

He gave an honest answer. 'I couldn't say.' And he sighed again.

'Marry first and be a poet later,' Joseph said. 'That's my advice.'

Emmeline gave him a little warning grimace and turned her full attention to her sighing brother-in-law. 'How have you been faring in London?' she asked him.

It was the perfect opportunity to tell them his news. 'I have met up with an entire branch of this family that I never knew existed,' he said, 'which I find mighty mysterious.'

'Ah!' his brother said easily. 'They would be the news-agents I daresay.'

'The same.'

'Did you visit?' Joseph asked.

'A few times. Why don't we know them, Joseph?'

'Couldn't say, old thing,' Joseph said without much concern. 'Never have as far as I can remember. Some sort of feud, I believe. Ages ago of course. Before our time. I think it was our great-grandfather started it. Quarrelled with a woman called Anne or Nan or somesuch. Was there a woman called Anne or Nan d'you know?'

'There still is. Nan Easter. She's the manager of the firm.'

'Good Lord!' Joseph said. 'Fancy that, Emmeline. She must be a hundred. What is she like? Did you get to see her?'

'She's like Sheffield steel,' the poet said, 'sharp and grey, with a cutting edge.'

'Oh I say,' his brother applauded. 'That's very good. And what about the others? What are they like?'

So Henry told them all about Will and Euphemia and Caroline, describing the latter at such length and with such warmth that Emmeline understood the state of his affections at once. 'We must invite them here, Joseph,' she said. 'It would be interesting to meet a whole family of new relations all at once.' She was rewarded by the eagerness on Henry's face.

'Can't say I fancy Sheffield Steel,' Joseph said, gulping the last of his brandy. 'But the younger members of the family sound as if they would be good company. Ask 'em, Henry.'

'Oh, I will. I will,' Henry said. 'On the very first opportunity. Depend on it.'

'And if you don't find an opportunity, make one, eh?' his brother said.

But in the event it was Joseph who made the first opportunity and he made it for his brother. Although because it was an act of charity, he made it secretly. The day after Henry returned to town he rode up to London himself to seek out an old friend of his from his Oxford days, an old friend who was now the editor of the *Weekly Herald*.

After pleasantries and an ample lunch he came straight to the point. 'It's about my young brother,' he said. 'Fancies himself as a poet. I'd take it uncommon kindly if you would throw the odd job in his direction, just now and then.'

So an odd job was thrown. On the morning of the next ball of the season, after two days spent miserably indoors because of torrential rain, Henry received a letter commissioning him to compose a series of three odes on British heroes: Sir Francis Drake, Admiral Lord Nelson and the Duke of Wellington. He was cock-a-hoop about it, for it meant that he was being recognized at last. And he couldn't wait to tell Caroline.

He spent the entire day in a fever of excitement, looking forward to the ball, which was easy and pleasant, and trying to compose, which was far more difficult than he had expected. Inspiration did not descend from the clouds. In fact by the end of the afternoon he was beginning to suspect that he'd been given an impossible subject because he really didn't know very much about this long-dead hero except that he'd fought the French and been killed at the battle of Trafalgar. And rhyming was impossible too. The only one he could think of for hero was Nero, which wasn't appropriate, while as to finding a rhyme for Nelson . . . Nevertheless he took his notebook to the ball. Perhaps Miss Easter would inspire him.

It took him some time to discover where she was, for the ball was being held at the Montacute's and their ballroom was enormous and gave out into a series of terraces that led to the garden. But eventually he saw her standing on one of those terraces, leaning her arm against an urn full of roses and honeysuckle, talking to Euphemia, with her grandmother and Mr Brougham and her brother beside her.

He walked over to her at once, his notebook still in his hand.

'I do declare you're composing a poem,' she said, addressing him without preamble, in that forthright way of hers, and gazing at him so directly she quite took his breath away. She really is a very pretty girl, he thought. Her eyes are so fine, so dark and passionate, and her hair quite beautiful, clustering thickly about her forehead and swinging beside her cheeks in ringlets so glossy I can hardly bear not to touch them. While as to her mouth, why that really is most delicious, so wide and generous and outspoken . . .

'Yes,' he said as casually as he could. 'A commission, you know. From the *Weekly Herald*.'

'How thrilling,' she said. 'What is it about? Do tell. Are we allowed to see it?'

'Not just yet,' he said, closing his notepad quickly before she could see the mess he was in. 'Takes a bit of doing, does an ode.'

'What is it about?'

'Admiral Lord Nelson.'

'A great hero,' Nan Easter said. 'But the man was small.'

'Did you *see* him?' Euphemia asked, eyes wide. 'Did you actually see Lord Nelson with your own eyes?' What a marvellous thing to meet a hero face to face!

'Several times,' Nan said.

'What was he like, ma'am?' Henry asked. 'If I may make so

146

bold as to ask.' Now this was more like. This could turn out to be the inspiration he needed.

'He was quiet,' Nan remembered. 'An unassuming sort of feller, riding about town with his lady-love. He wore a patch over his blind eye, I remember. A gentle looking man. You'd never have thought he was a hero. Not to look at him.' What a long time ago it all was, that terrible battle of Trafalgar. Before these children were born, when John and Billy and Annie were little more than children themselves. And yet she remembered it all so clearly as if it were yesterday. 'We've took an unconscionable time to honour him.'

'He was our greatest hero, wasn't he?' Euphemia said. Mrs Flowerdew had told them all a great deal about him. In fact he and the Duke of Wellington were the only two men she'd ever approved of.

'Without Lord Nelson,' Mr Brougham told them, 'Napoleon would have invaded this country in 1805. We had troops stationed all along the south coast waiting for him but, even so, if he'd landed we would have been hard put to it to defend ourselves. I dread to think what would have become of us.'

And one of those troops, Nan thought, was my Calverley Leigh. I wonder where the old rogue is now. Now he *was* a handsome crittur and no mistake, the love of her youth and such fun.

The fiddles were striking up the quadrille.

'You could dance with me if you wished,' Caroline said to Henry. Papa hadn't arrived yet, so this was just the chance, even if she did have to be – well, rather forward to take it. It was just as well Bessie was out of earshot.

'Honoured,' he said, bowing to her. And he led her happily away.

As their feet followed the complicated patterns he told her that his family would like her to visit them at Ippark and she told him, most diplomatically, that her father was rather busy and that it might not be possible to arrange a visit just at present. And they spoke of the quarrel that had kept their two branches of the family apart for so long and agreed that it was positively ridiculous, indeed it was. And when the dance was done and they walked out onto the terrace again, they returned to the subject of the ode.

'How much have you written?' she asked.

'Not a great deal,' he confessed. 'It's uncommon difficult to find the rhymes.'

'Poor Nelson,' she said. 'I always think he must be jolly cold on his column.'

Cold on his column, Henry thought. How extraordinary she is to think of a statue being cold. But it was the perfect first line.

' "Cold on his column Nelson stands",' he declaimed, pulling his notebook from his pocket and writing as he spoke. ' "His iron sword in iron hands." What do you think?'

'Wonderful,' she applauded, admiring his dark eyes. Oh, he looked every inch a poet. 'Except . . . '

'Except?'

'Well, he only had one, you know.'

'One what?'

'One hand.'

'Poetic licence,' he said, suddenly feeling quite cross. It was the first good couplet he'd been able to conjure up and he wasn't going to reject it for mere verisimilitude. Now she'd spoilt herself, pretty though she was. There was no need to go pointing out every single little error.

'He only had one eye too,' she observed.

'Yes. I know that.' Everybody knew that.

She looked out at the ballroom, checking to see whether her father had arrived. 'Nan says he could see a deal better with one eye than most of us can see with two.'

The second couplet materialized. He wrote again. 'With one eye he could see. A great deal better than you and me.' It wasn't perfect but it was a start.

'You are a muse,' he said, feeling quite warm towards her again. 'A poet's muse. Before I danced with you I could hardly write a word. Now. Well, you see how it is.'

Caroline was thrilled. 'A muse!' she said, enraptured. Why, it was like something out of a romance.

'All the great poets have been inspired by women,' he told her, sliding his pencil behind his ear. 'Dante, Shakespeare, Shelley, Keats, Byron . . . '

'Henry Osmond Easter.'

'If you were the woman,' he said, feeling full of power and

148

daring. 'Oh, how splendid creation is! You see how I write now that you are with me.'

'It is an honour,' she said, wondering breathlessly just where this extraordinary conversation was leading them.

But neither of them were to find out, for at that moment Will suddenly strode through the crowd to join them, talking as he came and signalling to his sister with a stern glance sideways that she was to be discreet. 'My dance, I believe, Carrie.'

'Such a splendid evening,' Euphemia said, panting up behind them to take Caroline by the arm and move her two steps sideways and out of danger. 'Your father has arrived,' she whispered.

But John Easter was already upon them. 'You will please to follow me, Caroline,' he said. 'Your grandmother wishes to speak with you.'

He was walking her away before anyone had a chance to say anything else.

So many emotions eddied within the little space they enclosed with their bodies, John's fury, Euphemia's anxiety, Henry's confusion, Will's embarrassment, all so strong and so sudden that Caroline had no time to respond to any of them. It was hard enough to cope with the force of her own emotion which was something new and powerful and very disturbing and yet reminded her of the feelings she had at a wedding. She wanted to go on talking to Henry, to go on feeling this new excitement, whatever it was, to go on. But the force of her father's anger pulled her away, drew her feet after him, so that she followed almost without volition. She sensed that Will was saying something to poor Henry, because she could hear his voice, soothingly polite, but everything was happening much too quickly. Euphemia was holding her arm, her head so close that they were cheek to cheek, smiling sympathy and warning and affection all mixed up together. I can't just walk away like this, she thought, and she turned her head to glance back at her poet and was thrilled and upset to see how bleak he looked, standing tall and white-faced on the terrace with his notebook still in his hand.

'I will ride tomorrow,' she mouthed at him. And then they were inside the ball room and the crush was between them and she couldn't see anything except backs and shoulders and head-dresses that were much too tall, wretched things. 'Why do people have to wear such ridiculous head-dresses?' she said crossly to Euphemia. 'Sticking up in the air, getting in everybody's way!'

'Come and dance,' Will urged. 'It's no good getting cross.'

But although she soon danced herself into a good humour again she was still annoyed by her father's peremptory interruption and hurt to think how much it must have upset poor Henry. And she made up her mind that she would apologize to him on her father's behalf the minute she saw him again.

The next morning it was drizzling with rain.

'You don't want to go riding in this,' Bessie said with obvious satisfaction.

'Yes, I do,' Caroline said. 'It will soon clear. You'll see.'

And it did. After the first half hour or so. But by then Caroline didn't care what the weather was doing, for Henry was already in the Park when she arrived.

'I am so sorry for the way my father behaved yesterday,' she said, trotting up to him. 'It was most ill-mannered to cut you. He makes me ashamed.'

'It's of no consequence,' he said gallantly. 'No consequence at all.'

'It's all on account of that stupid quarrel,' she said. 'I do think it's ridiculous.'

'So it is,' he agreed, riding as close beside her as his palamino would allow. 'But we are above such folly, are we not?'

'No,' she admitted ruefully, 'I'm afraid we're not. The truth is, he forbade me to spend any time with you at all. I may greet you when we meet, out of common politeness, he allowed that, but we ain't supposed to talk. He don't approve of you.' And then, aware of the stiffening of his expression and afraid that she'd upset him, 'Oh, not because of anything he's heard about you, just because of who you are. An Ippark Easter, you see.'

He should have been annoyed, but he wasn't. He was thrilled to be the subject of such a ban. It was romantic, the sort of thing a struggling poet ought to expect. 'The slings and arrows of outrageous fortune,' he said, sitting straight and proud on his palamino.

'I think it's downright hateful,' she said. It had upset her to have to tell him. 'I don't share his opinion at all, do I Pheemy?'

'No,' Euphemia said, 'neither of us do.'

'I think he's quite wrong,' Caroline said emphatically. Now that the truth was out she wanted Henry Easter to know exactly what her feelings were. Even though she wasn't entirely sure herself. Oh, it was hideous to cut him. Indeed it was. Especially when he was so noble and handsome.

'He has been alone for a very long time,' Euphemia explained. 'Living alone, I mean, with no wife, you see. I think that may be why he is harsh sometimes.'

'He had no right to cut you,' Caroline said passionately. 'Nor to forbid me to talk to you. That ain't natural.'

'No,' he said with equal passion, gazing straight into her eyes. 'Nor possible.'

That odd excitement wriggled in her belly and for a second or two she found she was breathless and didn't know what to say. Then her horse shied and had to be coaxed and the three of them walked on without speaking for a yard or so.

'You don't mean to obey your father,' he said, breathless with daring and exertion.

'Not in every particular,' she said, feeling very bold even to be saying such a thing.

'I think you are quite right,' he said. 'Sometimes it is necessary to take a stand. All poets take stands. Think of Lord Byron.'

They all thought of Lord Byron for several further yards.

'Where shall you be tonight?' he asked.

'At the Drury Lane Theatre,' Euphemia said, 'with Nan and Mr Brougham.'

'What good fortune,' he said, beaming at them. 'I shall be there too. Who knows, we might meet in the interval.'

'You see what a noble spirit he has,' Caroline said, as she and Euphemia were driven home after their ride. 'It's downright ridiculous of Pa to forbid us to meet. He's a splendid young man, don't you think so, Pheemy? So forgiving and kind.'

'And artful,' Euphemia said.

'Oh yes, indeed. Wondrously artful. What shall I wear tonight?' And then as another thought struck her, 'I wonder if I could persuade Aunt Matilda to invite him to Edward's wedding?'

But Aunt Matilda was horribly resistant, even to the very broadest hint her niece could devise, and Henry Osmond wasn't invited.

Caroline was jolly annoyed. It was too bad. It really was. Especially when everybody else was there. And especially when she couldn't comment on the lack of invitation without appearing to show too familiar an interest in the young man. Which wasn't the case at all, of course. Her interest in him was purely literary. Wasn't it? But really? Out of common politeness, you'd have thought Aunt Matilda could have made an effort, no matter what Papa might say.

It was a boring wedding too, on a freezing cold day and with everything veiled and hidden as if nature had dropped a shroud across the whole affair. There was a heavy mist that morning rolling against the doors and windows in great clouds of objectionable dampness and all the trees were dripping.

The wedding guests arrived at the church under umbrellas, and the women all covered their bonnets with scarves so that it was hard to tell who they all were, and the bride wore a veil so thick you couldn't see her face at all. She and Edward gave their responses in silly little voices as though it were all a great secret. Not that anyone could hear them anyway with so many people coughing. Uncle Billy was making a noise like a cracked trumpet, which didn't please Aunt Matilda. And when the ceremony was over and the new Mr and Mrs Edward Easter walked in procession to the porch, what with guttering candles and seeping mist, the light in the church was so poor it was impossible to do more than catch a glimpse of their frozen faces.

And then as if that wasn't bad enough, it was raining when they came out of the church and the waiters at the reception were so slow that all the food was congealed and cold long before it reached the table. Caroline was jolly glad when the whole business was over and the bride and groom had been tucked into his new carriage under her new travelling rug and brisked away towards their honeymoon with the rain spraying from their wheels.

'Thank heavens that's finished,' she said to Euphemia as they trotted back to Bedford Square. 'Now we can get on with the rest of the season. If it ever stops raining.'

Her father was glad to have the wedding over and done with too. 'The sooner it is autumn and Caroline is safely away in the country the better,' he said.

'Poor old John,' Billy commiserated. 'Children are the very devil. Don't I know it.'

'Yours,' Matilda told him sternly, 'have always been exceedingly easy, all things considered.'

Nan and Billy grimaced at one another, remembering Edward's debts, and John squinted at his own furious thoughts.

'I must confess,' Matilda went on, ignoring them all, 'that it's a relief to have both my darlings happily settled and with all their little childish problems over and done with. How happy my dear Edward must be now, away on his honeymoon, without a care in the world.'

Chapter 11

Married life wasn't quite what Mr Edward Easter had expected it to be. It had been pleasant to court a rich woman and to know that his friends envied him a wealthy match, and it was flattering to see her sitting beside him at the reception in her elegant gown, entertaining the guests with her tales of writers and poets, but he hadn't really imagined she would be silent once they were alone together.

Mirabelle's aunt had put her country estate at their disposal for the month of their honeymoon. It was out in the wilds of the Wiltshire countryside and the journey there was long and damp and uncomfortable. During the first half hour he had tried to make conversation, passing witty comments upon the wedding guests and holding forth about his ambition to live like a gentleman now that they were married and to run a town house and a country seat and keep a carriage and pair and a dog-cart. But she said nothing in reply except, 'Yes, dear' and 'No, my love', and after a while his monologue became embarrassing, so they finished their journey in silence.

And dined in silence. And sat by the drawing room fire in silence, while the chambermaids prepared their room, clattering about with warming pans and sweet herbs and scuttles full of coal, and the housekeeper fussed over the number of pillows they might require and whether or not she should serve them hot toddy as a night cap, 'on such a cold evening'.

'They are very attentive, my dear,' he said, when they were finally allowed to enter their bedroom.

'Yes, my love.'

'We should retire, I think,' he suggested. 'It grows very late.' And he gave an exaggerated yawn to help her to agree with him.

'As you wish,' she said, ringing for her maid.

He retreated to the dressing room while she prepared for bed, because that was the correct thing to do, and because it gave him a chance to peek through the crack in the door and watch her without her knowledge.

She undressed deftly, folding her clothes before she handed them to her maid, lace cap, bodice, skirt, and then one petticoat after another, while her husband wondered however many more there would be. She was so thin once all her padding was gone that her stays were really unnecessary. But she removed them neatly too, reminding her maid to powder them thoroughly. And then the only thing between her and the flesh he now owned was a fawn chemise trimmed with expensive blonde lace.

All the whores he'd used had looked mighty alluring in their stays, with their waists so ridiculously slender he'd felt he could snap them in two if he wanted, and their breasts pushed up into tempting mounds of pliable flesh ready for his hands. In fact almost the best part of the procedure had been watching them strip and waiting for the gradual revelation of breast and thigh. But as far as he could see through the crack, Mirabelle had no breasts at all. It was a disappointment. And it would make their first night rather difficult, because he simply couldn't feel any desire for her at all. Perhaps things would improve when she took off her chemise.

But to his frustration she left the undergarment where it was while her maid lowered a voluminous nightgown over her head, past the wall-eye, cloaking her narrow neck, falling like a stage curtain across flat bosom, wide waist and narrow hips until it reached her long white feet, which he watched stepping delicately out of a pile of fawn linen, which was then lifted from the floor and folded, and turned out to be her chemise. What amazing modesty! he thought. Somehow or other she had contrived to take off her chemise underneath her nightgown. Imagine that!

Then her hair was unpinned and brushed out of curl and arranged in a neat plait over one shoulder. And at last the maid was dismissed. Edward was quite intrigued to see what she would do next. Would she get into bed and wait for him there, or sit by the fire, or stay where she was before the dressing table?

But no. She did none of these things. She walked across to the wash-stand, took a candle from the sconce and left the room. Gone to the closet, he thought, and was annoyed to be reminded of something so vulgar at such a time.

She was a long time gone. Long enough for him to undress, ring for his man, have his clothes taken away, and climb into bed. And by then he was getting impatient. What did she think she was doing, keeping him waiting? And on his wedding night too.

But at last she returned, pale and expressionless behind the yellow star of her candle. She climbed into the bed beside him, without looking at him or saying a word and snuffed out the candle without consulting him, as though she was sleeping on her own.

It was disconcerting to be suddenly marooned in darkness like that. He felt so aggrieved that he reached out and grabbed at her roughly. 'You are my wife,' he said angrily.

'Yes,' her voice came softly out of the darkness. 'Of course, my dear, that is perfectly understood.'

Her calm was infuriating. He would rather she'd wept, or sounded afraid, or pleaded with him to treat her gently. Very well, he thought, if you give me nothing I will take what I want, and it will be all your own fault for behaving in such an unwomanly way. Feeling angry with himself because he knew he was treating her badly, angry with her because she had provoked his harshness, he ran his hands roughly over her body, pushing the nightgown up and out of his way, exploring for soft flesh and finding bone, for endearments, clinging arms, welcoming breasts, finding none, angry with everything in a vague generalized way, growling discontentment.

But she said nothing. She lay quite still and let him do whatever he wanted and made no sound, except for an odd intake of breath at the moment of entry, as though she was wincing. He took her in a rush of angry desire and very limited pleasure. And was more angry than ever when the deed was done.

She lay beside him in the darkness until he had recovered his breath and then she sat up, rearranged her nightgown and lit the candle.

156

The sudden light hurt his eyes. 'Blow that out,' he said.

'Not yet, my love,' she said calmly. 'We have things to talk about.'

After all that silence, he thought, she chooses this moment to talk. The perversity of woman. 'No, we don't,' he said. 'Blow it out.'

She lit the second candle in the holder. And then the third. The light was blazing. 'We have things to talk about now that we are one flesh and truly married,' she said.

'I want to go to sleep,' he said, sulkily, closing his eyes against the glare.

'I've no doubt you do, my love,' she said, 'and so you shall when we've decided how we are to live our lives.'

What was she talking about? 'Live our lives?' he said, thickly, opening his eyes to squint up at her.

'Indeed yes,' she said, and she smiled at him, her head half turned away from him so that he could only see her good eye. 'We have to decide what we are going to do with the money.'

'The money?'

'Yes indeed. The twelve thousand pounds, my love. The money you married me for.'

He was so shocked his mouth fell open. 'How can you say such a thing?' he spluttered. 'I'm sure such a thought never crossed my mind. I'm sure I never . . . '

'Yes, you did,' she said coolly. 'All my suitors did. Every single one. And you as much as any of them. I am not such a fool as to imagine that you married me for my beauty. No, no you married me for the money. That is perfectly understood. Now we have to decide how it is to be used.'

He couldn't think of anything to say to her after such coarseness. He couldn't bear to look at her. That one eye was altogether too direct and unblinking. So he listened, scowling at the sheet.

'At present the money is invested in government bonds,' she said, 'which bring me in a comfortable return, sufficient to keep me in clothes and books and newspapers and trips to the theatre and suchlike commodities, and to pay for my maid and such personal bills as I might run up from time to time, the hairdresser, milliner, dressmaker and so forth, and still have enough over to run a literary salon should I so require. Left to accumulate they could continue to provide indefinitely, with careful re-investment whenever necessary, of course. That is what I would advise us to do.'

'You talk like a banker,' he tried to joke, glancing up at her to see if his words would soften her at all.

But she took the joke as a compliment. 'You flatter me,' she said, smiling at him again.

'However, my love,' he said, 'it ain't for you to say how the money's to be used. Not now. Not now when you have a husband to attend to it for you.'

'Not according to the law,' she said calmly. 'No, you are right. In law you own the money just as you own me. But law ain't the only thing you have to consider tonight, my love.'

'Why no, indeed,' he said, smiling back at her and deciding to try tenderness this time. 'This is a night for love, not law. Our wedding night, my love.'

'Hum,' she said, and the little sound wasn't encouraging. 'Well, we'll not speak of that. At least not now. There is time enough to amend those matters later. At present we have to decide about the money. As you say, by law the money now belongs to you and you could spend it in any way you chose, if you decided to be so foolish. But I do not think you a foolish man, or I would not have married you.'

'I hoped you married me for love,' he said weakly.

'Oh dear me no,' she said. 'Although I daresay we shall come to love one another in time if we treat one another well enough. Oh no, I married you, my dear, because you are an Easter, and a name in the newspaper world, and consequently a man who would not wish the newspapers to know anything to his discredit, which they most certainly would if you were so foolish as to squander my money on selfish luxuries.'

It sounded uncomfortably like blackmail. 'Oh come,' he tried. 'A man's finances are his own concern. How could they possibly know how I spent my money?'

'They would know,' she said firmly, 'because I would tell them. The editor and owner of the *Daily Record* is my mother's cousin.'

It was blackmail. Dear heavens! Blackmail, from one's own wife!

'The decision is yours, of course,' she was saying. 'Sleep on

158

it, my dear. You have no need to say anything now. You can tell me what you have decided in the morning. We have all the time in the world.'

And I have none of the money, he thought, bitterly. And he turned on his side and pulled the covers over his head, boiling with anger and frustration. To be caught so. And by a woman too, an old ugly woman who had no right to be behaving in such a way.

He was still furiously angry when he woke up in the morning, and his anger increased when he saw how peacefully she was sleeping, and went on sleeping despite all the noise he made getting up and washing and dressing.

It was a foul day but he went out for an early morning stroll despite the weather. He could hardly stay in the bedroom with such a wife. Mist lay across the meadows like a white sea; the paths in the gardens were ridged with mud and treacherous with puddles; and the boughs above him dripped moisture like miserable tears. So he was cross and wet when he finally returned for breakfast.

Mirabelle was at the table, enjoying steak and eggs. The sight of her pleasure removed what little appetite he had.

'Have you come to a decision?' she asked.

He walked across to the sideboard to get away from the unpleasantness of such talk, not wanting to speak at all because he was so cast down. 'Yes,' he said at last. 'I suppose the money must stay where it is.'

'Very wise,' she said, cutting the steak.

'I want to go home,' he said petulantly, lifting the covers from the dishes on the sideboard and sniffing their contents.

'Of course, my love,' she agreed.

'Today,' he said, helping himself to bacon.

'Would that be wise?' she asked mildly. 'If we return too soon people might think all was not well between us, and that would be bad for trade, would it not?'

Right again, he thought bitterly. Aggravating woman. 'We will stay a week then,' he said.

'A fortnight would be better.'

'A fortnight would be interminable,' he said.

And it was.

But at last they were back in London in their new home in Bayswater and he could escape to the Strand and leave all his annoying troubles behind him. It was a relief to be back on home ground, with men to obey him and the knowledge that poorly paid as he was he still had power in the firm. But his temper was easily frayed. It made him cross just to think of all that capital lying in Mirabelle's banking account untouched and untouchable. The slightest fault or the faintest insult, real or imaginary, had him bull-roaring in an instant. Within a day of his return people who could were avoiding him.

Not that marriage to Mirabelle was all loss. She ran their house extremely well, and was an excellent hostess at their dinner parties. So good, in fact, that they were soon to become quite renowned for the excellence of their hospitality.

But public success, however sweet, didn't bring curves to Mirabelle's flesh nor joy to their marriage bed. He made love to her whenever he could, but the little pleasure it gave him was rarely worth the effort.

Until the day he discovered Mr Leonard Snipe.

It was a fine summer afternoon. He had finished his work in the warehouse and was strolling down the Strand towards the Somerset coffee house, enjoying the sunshine and feeling pleasantly idle, when he saw an old college friend of his just ahead of him. He quickened his pace to catch up with the fellow, but instead of continuing along the Strand as he expected, the young man cut across the churchyard of St Clements' Danes and disappeared into the crowds that tangled in the narrow lane behind the church. As he had nothing better to do, Edward followed.

Holywell Street was narrow and old and chronically run down. Several of the houses were clumsily buttressed but their inhabitants had turned this particular misfortune to advantage and used the slanting beams to display the second-hand clothes they hoped to sell. Most of the shops in the alley were small and poorly lit, so a great deal of trade was done in the street among the mounds of rubbish and the carefully gathered manure stored there by the street sweepers. Whores watched for custom from the upstairs windows, and small pickpockets mingled with the customers, dark hands at the ready. It was a busy, pungent, noisy place, and until that afternoon Edward had avoided it. Now looking in vain for the blue top hat of his friend among the welter of old clothes and dirty faces, he was convinced he'd been wise to do so.

There was no sign of the top hat, and he was just about to turn round and fight his way out of the crowd when he saw a neat hand-printed notice in the corner of an otherwise blank shop window. 'Literature for discerning gentlemen of quality' it said. 'Full colour plates of delectable beauty. Academic erotica. For list of titles enquire within.'

He was interested at once. Literature for discerning gentlemen could only mean one thing, and colour plates sounded too good to miss. He lifted the latch and stepped down into the shop, closing the door upon the stink and racket outside.

There was incense burning in a brass censer just inside the door, but no sign of a shopkeeper and no books, but that was encouraging too, for given the work of the Society for the Suppression of Vice, books of this kind would hardly be on open display. But there was a small desk in one corner of the room with an ink well, a pen, a magnifying glass and a hand bell laid neatly upon it. He rang the bell.

There was a shuffle behind the blue baize curtain in the corner of the room and an eye appeared through a small hole in the curtain and glared at him balefully for several seconds. Then it disappeared and the curtain was held back and a man stepped into the room.

'I can see that you are a gentleman of distinction, sir,' he said, 'so I know you will forgive my – um – scrutiny. There is such a need for caution in these – um – unfortunate days. Not that a gentleman like yourself would require instruction in such matters. No, no, no. I would not presume even to suggest such a thing. Can't be too careful, can we, sir? People have such nasty minds. I *do* have the honour of addressing a connoisseur, do I not?'

Edward agreed that he did.

'Leonard Snipe,' the gentleman said, bowing deferentially.

He was an unremarkable looking man, straight as a wooden doll and with the same blank rotundity, a pale brown man, neatly dressed in a buff cloth coat, brown cloth trousers and two quiet waistcoats, one buff, one snuff and both faded. An unobtrusive man, with buff fingers and scant, straight, pale brown hair like a baby's and a face as bland as a hard boiled egg, unblinking and almost totally devoid of expression. 'Leonard Snipe, printer and publisher.'

'Pleased to make your acquaintance,' Edward said, as the words seemed to be expected of him.

'Ah, pleasure!' Mr Snipe said, lifting both his hands before him as though he were about to pray. 'What a crying need there is for pleasure in this weary world of ours! Pleasure and beauty, sir, where would we be without 'em? I consider it an honour, sir, to be able to provide such necessities to my discerning public. Did I say an honour, sir? Nay, a duty. I am a man of principle, sir.'

'Quite,' Edward said, because he didn't know what else to say.

The word seemed to satisfy. 'I can see that you are a gentleman of true distinction, sir,' Mr Snipe intoned. 'And discretion, dare I hope?'

'Of course.'

'It is so necessary in these matters to be sure of discretion. People have such very nasty minds, sir. Positive cesspools, and no appreciation of art or the artist, who has a very different view of things, as I hardly need to tell you, sir. Would you care to see my current list?'

'Yes,' Edward admitted, trying not to sound too eager nor to show how impatient he was getting. What a long time this man took to get to the point.

The list was finally produced, after a brief disappearance behind the baize curtain. And a very tempting list it was. He read it with rising pleasure at the titillation it promised.

'*Tales of Twilight*: or the amorous adventures of a company of ladies before marriage 10/6 (8 colourplates)

The Royal Wedding Jester: or all the fun and facetiae of the wedding night with all the good things said sung or done on that joyous occasion 2/6 reduced

The Wedding Night: or the battles of Venus

The Voluptuarian Cabinet: or Man of Pleasure miscellany 3/6 (5 plates)

Julia: or I have saved my rose 10/6 (8 plates)

The Jolly Companion: women disrobed.'

'Of course, I have other publications,' Mr Snipe smoothed, 'should these not be to your taste.'

'No, no,' Edward said. 'These are very much to my taste, Mr Snipe.'

He chose *The Jolly Companion* and he wasn't disappointed. At least not until he'd made use of it on half a dozen occasions. Then he had to admit its effect began to pall, but that was only to be expected, and now that he knew where to find them other books could be bought.

Soon he had acquired quite an extensive library to lock away in the cupboard in his dressing room, a repertoire of delectable images that enabled him to make love to his poor plain wife far more often and with much greater pleasure, providing he could rouse himself by gazing upon the pictures as he disrobed. Oh yes, life was decidedly more enjoyable now that he and Mr Snipe were regular acquaintances. In fact as the weeks passed he wondered whether he might not ask the gentleman to dine at his house. After all he *was* a publisher, which made him acceptable providing nobody knew what additional material he published. And besides, it would jolly well serve Mirabelle right.

I will put my mind to it, he promised himself, as he drove home with a copy of *The Man of Pleasure* wrapped in plain brown paper and tucked inside his inner pocket.

In the event Mirabelle saved him the necessity. That evening, when her excellent dinner had been enjoyed and cleared, she told him that she intended to hold her very first literary salon in six days' time.

'It is all arranged,' she said, with that infuriating calm of hers. She was looking so pleased with herself it quite upset him. 'I have had the great good fortune to secure the presence of Mr Charles Dickens, my dear, and if that isn't guaranteed to ensure success I'm sure I don't know what would be. He and his friends have promised to perform a short play, and Mr

163

Dickens has very kindly consented to give a reading from one of his novels.'

'I congratulate you,' he said. 'Whom do you mean to invite to this occasion? Have you drawn up a list?'

'I thought we might do that this evening,' she said, smiling at him.

So the list was drawn up and the name of Mr Snipe, (publisher) included, immediately below the names of Caroline, Euphemia, Will and Mrs Nan Easter.

'I do so hope your grandmother will attend,' Mirabelle said, 'for of all the ladies of my acquaintance she is the one I most admire.'

'Do you?' Edward said with some surprise. He had always found Nan Easter a very difficult old lady.

'Indeed I do. I should be honoured by her company on this occasion.'

'She is a very busy woman,' Edward warned. 'I doubt if she'll have time.'

But Nan wrote back at once to say that she would be delighted to attend, and when the evening began the Easters were present in force. Only Mr John Easter was absent and that was because he had to be in York attending to negotiations with Mr Hudson the railway king who was about to open two more new railway lines in Yorkshire. It wasn't a job he could hand over to anyone else, for Mr Hudson was an overfed, ambitious bully, and accustomed to getting his own way in every particular, so the transfer of Easter freight to the two lines would have to be handled with strength and patience.

The literary salon was a dazzling event. Euphemia was quite overawed by it, for there were lots of people there she'd never seen before and she was always shy in strange company. Beneath the two glittering chandeliers, Mirabelle's vast red and gold salon was packed to capacity, and yet new arrivals were announced every second. The ladies were magnificent, glistening with jewels, fluttering their feathered fans, their arms and bosoms soft as powder, and their huge bell skirts taking up so much room, even when they were settled on one of Mirabelle's sofas, that it was almost impossible to move through the throng for the crush of silk and satin. And the gentlemen looked highly romantic too, for with one or two rather dull exceptions they were either in full evening dress or military uniform and most of them were loud with excited gallantry.

'My hat!' Will said, steering his two companions into the crush.

'Where's Mr Dickens?' Caroline wanted to know, peering about her as she hung onto his arm.

A stage was erected in one corner, ready for the players, but there was no sign of the guest of honour.

'He'll be the last to arrive,' Nan told them, 'seeing he en't the first.' With which cryptic remark she pushed her way through the mass of chattering bodies towards her son Billy, who was beleaguered beside the mantelpiece talking to Edward.

And of course she was right. Just when the crush in the room was so intense that Caroline said she would faint if anyone else arrived, and many of the ladies were draped over the sofas as if they were swooning already, there was a flutter of interest close to the door and somebody sounded a gong.

'Mr Charles Dickens!' the butler announced. And there he was, a young man in his early thirties, striding into the room, blue eyes flashing, dark hair on end, talking and gesticulating, all excitement and vitality and high-charged energy, like walking electricity. Every head turned towards him at once as though they were magnetized and the swooning ladies sat up and began to sparkle. 'Mr Charles Dickens!'

From then on the pace of the evening was entirely changed. The actors were upon the stage in a leap, so that the audience barely had time to settle into their gilded chairs before the performance was under way. And a rapid, dazzling performance it was, a farce called *A Good Night's Rest*, which, naturally enough, was as restless as its producer and was played on the trot, to squealing applause.

Then there was the reading, a marvellously dramatic rendering of the death of Nancy from *Oliver Twist*, and then wonder of wonders, the famous author was striding amongst his audience, talking and talking, kissing Nan on both cheeks, giving Caroline and Euphemia a glance of such open admiration that it made Euphemia blush, talking and talking, his entire face mobile, as one expression after another shunted across it, his eyebrows arching and dipping, his mouth constantly on the move, smiling, twisting, grimacing, stretching wide in booming laughter, those blue eyes flashing fire. The two girls were bewitched by him.

I wish Henry were here, Caroline thought. It would be such an opportunity for him. Mr Dickens is just the man to inspire him. I wonder if I could persuade Mirabelle to invite him next time. And she burrowed off through the crowd to find her new cousin and see.

Mirabelle was in the centre of an earnest group of gentlemen, one of whom was a dull brown creature with a hideous name, but she detached herself from them when she saw Caroline. 'It goes well, I think,' she said. 'The refreshments are circulating, are they not?'

Until that moment Caroline hadn't noticed the refreshments but now she helped herself to a glass of champagne from a passing tray. 'I do hope you'll hold another salon soon, Mirabelle,' she said.

'I have every intention,' Mirabelle assured her, smiling as two of her other guests eased themselves past her.

'For poets perhaps?'

'Ah!' Mirabelle said. 'You enjoy poetry?'

'Oh yes,' Caroline said.

'Then I shall hold a salon expressly for poets and poetry and your invitation will be at the head of my list. You have my word for it.'

'When will it be, Mirabelle? Oh, let it be soon. I know a poet I should like you to include.'

'Not this season, I'm afraid,' Mirabelle said. 'There is so little of it left. But at the very start of the next one. How would that suit?'

'That would be thrilling!' Caroline said. And she went off at once to find Euphemia and tell her the good news.

But the expression on her cousin's face almost put the entire plan out of her head. She was sitting quietly beside the stage, with an untouched plate of food on her lap and a full glass of champagne in her hand, gazing into the crowd. And her lovely madonna face was lit with such blazing affection that Caroline was quite startled by it. Why, it's as if she was in love, she thought. Surely she ain't fallen in love with Mr Dickens? And she turned her head at once to see who her cousin was looking at. And it wasn't Mr Dickens. It was her brother Will.

'Pheemy!' she said, sitting on the stage beside her. 'Why Pheemy, my dear. You are in love with Will.'

Euphemia was embarrassed to be discovered so. 'Oh hush!' she said, ducking her head to hide her blushes. 'Not so loud, Carrie, please, or he'll hear you.'

'Well, I hope he does,' Caroline said trenchantly. 'He ought to know.'

'Oh hush! Hush!'

'Ain't you told him?'

'No,' Euphemia said, quite shocked at the idea, 'of course not. It wouldn't be seemly.'

'Well, I know I would. Has he said anything to you?'

'No, no, of course not.'

How romantic this is, Caroline thought. My dear Pheemy and my dear old Will loving one another and too shy to speak. And she resolved to do something about it at the very first opportunity. It would be wonderful to play cupid, indeed it would.

'You mustn't say anything, Carrie,' Euphemia begged. 'You will promise me, won't you?'

'Of course,' Caroline said, kissing her. 'Your secret is safe with me. Let's go and join him.'

'Not now,' Euphemia said. 'I think he's going to talk to Mr Dickens. Look.'

And sure enough the guest of honour was striding towards him, hand outstretched in greeting. 'Well, fancy that!' Caroline said. 'Do they know one another already? Will never said they'd met, did he, Pheemy? What an old sly-boots he is!'

'Will Easter,' Mr Dickens was saying. 'Mr Walters tells me you are a journalist. Says you wrote a fine piece on the riot in the Bull Ring. Is that true?'

'I wrote the piece, yes,' Will confessed, yearning a little at the memory of his vanished career but full of pride that Mr Dickens should know of it.

'Then you're just the man for me, sir.'

That was such a surprise that Will couldn't find an answer. Not that it mattered, for Mr Dickens' mind worked at such speed that obvious answers were taken as said. 'I've plans afoot,' he said. 'It's my opinion that we need a new radical newspaper in times like these. What do you think?'

Will recovered himself sufficiently to agree that they did. He'd heard rumours that Mr Dickens had plans to start such a paper, and thought it an admirable venture.

'How would you like to work for me?' Mr Dickens asked. 'Should there be such a paper for me to edit and you to work upon.'

'There's nothing I should like better,' Will said with perfect truth. What an opportunity! But could he accept it? Would it be possible to extricate himself from the firm at last?

'Come and see me,' Dickens instructed, as he moved on to the next group waiting his attention. 'Devonshire Terrace.'

'Thank you,' Will said, feeling how inadequate the words were. His brain was spinning with amazement. To be offered a job with Mr Charles Dickens! Imagine that! Why, it was too good to be true. And much too good to be refused. A second chance, just when he least expected it. And such a chance. He'd be a fool not to take it. He would wait until his father got back from York and then he'd ask him about it. No, not ask. That was too timid. He would tell him. Papa would understand.

Chapter 12

The season was coming to an end. It was August and a glorious late summer evening, warm and dusty and luscious with the scent of honeysuckle under a sky the colour of lavender. The famous Vauxhall Gardens were being opened to the public for the last time that year and Caroline was going to put a secret plan into operation and see her handsome poet again at the same time while her father was away in York. What could be better?

John Easter had given Bessie most particular instructions before he went away. Whenever the family appeared in public, she was to accompany the young ladies and be sure never to let Miss Caroline out of her sight. She wasn't to allow her to speak to that Mr Easter, and she was to make her behave with decorum and to stay with Will and Euphemia all the time. Though how that was to be done when she ran about everywhere the way she did Bessie couldn't think.

She'd confided in Nan of course, that morning, because she talked everything over with her old mistress, but it hadn't helped her much.

'She en't like to come to much harm in Vauxhall Gardens,' Nan said. 'Not with the sort of crowds we'll see there and the entertainments they've laid on. It'll be quite like old times, Bessie. Do you remember the Ranelagh Gardens and the old Rotunda? My heart alive, they were grand old days.' And when Bessie sucked her remaining teeth and made a wry grimace, 'Don't 'ee fret, my dear. 'Twill be a great occasion, you'll see, and no harm done.'

It was certainly a very noisy one. And the crowds that streamed across Waterloo Bridge were in high good humour. They were like a travelling carnival, filling the road with wheels and horseflesh and every kind of traffic; cabs and hackney carriages; donkey carts and gigs; young women bright-faced and beribboned in two-horse chaises; young men on horseback trotting from carriage to carriage to greet their friends; and so many revellers on foot it was a wonder some of them weren't crushed in the crowd; shopkeepers and their wives cheerfully rotund; clerks as skinny as pipe cleaners; servants of every size and kind; in and out of livery. Why, there'd hardly be room for them all in the gardens.

But the new owners of the Vauxhall Gardens wanted crowds and had made provision for them. There were six entrance gates, and a band to play welcoming music and attendants in green to sell programmes and smile welcoming smiles, and behind them a blaze of welcoming light. There were two crescent-shaped buildings full of supper rooms golden with candlelights; a fountain sparkling with white light and the fish-flash of silver water; a dazzling variety of entertainments surrounded by flaming torches; and on every ancient tree in every glade and bower and avenue, string upon string of coloured lanterns, thousands and thousands of them, glowing and bobbing and beckoning in a vast whispering sea of enticing darkness. Half the people of London could have lost themselves inside the place with no difficulty at all. Which on that lavender coloured evening they very rapidly did.

The first of the Easters to go tumbling off into the dazzle was Caroline. Of course. She disappeared into the crowd, with Euphemia tripping behind her, long before poor Bessie could struggle out of the second carriage.

'Now look!' the old lady grumbled. 'You can't even see her.'

'She'll be back,' Nan said, looking out for Billy and Matilda who had arranged to meet her inside the grounds. 'The ball begins at seven and she won't miss that, I can tell 'ee. And we've tickets for the refreshment rooms afterwards. She'll be back. Don't 'ee fret.'

'How can I keep an eye on her when she runs off?' Bessie demanded.

'Will'll find her,' Nan offered. 'Won't you, Will?'

But Will couldn't see where she'd gone either.

'It's too bad,' Bessie grumbled. 'I'm getting too long in the tooth for all this jaunching about.' But she followed Nan into the grounds to where Mr Billy was waiting with Matilda and Matty and Jimmy. What else could she do when she hadn't got the faintest idea where her naughty Caroline could be?

In fact, her naughty Caroline was a mere hundred yards away, running at full tilt towards the fountains, skirts swinging and bonnet flying by its strings, because she had just seen her dear, dear Henry. He was waiting impatiently beside the pool, just as he'd promised, looking oh so handsome in his mustard coloured jacket, and as she ran towards him, hands outstretched, a rainbow shimmered into being in the waterdrops above his head, a bright theatrical night-time rainbow, like a miracle.

'My dearest, dearest girl,' he said, his long face lifting with joy to see her again, catching her hands, raising them to his lips, kissing them. Every time he saw her, smiling at him with those fine grey eyes, the pleasure of it was more extreme. 'My dearest girl.' Then he saw Euphemia and tried to control himself.

But Caroline was dancing about him, skipping on her toes, light in her excitement as a leaf in the wind. 'Ain't this thrilling!' she said. 'Papa's away.'

Euphemia tried to be sensible. 'Are you to attend the opening ball?' she asked.

'Of course. Of course. I can't wait to dance.'

But there were twenty minutes to wait, according to the programme.

'What shall we do in the meantime?' Caroline said, still skipping.

'There are instrumentalists playing in the bandstand,' Euphemia told her, reading from her programme, 'or we could see the Ballet of Spring and the Graces. Or there's an eruption of Etna in the Turkish Saloon.'

'Volcanos are just my style,' Henry said, seizing them both by the hand. 'Especially today. Lead on!'

So they went to the Turkish Saloon, where attendants of both sexes were dressed in turbans and sequined jackets and huge baggy trousers, and the crush was so extreme that Henry had to stand close behind Caroline with his hands about her waist to steady her, and she had to remove her bonnet and lean her head and shoulders against his chest, so that he could see the stage. Which was all a great deal more thrilling than the presentation.

Etna was plainly made of cardboard and rose in isolated splendour on the tiny platform while a flautist and drummer played 'Turkish' music in the pit below. It was three feet high and glowed in a splendidly sinister way from the pink lanterns not quite hidden in its interior. Presently, to cheers from the audience, two lines of wooden peasants, six inches tall, were slid onto the stage from the wings and performed a dance more or less in time to the wailing music. Or to be more accurate, swayed about rhythmically, for they were attached by their feet to two wooden poles, and had to dance in unison whether they would or no. In fact when Etna gave its first echoing growl, through a megaphone every bit as visible as the lanterns, one line fell over backwards and had to stay where they were for several seconds because their companions were trampling straight across them.

The audience were delighted by such chaos. 'Bravo!' they called. And when the dancers made trembling movements towards the wings. 'Encore! Encore!'

The megaphone roared again, 'A-raaa! A-raaa!', and was applauded for its efforts.

'It is remarkably leonine for a mountain,' Henry said.

'I think it has burnt itself on those lanterns,' Caroline laughed.

As if to prove her right, the pink lanterns were suddenly dropped into the bowels of the earth, leaving the stage in momentary darkness and giving Henry a chance to tighten his embrace. Then, just as the audience was getting restive, a paper rocket shot up from the crater towards the ceiling where it exploded with a stink of sulphur and a great deal of dark smoke and then showered the audience with thirty seconds' worth of dazzling white sparks.

Rapturous applause. But wait. More and better is to come. The rocket is followed by spurts of flame, blown into the air by two silhouetted heads, lips pursed and puffing. The flames intensify and now grit is being tossed upwards too, cascades of grit, larger and larger grit, and finally pebbles. Some of the pebbles are so large and thrown with such abandon that they land in the front ranks of the audience and are promptly thrown back. The chaos is total. Mount Edna bends under the onslaught, a gentleman has retrieved the rocket stick and is conducting the cheers, the lip of the crater appears to be on fire, it smoulders and sparks and is doused from the wings by a very full bucket of water, which overshoots the mark and drenches the red lanterns.

As a volcanic eruption the performance left rather a lot to be desired, but as a spectacle it was priceless. The three friends emerged into the gardens limp with laughter.

'Where shall we go next?' Caroline demanded.

But the trumpets were sounding for the opening ball, so there was no need to make a choice.

Dancing in the open air among all those magical lights was better than anything Caroline had ever experienced, especially as there was no need for caution in such a light-hearted crowd, and she could partner Henry as often as she wanted and he would ask. And she and Henry, and Will and Euphemia, and Matty and Jimmy, and dear old Nan and Mr Brougham were perfect company for an eightsome reel, even if Mr Brougham *was* a bit slow on the turn, and Bessie *did* scowl. Oh, it was a lovely ball.

And when the dancing was done, Nan winked at her and invited Henry to join them in the supper rooms, even though Bessie made furious faces to dissuade her, when she thought Caroline wasn't looking. And supper was fun too, even if the food was mediocre and the service much too slow. Euphemia sat beside Will and consequently lost her appetite for anything but the sight of him. But Caroline was so happy she ate everything that was put before her.

After supper, despite quite frantic grimacing from Bessie, Nan said she couldn't see any reason why her four young people shouldn't go and sample the delights of the gardens with Jimmy and Matty, providing they all stayed together. So they went skipping off to the 'attractions'.

They watched the famous Mr Green ascend in a balloon, which was ponderous and awkward and preferred dragging its handlers along the grass to actually rising into the air, and they

173

saw a gentleman called Signor Joel perform amazing feats on a very high wire, and they attended the ballet of Spring and the Three Graces, who were too plump to be the least bit graceful and couldn't spring more than two inches into the air however hard they tried. And towards midnight they all went romping off towards the central arbour because the fireworks were about to begin.

The fireworks were still being set in position when they arrived.

'We shall be hanging about here for a precious long time, if I'm any judge,' Will said. 'Let's go somewhere else, while we're waiting.'

It was a sentiment shared by a large number of the audience who were already drifting off towards the arbours and walkways.

'Perhaps Matty and I should remain here and wait for the rest of the party,' Jimmy said.

'As long as you don't ask me to sit about,' Caroline said.

'Got the fidgets, ain't you, Carrie,' Will teased.

It was true. She was too charged with energy to sit still. 'Come on,' she said. 'I want to walk to the end of that arbour.'

What she really wanted was a chance to put her secret plan into operation and to talk to Henry on her own, and this unexpected pause in the proceedings had suddenly given her the opportunity for both.

She waited until Will and Euphemia were several yards ahead of her in the arbour, with several other strollers between them. Then she began.

'Shall you be at the final ball on Friday?' Say yes, and then we can dance together again.

'Without fail if you are to be there.'

'Good,' she said. 'Now tell me do, have you had any more commissions?'

'I have to write a set of poems about the new railways,' he told her. The pride and importance of it made the neat curves of his little moustache lift like wings.

'What a curious subject,' she said. 'Railways ain't poetical.'

'Then I shall have to make them so.'

'You will do it, I'm sure. And then you will be one step

nearer to being an established poet and Papa will have to take you seriously.'

'I *am* an established poet,' he said. 'I've been printed.'

'Three odes in the *Weekly Herald* don't make you a poet,' she said, teasing him with her eyes. 'A poet has books printed.'

'Well then, so shall I,' he promised. 'You'll see.' Despite his pleasure at being with her he couldn't help feeling rather huffy. There was no need for her to say such hurtful things. Sometimes she had no tact at all.

He was just opening his mouth to try and tell her so, when she suddenly seized his hand and ran into the undergrowth, pulling him so that he had to follow her. Which he did most willingly, although with considerable surprise. They pushed through the branches, into the inner darkness of the copse, their feet swishing over grass they couldn't see, their free hands shielding their faces, and finally came to a halt behind the trunk of a sizeable hornbeam.

'Why have we run away?' he panted, still holding her hand. 'What is it?'

'Hush!' she said, peering behind her through the trees. 'I don't want them to see and follow us.'

'Who?'

'Will and Euphemia,' she said, still peering.

'There is no one there,' he said, after checking too. 'They haven't followed us. We are quite alone.' What rapturous knowledge. He could kiss her, if she'd let him. Would she let him? Oh, if only she would. 'But why have we run away from them?'

'I want them to be entirely on their own together,' she explained.

'Why?' Admiring her flushed cheeks and the splendid disorder of that dark hair.

'Hush! It's a secret,' she said. 'She loves him.' He was holding both her hands now and they were so close to one another that she could see the reflection of a distant red lantern glowing in the pupils of his eyes. And how red and full his lips were, parted ready to speak and so close she could feel his breath before his words. Just looking at him was making her heart turn somersaults again.

'I love you,' he said. It was the natural thing to say. The undeniable truth.

175

'Do you?' she asked breathlessly. But she knew he did. His face was glowing with love.

'Yes,' he said, drawing her towards him. 'So much.' Now he knew how much. There was no doubt about it at all. He loved her and he would have to kiss her. The bounds of correct behaviour were far, far away from this magical bower among the leaves. Here there were no rules, only fascination and instinct and this marvellous unexpected privacy. He bent his head and kissed her gently, but full on the lips. And to his great delight she kissed him back. 'Oh my dearest dearest Caroline.'

'Oh, kiss me again do,' she said, when he raised his head at last.

He needed no second bidding, but when they had kissed one another breathless he thought he ought to warn, 'I should have spoken to your father first, you know, even if he don't approve of me. Asked leave to court you and all that sort of thing.'

'I don't care,' she said, brushing her mouth gently along his lower lip and delighted to feel that she was making him shiver.

'You love me?' he hoped, taut with the most exquisite desire for her.

'Um.'

'You will marry me?' Was it possible? Would her father allow it?

'Um. Kiss me again.' She had surrendered herself to sensation. The most delicious sensation, that made her lips tingle and the whole of her body feel as if it were expanding and lifting, as if she were floating six inches above the ground. To be loved so, and by a poet too. It was a wonder she didn't swoon. And on top of all this, she thought, as he began to kiss her again, oh so slowly and luxuriously, she had given her dear brother the chance to declare his love to her dear, dear Pheemy.

In fact her dear brother was being horribly circumspect, walking at a respectable distance from Euphemia, and talking most properly of the high-wire act, and the balloon ascent, and those four well-upholstered dancers who had made them laugh so much. And finally telling her all about Mr Dickens' amazing offer.

'You will accept it of coursé,' Euphemia said. 'What an honour to be sought out by Mr Dickens.'

'It would mean leaving the firm,' he said.

'You have given the firm good service all these years,' she said. 'Mrs Easter would release you, I'm sure.'

But the problem was Mr John Easter as both of them knew just a little too well.

'Edward is in better humour at last,' he said, changing the subject.

'He should be happy now,' she said. 'Being married. It must be a great happiness to be married.'

His answer was unequivocal. 'Marriage doesn't always make people happy, Euphemia. In fact, most of the married people I know are jolly unhappy.'

That seemed very harsh. 'Jimmy and Matty are very happy and they love one another dearly,' she pointed out gently.

'Yes,' he agreed. 'But in some ways that is even more dangerous.'

'Dangerous, Will?'

'There are so many dangers in love,' he explained seriously. 'You might marry and then be unhappy, like Edward, which is bad enough, in all conscience. Or you might marry and be happy for a time and then lose your loved one, which would be a great deal worse. Think of it. I can remember how awful I felt when mother died and I can tell you there is nothing more dreadful. Oh no, if you have any sense, Euphemia, you will avoid marriage altogether.'

The words struck at her like an ice-cold wind. 'But you can't help loving people, Will.'

His firmness increased. 'Yes you can,' he said. 'It's a matter of will power, that's all. And good sense, of course. Oh no, it's much better to remain single, believe me, to keep away from Aunt Matilda's match-making and spend your time with your friends. Or your sisters.'

She was gazing at him attentively, looking extremely pretty in her green and blue gown, with her skin so creamy and her red hair glowing and those nice brown eyes shining in the lantern light, almost as though they were full of tears. A very pretty sister, he thought, and excellent company. Better by far than any sweetheart.

'Besides,' he said, 'You might love someone who didn't love you. Think how painful that would be.'

Oh it is, it is, she thought, sinking deeper and deeper into unhappiness. He doesn't love me, she grieved, and yet she ached to hold his arm and to tell him how very much she loved him. He will never love me. I am nothing to him except a sister, someone to confide in and dance with but not to marry. Oh, what is to become of me, when I love him so much? And the pain of it crushed her chest and made her feel bleak and alone as she had done on the long voyage back to England all those years ago. And she couldn't think of anything to say to him at all.

She was very glad when the band struck up the first notes of Handel's firework music to announce that the display was about to begin and they were caught up in the jostle of the returning crowd. She found herself a seat between Nan and Matty because she simply couldn't bear the torment of being beside him for another minute, then was torn with misery because he was talking to Jimmy and didn't notice what she'd done.

And so the evening came to a fire-spitting end, and the two girls drove home in velvet darkness to the quietness of their rose and white bedroom.

Caroline could barely wait for the maids to leave the room before she spilled out her good news. 'Pheemy! Dear dear Pheemy! I'm going to marry Henry Easter.'

'Caroline!' Euphemia said, torn by surprise and shock and delight, and, it had to be admitted, a searing, shameful envy. 'How can you be? Has he spoken to your father?'

'He's spoken to me,' Caroline said, wielding her hairbrush like a rake. 'And I've said yes. So Papa will have to agree now, won't he? He'll have to agree and stop being foolish. Oh Pheemy, I'm so happy, you'd never believe.'

'Oh I would, I would,' poor Euphemia said and then her emotions overcame her and she put her head in her hands and burst into tears.

Caroline threw down her hairbrush and rushed across the room to fling her arms about her friend. 'Pheemy! Dearest! What is it?' she said.

'It is nothing,' Euphemia sobbed. 'I am being foolish. Nothing. Nothing at all. Oh dear oh dear!'

'You must tell me all about it, whatever it is,' Caroline

insisted. 'I cannot have my darling in tears. Not when I'm so happy. And there's an end of it.'

And so she was told all about Will's terrible philosophy, haltingly at first and then in more and more painful detail. 'I love him so much,' Euphemia ended, 'and he will never love me. Never ever.'

'Well, he must,' his sister said fiercely. 'I shall speak to him about it.' To behave like that after all her cunning in leaving them alone together. It was too bad. It really was.

The very idea terrified poor Euphemia. 'Oh don't,' she pleaded. 'I beg you, Carrie. Please don't. I should be shamed before everybody. If he doesn't love me, and I know he doesn't, there's nothing you or I can do about it. You can't force love, my darling.'

'More's the pity,' Caroline said. 'Well, he's a fool. That's all I can say. We must work on him subtly, and make him change his mind. At least he ain't in love with someone else.'

But it was poor consolation, and Euphemia wept more hopeless tears before the two of them finally settled to sleep.

She was still pale and unhappy when they came down to breakfast the next morning. Will had been up more than three hours, as he told them cheerfully, and had gone to the stamping and come home again while they were still abed.

'You have the constitution of an ox,' Nan said, laughing at him.

'And the temperament of a mule,' his sister reproved, despite warning glances from Euphemia.

'Try the bacon rolls,' he said, not in the least annoyed. 'They're capital.' And he returned to his paper.

Caroline was just thinking up some stinging rebuke for him when the door opened and Bessie came in, looking horribly anxious.

'If you please, mum,' she said to Nan, 'Mr John's back from York and he's sent the carriage for Caroline. She's to go to Fitzroy Square directly, he says. Tom's to wait.'

'So early in the morning?' Nan said, frowning at the news. What was the matter? she wondered.

'Yes, mum. He was most particular, Tom says.'

Something is wrong, Caroline thought and foreboding

179

wriggled in her chest. But she put on a brave face. 'If that's the way of it,' she said, 'I'd best be off at once. It wouldn't do to keep him waiting, would it Bessie?'

'No, my lovey,' Bessie said sympathetically, 'I don't think it would.'

180

Chapter 13

The twenty minutes it took to drive Caroline Easter to Fitzroy Square were the longest twenty minutes of her life.

She had woken that morning still warm from a dream of remembered pleasures, dancing an eightsome reel with Henry's hands holding hers so lovingly, standing before him in that Turkish tent with the warmth of his body behind her, kissing him again and again in their lovely private darkness, hearing him say 'I love you'. The joy of it! She had dressed in a daze of happiness, convinced that it would only be a matter of time before she could persuade her father to allow Henry's courtship. And now this terrible summons, which was bound to be about Henry. What else could it be? There was such speed and anger in it, and she *had* disobeyed. She couldn't deny it. In fact she'd gone much much further than any proper young lady would ever have done, allowing Henry to kiss her like that. You weren't even supposed to hold a young gentleman's arm until you were engaged. Not that Papa could possibly know anything about those lovely kisses, and they *were* lovely kisses. It made her warm to remember them. But he couldn't, could he? They'd been quite private inside their leafy bower. Hidden from everybody. But she was alarmed about it just the same, and the nearer she got to Fitzroy Square the more anxious she felt. By the time she arrived outside her father's dowdy house and Tom handed her out of the carriage she was shivering with apprehension.

And the shiver became a shudder when she was ushered into the drawing room and saw the anger that was stiffening her

181

father's spine and had removed all expression from his face. Oh dear, oh dear, whatever it was, it was going to be terrible.

'Sit down,' he said. No 'Good morning', no 'Caroline dear', nothing. Just 'sit down'.

She sat in the corner chair beside the window, unconsciously putting as great a distance between herself and her father as she could.

'What I have to say to you is not pleasant,' he told her. 'You are a disappointment to me, Caroline, a grievous disappointment.'

Tell me quickly, she thought. Tell me quickly and get it over with.

'Where were you yesterday evening?' he said.

'I was at the Vauxhall Gardens, Papa. With Nan and Will and Euphemia.'

'And other company?'

She told him the truth. 'Henry Easter was with us, too, Papa. Nan invited him to supper.'

He was so angry his nose was pinched white. What folly, he thought. How could Mama be so foolish as to encourage this nonsense? Was it any wonder that the child behaved badly when her own grandmother set her such a bad example?

'At least you are honest enough to admit it,' he said, 'but not wise enough to behave with propriety whilst you were there, or so it would appear.'

Her heart contracted with fear. What does he know? she thought. He couldn't know *that* surely. Oh what *does* he know? 'I behaved as others were behaving Papa.'

'You danced.'

'With Nan and Mr Brougham, as well as Mr Easter. It was a country dance. Everybody was dancing.'

'If you had simply danced with your brother or your cousins I would not have been so angry. But you did not. You danced with a young man whom I neither like nor approve of, and what is more and much much worse, you behaved yourself in such a scandalous manner that your behaviour was certain to be seen and commented upon. You walked alone with this young man, did you not?'

She had to admit it, wondering who had seen her and carried tales.

'You were hanging onto his arm?'

'Yes, Papa, I held onto his arm, I believe. Most people were promenading arm in arm that evening.'

'With no bonnet on your head?'

'It was blown off. I put it on again straight away.'

'And where was Bessie Thistlethwaite? She is your companion. She should have been with you to chaperone you.'

'Nan said we could go and see the fireworks, Papa. There were six of us, me and Will and Euphemia and Jimmy and Matty, besides Mr Easter.' And she tried to smile at him because that expressionless face was frightening her more and more.

It had no effect on him whatever. 'You were seen,' he said, 'and no mention was made of any other companion except for Henry Easter. You were seen with no bonnet on your head and no chaperone, running in and out of the bushes like a hoyden.'

There was nothing she could say. For the first time in her life she dropped her gaze before her father's anger.

He was mollified, but only slightly, his shoulders dropping just perceptibly. 'You have shamed me, Caroline,' he said. 'Can you imagine how it felt to have two business acquaintances seek me out in the Strand this morning to report such scandalous things to me about my own daughter? How *could* you do such a thing?'

To see emotion on his face at last upset her. 'I did not mean to shame you, Papa,' she said. 'Truly.'

'If you did not mean to shame me, you should not have spent time in the company of that young gentleman. You know my feelings on the matter.'

She had to support her darling, no matter what her father might be feeling. 'He is a proper gentleman, Papa,' she said. 'Every inch an Easter. I can't see why you don't approve of him. You would if you knew him.'

'There are Easters and Easters,' he said sternly. 'The Ippark Easters are no fit company for anybody, and certainly not for you. You are not to know them.'

'This is all because of that stupid quarrel, years and years ago,' she blurted out. 'I can't see why we . . .'

'It is an old quarrel certainly,' he said, 'but not stupid. What happened was too cruel to be stupid. It was deliberate and heartless and has put all members of the Ippark branch of the family quite beyond the pale. And since you make an issue of it, you might as well know what happened.' And he walked across the room and sat himself in the other corner chair beside the window, facing her.

'When your grandmother married your grandfather,' he said, 'his family cast him out without a penny, because she'd been a servant and they were full of false pride. That was bad enough, in all conscience, but what happened later was worse. Your grandfather died when Aunt Annie and Uncle Billy and I were little more than babies, and he left your Nan very nearly penniless. Think of it. Naturally she went to Ippark for help, as anyone would in her position. And they turned her from the door. They turned her from the door, Caroline, callous, heartless, uncaring creatures that they were. They turned her from the door without a penny.'

'It was all a very long time ago,' Caroline tried. 'Things change, Papa. People change.'

'Not the Easters of Ippark,' her father said. 'They are leopards of the cruellest kind who never change their spots. Your Mr Henry Easter is the son of Sir Osmond Easter, my dear, and Sir Osmond Easter was every bit as bad as his forebears. When he married for the second time, he threw his two poor old cousins out into the world with no means of support except a small annuity. What would have happened to them if Mama had not taken pity on them I do not know. And even before that he had shown us what manner of man he was. There was never any doubt about his jealousy and spite. He did everything in his power to prevent my mother from making a success of Easter's. I was young at the time and I cannot remember the details, but I remember her distress and her anger, and I do not forgive him for it.'

'But he didn't prevail, Papa. It *was* a success, wasn't it?'

He was aggravated that she should argue against him. 'The success of the firm is immaterial to your present situation,' he said sternly. 'You have gone beyond the bounds of propriety, and you know it. Now I must take action.'

This time she faced him boldly, saying nothing.

'You are not to attend any further functions this season,' he said. 'You will not go to the final ball. You will not ride in the

184

Park. In short, you are not to see Henry Easter or communicate with him ever again.'

'Papa!' she cried, shocked by his harshness. 'How can you be so cruel?'

'It is for your own good,' he said. 'The association would only make you unhappy. Don't you see that?'

'No,' she said, 'I do not. I love him, Papa.' There it was. The words were said, openly and publicly. She was committed. Yesterday she hadn't been sure of her feelings, strong though they were. She'd been playing at love, thrilled to be kissed and told how much *he* loved *her*, but playing nevertheless. Now her certainty was strong as iron.

'You are too young to know what love means,' he told her.

Apprehension and shock and this new terrible, wonderful certainty gathered and became rage. 'I do too,' she roared at him. 'I love him with all my heart. I shall always love him. Always. And nothing you say will ever change that. You *can't* forbid me to see him. It's barbarous!'

He stood up and walked away from her anger. 'I have forbidden it,' he said, horribly calm again. 'You are not to see him and that is all there is to be said. Annie and James are visiting Mama in a day or two. You will return to Bury with them and remain there until you can see sense.'

'But Papa . . .'

'I do not propose to argue with you, Caroline. You will do as I say.'

'Very well,' she said, cold with anger and control. 'I will. But I shall go on loving Henry just the same. You can't stop that. I shall love him for ever and ever and when I come of age I shall marry him and I don't care what you say. And I shall hate you, Papa. I shall hate you for ever.'

He rang the bell. 'You will see sense in time,' he said wearily. Her words had stung him cruelly, but she was young yet. He had to remember how young she was. 'Tom will take you back to Bedford Square.'

But she'd already left the room. He could hear her feet, thudding down the stairs. It had to be done, he told himself. It had to be done. It was for her own good. She will thank me for it in the end.

*　　*　　*

Caroline kept her feelings under control until she was back in Bedford Square and had climbed the stairs to her own bedroom and closed the door behind her. Then she flung herself down across the bed and wept as if her heart was breaking.

Euphemia had been waiting for her return in a state of growing anxiety, watching at the bedroom window, as the square filled with departing carriages and street traders. Now she was terribly upset. 'What is it, my dearest,' she said, sitting beside her cousin and stroking the wild hair out of her eyes.

'He says I ain't to see Henry ever again,' Caroline wailed. 'Oh, Pheemy, I'm so unhappy. How could he be so cruel? I shall die if I never see my darling again.'

'He can't mean it,' Euphemia said, when Caroline had sobbed out the entire miserable story. Not Mr Easter. He was stern and distant, certainly, but not unkind. 'Did you tell him of Henry's proposal?'

'No,' Caroline sobbed. 'How could I? Oh, he's so cruel, Pheemy. How could he be so cruel?'

'He spoke in wrath, my dearest. I'm sure of it. He will think better of it tomorrow, you'll see.'

'No,' Caroline wailed. 'He meant it, Pheemy. Every word of it. Oh, what shall I do? He says I'm to go back to Rattlesden with Aunt Annie and be buried in the country. I shall die if I never see my darling again. I love him, Pheemy.'

'Yes,' Euphemia said, 'I know.' And as her cousin continued to weep. 'Oh pray don't cry, my dearest. I would do anything to help you.'

'You couldn't make him change his mind, could you?' Caroline sobbed.

And it was true. Neither of them could think how to do that. And Nan and Will had gone to the Strand and wouldn't be back until dinner time. Euphemia sped off to find Bessie.

'This is what comes a' disobeying yer father,' the old lady said, but she came toiling up the stairs at once, of course, to wash her Caroline's tears and brush her hair and croon commiserations.

'Perhaps you'd better put a brave face on it,' she cajoled, as she emptied the dirty water into the pail, 'and do as he says. Jest fer a month or two, eh? Till it all dies down. After all, he is yer Pa when all's said and done. He's got a right ter know what you're a-doin' of.'

That made Caroline fierce with anger. 'No,' she said, 'I won't. It's so unfair, Bessie. Henry is a dear good man, *and* a poet. Papa should be proud of him like I am. Oh no, no, no, I most certainly will *not* do as he says.'

'Then what will you do?' Euphemia asked.

'Oh, I don't know!' Caroline wept, throwing herself across the bed again.

'I know you think your Mr Easter's a fine young man,' Bessie said, 'but is he worth it?'

'Yes,' Caroline said, looking up fiercely. 'He is. And don't you ever say another word against him. You were the one who told Papa I was dancing with him in the first place, weren't you?'

'Well, if that's how it is,' Bessie said crossly, and hobbled out of the room.

'Oh, my poor Henry,' Caroline said. 'He'll be riding in the Park by now. He won't know what's happened to us.'

'Your father may have written to tell him,' Euphemia said regretfully.

'You think so, Pheemy?'

'I fear he might have done.'

'Oh, I do hope Nan knows what to do.'

'Or Will,' Euphemia said. 'He'll plead for you, Carrie. I know he will.'

But when he got home that night, Will's reaction to the crisis was not at all what either of them expected. Instead of rushing to his sister's defence, he was cool and critical. In fact he almost seemed to be blaming her for what had happened.

'It was jolly silly to go off on your own, if you ask me,' he said. 'You might have known someone would see you. Why didn't you stay with Jimmy and Matty?'

'I walked off on your account,' Caroline said, angrily, and was just going to tell him exactly why when Euphemia intervened.

'Could you speak to your father, Will?' she hoped. 'I'm sure he would listen to you.'

'What a time you've chosen,' Will said to Caroline. 'Just when I wanted to leave the firm.'

'That has nothing to do with it,' she retorted.

'On the contrary,' he said. 'It has everything to do with it.' How could he possibly broach the subject with his father now that she'd put him in such a bad humour. And just when he was going to visit Mr Dickens too.

'But you will speak to Mr Easter,' Euphemia said. 'Won't you?'

'I will if the right moment presents itself,' he promised grudgingly.

'If you have to wait for the right moment then I'd rather you didn't bother,' Caroline said, glaring at him. 'I thought you loved me more than that, indeed I did.'

'I do love you Carrie,' Will tried to explain. 'It's just rather awkward at the moment, that's all.' But even though he felt ashamed of himself to be thinking of his job rather than her needs, he couldn't offer to help her. There was too much at stake. And besides, she had brought this all on herself. She should have known better.

Strong emotions bristled in the air between them, her misery and fury and incomprehension, his disappointment and self-disgust and a vague generalized anger that was all the more potent because he didn't know where to direct it.

'Here's your grandmother come home,' Euphemia said, recognizing the approaching sound of Nan's carriage with great relief. 'She'll know what to do.'

But Nan had already done all she could, entirely without success.

John had come into her office not long after she arrived in the Strand that morning to tell her of Caroline's misbehaviour and his decision.

'She will return to Rattlesden with Annie and James,' he said, 'and stay there until the spring, out of harm's way.'

'Has James agreed to it?'

'I see no reason why he shouldn't. I wrote to him at once, of course.'

''Tis a harsh punishment, for such a little folly.'

'Of necessity,' he said sternly. 'If I don't take action now, she might end up marrying the fellow, and we don't want *that*.'

'I could think of worse partners,' Nan said lightly. 'He's a nice enough young man and uncommon fond of your daughter. Fancies himself a poet, which he en't, but you can't hold youthful conceit against him.'

The gentle joke fell flat. 'He's an Ippark Easter,' John said.

'And rather a pleasant one.'

His face hardened. 'You may forgive them if you please, Mama, although I cannot understand how you bring yourself to do it, but I have more pride. The young man is beyond the pale. Caroline has misbehaved and now she must take the consequences. We will not speak of it again if you please. Here are the invoices from the Darlington branch line.'

'You will have to do as he says, I'm afraid,' Nan told Caroline, when she'd taken off her bonnet and gone up to see how the child was.

'Well I won't,' Caroline said, stubbornly. 'I'll sit here in this bedroom and starve myself to death rather than do as he says. It's cruel and unfair.'

'She don't mean it,' Bessie said. 'Not with her appetite.'

But Caroline could be as adamant as her father, and stayed in her room for the next twenty-four hours, eating nothing, until Annie and James arrived, full of anxiety to know what had really happened. And to the relief of the household, Annie took charge of the situation, springing into action like Hope from Pandora's box.

'You are not to make any more fuss,' she said to Caroline firmly, 'or you will make matters worse and worry your father into an apoplexy and I can't have that. One in the family is quite enough. Come downstairs and dine with Will and Nan and Euphemia as you always do, and then James and I will talk to your father and see what may be done. We dine with him this evening, so what better opportunity? Your behaviour is to be impeccable, though, otherwise I cannot plead for you. Is that understood?'

To have an ally at last, and such a staunch one, was enough to lift Caroline out of her misery and release her from her self-imposed fast. She came down to dinner, with a subdued appetite but quite good grace, and Annie and James went to Fitzroy Square.

They found their brother downcast and the dinner he served no more than passable.

'You will take her back to Rattlesden, won't you?' he asked.

'Of course,' Annie assured him, 'if that is what you want.'

'I can't understand her,' he confessed, cutting his mutton chop with difficulty. 'Of all the young men Matilda put her way, why must she choose this one? It's downright perverse.'

Annie didn't defend her niece's choice. She had another matter for John to consider. 'History is repeating itself, I fear,' she said. 'I remember what a scene there was when I first told Mama that I meant to marry James.'

He gave her a puzzled glance, and that pleased her because it showed that he couldn't remember what had happened, and if he couldn't remember, that would give her story all the more impact.

'A scene?' he said.

'Oh yes, indeed. A fearful scene. She didn't approve at all. She said I could do better for myself than to marry a curate.'

'Mama said that?'

'She did.'

'Of James?'

'Yes, yes, indeed,' James said easily. 'When I went to ask her for Annie's hand, she told me I was no catch for a daughter of the great Nan Easter. I remember it to this day.' His eyes were twinkling with amusement at the memory. What an interview that had been!

'But that is ridiculous,' John said. 'What possible reason could she have had for such an opinion?'

'There is no reason in such matters,' Annie told him gently. 'Parents require perfection when it comes to marriage partners for their children. I know I had a low opinion of poor Mr Meredith at first, because he was always so slow to speak, but you see how happy he has made my Meg and what a good father he is to young Jonathan.'

Now John understood the import of this conversation, and although it annoyed him that she was questioning his decision, he was touched by the delicacy with which it was being done. 'It ain't the same thing, Sis,' he said, giving her his lop-sided grin. 'The man in question this time is the son of Sir Osmond Easter. I cannot tolerate an alliance between that man's son and my daughter.'

'Happily, sons do not always resemble their fathers,' James pointed out. ''Tis a wise father that knows his own child.'

'Or his own daughter, it would appear,' John said, smiling at them both for the first time since their arrival in his house.

He will agree, Annie thought, acknowledging the smile, dear dear John, grieved though he is, he will agree with what I'm going to propose, because there is still love in him for all his gruff ways. And the thought made her feel protective towards him, as though he were her son and not her brother. Dear John. 'However much our children may need punishment,' she said, 'and I'm the first to admit that they all need punishment at some time or another, I do not think we should deprive them of hope. Life is so utterly bleak without hope, is it not, John my dear?'

'Yes,' he said, remembering the bleakness he had felt when Harriet died. And still felt even now, sitting in this faded room that she had decorated and he had never changed. 'Yes, Annie, that is true. We all need hope.'

Annie took a deep breath and began her appeal. 'That being so,' she said . . .

Annie and James returned to Bedford Square at a little after eleven o'clock with their good news.

'We have prevailed upon your father to revoke 'for ever', Annie said, 'haven't we, James? Providing you are prepared to show your love for Mr Easter by waiting a twelvemonth before you see him again.'

'A year!' Caroline said, sucking in her breath ready to protest.

'A year,' Annie said firmly, 'which is a good deal better than never at all. Especially when you know where and how it is to be spent.'

'Where?'

'In Saffron Hill with Matty and Jimmy. Not buried in the country, my dear, but right here in London, in the heart of things, with good works to keep you occupied and make the time pass quickly, and Matty and the children for company. There now, what do you say to that?'

It was a reprieve and Caroline had to admit it, even though a twelvemonth seemed a parlously long time.

'I will keep you company, Carrie,' Euphemia promised. 'I

may, mayn't I, Mrs Hopkins? I could help with the good works too.' It would give her an excuse to escape from Will, for ever since that evening at Vauxhall she had found his presence more painful than she could bear.

'I see no reason why not,' Nan said, 'although why you should wish to share her punishment I cannot imagine.'

'You may write one letter to Henry to explain what is happening,' James said, 'but then you must promise not to write again until the year is up.'

So the letter was written, with great care and several quiet tears, and then plans were made. And two days later, the carter called to take Caroline's travelling box to Clerkenwell Green, and she and Euphemia kissed Nan and Annie and Bessie goodbye and were driven off to their new life by a cheerful Tom Thistlethwaite.

'You'll have a fine ol' time with Mr Jimmy,' he said encouragingly, because Miss Caroline was looking decidedly down, 'and Mrs Jimmy and their little boys an' all.'

But it was the 'an' all' that was worrying Caroline.

'If only I could have seen him, just once,' she mourned to Euphemia as the carriage turned out of the square.

Chapter 14

Small dirty feet swung above sand-scrubbed floorboards, or splayed against the foot-rests of long benches to be surreptitiously scratched by black-rimmed broken fingernails. Their ankles were coated with grime, black tar oozed between their toes, and the skin on their heels was hardened to a scaly grey hide as if it belonged to an elderly elephant. Only their insteps were pink and young. It was afternoon and the Reverend Jimmy Hopkins' ragged school was in session.

The room they occupied was an empty warehouse, its brick walls still dusted with grey flour. It was poorly lit by two long windows just below the ceiling and sparsely furnished with eight rows of benches, a Bible, a chair, a blackboard and a line of plain deal chairs. Each child had a slate and a stick of chalk, finger-marked with grime, and when Caroline and Euphemia arrived they were all busy copying their letters from the board. The stink of unwashed bodies and filthy clothes gradually heating was so awful it made Caroline gag.

But Jimmy Hopkins didn't seem to notice it. 'Children,' he said, stooping before the blackboard in his usual mild way but holding up his right hand for silence with gentle authority. 'I have come to give you the most splendid tidings.' Then he paused to allow his scholars time to slide their soiled feet to the ground and stand politely before him. 'We have two new teachers, come to help us in our work,' he said. 'Miss Easter and Miss Callbeck. Are we not blessed?'

Blessed! Caroline thought, still covering her nose with her hand. Blessed! In this stink? That's not the word I'd use.

An urchin in the front row was quick to see the implication of his announcement. 'Can our Joanie come ter school now, sir?'

'Very likely,' Jimmy said, 'very likely. I will tell you on Monday afternoon. Meantime Mrs Hopkins and I will divide the class into four groups instead of two, now that we have four teachers. But first we will say a prayer to thank the Lord for our good fortune. Bow your heads.'

During the prayer Caroline sneaked a look at her new charges. They were like creatures from another world, dark and quick-eyed and horribly thin in their evil-smelling rags, their faces as dirty as their feet, and their hair so rough and un-combed it looked as dead as old twigs. But at least they stood quietly, eyes closed and palms pressed together, with a meek-ness and earnestness about them that she actually found quite touching, despite her abhorrence of their stench.

The quartering of the class was done very quickly and with no fuss. Five minutes after their arrival in the room, Caroline and Euphemia were taking their first class. Caroline's was a group of 'big-uns' eager to read from the Bible, sitting up as straight as any teacher could possibly desire, wide-eyed as owls. Ah well, she thought, as I'm honour bound to stay here for a year, I'd better make the best of it I can. But I wish they didn't smell so dreadfully.

'The Gospel according to St Matthew, Chapter 24,' she said, remembering Mrs Flowerdew. 'The parable of the talents.' And she handed the Bible to the first boy in the line. 'What is your name?'

'If you please, 'um, Josser. Josser Turner.'

She was rather taken back by such a peculiar name but she tried not to show it. 'Very well, Josser,' she said. 'Start at verse 14, if you please.'

She was surprised by how well these scruffy children could read, and how hard they struggled to decipher words that were new to them. And when the lessons finally came to an end and Matty's two scullery maids arrived to serve them all with lentil soup and hunks of bread, her surprise increased even further, for although they were obviously and ravenously hungry, they were all careful to eat politely and not to bolt their food. She noticed that every child retained a piece of bread to mop the last, least trace of soup from its bowl and when all the dishes and spoons were collected and carried away they followed the bowls with yearning eyes and were clearly wishing them full again.

'I'll wager your soup was the only meal those children had today,' she said to Matty when the four of them sat down for their own meal later that evening, back in Clerkenwell Green, washed, and dressed in clean clothes, and rested and refreshed from the stink of the afternoon.

'I'm sure of it,' Matty said. 'There's precious little food to spare for children in Saffron Hill. In fact I've always thought they come to school as much for the soup as the learning.'

'However, they *do* come for the learning, my love,' Jimmy said, passing a plateful of roast beef across the table to Euphemia, 'and make good use of it, what's more.'

'Thank you,' Euphemia said, taking the plate. 'So they do, poor little things. And they work so hard. I'm sure we never did half so much work at Mrs Flowerdew's seminary, did we Caroline?'

'I couldn't say,' Caroline said, rather crossly, spreading her napkin across her knees. It was foolish to compare these scruffy children with Mrs Flowerdew's well-dressed pupils. They lived in different worlds. Why, you might as well compare them to Everard and Emmanuel, Matty's two dear little boys, who'd been brought down to be kissed goodnight just before the meal, all pink and clean and delectable in their pretty night-gowns.

'They might learn a little better if they were clean,' Euphemia said. 'I can't bear to think of all the dirt they were putting into their mouths when they ate their bread.' It made her shudder just to remember it.

'We all have to eat a peck of dirt before we die,' Matty said, cheerfully, spooning her nice clean vegetables onto her nice clean plate with her nice clean spoon.

'That's true, I suppose,' Euphemia said, 'but I can't help feeling the dirt they ate was rather excessive. Could we not provide them with soap and water just to wash their hands?'

'We couldn't afford to, I fear,' Jimmy explained. 'It would cost more money than we could spare. Lord Shaftesbury provides us with slates and benches and so forth, and the Church Commissioners pay the rent of the warehouse of course, since we are a church school, but I doubt whether I could prevail upon either of them, good and generous though they undoubtedly are, in a matter of soap and basins and such. What argument could I use to persuade them?'

'That cleanliness is next to Godliness?' Caroline suggested, half teasing, half cross.

'Mr Chadwick of the famous report would certainly agree with you as to that,' Jimmy said, smiling at her.

Neither Caroline nor Euphemia knew who he was talking about. So he explained.

'Mr Edwin Chadwick,' he said. 'The author of the report on the sanitary conditions of the labouring poor. There was a great to-do about it in the papers when it was first produced.'

'Ah, now I recall it,' Euphemia said. 'Mrs Flowerdew read us extracts from it, on the day she told us about that lady called by God to nurse the sick and succour the poor. You remember, Carrie.'

'I can't say I remember the report,' Caroline admitted, 'but I remember the lady. She had the same name as a bird. Skylark or Mistlethrush or some such.'

'Her name was Miss Nightingale,' Euphemia told her. 'She wanted to start a school for nurses. I thought it was an admirable idea.' Then she turned to Jimmy. 'But you were speaking of Mr Chadwick's report.'

'I have a copy of it should you care to see it,' Jimmy told them.

'Yes,' Euphemia said seriously. 'We should like that very much.'

You would, Caroline thought, but you speak for yourself. It'll be some dry dusty old thing, I'll lay any money, and I shall be bored to tears by it. Oh, if only I could see my dear Henry again. And she ate her last mouthful of beef and horseradish, sighing with self-pity.

After dinner they adjourned to the parlour and the book was lifted down from the top shelf of the bookcase. It was a weighty tome, in every sense of the word, just as Caroline had feared. Even the title was so long it covered more than a quarter of the front cover. 'Report to her Majesty's principal Secretary of State for the Home Department for the Poor Law Commissioners on an inquiry into the sanitary condition of the labour-

196

ing population of Great Britain,' by Edwin Chadwick, July 1842.

Euphemia was fascinated by it and she and Jimmy spent the rest of the evening reading the wretched thing. 'Look at this, Caroline,' she said. ' "Evidence given by Mr John Liddle, medical officer Whitechapel." Why, he could be describing our pupils here.' And she read the words aloud.

' "How do they get the water they use? – they get it for the most part from a plug in the courts. When I have occasion to visit their rooms, I find they have a very scanty supply of water in their tubs, consequently they do not wash their bodies and when they wash their clothes the smell of dirt mixed with the soap is the most offensive of all smells I have to encounter. It must have an injurious effect on the health of the occupants." '

'And on everyone who comes into contact with them,' Caroline said sourly. It was bad enough to have spent the afternoon among smelly children without reading about them all evening.

'Oh, we really should try to make some provision for them here,' Euphemia said. 'How can we expect them to keep clean when they have no water in their homes?'

'Read the section headed "Conclusions and suggestions",' Jimmy said, taking the book and turning the pages.

Euphemia thought that the most sensible part of the report, for here the authors suggested that all slum houses should be provided with a clean water supply and that refuse and sewage should be removed from their homes 'by suspension in water in cylindrical glazed bore sewers'.

Well really, Caroline thought, what a topic for an after-dinner conversation!

'It seems so sensible and so obvious,' Euphemia said. 'Nothing but good could come of cleaning the slums.'

'I would pull them all down,' Caroline said, scowling at the thick boring mass of the report where it lay in her cousin's lap. It was creasing her skirt quite horribly.

'But what would happen to the people then?' Euphemia said.

Caroline was just about to tell her she really didn't care what happened to the people when the door opened and Mary Ann, the parlour maid, came in with a letter on a tray.

'What a very late post!' Matty said, glancing at the clock.

'If you please, mum, it ain't the post,' Mary Ann told her. 'The young gent'man delivered it puss'nal. Onny 'e wouldn't give 'is name nor a card nor nothink. 'E jest said I was ter be sure ter give it in ter Miss Easter directly.' Which she did.

Inside the envelope were two sheets of paper. The first was a letter from Henry. 'It's Henry,' she explained rapturously, reading as she spoke. 'My dear, dear Henry.'

'Take courage, my dearest love,' he wrote. 'I know the worst. Your father's letter arrived in the same post as your own dear note. I cannot tell you how glad I was to receive it (your note I mean, not your father's) and to know that you love me and will wait out this dreadful year for me, as I love you and would wait for you until the end of time if need be, which please God it need not be.

'All the greatest lovers in history have been parted, my dearest, Eloise and Abelard, Dante and Beatrice, Romeo and Juliet. It is as if the greater the love we feel the more we have to suffer for it. This year will pass, watered by our tears and blown along by our sighs. You must never despair, nor ever doubt,

That I am, your most loving,

Henry.

P.S. I enclose a poem I wrote for you last night.'

Underneath that another postscript was added in pencil.

'P.P.S. If you look out of the window you will see me standing underneath the chestnut tree in the centre of the green. I will wait there every evening at this time, no matter what the weather, so that if we may not speak we may at least see each other. I love you. H.O.'

'Oh, my dear Henry,' she said, beaming at her cousins. 'He's out there on the green this very minute, waiting to see me.' And she ran to the window and pulled back the curtains.

And there he was, standing under the tree with a lantern held aloft on a pole to light his dear handsome face. She could see him smiling at her quite clearly. 'Oh quick, quick,' she said, 'fetch a lamp so that he can see me too.'

Eager hands set the lamp beside her on the window sill. And

Henry looked up and saw her and waved and blew kisses. She still had his letter in her hand, so she kissed that and waved it at him, to show how much she loved him and how glad she was to receive it. For several blissful minutes the two of them waved and yearned at one another. But after a while their speechless communion grew rather difficult and continual waving felt foolish, so he began to walk out of the green, pausing at every third step to wave again and smile and blow yet another kiss. And his visit was over.

But the glow of it stayed with her, bright and warm as the lamp beside her fingers. And there was still the poem to read. She drew it gently from the envelope and read it still standing at the window.

> 'You are my love and always will be so
> Until the mighty sea runs dry,
> Until the bright stars lose their everlasting glow
> And the eternal moon falls from the sky.
>
> When you are sad and tears bedim your sight
> Look up and see the moon still shining in the sky
> And know that we will be together at the end of our
>   long night,
> And I will love you till the day I die.

It doesn't quite scan properly, so I shall have to work on it further. However I thought you would like to see it. H.O.'

Oh she did, she did. It was the most wonderful, romantic, loving poem, and she didn't care a bit whether it scanned or not.

'Now,' she said, turning back to her family, 'we will plan how to clean those children. I will write to Nan this very evening, that's what I'll do, and we'll ask *her* to provide us with soap and basins. And the minute they arrive we will set about it. What do you think of that, Euphemia?' She was charged with triumphant energy.

'Will she agree?' Euphemia said, looking from one to the other.

But Caroline had no doubts at all. Not now. 'Of course she will,' she said.

*   *   *

'You'll be pleased to know that Caroline is in a better humour,' Nan said, passing her letter across the boardroom table to John at the end of their September meeting. She was in high good humour herself, having just announced her intention to extend their headquarters by renting the property next door and knocking down the intervening walls. The stationery business was booming and their warehouse was full to overflowing.

'Yes,' John agreed when he'd read the letter. 'That seems encouraging.' At least she'd made no mention of the Ippark boy. 'Shall you send her the things she needs? It's a civil request.'

'They were ordered this afternoon,' Nan said. 'Will is to deliver them this evening.'

'Then perhaps he will deliver a little parcel for me.'

'A peace offering, eh?' Billy smiled.

'Something o' that,' John admitted. But he didn't tell them what it was.

'She'll come round,' Billy said comfortingly. 'There's a deal too much affection in the girl for her to keep up a quarrel for ever.'

'Yes,' his brother agreed, with unhappy patience, 'that is true, Billoh. We shall reconcile in time, I know it. She's a most loving child even if she *is* headstrong.'

'There you are then.'

'I *had* to forbid this marriage, Billoh. I love her too dearly to let her make such a match. But I miss her cruelly.'

'She'll come round,' Billy promised again, nodding encouragement.

When Will arrived in Clerkenwell Green that evening he needed the help of all Matty's servants to carry his parcels into the house. And when they were unpacked they filled the parlour; two dozen basins in crates, four boxes full of cheap towels, a dozen cakes of carbolic soap, and, set down with particular care upon the table, a small flat parcel labelled, 'Caroline'.

Matty said it was like Christmas, and all of them were intrigued to see what Caroline's parcel would contain.

It was a set of cards tied together with ribbon to make a small, hand-painted, hand-printed book. There were two letters of the alphabet on each card with two pictures and a rhyming couplet to accompany them. 'A is for apple that grows on the tree. B is for bread that we eat for our tea.' It was a child's primer.

'How delightful!' Euphemia said, as Caroline turned the pages. 'Where did it come from? It's beautifully painted.'

'Papa sent it,' Will said. And now that it was unwrapped, he could see why. 'I remember it, Carrie. Mama made it to teach me and Matty and Edward to read. We used to sit in the garden in Rattlesden, under the cherry tree, learning our letters.' The sight of the little forgotten book was making him yearn with loss, as if he were a child again, and she were newly dead. Dear patient Mama. Oh, how well he remembered her.

'Just look at this drawing of a lion,' Euphemia said. 'It's very realistic, Carrie. Your mama must have seen a lion somewhere and sketched it from the life.'

'I like the weaver "who works at his loom",' Caroline said. It was the picture of a dark squat man bent over an old-fashioned wooden loom, and there was something dogged and dependable about him that she found most attractive.

'It's a peace offering, Caroline,' Matty said. 'You must write and thank him.' It would be the first step towards a reconciliation.

'Will may thank him if he likes,' Caroline said, 'but I ain't writing and that's flat. If I can't write to Henry then I can't write to Papa.'

'But it's a lovely gift,' Euphemia said. 'Think how useful it will be.'

'So it will,' Caroline agreed, 'and we'll all use it with the littl'uns, but I ain't writing, so don't ask me.'

'It will upset him,' Matty said.

But the answer was adamant. 'That is inevitable. Consider how he upset me.'

It was no use pursuing the topic. 'Time for dinner, I think,' Jimmy said. 'Shall we go in?'

He did his best to keep the conversation light throughout the meal, for there was no sense in provoking disagreement and giving them all indigestion. So Will told them about Nan's new

201

extension to the Strand headquarters, and Matty spoke well of the new maid she was training up, and Jimmy was delighted to inform them that he'd been able to take on ten new pupils since Caroline and Euphemia had arrived, and they reached the pudding quite amicably.

But then Caroline altered the tone by asking her brother if he'd been to see Mr Dickens yet.

'In point of fact, I have,' he admitted, looking uncomfortable, 'but please don't say anything to anyone else yet, because I haven't spoken to Papa.'

'Why not?' Caroline said bluntly, ignoring Euphemia's pleading expression. She still hadn't forgiven him for being so lukewarm in his support of her.

'Mr Dickens means to start a new radical newspaper in January,' Will explained. 'It's to be called the *Daily News* and he is to be the editor, and he's offered me a job as a reporter, if everything goes according to plan.'

The news was greeted with delight all round the table.

'But how wonderful!' Euphemia said. 'I'm so glad for you.'

'It might come to nothing,' Will said, 'and in any case it's all a great secret. That's why I haven't told Papa. Or anyone at all except you.' Time enough for that when the paper was founded.

'Your secret is safe with us,' Matty promised. 'We've all got too much to do to be gossiping, especially now that the soap and towels are here and we can get our scholars clean.'

'I wonder how they'll take to the idea,' Jimmy said. 'Another slice of tart, Will?'

They were to find out the next afternoon, when the three young women put on their holland aprons to protect their clothes and set about the task of instructing their pupils in the civilized art of hygiene. Each and every child was presented with a basin of fresh warm water and required to apply soap to their hands and faces until their skin was pink.

Some obeyed meekly, but others were annoyed. 'We come 'ere ter be learned,' one boy protested, 'not fer none a' this caper.'

'You'll learn better when you're clean,' Caroline told him firmly. 'Put your hands in the basin if you please.'

It was very hard work but the transformation they achieved was spectacular.

'That boy they call Josser is really quite handsome when he's washed,' Euphemia said later.

'He's a clever boy,' Jimmy told them. 'He will make a good monitor when he's older.'

'The littl'uns loved their new primer,' Matty said. 'It *was* kind of your father to send it.'

'Yes,' Caroline said. 'It was.' But she still didn't write to him.

The only letters that interested Caroline were the ones that were delivered at the door every evening by Henry Easter. His familiar knock was the highlight of her day. She would rush to the drawing room window at once, lamp in hand, to watch him as he stood beneath the chestnut tree with his own lantern held aloft to remind her. And when he was gone she would feel quite bleak for an hour or two, missing him painfully and feeling the full impossible weight of her father's punishment.

'How wonderfully patient he is,' she would say.

But on the eighth evening, his letter was written with such a furious lack of patience that she could barely decipher it.

'I cannot bear this,' he wrote. 'To see you and not speak is torture to my innermost being. Could you not slip from the house for just a minute? Your father need never know of it.'

It was a terrible temptation, but it had to be resisted. And at once, while her resolve was wrong.

'Dearly though I wish to speak to you,' she answered him, sitting beside the window so that he could see her as she wrote, 'I cannot do as you suggest, although I will write to you, just this once, to explain to you. I have given my word to my father and an Easter's word is her bond, as you must know. I love you more dearly than ever and shall never waiver in my intention to be

Your own

Caroline.'

Then she sent Mary Ann to run out of the house and give it to him, watching in her turn as he took it and read it, holding the little paper up to the lantern. When he'd finished reading it, he looked up at the window for a long time, his face pale in the lamplight. Then he seemed to be tearing the letter in two. Oh dear! Had she upset him so much? But no. It was just a corner he'd torn off and now he was writing something on it, leaning it against the trunk of the tree.

'You are quite right,' he pencilled. 'I was wrong to ask. I love you. H.O.' He was saying the right thing, but the effort it was costing him was making him hot with frustration and bad temper. She could have sneaked out just once to see him. It wouldn't have hurt. There was no need to be quite so proper, devil take it. Oh, this was a preposterous situation!

He gave the note to her servant and watched as she went trotting back to the house with the little scrap of paper in her hand.

Caroline read her second note with mounting affection and was just about to tell Euphemia how noble she thought he was, when she looked down into the square again and saw that he was kicking the tree. It was such a violent outburst and so unexpected that she didn't know how to respond to it. She would have liked to accept it as romantic evidence of his great love for her, but she recognized that temper just a little too clearly, remembering the way he'd sworn when his horse threw him on that first afternoon. And even when he'd recovered himself and taken up the lantern and waved goodbye and gone, the memory of those stabbing legs still disturbed her.

For the first time in her life, she didn't tell Euphemia what she was feeling. These emotions were too raw, too muddled and too private. So they went on disturbing her for several long slow days. And to make matters worse, the one person she could have talked to, who would have understood how she was feeling, was over a hundred miles away from her and not likely to be back in London for months and months.

Nan Easter was in Penrith with Mr Brougham, as usual, wintering at his house on the edge of the great Brougham estates in Westmoreland.

Frederick Brougham had inherited the land when one of his cousins died some twelve years earlier, and had built himself a house on the bank of the river Eamont, well away from the

204

town and with a breathtaking view of the distant fells. It was an isolated place and when she first went there, Nan, the town dweller, had felt ill at ease in such a wilderness, although she had to admit that the scenery was magnificent.

But over the years she had grown to appreciate it almost as much as Frederick did. The local people kept themselves to themselves but were friendly enough when they chanced to meet. The food was excellent, the water sweet and pure, which made a refreshing change after the stale waters of London, and although most parts of the house were extremely cold in winter-time, particularly first thing in the morning, the parlour and their bedroom were always warm, since Frederick gave orders that the fires there were to be kept going day and night. She liked the spaciousness of the rooms with their thick carpets, and their chandeliers and their marble mantelpieces, the kitchen with its two ranges and its two huge dressers, the drawing room on the ground floor and the stepped terraces that rose before it into their steep garden, each with its own hidden delight – sundial, dovecote, fish pond.

And then there were the Broughams, a tribe of aristocratic cousins with whom they visited and gossiped and dined in the leisurely way common to most people who lived among the fells. There was no rush or fret in their isolated tranquillity, and with those magnificent folded hills brooding above them it was impossible to fuss about trivialities, which was refreshing and restful to a woman as busy as the great Nan Easter. So it soon became her habit to spend two or three months there every year.

However, this year proved rather less idyllic than usual. In her second week Frederick took a chill and within two days was racked by a feverish cough that kept them both awake most of the night and worried Nan more than she admitted. She kept her Frederick in bed and dosed him with calfs-foot jelly, but he didn't improve, and finally she gave the butler orders to send to the village for a surgeon.

The gentleman who came was a quiet wizened man, who examined his patient slowly and then pronounced him very sick indeed. 'He has a congestion of the lungs, ma'am,' he told Nan. 'I will bleed him directly which should ease the condition somewhat but the prognosis is not happy.'

So Frederick was bled, first by the application of leeches and then, when that didn't seem to improve his condition at all, by cupping, which reduced him to panting exhaustion, which alarmed Nan but which the doctor assured her was 'a most excellent sign'. But although his fever did drop a little, poor Frederick still coughed incessantly, and now there was no doubt that he was very ill indeed, just as the surgeon had said.

That night she wrote to John and Billy to tell them that she would be staying in Penrith until Frederick was better. 'The firm is in your capable hands,' she said. Then she returned to the sick room.

'I keep you,' Frederick worried between bouts of tossing fever. 'I keep you, my dear. You should be in London.'

'You en't to talk squit,' Nan said lovingly. 'I shall stay with 'ee till the fever's gone, my dear. Don't 'ee fret. Billy and John can run the firm for a day or two, surely to goodness.'

But it wasn't a day or two, it was more than six weeks. In fact by the time he was able to tremble out of bed and totter across the room on his pathetically shrunken legs and sit most gratefully by the bedroom fire, it was well into November.

'Now you must go to London, Nan my dear,' he urged. 'It increases my guilt that I keep you here so long, and a guilty man makes a slow recovery.'

She was relieved that his wit had returned. 'If that's the way of it, I shall travel tomorrow,' she grinned at him.

But in fact she took time to check all the household stores and give detailed instructions to the housekeeper and the cook, and to impress upon Frederick's manservant that she was to be informed at once if he took so much as a fraction of a turn for the worse. Then she took the closed carriage to Lancaster and the railway.

It was a very cold journey, for the first snow of the winter had fallen overnight, and even in the relative comfort of a well-upholstered first class carriage her hands and feet were soon chilled, despite her fur muff and stout leather boots. Fortunately she had the carriage to herself for the first twenty miles, so she curled herself up like a dormouse for warmth and tucked her feet under her petticoats.

The white hills rolled past her little misted window, black trees spiked the horizon like wild hair, the occasional black homestead crouched under its white roof, black and white, white and black. There is no colour in the world, she thought, as the engine chuffed white steam into the grey sky and the wheels clacked clicked clacked over frost-black rails. The spring seemed a long way away. She realized that she was exhausted. I must be growing old, she thought, to have so little energy and to feel the cold so acutely. Until then she hadn't thought of herself in terms of age at all. She was simply Nan Easter, busy running her great firm and happily involved in the complicated affairs of her huge family. Now, and for almost the first time, she was aware of her seventy-three years. As the train rocked her into sleep, she knew she would be glad to be back in London with her work to occupy her and the renewal of spring just round the corner.

Chapter 15

'You've just got back in time for bad weather,' Will said, as he handed his grandmother out of her carriage outside the Easter headquarters. The sky above the Strand was the colour of blue ink and seemed to be pressing down upon the buildings as though the air were weighted.

'I shouldn't be a bit surprised,' Nan said, walking briskly into the building. 'It's been snowing in the north. When that lot starts a-falling we shall know about it.'

It started a-falling at three o'clock in the afternoon, and by then a strong wind was gusting, so the first downpour was hurled sideways into the open doorway of A. Easter and Sons and blown underneath the tarpaulins that covered the exposed joists in the new extension.

John and Nan were inspecting the site. The first floor of the building, where they now stood, had been completely gutted, with all the inner walls removed and the central stairway left as a perilous ladder. A hoist had been fitted on the floor above them, and a large hole, which would eventually become a double loading door, had been made in the wall overlooking the courtyard. Most of the labourers were on the ground floor converting the rooms to offices, and the foreman was nowhere to be seen, having taken himself off through the back door the minute he heard Nan's voice.

'Off to buy wood at four o'clock in the afternoon? That's a likely story!' Nan was complaining, when the sudden shower swooshed through the loose tarpaulins that were supposed to be covering the hole. She was drenched from shoulder to thigh.

'There you see!' she said, shaking her skirts. 'That should

never have happened. Shoddy workmanship, that's what that is. Oh, I shall have something to say to that foreman when he gets back.'

'You must get into dry clothes, Mama,' John said anxiously. 'You are soaked to the skin.'

'Tosh!' she said. 'I en't a baby. Bit of rainwater never hurt nobody.'

He gave her his wry grin. 'And here you've been telling me all about poor Mr Brougham and how ill he's been with the congestion of his lungs, and what caused that if it wasn't the damp?'

'I'm made of tougher stuff,' she said. But she *was* wet. There was no denying it. Wet and beginning to feel cold in consequence. So she allowed herself to be persuaded and went back to her office to change into the clean clothes she kept there for emergencies.

She was sitting at her desk afterwards, feeling a great deal warmer and checking through the order books, when Will arrived with a pot of tea and a dish of fancy cakes.

'Papa thought you might need sustenance,' he said. The gale was still blowing, roaring so loudly outside her window that she could hardly hear what he was saying.

There were two cups set on the tray, so he obviously wanted to be asked to join her. 'Come in, come in,' she said, beckoning him towards her.

'What weather,' he said, as she poured the tea. 'I've just been down to the Isle of Dogs. You should see the tide that's running. They've been trying to tie all the colliers to their moorings there, tiers and tiers of them. I've never seen them all tied up before. There must have been about eighty of them along the Mill Wall. They were like an armada. I'm going back again presently. I think there's a story in it.'

'You still write then?' she said, sipping the hot tea.

'Now and then,' he admitted, 'just to keep my hand in.'

'Is this a commission?'

'Well, yes.'

'Who is it for?'

'Well actually,' he said, in that deliberately casual way that showed how very important it was, 'it's a commission for Mr Dickens.'

'The novelist feller?'

'The same,' he said. But then his casual façade was breached by excitement. 'He's offered me a job, Nan. On his new paper. He's been planning it for months and now it's all set. The first issue will be out in January. He'll be advertising in the trade in two weeks' time.'

'Does your father know?'

'Not yet. I thought I would tell you first. See what you think.'

'Curry support eh, you rogue?' she laughed at him.

'Something of that.'

'Is the pay good?'

'Phenomenal. Almost as much as you pay me here.'

'Then it is good,' she said, laughing again. 'Very well. I'll plead for 'ee. Tomorrow perhaps, when Billy and your father come to dine with us. 'Tis time you went back to your true love, my dear. You've played fair by us all these years. You've earned your reward.'

He stood up and rushed round her little fireside table to kiss her. 'You're a brick, Nan,' he said.

'Quite possibly,' she agreed. 'Now run off, there's a dear boy. I've work to do.'

'And I may go back to the river later?'

'If your father can spare you.'

In the event Will didn't have to ask for permission, because John Easter was sparing everybody. By five o'clock the gale was so bad it was blowing tiles from the roofs, and two of the Easter delivery vans, which were being chocked into position beside the warehouse gates ready for the morning, were blown right over and with such force that one of them had its side caved in.

John heard the crash and came out at once, lantern in hand to inspect the damage. He'd been so busy that until that moment he hadn't noticed how bad the storm was. It was like stepping onto the deck of a ship far out at sea. The darkness was so intense that his lantern was virtually useless; the rain whipped like a lash and the gale roared upon him with such ferocity that it was all he could do to stay on his feet.

As his eyes grew accustomed to the storm he became aware that the street was full of struggling figures, some hump-backed with effort, trying to heave the two carts back onto their wheels; some holding the heads of the terrified horses; some too buffeted to move in any direction at all; and two staggering after a tumbling shape that turned out to be the apron of a hansom cab which was being blown along the street cracking like a sail. Why, it's a hurricane, he thought. I must take action.

'Leave the carts!' he yelled. 'See to the horses. Where's Mr Mellor?'

Mr Mellor surged towards him, clutching his hat and with his greatcoat flapping his legs. 'Sir?'

'Get those horses back to the stables,' John ordered. 'They shouldn't be on the streets. Not in that state. No more carts, tell Joe. And fetch Mrs Easter's carriage. With the cobs. They're steady.'

'Sir!' Mr Mellor agreed, struggling back to the horses.

Mama must go straight home, John planned as the rain needled his face. I shall have to persuade her. The shutters must go up directly or the gale will blow the windows out. I'll shut the shop and send all the men home except the night porter. There's no sense in staying open in weather like this. There'll be no more business done until the morning. His mind was working like clockwork, checking off chores. Those tarpaulins must be made safe or the extension will be flooded. He was still thinking hard as he pushed his way back into the building.

When Will approached him for permission to leave the premises, he gave it at once almost without thought. 'Be careful how you go,' he said. 'The wind is uncommon strong. Is Mama still in her office?'

She was, and to his great relief she agreed that the shop should be shut and that she would go home as soon as her carriage arrived. 'It's a foul night,' she said. 'We'd all be a deal better at home in the warm. Where shall you dine?'

Dinner was a long way from his thoughts. 'At home I daresay,' he said vaguely.

'Shall I wait for 'ee? Would 'ee care to dine with me?'

'No, no,' he said. 'There's a lot to attend to. I could be late. Thank you all the same, Mama. I'll dine at home.'

'As you wish,' she said, kissing him. Her fire was giving no heat at all. It would be good to be home beside a real blaze. 'Goodnight, my dear. I shall see you in the morning.'

Over in Clerkenwell Green, Jimmy and Matty were glad to be back in the warm too. They had been to evensong, of course, gale or no, and the short walk back to the rectory had been so difficult they'd arrived home wet to the skin.

Caroline was at the drawing-room window, watching for Henry.

'He may not come,' Euphemia warned. 'It's a terrible night.'

The green was completely empty. There was no sign of any of the usual street sellers; the inhabitants were all indoors and even the sheep, who usually cropped the grass all year round whatever the weather, had been rounded up and herded into the barn. And since the night when he kicked the tree, Henry had only appeared in the green once or twice a week, although Caroline looked out for him every single evening, just in case.

'If he stays at home tonight it will be jolly sensible of him,' she said, as the wind hurled rain against the window. 'It wouldn't do to go catching the pneumonia.'

'I feel so sorry for our poor children on a night like this,' Euphemia said, adjusting the lamp on the side-table. 'What they must be suffering, in those awful rooms of theirs, with no food and no fires. It doesn't bear thinking about.'

'Then don't think about it,' Caroline advised practically. 'I'm ready for dinner, aren't you? Doesn't it smell good?'

'Do you think Will will dine with us again soon?' Euphemia said as they left the room.

'How you must miss him,' Caroline said, torn with sudden sympathy for her cousin. At least she saw her Henry every week at some time or another but Pheemy had to wait ages to see Will, and all through no fault of her own. 'You are very dear to stay here with me the way you do! We will tease Matty to ask him to dinner tomorrow.'

'I wonder where he is now,' Euphemia said wistfully.

*　*　*

He was striding down Fleet Street, head down, feet determined, storm lantern in hand. The wind was howling up all the narrow alleys that led like canyons down to the Thames, and even at this distance he could hear the crash of waves and a hideous grinding noise like trees being felled. It was extremely difficult to make progress for the gale stopped his breath and hurled him sideways against the walls, but at last he emerged at the water side. He was thrilled and horrified by what he saw. Oh, there was a story here and no mistake.

The river looked like a rough sea, with huge waves thudding together in the darkness and crashing against the bank so that spray spat high in the air against the warehouse walls. But what was worse and more drastic, the ships that he'd last seen lying at anchor with their holds well battened down, were now being tossed about in the middle of the river as helpless as corks. It was impossible to estimate how many there were for they were thrown above the waves one minute and lost to sight the next, but there must have been at least twenty in the short stretch of river above Blackfriars Bridge.

Beneath the cliff face of the warehouse, a group of men in oilskins and sou'westers were sheltering together watching the destruction. They had hung their lanterns on the wall behind them, where they swung frantically to and fro, their little intermittent light making the oilskins gleam like fish and spiking the heaving water with eerie darts of fire.

'A bad night,' Will shouted to the watchers as he stumbled towards them.

'Never known nothink like it,' one man replied, making room for him on the doorstep. His face was shining wet in the lamplight. 'Thirty years I been a waterman. Never known nothink like it. My boat's stove in.'

''Undreds a' boats sunk,' another man shouted. ''Undreds! Gravesend steamer's gone aground, so they say. Hit a fishin' smack, be all accounts. Crew run 'er ashore. An' there's scores a' coal barges gone down be London Bridge.'

Will could well believe it, for now he could see that there was a large cargo ship wallowing in the middle of the river with its top mast broken off and its stern completely caved in.

'Never seen the like,' the waterman mourned.

Will hung his lantern with the others, and pressed well back against the door. The pull of the churning water looked very strong. Even in the doorway they were in real danger of being sucked into the river.

'Are we . . . ?' he was beginning.

But the watermen were groaning. 'My dear Lord! Look at that, sir!'

A barge, piled six feet high with long planks, was being lurched towards the second arch of the bridge. They watched as the river heaved it nearer and nearer, tossed it almost vertically into the air and finally hurled it against the stonework. The impact was so savage it could be heard above the scream of the wind.

Will blinked the moisture out of his eyes, excited and appalled to see how easily such a sturdy boat could be destroyed. The tide was beating over the sides of it, washing away the planks as though they were no weightier than matchsticks. We don't stand much chance against the elements, he thought, for all our new inventions. A tide like this could demolish a steam train. And what with the thought and the danger and the penetrating cold, he began to shiver.

There were two dark figures on the bridge, waving and beckoning to them. They looked squat and bulky, even for men in oilskins but their signal was unmistakable.

'All hands!' one of the watermen called to his mates, but they'd taken their lanterns already and were trudging off towards the bridge, slithering in the river mud, and leaping back from the impact of the waves, with Will sliding after them.

'What's up?' their leader called as they reached the road.

'Horse and rider gone in.'

On the other side of the bridge the Thames looked as though it was boiling. There was so much foam on the water and so much spray in the air that it was several minutes before Will caught sight of the horse, flailing wildly, about three yards off shore, and being carried along at an alarming speed with his rider clinging to his neck, despite a rope that seemed to be tangled about their bodies and spread whitely out across the black water to where four men struggled to hold it.

A second rope was uncoiled and hurled, and a white hand grabbed into the air for it, missed and disappeared under the waves. It was hauled ashore and flung out again. And missed again. But the third throw was successful. The hand grabbed, scrabbled, clung, struggled, looping the rope above the horse's head, as the tide carried them both several yards further on with their rescuers dodging along the shore to keep up with them.

Then there was a faint bubbling shout, as the first rope was secured and at that Will and the watermen took a stand, as close to the warehouse walls as they could get, and began to heave upon the second rope, working as a team, as though they were playing tug o' war. Will was the fourth man behind the leader and pulled with the best, but it was a long exhausting struggle, and a terrifying one, for the waves broke over them as they hauled and they all knew how horribly easy it would be for them to be dragged off their feet into the river.

But at last their rope suddenly grew slack and they were handing it in almost freely. And the horse was scrambling onto the bank with his rider still clinging to his mane.

Then there was a roar of relief, and one of the watermen went running off to fetch a rug and two penn'orth of gin, and the horse shook and trembled, and the rider tried to tell them his name and address and couldn't do either because his teeth were chattering so violently. And Will found he was covered in mud and so tired that he had to lean against the warehouse wall for a few seconds to recover.

I've got myself a story now and no mistake, he thought.

'Come along, sir, if you please,' one of the watermen said close to his ear. 'Best get out of here sharpish. That tide's rising by the second.'

They were already leading the horse into the alley behind the warehouse. 'There's an alehouse in the Strand,' the waterman said. 'Jest a few yards, sir.'

Back in the Easter headquarters, John and the night porter were checking the shutters and damping down the remaining fires. It was very cold in the empty building and the reverberation of the wind was like thunder.

'You'll be glad to get home, I shouldn't wonder,' the porter said.

'Yes,' John admitted, 'I shall.'

But his long day wasn't over yet. As he and the porter walked wearily downstairs to the ground floor, there was a crash from the new warehouse next door.

Despite his fatigue John reacted automatically, taking the keys from the hook in the porter's lodge as the echoes of the crash merged with the howl of the gale, putting on his greatcoat and his hat and muffler as the rain drummed against the window, taking the lantern the porter had lit for him and walking out calmly into the tempest and the crowd that was rapidly gathering outside the door.

He was surrounded by people eager to tell him what had happened. 'That's the chimbley gorn, guvnor.' 'Half the house more like.' 'Tiles, that's what that was.' But they made way for him, awed by his calm and the gentle determination of his gait.

'If you would please stand back,' he begged, speaking loudly and clearly to be heard above the wind. 'The structure could be dangerous, I think. I would not wish any of you to be hurt.'

They stood back respectfully while he wrestled with a combination of stiff lock and flapping greatcoat. Two of his carters were among the crowd and when the door was opened they shoved forward to offer their help.

'Joe, is it?' John said, peering through the rain at him.

'Yes, sir, Me an' Charlie.'

'I thought I'd sent you home.'

'Stopped fer supper, Mr Easter sir. D'you need any help?'

'No, no,' he said. 'It is better that I go in alone.' And giving them his wry smile in that howling darkness, 'You never know what I might find. I will leave the door ajar and call you if I need you.'

The ground floor was the same as it had been when he had left it that afternoon, but when he lifted the lantern he could see a dust-cloud swirling across the top of the stairs. There's masonry down somewhere then, he thought, climbing carefully. That won't please Mama.

At first sight the floor seemed to be covered with bricks. He stepped gingerly across them to investigate. Was it the chimney? But he couldn't see for all the dust, which was trailing across the light of his lantern red as hell-fire. There was something hateful about this place, something menacing. The tarpaulin was flogging like a cat-o'-nine-tails, and the scream of the wind was the agony of a creature trapped.

'Come now,' he said aloud. 'You have work to do.' And he tried to shake these morbid imaginings from his brain, deliberately conjuring up images of his dear, dead Harriet, so as to comfort himself, Harriet cool as a lily in the portrait he knew so well, sitting in the garden at Rattlesden, primer in hand, with the children grouped about her, striding through the field of Peterloo, dishevelled and brave and blood-stained, tripping towards him on their wedding day, like a spring flower in her yellow gown and her green stockings, that pale face glowing, his own and only dearest.

There was a sharp cracking sound above his head, like a pistol shot. He dragged his mind back from his dreams and glanced up, raising the lantern. And the ceiling was falling towards him in horrible slow motion.

That second roaring crash made the crowd jump with alarm. 'Now what?' they said to one another.

'I reckon we oughter go in,' Joe said.

But Charlie thought they ought to wait for Mr Easter to come out again.

'I'm off home,' another man said, moving away as well as he could for the force of the wind. 'We shall have the whole damn kit and caboodle down round our ears, you ask me.'

'Here's Mr Will,' Charlie said. 'He'll know what ter do.'

Mr Will's decision was as quick as his father's had been. 'We'll go in and see,' he said to the carters. 'Will someone lend me a lantern? I've left mine down by the river.' And when one was produced, 'Follow me.'

The hall was so full of dust that for a few seconds none of them could see anything else. Then Will realized that it was all billowing down upon them from the upper floor and he leapt up the stairs two at a time, with the carters running behind him.

The place was full of bricks and mortar, huge dust-steaming piles, like rubbish dumps, the ceiling was gone and so was the tarpaulin and the wind was howling and screaming through the hole in the wall. There was no sign of his father.

'Shall I go up ter the next floor, sir?' Joe asked.

'There's no floor left,' Will said, stepping round the nearest pile of rubble, his heart thudding with the most terrible alarm. Where was Papa? He must be here somewhere. 'Papa! Papa! Answer me, for the love of God!'

There was something soft and squashy underneath his foot. Something soft and squashy. Dear God! He recoiled from it, swinging the lantern so that he could see what it was. Wanting to know. But dreading it too. And it was a hand. Streaked with dirt and blood. A hand!

'Over here!' he yelled, tearing at the rubble with both hands. 'He's under here. Quick! Quick! Get the others Joe. Send for a doctor. Oh, quick! Quick! We must get him out.'

Charlie's hands swung into the lantern light, clawing frantically. There were feet on the stairs, voices shouting, somebody with a spade. 'Oh take care, for pity's sake!' Long, long minutes of appalled effort, dust everywhere, choking them all, somebody spitting and coughing. And finally, inexorably, terribly, shatteringly, the body was revealed.

The doctor was elbowing his way through the rescuers. But there was no need of a doctor now, for John Easter was dead.

Chapter 16

By the time Will got back to Bedford Square the storm had blown itself out. It was four o'clock in the morning and pitch dark.

He had come home by instinct, too weary to think and too drained of emotion to feel. All he knew was that he wanted to be with Nan, with dear strong dependable Nan, because she would make everything all right. If he could just be home with her, she would kiss away the pain like she'd done when he was a little boy, and the horror would go away. Somewhere in a very distant part of his mind he knew that his father was dead and lying in a coffin in an empty office room and that the undertakers would be taking him to Fitzroy Square in the morning and that nothing would ever be the same again, but he walked on in a daze, full of illogical, unreasonable, childish hope. Nan would know what to do.

The house was in darkness. Even the lantern above the front door was out. It took him a long time to get his key into the lock and let himself in. Then he stood in the hall with his fists in his pockets, quite unable to move, as the tears spilled out of his eyes and rolled down his cheeks and fell onto the filth that covered his greatcoat. Although he didn't know it, he was groaning with grief.

Nan came out onto the landing almost at once and was down the stairs soft and quick, with Bessie hobbling behind her, candle in hand.

'My dear, my dear,' she said. 'What is it?' Putting her arms round his neck, pulling his head down and down until it lay on her shoulder. 'Tell your old Nan.'

'Father is dead,' he said, and then he was too choked with sobs to say anything else.

She took charge of him, as he'd known she would. He was undressed, still weeping, and the blood and grime was washed from his face and hands and he was put to bed and given a beaker full of bitter liquid to drink. And gradually, bit by bit, his grief subsided and he told her the story, because she was attending to him so gently and listening so calmly.

She said very little, nodding her head, waiting, patting his hand. She didn't question and she didn't comment, she simply listened. And when he'd told her all that he could bear to, she kissed him and tucked him in the covers comfortingly as though he were a child who'd been confessing to some schoolyard brawl. 'Sleep now,' she said. 'We will talk again tomorrow.'

Her bitter brew was drowsing him. I shouldn't sleep, he thought, not after all that, but he was already far away.

When she was satisfied that her opiate had taken effect, Nan turned the gaslight down to a bead and she and Bessie went softly back to her bedroom.

Then it was Bessie's turn to comfort, for neither of them could hold back their own grief any longer.

'I have lost my right arm, Bessie,' Nan wept. 'My right arm. He was the best of the bunch.'

'Yes, Mrs Easter mum. You have. You have.'

'It en't right, Bessie.'

'No, mum.'

'He should have survived me, my poor John.'

'Yes, yes, he should.'

'That foreman will never work again. I swear it!'

'I'll get the fire lit, shall I mum?' Bessie said. 'Your poor hands are as cold as ice.'

Her practical concern drew Nan away from the anger of her grief. 'We'll light it together,' she said. 'It's nearly six, and there's a deal to do. We must start the day, howsomever we feel. There's letters to write and clothes to prepare. Oh, my dear heart alive, I never thought to wear mourning for my Johnnie.'

So they lit the fire, kneeling before the grate together, and they drew Nan's fireside table right up close to the fender. Bessie left her to write her letters, while she set a kettle on the hob, and warned the waking household, and saw to it that all the blinds in the front of the house stayed drawn, and bustled about the bedroom looking out Nan's mourning clothes and preparing a bowl of warm water for her so that she could wash and dress.

They were difficult letters to compose, to *The Times* to announce the death; to Frederick Brougham to urge him to write and tell her how he was, and to drop a hint that there were 'things' she had to attend to in London that would keep her for 'rather more time' than she'd intended, that one of those things was a death, and finally after much preamble, that it was John who had died, for she couldn't tell him the truth straight away, not in his weakened state; to Billy and Matilda and Edward, and Annie and James, oh so carefully worded, for they had to know what had happened, but not too suddenly or shockingly; to Annie's two daughters who'd always been so fond of their uncle; to all the regional managers who'd worked with him for so long. And each letter was worse than the last. Dreadful, impossible letters.

'Shall you write to poor Caroline?' Bessie asked when the last envelope had been addressed and trembled upon the pile.

'No,' Nan said. 'I shall take the closed carriage and go and tell her myself. It en't a thing she should hear in a letter. She'll take it hard, poor child, after that foolish row.' She was bowed under the weight of this nightmare, her shoulders drooping, her face drawn, her eyes shrunk to half their size, and the lines on her cheeks and forehead etched dark grey even in the gentle glow of the gaslight.

'I'll make some tea,' Bessie said, lovingly. 'Could you fancy anything to eat?'

Caroline and Euphemia were up early that morning too. Nobody in the house had slept very much during the storm, and now that the rain had stopped and the wind had died down, they were all eager to be out and about, to inspect the damage and see what help their neighbours might require. There was a plane tree lying across the centre of the green, torn up by its roots, which was very exciting, and the house on the corner had a gaping hole in its roof, and as Matty said, there was no knowing *what* might have happened just around the corner.

The two little boys were thrilled to be going out so early. Everard, who was four and very venturesome, looked happily at the fallen tree, telling baby brother Manny, 'Us'll climb up there Manny, shall us?'

So they had an early breakfast and were just about to put on their coats and caps when Nan's carriage drew up at the gate.

All four of the adults assumed that she had come to tell them about the storm, but her opening words and the expression on her face soon alerted them to something worse.

'I think these two babbas should be in the nursery,' she said.

'We're a-going to climb a fallen tree,' Everard told her importantly as their nursemaid led them away.

'Yes, my love. Presently.'

'What is it?' Jimmy said when the two little boys had been coaxed out of the room.

'Someone has been hurt,' Matty guessed.

But Caroline, all sharp wit and intuition, knew the worst. 'Someone has been killed,' she said. 'Tell us quickly.'

'It's your father,' Nan said, and told them quickly, while they could cope with it.

The howl that Caroline gave when she understood what was being said was too awful to hear without weeping. 'No, no, no!' she cried. 'He can't be dead. I haven't said sorry to him. He can't possibly be dead. He can't. He can't.' And she put her head in her hands and ran from the room, howling and howling.

'Leave her,' Nan said, when Euphemia began to run after her. 'Let her get over the first of it on her own. Sympathy'll make it worse.'

But the extremity of Caroline's grief persisted. She cried all the way back to Bedford Square and she continued to weep for three more days, refusing food or comfort, even from Euphemia, sitting in a twilight of drawn blinds and hopelessness in Nan's empty parlour on the ground floor of the house.

On the second morning when letters of condolence started to arrive, she wouldn't look at them. And the next day, when a letter from Henry arrived, addressed to Nan, she merely glanced at it and let it fall. Nan was most upset, particularly as the letter was written with an honest regret she found rather touching, given the young man's circumstances.

'He would like to visit,' she said to her granddaughter. 'What shall I tell him?'

'What you will,' Caroline said listlessly. She was so unlike herself it was really rather alarming.

So Nan wrote back by return of post to tell Mr Easter that he could call whenever he liked, and privately hoped that he would make it soon. Perhaps he could cheer the poor child.

He was on the doorstep at eleven o'clock the following morning. And not a minute too soon, for a mere half an hour before his arrival Billy brought them a letter from the company solicitor, which had stirred Caroline's guilt and misery all over again. It enclosed her father's will, which she and Nan and Will and Billy had read together, and in which he asked to be buried at Rattlesden 'alongside my darling wife Harriet' and instructed that his fortune should be divided equally between 'my dear son Will and my dear daughter Caroline so that they may live in comfort and without worry'.

'I was so unkind to him,' Caroline sobbed, when the last word had been read. 'I said I would hate him till the day I died. And now he leaves a will so that I won't worry. How could I have said such a dreadful thing to him when I loved him so? I shall worry about it for the rest of my life.'

'We all say things we don't mean,' Nan tried to comfort.

'But I *did* mean it. I wouldn't have said it if I didn't mean it. I haven't said sorry to him. That's the awful thing. I'd have said sorry when he sent the book if I'd known this was going to happen. I should have said sorry when he sent the book. But I didn't, and now he'll never know. Oh, I wish I hadn't said such dreadful things.'

'He knew you didn't mean them, Carrie,' Billy said, patting her shoulders. 'Told me so himself.'

'Did he?' she asked, turning swimming eyes towards him.

'Yes, my dear. He did. He said you were the most loving child alive and he knew you didn't mean what you said and he knew you'd be reconciled. Told me so himself.'

But that made Caroline weep more passionately than ever.

'Don't cry so, Carrie,' Will begged. 'You'll make yourself

ill.' But he couldn't bear her grief because it unleashed his own so terribly. 'Please don't cry.'

But her tears seemed endless. So Nan and Will were very glad when Henry Easter was ushered into the darkened room.

He was completely composed and to Nan's surprise and interest he seemed to know exactly what to do, as though he'd been comforting grief all his life. He took his weeping Caroline into his arms and smoothed her hair out of her eyes and wiped her face with his handkerchief and told her everything was going to be all right. Then he led her to the sofa and coaxed her to sit down, which he did without words by simply sitting down himself, very gradually and with his arm still about her waist so that she swayed, following the movement of his body, and finally sat too. It was skilful and it was loving. Nan approved of it all very much.

'We will leave you,' she mouthed at him over Caroline's bent head. And when he nodded, she and Will walked quietly out of the room and closed the door behind them.

'I know how you feel,' they heard him say, 'but it will pass, believe me my darling. It will pass.'

'I was so horrid to him,' she wailed.

'Yes,' he said in the same composed voice, 'of course you were. You wouldn't have been human if you hadn't been. We're all horrid to people at some time or another, I know I am. But you were loving to him too, don't forget that. You loved him dearly.'

'Oh, I did. I did.'

'There you are then. Dry your eyes, my dearest.'

'What an excellent young man!' Nan said as she and Will went upstairs to the drawing room. 'If they marry, he will make a splendid husband.'

'I suppose they *may* marry now,' Will said, 'since Papa ain't here to disapprove.' It was the first time he'd spoken of his father since, and it pained him that his first words should be so critical, as Nan could see by the strained expression on his face.

'He'd have come round to it in time,' she assured him. 'He was a good man.'

'Yes,' he said bleakly. 'A very good man. How shall we manage in the firm without him?'

Neither of them had given the firm a thought until that minute.

'I shall go in this afternoon and see how things are,' Nan said. 'It'll be the quarterly meeting soon. We shall have to make plans, find a replacement. There's a deal of work to be done.'

And I suppose I shall have to do it, Will thought with weary resignation, for who else is there? He would have to turn down that job with Mr Dickens. And he sighed most miserably. 'Should I come with you?' he asked.

'Not today,' she said kindly. 'Time enough when the funeral is over.'

Downstairs in the parlour Henry was urging Caroline to get out of the house too. 'We will walk out into the countryside,' he said. 'The air will do you good.' The countryside would cheer her. She might see a fallen tree or two but there would be few damaged buildings to remind her of her loss. 'And tomorrow we will ride together. If you sit about brooding everything seems worse.'

In her listlessness Caroline agreed with him. It was the oddest sensation to be taken care of, when she'd always been so independent and so sure of herself, but it was very comforting. Oh, how dear he was, her Henry, how very dear.

'I don't think I shall ever feel happy again,' she said.

'Yes, you will,' he assured her. 'You will. Things will start to get better once the funeral is over. You'll see.'

'But how shall I ever make amends to him?' she said.

'We will find a way,' he promised.

'How do you know all this?' she asked, impressed and intrigued by his confidence, for it was a side of his character she'd never seen until now.

'I am an orphan too, if you remember,' he said, smiling at her.

'You felt like this when your father died,' she said, understanding.

His grief hadn't been at all the same. He'd been afraid of his father who'd always been distant and unapproachable and often cruel. But he didn't tell her. It wasn't the right moment. 'Something similar,' he compromised. 'Now get your coat and bonnet and we will take a walk.'

'Should I be chaperoned?' she wondered. If Bessie had to come with them they wouldn't be able to walk very far.

'No,' he said. 'Your sorrow is chaperone enough.'

Upstairs in the bedroom she shared with Caroline, Euphemia sat at the window with her sewing. It was difficult to see the stitches in the half-light of those drawn blinds, so from time to time she held her work to the window and lifted the nearest blind just an inch to get a better light. Which was how she saw Caroline and Henry leaving for their walk.

Thank heavens, she thought, watching them as they strolled through the gardens, she so pale and small and woe-begone in her heavy mourning clothes, her black gloved hand in the crook of his elbow. It had upset Euphemia to see such a change in her lively cousin. Now that Henry had come to visit her, perhaps she would regain her spirits. And she decided that she would go downstairs and see if she could find Will and tell him what she'd seen. If he knew that Caroline was a little less unhappy, it might cheer him a little too.

He was in the library, sitting at the table with a lamp lit beside him and a blank sheet of paper before him, gazing miserably into space.

'Will?' she said, tip-toeing into the room.

He turned his handsome head towards her wearily, as though it were too heavy to be moved with ease. 'I've been trying to write an article about the storm,' he said, 'and I can't do it.'

'No,' she said. 'Of course you can't. Not now. You shouldn't expect to.' But how dear and foolish he was to try.

'It's a commission,' he said. 'For Mr Dickens. He suggested it when he offered me the job. I thought . . . ' But then he hesitated, looking away from her, seemed confused.

'What did you think?' she encouraged.

'You will say nothing about this to anyone if I tell you.'

'You have my word.'

'I thought that if I could write the article I might still be able to take the job. Oh, it's all folly. There is no real hope of any such thing. No hope at all. I do know that. Everything is changed now, I'm afraid. I must work for the firm. It is inescapable. Who else could replace Papa? But I thought . . . '

How much this job means to him, Euphemia thought, yearning with sympathy. 'It might be possible,' she said.

'No,' he said. 'There is no chance of that. I must face reality.'

It would be unkind to argue with him, Euphemia thought. And she decided to change the subject. 'I have some good news,' she said. 'At least I think it is good news. Caroline has gone out for a walk with Henry.'

He pulled his mind from his troubles to hear of it. 'Has she though? That's an improvement.'

'Yes,' Euphemia said, admiring the effort he was making. 'It is.'

'They will be able to marry now,' he said. 'Poor creatures. What unhappiness there is in store for them.'

'Unhappiness?' Euphemia said. 'Oh, surely not. I think they will be very happy together.'

'While they *are* together perhaps,' Will conceded. 'But they cannot be together for ever. One of them will die, sooner or later, and the survivor will suffer the torments of the damned. Like Papa. He lived in misery for more than nineteen years. In misery. Well, you saw how it was. He wouldn't change a thing in that house, the wallpaper faded on the walls, the clocks didn't work, the furniture split, there were legs off the chairs, but he wouldn't change a thing. He was locked in misery because Mama had died. It is always the way.'

'Oh, not always, surely,' she tried to argue. 'He didn't seem miserable to me.'

'Always,' he said, with the terrible, unreasonable finality of his grief. 'Always.'

'Not all change is for the worse,' she said, trying to reason with him because she could see that it was grief that was making him speak so wildly. 'My life changed out of all recognition when I came to England, and that was a change for the better, you must admit.'

'But that was different. That wasn't due to a death.'

'No,' she admitted gravely. 'But then death is not always a bad thing. It hurts us all most terribly but it is natural, part of a natural cycle, birth, growth, decay, death. We have to accept it. Plants die, just as we do, and yet new plants grow from the

227

compost of their leaves. There is always rebirth, always new life.'

'There is always death.'

'Yes,' she agreed, 'always death. But life goes on, Will, truly it does.'

'The phoenix from the ashes, eh,' he said, giving her the faintest flicker of a smile. 'You are such an optimist, Pheemy.'

'Perhaps that's just as well,' she said, smiling back. And she made up her mind that she must do something to help him if she could, for she had never seen a melancholy before and she found it very upsetting.

Over in the Strand, Nan Easter was examining the books. In three days the affairs of the firm had snarled into a parlous muddle. Papers hadn't been delivered, bills weren't paid, business meetings had been missed, several of the regional managers had written wondering if the December meeting would be cancelled.

'It's just as well I'm back,' she said to her clerk. 'There's a deal of work needs doing. Tell 'em the quarterly meeting stands. And fetch me Mr John's folder, the green one labelled ''Deliveries''.'

But she'd only been studying it for ten minutes or so, when Matilda arrived, wearing black silk and a strained expression.

'I saw your carriage as I was passing,' she said, settling herself beside the fire. 'I'm so glad you're in today. A terrible business, my dear. Terrible. Billy is devastated.'

Nan left the problems on her desk and joined her daughter-in-law by the fire, for it was plain that this was no mere courtesy call. And sure enough after a few minutes Matilda came to the point. 'Have you considered a replacement?' she asked, her face more strained than ever.

She's going to suggest young Edward, Nan thought, and began to marshal her arguments against him, too young, not sufficiently interested in the firm, still too much of a spendthrift.

'Billy is quite out of the question,' Matilda said. 'His health is very poor, you know. Worse than we tell you. Oh, I daresay he will work on for a few years yet. He is too conscientious to do anything else and that's the truth of it. But on no account should he even consider taking on any more burdens than he does at present.'

'Quite right,' Nan agreed. 'No more he shall, my dear. You have my word.' And now she'll offer young Edward.

But she was mistaken. 'And I do hope you won't think of Edward either,' Matilda said. 'Oh, he seems the obvious choice. That I'll grant you. But he ain't, my dear, indeed he ain't. He's a deal too young, and a deal too extravagant. And besides, if he took over John's position, who would do my Billy's job during the summer? Three months is a long time to hand over to a stranger.'

So that's it, Nan thought. She is protecting Billy's long summer holiday. What a choice she's had to make, Billy's health or Edward's ambition. No wonder she looks strained. 'Quite right,' she said again. 'Billy and Edward should remain as they are. There en't a doubt in my mind about that.' Which was true.

Matilda sighed with relief. 'Then how will you manage, my dear?' she asked.

'Well, as to that,' Nan said briskly. 'I shall do the work myself for a while, being there en't much else I can do. Then we shall see.' And she looked back at the pile of papers on her desk.

'I disturb you, my dear,' Matilda said. 'I must be on my way.'

'Yes,' Nan agreed. 'You must. There's a deal to do.'

So Matilda kissed her gratefully and left.

Nan worked until her desk was cleared, all through her lunch hour, past tea time, well into the evening. And she'd have gone on even longer, if her weary clerk hadn't come knocking at her door to tell that 'a young gentleman by the name of Easter' was waiting to see her.

'A young gentleman by the name of Easter?' she queried.

'If you please, ma'am, he *said* he was Mr Henry Easter, but being as I've never seen the gentleman before . . . '

'Show him up,' she said. 'He's a distant relation.' And likely to be a deal closer now.

He seemed less sure of himself in her impressive office. She noticed that he hesitated at the door and had to clear his throat several times before he could tell her why he'd come.

229

'It's on Caroline's account,' he said, finally. 'She is very unhappy.'

'That is only to be expected.'

'Yes,' he agreed, 'but I think I know of a way to help her.'

'Then you'd best tell me.'

'She has such a strong character, you see,' he urged. 'She needs something to occupy her, something demanding.'

'And what would you suggest?' Nan asked, seeing that he had some particular occupation in mind, and guessing that it would be marriage.

His answer surprised her. 'With respect, ma'am,' he said, 'I think you should give her a job in your company.'

It was such an obvious solution, now that it had been said. Work. But of course. And why not? She was another Easter to take into the firm. And her presence there would certainly ease the present situation. 'What would she like to do?' she asked. 'Does she have a job in mind?'

'Yes,' he said, smiling at her. 'But she should tell you that herself, I think. She might not take it kindly if she thought I was arranging her life for her.'

How well he understands my headstrong Caroline, Nan thought, admiring him more than ever. 'I will speak to her tonight,' she said. 'It'll be the first thing I do when I get home. I'm uncommon grateful to 'ee, Henry Easter. Would 'ee care to join me for dinner tomorrow?'

In the event it wasn't Caroline she spoke to first that evening. It was Euphemia.

The two girls came tripping down the stairs the minute the front door was opened to her. They looked almost themselves again, alert and bright with a deal more colour in their faces.

'Could we talk to you before you dress for dinner?' Euphemia asked.

'If there's a good fire in the parlour,' Nan said, handing her mantle to the maid.

'Oh, there is,' Caroline said. 'A roaring fire.'

They sat beside it, toasting their toes on the fender. 'Well now,' Nan said. 'What is it?'

'It's Will,' Euphemia said earnestly, her madonna face gilded by the firelight. 'He's terribly unhappy.'

I've had this conversation before, Nan thought, answering with the same words she'd used earlier that evening. 'That's only to be expected, Pheemy.'

'Oh yes,' Euphemia said. 'I know that he must grieve. That's only natural, but there is something else in his grief. Something more.'

Nan waited to be told what it was.

'He feels he is doomed to work in the firm for ever,' Euphemia said. Then realizing that her choice of words might sound insulting, 'Well, not doomed exactly but . . . '

'Trapped,' Caroline said. 'That's how he feels. Trapped.'

'It's the job he's been offered,' Nan said, remembering and understanding at once. 'Mr Dickens' job. You think he should take it, Pheemy?'

'Yes,' Euphemia said seriously. 'I do.'

'Um,' Nan said. 'You could be right. We will talk of it over dinner.'

'You won't tell him that we spoke to you,' Euphemia pleaded. 'I promised not to say anything to anybody.'

'I shall speak of it generally,' Nan promised. 'I have other things I want to discuss too. There's a deal to think about. Howsomever, now I must go up and change, or I shall keep the meal waiting and Cook won't like that. I'm late enough as it is.'

'Will she let him go, do you think?' Euphemia asked her cousin when Nan had gone upstairs.

'We shall soon know,' Caroline said. 'If she talks about it before the roast, she'll do what we want, if it has to wait for the sweet, she won't.'

It was talked about as soon as the first course was served.

'Have you seen Mr Dickens yet?' Nan said to Will, as she raised her spoon to her lips.

'Not since . . . ' Will said.

'Well, then it's high time you did,' his grandmother said, cutting into his hesitation in her decisive way. 'You don't want him to go offering that job of his to somebody else, now do you?'

'But I thought . . . '

231

'I told you you should work with Mr Dickens, did I not?' And when he nodded, 'Very well then. I still think you should. And I think you should tell him so.'

'But who will do Papa's work?'

'Well now, as to that,' Nan said, grinning round the table at them in her old familiar way, 'I've a mind to take another member of my family into the firm.'

They were all puzzled and looked it. 'But who?' Will said.

'Why, Caroline, who else? I've granddaughters as well as grandsons.'

'Nan!' Caroline said with awed astonishment. 'Do you mean it?'

'Never say things I don't mean, child. You should know that by now. Besides I can remember you a-telling me once that you'd join the firm when you were grown up, and what's more, you said you'd extend our trade. Or had 'ee forgot?'

'No,' Caroline said, eyes shining. 'I ain't forgot.' How extraordinary that her grandmother should be talking about all this today, on the very day she'd been remembering it herself, walking in the country with Henry.

'So what will you do, eh?' Nan said. 'Tell me that?'

Oh, that was simple. She'd known what she would do for a very long time. 'I will sell newspapers and books on every railway station. That's what I'll do. It's so bare on those long platforms. A nice little stall would be just the thing to cheer them up. They would make them look more homely and give people something to do while they are waiting. Books would sell like hot cakes.'

Nan could well believe it, but she pressed her further. 'How do 'ee make that out, pray?'

'Haven't you noticed how people behave on trains?' Caroline said. 'They sit there in their seats, and they read their papers if they have them, and they look out of the window, and they fidget, but they don't talk to one another and they never ever look at one another. They'd do anything rather than do that. They need something to occupy their eyes, that's what it is. On a coach journey we used to stop at all sorts of places along the way. You could get out and stretch your legs and buy something to eat and drink while the horses were being changed. But trains don't stop. They just keep on going until you're there. Sometimes you travel for miles and miles before you ever get out of the carriage, and newspapers don't occupy you for very long. So there you all are, with nothing to read, trying not to look at one another. If we offered railway passengers some books to buy for the journey, they would snap them up.' Her cheeks were pink with enthusiasm.

'You could be right,' Nan said. 'We would need to negotiate the concession with the railway owners.'

'And design the stalls,' Caroline said, 'with a nice wide counter and a roof to keep the papers dry and our sign along the top.' Oh, this was the way to make amends to Papa.

'You shall start work after the funeral,' Nan said, and when Euphemia drew in her breath quite shocked at the idea, 'Her father will understand entirely, my dear. He always said work was a sovereign cure for grief.'

'Will people not be offended?' Euphemia worried. 'If Caroline comes out of mourning so soon, I mean.'

'She won't come out of mourning,' Nan said. 'None of us will. No, no, we shall wear black for the full six months, and half mourning for the six months after that, which is only right and proper. Howsomever, a great firm cannot cease to function, even when it loses one of its managing directors. Work must go on. We will speak more of this after the funeral, Caroline. Eat up, my dears. There's saddle of beef to follow.'

It was an extraordinary funeral. There were so many guests there was barely room for them all in the churchyard but they all stood very quietly to listen to the service, murmuring agreement at the fine, true things the Reverend Hopkins was saying in his eulogy.

'John Henry Easter was an honourable man. He was dependable and thorough and responsible. It is ironic that these most admirable traits were the ones that led him to his death, for in his last hour he chose to walk into danger himself rather than to risk the life of another person. We are all impoverished by his death, just as we were enriched by his life. We must give thanks to God for a life so honourably led, and for memories of that life that will stay with us all until we are called to God's Glory in our turn.'

'Amen!' his huge congregation growled. 'Amen!'

And then they all went trooping off to Nan's house in Angel Square, in a clatter of hooves and carriage wheels and a torrent of talk. They brought such a change of mood with them, it was impossible to stay sad, for they filled the house with conversation, with commiseration certainly, but with reminiscence and memory too, tales of old endeavours, remembered jokes. 'A good man,' they said to Nan and Will and Caroline, over and over again. 'A very good man.'

When they finally left, the house was peculiarly quiet.

'Back to London tomorrow,' Nan said. 'It's the quarterly meeting on Thursday week. Just the right time to tell 'em what we're a-going to do.'

Chapter 17

Nan Easter's twenty-seven regional managers were none too pleased when they heard her plans. It was bad enough that Mr William had decided to leave the company, as they told one another afterwards, but to appoint a woman to replace him! Well, that really was the height of folly. Mr Jernegan of the City of London and his friend Mr Maycock of the County of Middlesex were so aggrieved by it that they took themselves off to the nearest hostelry for several pints of porter and considerable complaint. And at their particular invitation 'their very dear friend and valued colleague' Mr Edward Easter went with them.

'You should have been asked to replace Mr John,' Mr Maycock said to Edward. 'That's my opinion of it.' He was a plump gentleman with very slack, rubbery-looking lips and consequently every word he said had to be thoroughly munched. 'You should have been the one.'

'Very true,' Edward said miserably. Because it was. There was nobody so well suited to take command of the firm. His father was too weak and Nan was too old, for all her tough ways. And yet there she'd sat, telling them all she would be 'running the firm for the time being' as if he, Edward Easter, didn't exist. It was deeply hurtful to be overlooked like that. And all done so quickly too, before he'd had the chance to suggest a better arrangement.

'We don't want women in the firm,' Mr Maycock said, stroking his mutton-chop whiskers so as to pull his mouth back into realignment. 'You should have taken Mr William's position, Mr Edward, sir, at the very least, and after that *we* should have become a full management committee, with voting powers. That's what I say.' He'd been saying the same thing to the other regional managers for more than a year now, but he'd never found one brave enough to suggest it to Mrs Easter. Lily-livered lot!

'Petticoat government,' Mr Jernegan said, signalling to the pot-boy that their glasses needed replenishment, 'petticoat government is the very devil. No good ever comes of it, on account of it ain't natural.'

'No good will ever come of Miss Caroline Easter and her meddling,' Mr Maycock agreed. 'That's a certain sure thing. Bookstalls on railway stations! I ask you! New-fangled nonsense, that's what it is. The public won't stand for it.'

'I agree with you, Mr Maycock,' Edward Easter said, nodding his fair head so energetically that his hair bounced up from his forehead. 'I tell you if there were any way I could persuade her straight out of the firm again I would take it. No matter what the cost.' He was more than a little drunk, his speech slurred and his blue eyes bleary, but there was no doubting the sincerity of his sentiments. Now that cousin Will was leaving, he *should* have been the one to take his place. It was insulting to give such a position to cousin Caroline. Downright insulting.

'Scandal,' Mr Jernegan said, slopping his next glass of porter as he tried to raise it to his lips. 'A nice juicy scandal to frighten her off. That's what we need. Petticoat government is the very devil.'

'Perhaps she'll get married,' Edward hoped, 'and settle down with her husband, a nice long way away, and raise a few kids.'

'Meantime,' Mr Maycock said, munching moistly, 'we've to watch her wasting the firm's money on that hare-brained scheme of hers. Bookstalls! I ask you. Your very good health, Mr Easter sir.'

'Nothing will come of it,' Mr Jernegan promised, belching slightly. 'Because nobody will take it seriously. And for why? Because it's a stupid idea. A very stupid idea. The stupidest idea I ever heard. Railways are nothing. A flash in the pan. That's what railways are. Never amount to anything, won't railways.' He fumbled his watch out of his waistcoat pocket and tried to focus his eyes upon it, and failed, frowning at the mist of shifting numerals. 'I tell you what,' he said importantly. 'We were better off in the old days with the coaches. You knew where you were with coaches. Coaches didn't mean having *women* foisted on you.'

'All this change is so unnecessary,' Mr Maycock complained, spraying spit into his porter. 'Much better off – things stay as they are.'

In the Strand outside the window, carts and carriages and coaches clogged the road as they'd been doing all his life, struggling through the crush a few feet at a time, rough with bad temper and worse language. 'Much better off – things stay as they are.'

It was unfortunate for Mr Maycock that the managing director of the mighty London and Birmingham railway didn't share his opinions. and doubly unfortunate that the same managing director was none other than Mr William Chaplin, Sheriff of the City of London, who was a life-long friend of Mrs Nan Easter and a man who not only accepted change but encouraged and caused it. He had once been known as the coach king, because he ran the largest fleet of stage coaches in the country, but being a shrewd business man, he was one of the first to see the potential of Mr Stephenson's invention. He had sold his coach companies while he could still command a good price for them and transferred all his capital and all his energy into the railways. Now he was a managing director of two London based companies, held shares in several others, and was constantly on the look-out for ways to increase his trade and influence.

So when Nan sent him a note to his office in Fleet Street requesting a business meeting 'at your earliest convenience' his answer was prompt and positive. If Mrs Easter and her granddaughter would care to meet him at four of the clock the following afternoon, he would be more than happy to see them.

'I will strike this first bargain,' Nan said to Caroline as they walked along the Strand towards the meeting, 'as Mr Chaplin is an old friend. Watch closely. See how 'tis done and when you've learned the art you shall manage the next.'

'Yes,' Caroline promised breathlessly. Oh, she would watch most carefully, for so much depended on this meeting. It was her chance to make good. To show them all that she was every bit as valuable to the firm as that wretched Edward. Maybe even as good as Will. And why not, when they were brother and sister? But most important of all it was the way to redeem her unkindness. She would increase trade in Papa's firm and do it so well and so dramatically that nobody could fail to notice. He would see it too, wherever he was, and know that she loved him and was trying to make amends.

'Here we are!' Nan said, and whisked them into a brown hall and up two flights of scrubbed stairs and straight into a wide office full of wide furniture where an elderly gentleman in a beautiful brown cloth coat was holding out his hand in greeting. 'Nan, my dear, I'm glad to see you well. I heard your sad news.'

'A bad business,' Nan said, briefly. 'The storm, you know. This is my grand-daughter Caroline.'

He seated them before the fire and listened, sombre-faced and attentive, while Nan outlined her proposition. And Caroline sat in the warm and watched and listened too. It was a fascinating experience, for there were so many undercurrents beneath the words, so many moments when she could see them both struggling for mastery even though neither moved or said a word. They were like two lions she'd once seen in the Zoological Gardens poised for a fight; they'd been so still that she'd thought them sleepy until she noticed the tips of their tails twitching.

The deal was struck in twenty hard-thinking minutes. For the princely rent of £1,320 per annum, A. Easter and Sons had acquired the sole concession to open a large bookstall on Euston station and lesser ones on all the other stations along the full length of the London to Birmingham railway.

'Now,' Nan said to Caroline, when their carriage had arrived to collect them as arranged, 'you must tell me all you've learned.'

Caroline settled herself onto the upholstered seat and collected her thoughts to answer. 'First,' she said, 'you ask for more than you expect so as to leave room for your opponent to bargain.'

238

'Bravo!' Nan applauded as the carriage began to move. 'First rule of good business.'

'Which means that you need to know the sort of price he expects to pay before you start negotations.'

'Of course.'

'And also the lowest price he would accept and how much he will want to negotiate?'

'Yes.'

'How is it done, Nan?'

'By knowledge of his other deals, knowledge of the man, information about the financial state of his company. And instinct. What else did you notice?'

'That you chose a straight annual rent rather than a percentage of the profits.'

'Aye, I did. Can you imagine why?'

'Because you expect a percentage of the profits to come to a higher figure, I daresay.'

'I made a wise decision when I invited you into the firm, my dear,' Nan said with great satisfaction. 'You have a business head on your shoulders and no mistake. We will write to the London and South Western tomorrow and see how you make out there.'

For the first time since John's death, dinner that evening was quite a jolly occasion, for Henry was invited and everybody about the table had been out of the house that day and busy with matters they enjoyed.

Euphemia had gone back to Clerkenwell Green and was full of news about her pupils. 'Josser has been taken on as a monitor,' she told them. 'He's horribly conscientious, but Jimmy thinks he will calm down with experience.'

Henry had been to see the Editor of the *Weekly Herald*, in some trepidation, he had to admit, because he hadn't managed to write a single poem about the railways, what with one thing and another. To his great relief he'd been granted two more months to complete the work, 'and that should be ample. Now.'

And Will had been to Devonshire Terrace to see Mr Dickens, and was full of subdued excitement because he was going to be sent to Ireland to report on the potato famine there. 'I'm to leave in the New Year,' he said, 'and if I do well I'm to be sent abroad again.'

'Then you will need a valet,' Nan said. 'And here's Tom Thistlethwaite ready and to hand.' She'd taken several of John's servants into her household where most of them had settled usefully, but so far she hadn't found work for Tom, who very plainly needed a master to care for.

'I could do worse,' Will said.

So that was settled.

'What plans do you have for tomorrow?' Nan asked them. She was delighted to hear that they all knew exactly what they would be doing. They would ride together in the morning, as they usually did when the weather was good enough, and then they all meant to go their separate ways. Euphemia would be back at the school, Henry would compose a poem, Will intended to write an article on the damage the storm had done on the Thames and in the London docks, and Caroline said she was going to visit a publisher called Mr Longman.

'He is producing a new popular series of well known works,' she said. 'Coleridge's *Table Talk* for instance, and some of Mr Wordsworth's poetry and Mr Tennyson's. If it is the right price, I think we should buy.'

'And what is the right price, pray?' Nan asked, spreading horseradish sauce on a long lean slice of beef.

'Sixpence,' Caroline said at once. 'Sixpence per book. That's quite enough to spend on a journey. A sixpenny book from a sixpenny stall.'

And she will do it, Nan thought, beaming at her. She's a child after my own heart.

The next few weeks were intensely busy. Euphemia spent every afternoon in Clerkenwell and returned home dirty and exhausted but so well pleased with her endeavours that they were all happy for her, despite her dishevelled appearance. Henry worked diligently at his poetry and completed one verse almost to his satisfaction and came to dine with them three times a week. The first edition of the *Daily News* was published to great acclaim and with one of Will's articles on the last page.

And Caroline negotiated with all three of the remaining London railway companies, designed the stalls and contracted two companies to make them and erect them, ordered her sixpenny books from Mr Longman, and persuaded Messrs Chapman and Hall to produce a 'Select Library of Fiction' especially for Easter's.

By the middle of February, when Will left for Ireland, with Tom in attendance, the first six stalls were up and doing business.

'I suppose I shall have to buy a book for the journey now,' he teased, as he and Henry and Caroline and Euphemia arrived at Paddington station. 'If I can get near the stall!' For they could barely see the sides of their little wooden shop for eager customers, gloved hands stretched out to buy, hats and bonnets nodding, and the huge skirts of the ladies swaying and rotating with excitement. 'Now there's a subject for a poem, Henry.'

Henry didn't think much of it, but he didn't say so, for that would have meant admitting that he was finding it very hard to compose his commissioned odes. It was all very well for poets like Keats and Shelley. They could choose poetical subjects, like skylarks and autumn and the wild west winds. But there was nothing poetical about railways.

Above his head the glass roof of the station curved like a wide white sky, full of reflected light and risen steam and an accumulation of captured sound, the rhythmical chuff and clatter of departing trains; brakes squealing arrival; the wheel-tapper's clang; the shriek of whistles; and the cheerful hooting of the engines reverberating like owls. Carriage wheels crunched the cobbles, horses snorted, and the high cavern echoed with a cacophony of voices, porters' cries and the newsvendors' repeated song, the murmur of goodbyes and the delighted shrill of greeting. How could he be expected to make a poem from such chaos?

The guard was blowing his whistle. People were rushing about him, climbing aboard. Tom Thistlethwaite had the door open for Will.

'You must write to us, Will, as soon as you arrive,' Caroline instructed, because she knew that was what Euphemia wanted to say and couldn't.

'I promise,' he said, climbing aboard.

'Well, see that you do,' she scolded, teasing him. 'If I know you at all, brother Will, you'll be so busy reporting, you'll forget all about us slaving away at home.'

'I promise,' he said again. And he kissed both the young women, warmly but absently, his mind already travelling on ahead of him.

It was a wasted vow. Departure brought such an overwhelming sense of release that he'd forgotten what he was saying before the train pulled out of the station. He was on his way to Ireland. Mr William Easter, foreign correspondent of the *Daily News*. It was like beginning his life all over again.

It was a long cold journey to Chester; the coaches that carried them along the north coast of Wales were horribly uncomfortable; and the crossing, in a rank, tossing cockleshell of a boat, was every bit as bad as he had expected. But even then he didn't care. The coast of Ireland was visible on the western horizon, a dark smudgy promise of fame and fortune. Mr William Easter, foreign correspondent.

Dublin seemed a settled city after the noise and bustle of London, quiet and staid and rather old-fashioned and with no sign of famine anywhere, as far as he could see. There were beggars at every corner, the usual stinkingly dirty creatures, but they didn't look as though they were starving, and although the street sweepers were even filthier and more ragged than their London counterparts, they seemed to be fed.

But the Irish journalists had another tale to tell. 'Sure,' they said, ''tis a terrible situation. Total failure o' the crop so 'tis. Tree quarters of it gone to ruination.' There was typhus in County Cork and the flux in Kilkenny. The workhouses were filled to bursting, and people were dying like flies. 'A terrible situation. You ask Mr O'Connell here.'

Mr O'Connell was a tousled man with a frizz of ginger hair and a bristle of ginger whiskers.

'You'll need to see it yourself to believe it,' he said. 'That's about the size and scale of it. If you'll meet wit' me here tomorrow morning, I'll escort ye, so I will. 'Tis time the British knew the trut' of it.'

He was as good as his word, although the cart he'd hired for their journey was a ramshackle affair drawn by a dispirited donkey who had to stop every few hundred yards to cough and wheeze. It was still raining, in a continuous drizzle that had them all well dampened before the donkey coughed to its last halt out in the countryside.

The green fields rolled like breakers all around them and to the south the Wicklow mountains were blue with rain, but there was no sign of life in any direction, no beasts in the fields, no standing crops, no labourers, nothing except the rough grass sighing in the wind and a pungent sickly smell that pulsed towards them through the rain.

'Tatties,' Mr O'Connell explained when he saw Will sniffing the air. 'From that pile over there, d'ye see?'

There was a dark hump among the grasses. They walked across to examine it and the stink grew more nauseous with every step. There were hundreds of potatoes in the heap and every single one was black and rotten and scored with oozing sores.

'Don't touch 'em,' Mr O'Connell warned, 'or the air will be too foul for us to breathe.'

'No fear of that,' Will said, recoiling. 'They're bad enough just to look at.'

''Tis the same all over Ireland,' Mr O'Connell said, backing away from the heap with his hand covering his mouth. ''Tis the quickest disease that's ever been known to man. They come out o' the earth as sound and sweet as a bell and wit'in the hour they're stinking to high heaven. Nobody knows the cause or the cure. And the people die like flies by the rubbish dumps of them.'

'Are there people hereabouts?' Will asked, following his new friend away from the smell.

'There may be,' Mr O'Connell said grimly. 'If we're not too late. Come wit' me.'

Now Will saw that there was a low dry-stone building further down the field. He'd done little more than glance at it when they arrived, because he'd assumed it was a ruin. Half the roof had fallen in and there was a gaping hole in one of the walls, but that was where they were headed.

As they approached Will saw that there was a dirty piece

of sacking nailed across the hole where the door should have been, but apart from the patter of rain on the stones, there was no sound. The two men stooped beneath the sacking and crept inside, moving slowly and with caution, for neither of them were at all sure what they would find. Despite the hole in the roof it was dark between the walls and the air was foetid with decay, but to Will's relief the place appeared to be empty. There was foul straw scattered on the earth floor and a pile of grey rags in one corner, but that was all.

'They've gone,' he said to Mr O'Connell.

The rags stirred and coughed, with a dry harsh rattle like the cough of sick cattle, and the hair stood on the nape of Will's neck, as a long, grey, bony arm rose from the midst of the pile and a skeleton's hand uncurled to claw at the air.

'Water,' a faint voice pleaded. 'Water, for the love o' God.' A gaunt face lifted slowly from the rags, a gaunt, aged face hauling itself up as though it were being held down by some fearful invisible weight, blue eyes glazed in deep black hollows, every bone clearly visible beneath slack grey skin, a gaunt, aged face framed by the long black hair of a young woman.

Mr O'Connell was at her elbow with a stoop full of brackish water, and the woman drank, sucking the liquid into her mouth as if it pained her, and falling back afterwards totally exhausted. And now that his eyes had adjusted to the light inside the hut, Will could see that there were other bodies among the rags, small legs like sticks, a distended belly trembling, an emaciated baby lying on its back with its mouth wide open in a soundless wail.

'This is a nightmare,' he said to Mr O'Connell, staring in horror.

'Then see that your countrymen share it,' Mr O'Connell said.

That afternoon Will wrote the first of his dispatches, describing the hovel and the rotting potatoes and the warehouses full of corn that the starving couldn't buy. He wrote with such passion and speed that he made his fingers sore.

'We talk of the power of England,' he concluded, 'her navy,

her gold, her resources – Oh yes, and her enlightened states-men – while the broad fact is that she cannot keep her children perishing by hunger. Something must be done!'

The next day he and Tom set off on their travels, journeying south. He would see this starving country for himself and report upon it as fully and accurately as he could. It was his job. At last.

Back in London Henry Easter was still finding it a struggle to find any words at all. He'd made more than twenty attempts to finish his ode to Euston station and none of them were any good. They didn't scan and they didn't rhyme. In fact if he was honest about them, they didn't even make sense.

It was miserably disappointing, and especially now, when he'd been accepted as Caroline's suitor and it was more impor-tant than ever to make his mark upon the literary world. When her first six months' mourning was over and they got married, he had to be in a position to keep her, and what was more, to keep her in Nan's high and rather extravagant style. And how could he do that on his annuity? Why, it hardly kept him. It was all very demoralizing.

All through the spring he tried to compose, prowling about in his sitting room every evening with a cold compress held to his aching head. During the afternoons, while Caroline was busy with publishers and railway tycoons, probably making more money than he could envisage, he haunted the stations, notebook in hand, hoping for inspiration that never came.

When Caroline or Euphemia asked him how his work was progressing he told them it was going well, of course, for it would never have done to appear incompetent. But the dead-lines passed one after another and he hadn't finished a single poem or earned a single penny, and he was no nearer to being in a position to support a wife. And to make matters worse he couldn't court Caroline while she was in mourning, that would have been improper, and the busier she became the less inter-ested she seemed in their future together.

His brother Joseph told him not to worry, which was no help at all, and his sister Jane suggested that he might consider some other way of earning a living, but that didn't help him either because he couldn't do it. Finally and in some despair he decided to go and talk to Nan Easter. She was fierce and she was powerful but she understood how very much he wanted to marry Caroline and her advice would be sound.

'She's in a powerful bad temper,' her clerk said, when he presented himself at the Easter headquarters. He'd had an inkwell thrown at his head not half an hour before. His jacket was splodged and stained to prove it. 'A-studyin' Mr John's timetables, she is. I'd give her the go-by if I was you.'

But he'd already been heard.

'Who is it?' Nan's voice shouted from behind her door.

'It's only me, Mrs Easter,' Henry said putting his head round the door, but keeping his feet in the corridor just in case he had to make a run for it.

'Well, come in, come in,' she said tetchily. 'Don't dither.'

'I could come back another time if it's inconvenient,' he offered.

'Damned timetables,' she said, scowling at the pile of books that littered her desk. 'Can't make head or tail of the beggars.' John's meticulous work was too thorough and subtle for her quick mind. And besides, she was cross and ill-humoured that day because Frederick had written to tell her that in October he was going to relinquish his seat as a member of parliament so as to spend more of his time in Westmoreland. And how he imagined she could afford to take six months away from the business every year and join him there as he suggested was more than she could bear to contemplate. Blamed fool!

Her distress was too plain to be ignored. 'Could I help you in any way?' he offered.

'You'd need to be a genius to understand all this,' she said, stirring the paper about in anger. Her white hair sprang above her forehead in furious curls, and the two deep frown lines above her brown eyes were thunder black. 'A nice, simple summary. That's what we need. Something to tell us where to send our merchandise and when, so's I don't have to go a-rummaging all through this lot every day. My heart alive, 'tis enough to make a saint wild, so 'tis.'

'I can't claim to be a genius,' he said, smiling at her, 'but I could look at it if you'd like. See if it made sense to me. I've a good head for mathematics.'

'Do as you please,' she said ungraciously. ''Tis all one to me. I'm sick to death of the blamed things. I'm off to the warehouse to see Billy.'

And she was gone before he had a chance to say anything else, leaving the room in a sudden silence, with the fire licking in the grate and the folders sliding from her desk.

He should have been shocked by her bad temper, but he wasn't. He was full of admiration for her, because she was renowned for being old and tough and yet she could admit defeat and weakness. If I can help her, I will, he thought, for she is a very great lady.

He spent the rest of the afternoon poring over John's careful plans, following them from the very first entry on the very first page. When the clerk came tip-toeing in to light the lamps and bank up the fire he was so immersed in their complications that he didn't even look up, and when the building closed for the night he gathered up all the folders and took them home with him, leaving a note for Nan to explain what he'd done and to promise he would return them in the morning.

They kept him awake all night, following the thread of each timetable year by year, and gradually unravelling the pattern of John Easter's plan. Although Henry had suffered from John's intransigence, the further he read the more he understood the man. Secretive and biased, certainly, but painstaking too, and as determined in his own way as his daughter was in hers. It was an admirable, adaptable plan, and would run as well in 1846 as it had done in 1820. As daylight dimmed the candles and he finished the last page of the last book he realized that he not only understood the plan but could put it into operation. Mathematics had always come easy to him but until that moment it had never occurred to him to value that particular skill.

'My heart alive!' Nan said, when he told her. 'Could 'ee so? Then I suggest you do it, my dear. I'd be uncommon grateful to 'ee. Providing you can spare the time from your poetry.'

'To tell you the truth,' he said, 'I ain't so much of a poet as I thought.' Somehow or other it was possible for him to confess it to her, especially now that he could see that there might be another way to make his mark on the world.

She grinned at him like a conspirator. 'Aye,' she said. 'I

thought as much. Well then, there's a job tailor-made for 'ee if ee'll take it.'

He hesitated, even though he knew it was what he wanted. 'I'm honoured to have such a position offered,' he said, smiling at her, 'but I wouldn't want to cause any difficulties.'

'Difficulties?' she said, as though such an idea was ridiculous. 'Why should there be difficulties?'

'It is a post of some responsibility,' he said. 'It might be more proper for it to be given to a member of your immediate family.'

His delicacy pleased her. 'None of 'em want it, my dear, or they'd have took it long before this. And besides, if you en't a member of my family now, you very soon will be.'

So he accepted her offer, moving in to John's old office, and with a salary the same as Will's had been when he started in the firm. For as his new employer said, 'We must all be fair, square and above board in this.'

To his relief Caroline was very pleased with the decision, welcoming him into the firm as her equal and saying she couldn't think of anything more fitting, and by the time Will came home from Ireland at the beginning of April he was settled and almost entirely accepted. Only Edward and his two discontented cronies on the regional board had reservations, and for the time being they were keeping them to themselves.

Chapter 18

'I'd almost forgotten what I looked like out of mourning,' Caroline said, admiring her reflection in the cheval mirror. Her grief for her father's death and the custom which required her to wear ugly clothes had always been two quite separate things in her mind, one an intense daily misery and the other merely a social necessity she was glad to be done with. 'We've been in black for ages.'

'Six months,' Euphemia corrected mildly.

'Well, it felt like ages,' Caroline said. 'And now it's summer and we can wear some of our pretty things again. I feel like a new person.' And it was true, for even her misery had lifted. The dress she had chosen for her first day out of purdah was a lovely thing, a creamy muslin with a triple-tiered skirt delicately printed with tiny lilac leaves. It had been a favourite when she first had it made three whole years ago, and she liked it more than ever now that she was in half-mourning after all that depressing black. 'Ain't you glad it's June, Pheemy? I shall wear my white silk for dinner tonight.'

Euphemia had chosen a lilac and white striped cotton for her afternoon at the ragged school and she'd been dressed and ready a good half an hour before her cousin. Now she sat beside their bedroom window enjoying the green of the gardens. 'I suppose you and Henry will be married soon,' she said.

'Oh, I'm in no hurry,' Caroline said lightly, smoothing the frills on her skirt.

'But he is, I daresay.'

'He don't say so. No, no, Pheemy. It'll be time enough to think of marriage when I've got all these deals settled. Mr Chaplin is the major shareholder of the London and North Western, you know, and that's bound to be a help to us. Even so, it's a very big company. It could be difficult. Do I look business-like, do you think?'

'He loves you so dearly, Carrie.'

'Yes,' Caroline admitted. 'I know he does. He's a dear loving creature even if he does have a short temper, and the firm couldn't run without him. I daresay we shall marry by and by and be very happy together. But not just now. I've a deal too much to do.'

'You sound just like Nan,' Euphemia said, intending a gentle rebuke.

But Caroline took the words as a compliment. 'Do I?' she said, grinning at the thought. 'Well, if that ain't the nicest thing you could say to me then I don't know what is. Especially now with this North Eastern deal to manage. If I can be like Nan in Mr Wellborough's office this afternoon, then I shall do well enough.'

'Poor Henry,' Euphemia said. 'I don't believe you want to marry him at all.'

Caroline left the mirror and walked across to the window to join her cousin. 'To tell you the truth,' she admitted seriously, 'I don't really know what I do want. Sometimes I think I love him dearly, and I'd marry him tomorrow, if he asked me, and sometimes I'm so busy I barely give him a thought. When he first said he loved me, I was so happy it made me tremble, but now I feel so little emotion, even when we are sitting side by side at dinner or the theatre. I sometimes wonder whether I ain't gone cold towards him.' All that wonderful, tremulous excitement was missing. He could take her hand and raise it to his lips when they said goodbye and she felt nothing. It was so disappointing she preferred not to think about it. 'Oh dear!'

Euphemia caught those hands and squeezed them comfortably. 'Grief turns the world topsy-turvy,' she said. 'That's what it is. Things will come to rights now that we are out of mourning. When we go to the Vauxhall Gardens, perhaps.'

* * *

Will and Henry decided against their proposed trip to the Gardens. They wanted to go to Richmond instead, to meet the Four In Hand Club at the Star and Garter, because they both drove a four in hand and this was the first meet of the season.

'Well, why not?' Caroline said, when the change of plan was mooted. 'Vauxhall will wait and it will be a treat to be driving in the country.' Her meeting with Mr Wellborough had been extremely successful and she was in an expansive mood.

So they went to Richmond, with Tom Thistlethwaite riding as footman and chaperone to the ladies.

The Star and Garter always served the best lunches they could contrive for the Four In Hand Club, for they were valued customers with plenty of money to spend, and the better they were fed the more often they came. On that Saturday the cooks had excelled themselves. There were oyster patties, and eel pie with brown bread and butter, there was lobster salad, and pickled herring, there were veal pies and honey-roast hams, little roast capons and a side of beef big enough to feed an army, and port and claret and hock and moselle on every table. It was, as Will said when he proposed the toast, a reward for the hard work they'd all been doing during the winter.

Caroline tried every dish, to Will's delight and Henry's astonishment. And even Euphemia had a good appetite for once, although she said it upset her to think how well they were eating when the children of the ragged school had so little. And after the meal they went strolling out into the gardens to admire the view.

The Star and Garter was a solid Georgian building, three storeys high and two colonnaded entrances, a central semi-circular bay and its own artesian well, no less. It stood at the top of Richmond Hill opposite the park gates and its gardens sloped down to the river in a series of well-kept terraces. The view from the top terrace was spectacular. After the speed and excitement of their ride and the cheerful company of their meal Caroline and Euphemia were quite stunned by it.

Below them the River Thames curved between lush meadows, here skirting a green island with a froth of foam, there providing a gentle watering place for a herd of brown-backed cattle. Its waters mirrored the blue of the sky above it and the luscious greens of the trees beside it, and were dappled with olive-coloured waves that fanned out from the triangular wakes of the skiffs and barks that drifted lazily upon it, their sails cloud-white and their hulls bright with rich colour, chestnut, scarlet, royal blue, grass-green, gold and purple. Between them, scores of swans trailed their lesser wakes like black-edged darts, and the air was shrill with black and white housemartins swooping over the water.

Beyond the river they could see the entire valley of the Thames, spreading for mile upon mile, from the heaths and downs of Surrey to the beechy hills of Buckinghamshire and the haze-blue heights of Berkshire, countless meadows, where sheep and cows wandered at will, thick woods and copses, the variegated green of their foliage shadowed with purple and indigo blue, and here and there among the trees the turrets and towers of new villas and ancient palaces, the dark shapes of Hampton Court, the Queen's white house at Kew, the long chestnut avenues of Bushey Park. Neither of the two girls had ever seen so far, so clearly.

'Why, it's wondrous,' Caroline said, 'and so beautiful. Don't you think so, Pheemy?'

'It is so peaceful,' Euphemia said. 'What a marvellous thing it would be to live in a house on this hill, and see this view every day of your life. It would be a daily blessing.'

'Better than travelling the world?' Will asked, teasing her.

'Oh much, much better, although I don't suppose you would agree with me.'

'When I was young,' Henry confessed, 'I used to look at the view from my room at Ippark and think how wonderful our estate was. I used to wish the land could be mine, you know, so that I could live there for ever and never move away from it. Land you see. Has a hold on you.'

Caroline glanced sideways at him and was moved to see that his face wore the same haughty expression she'd seen on the day they first met. And she understood, without words or conscious thought, that she was looking at sadness and vulnerability, not hauteur, and suddenly she yearned to comfort him.

'But this view is even better,' he said, making an effort to recover his humour, 'damn me if it ain't.'

'I don't see why the older brother always has to inherit,'

Caroline said, springing to his defence. 'Why couldn't the estate have been shared between you?'

'Never is,' Henry said, with studied cheerfulness. 'The eldest always inherits. That's how it is. Always was, always will be. Younger sons have to fend for themselves.'

'Well, it's not fair. Papa divided *his* capital in two equal halves.'

'That's capital. Land is different.' And again that vulnerable hauteur.

Affection for him welled up into Caroline's throat like tears. How terrible to be treated so, denied an inheritance and left to fend for himself. How unfair. He should never have been treated so badly. She would make amends to him, here and now. 'When we marry,' she said, 'this is where we will rent a house. Right here on this hill. And you shall have this view to lift your spirits every single day. That'll be a jolly sight better than Ippark, now won't it?'

The haughty expression was gone, washed away by a current of other emotions, amazement, disbelief, hope, love. He caught her hands in his, crushing them, his eyes suddenly moist and his mouth as red as wine. The patience of that long, long mourning was breached beyond repair. 'When?' he said. 'Oh my dearest girl, when will it be?'

He loves me so much, Caroline thought, dazzled by his emotion. There was only one possible answer to such a question and she gave it at once. 'Now,' she said. 'As soon as we can. We will find the house this afternoon.'

'Oh Carrie,' Will said, laughing at her, 'you can't just walk off and find a house, just like that.'

'Yes, I can,' she said.

And being Caroline Easter, she did.

It only took her one visit to one estate agency to discover that there were three suitable houses available on Richmond Hill and that she could inspect them all that afternoon. Will protested that this was not the way he'd intended to spend his time, but they all went along with her just the same because she was so determined. And the second house she saw was ideal.

It was a corner house, and from the front it appeared to be

rather plain, three storeyed and double fronted with the rather dull balance of all Georgian buildings, but the interior was a revelation. Because of the slope of the land the rear of the house had four storeys, not three, and in order to make the most of the view all the most important rooms were at the back and designed around sweeping bow windows. There were twelve bedrooms and a nursery suite, a vast kitchen and very adequate accommodation for housekeeper and butler, servants' quarters in the attics and the basement. And in addition to all that, three superlative rooms in which to entertain, a dining room with two dumb waiters in cupboards on either side of the fireplace, a withdrawing room and library lit by that splendid bow window, and a ballroom with no less than three bow windows all giving out to a paved terrace where steps led down to the garden.

'With new decorations and suitable furnishings it will be perfect,' Caroline decided. 'Don't you think so, Henry?'

Henry really didn't know what he thought. The speed of her decision had left him far behind. He had a vague feeling that he would rather have found their house himself and told her about it afterwards like any other husband would have done; and he wasn't at all sure that a home as expensive as this one was really within his pocket, even on the salary Nan was paying him; and for a few wistful seconds he found himself wishing for a reappearance of the vulnerable Caroline he'd loved so much and so easily when her father died, so that he could look after her again and make decisions on her behalf. But there was no time for such thoughts. So he said yes, it was a magnificent house, but shouldn't he have spoken to Nan first?

'Whatever for?' she asked, laughing at him.

'Why,' he said, speaking as softly as he could because he was mindful of the ears of the estate agent, who was trying to make himself unobtrusive over by the bay window, 'to ask for your hand.'

She laughed more than ever. 'Why, we're long past that,' she said. 'Ain't we, Will? You've been my accepted suitor for months and months, Henry Osmond. All we have to do now is to decide where we mean to marry and to agree upon the date. Now, shall we take this house?'

So the house was taken and then the four of them set off for a drive about the town, down Richmond Hill to the green, which was a wide grassy square surrounded by elm trees, and bordered by a terrace of fine red brick houses called Maids of Honour Row. Sheep grazed quietly in the sunshine and blackbirds sang among the leaves as the four in hand trotted past, heading towards the parish church and the centre of the town, where there were several shops that Caroline said looked 'most promising'.

'Would you wait here for us,' she said to Will, 'while Henry and I take a little look?'

So Tom put the chocks down and looked after the horses while Will and Euphemia took a stroll towards the river and their two companions went striding off along the High Street.

'She's so quick,' Euphemia said, adjusting her parasol against the glare of the sun. 'I can't keep up with her.'

'She always was,' Will said. 'Even as a little thing she was always making snap decisions. She ran away from home once in the middle of a blizzard. It was nothing short of a miracle she wasn't killed. Still, there it is. We shan't change her now, even if we wanted to, and I'm not at all sure we'd want to, would we? She's darling as she is. We must just hope rashness don't lead her astray, that's all.'

'She has made the right decision today, surely?'

'To marry?' he said wryly. 'Well, you know my views upon that subject.'

The excitement of the day made Euphemia bold. 'I do,' she said, 'but I think you are wrong.'

'It's a matter of opinion,' he said easily, 'and of no consequence either way.'

Then there was a long silence as neither of them could think what to say, he because he had no intention of pursuing the subject, she because she was afraid she might have spoken out of turn. They had reached an elegant bridge across the Thames and there was no sign of Caroline and Henry.

'Mr Dickens is to leave the *Daily News* at the end of the month,' Will said at last, as they stood upon the river bank together.

'Oh dear,' Euphemia commiserated. 'Why is that? Is it failing?'

'Failing? I should just think not. It's doing very well. We

255

started with a circulation of four thousand at fivepence a copy and now we are selling to more than twenty thousand people and we've halved the price. Oh no, it's in a very healthy condition, our paper.'

'Then why is Mr Dickens leaving?'

'I don't think he ever intended to stay for long,' Will said sadly. 'He meant to get us started and then leave us to our own devices. He told us his business was writing novels, and that's true enough in all conscience.'

'You will miss him.'

'Yes, we will,' Will admitted, smiling at her. 'He'll be in and out, I daresay. He ain't a man to cut his friends.' But the sigh he gave belied his optimism.

'I wonder what Nan will say when she hears about the house,' Euphemia said, feeling it might help him to change the subject.

'She will applaud,' Will said. 'Being they're two of a kind, our Nan and Caroline.'

And of course he was right. Wedding plans were made at dinner that very evening, brisk and business-like. Rattlesden church for the service because that was what Caroline wanted, Euphemia for bridesmaid, Will to give the bride away, Henry's brother to be best man, and all on the first Thursday in July, because all the current deals should be completed by then, and Will would be in England, and it was the day of the week when the Easter family could be most easily spared from their work. By ten o'clock the guest list had been drawn up, ready for the invitations to be sent in the morning.

'July,' Euphemia said happily, when it was all arranged. 'It's a perfect month to get married. Think of all the lovely weather you'll have.'

As it turned out, it was the hottest July for fifty years and on most days the temperature was over ninety in the shade. The prestigious people who crushed into the church of St Nicholas at Rattlesden that Thursday afternoon were soon hot and sticky in their fashionable clothes and the ceremony was wafted by the rhythmical whirr and flutter of their fans.

Not that the bride and groom paid much attention to any of it, she because she was still locked away from all emotion, he because he was too dizzy with desire to concentrate on anything except her delicious proximity. He was so overpoweringly aware of her it was painful to stand still beside her, breathing in the salty scent of those lace covered arms, watching a tremulous pulse throbbing under the milky skin of her throat, and her mouth so soft and as red as raspberries, and her breasts full and tempting in her beautiful white gown.

But with careful prompting from her Uncle James they managed to make their vows with only a few mistakes, and to sign the register with nervous hands but more or less legibly, and Miss Caroline Easter was declared to have changed her title if not her name. And then the entire company exploded out into the sunshine and the hot air was a-bubble of rose petals and a photographer was waiting with one of those new camera contraptions all set up on its tripod, like some squat long-legged bird, and bride, groom, best man, bridesmaid and brother were lined up in the porch to have their picture taken. It was a very long-winded business which required them all to stand perfectly still while the photographer counted to sixty, so when it was over and their guests gave them a cheer, they were all quite giggly with relief. Except Caroline.

While the rest of the group went chattering towards the carriages that would take them back to Bury and the reception at the Athenaeum, she went quietly off by herself to find her father's grave. And her new husband stood back and let her go, because he knew what it was she wanted to do.

It was blisteringly hot in the churchyard. Even the headstones were warm to the touch and the grass was burnt brown. Caroline laid her bouquet on her parents' grave, and knelt down on the rough ground in all her finery to say a prayer to the mother she'd never known and to ask forgiveness of her father for the last time.

'I am married now,' she said, when the prayer was done. 'I will be a credit to you both, I promise. I've done well by you already, haven't I? Oh, you must think I have. And I will do even better now.'

A frond of maidenhair fern curled about her mother's name, 'Harriet Easter 1799-1826, who departed this life aged 27 years', and two moss roses drooped in the heat against the newer inscription 'also her husband, John Henry Easter 1792–1845'. But she couldn't feel their presence at all. She couldn't feel anything. No sorrow, no happiness, no relief. Mama was just a painted face in the portrait that now hung in Nan's drawing room, Papa a remembered figure stooped over his books at that great desk of his. It was a great disappointment, because she'd arranged to have her wedding in this place so that she could lay the ghosts of her unkindness to him for good and all. And now she couldn't do it.

At the top of Aunt Annie's may tree a blackbird fluted, its high clear joyous song echoing into the shining sky. 'Married. Married. For better for worse, for richer for poorer, in sickness and in health . . . God's Holy ordinance . . . give thee my troth. Treeee. Treeee. Two-eeee.' I ought to be happy about that at least, she thought. But she couldn't feel anything.

Henry was standing behind her, his hands warm on her shoulders. 'We must go now,' he said gently, 'or we shall be too late for the reception. All the others have left.'

She rose to her feet, sighing slightly, her face pale and withdrawn.

'I love you so much,' he said, wishing he knew how to comfort her. He wanted to hold her in his arms and smother her with kisses. But he could hardly do that in the middle of a graveyard. 'So much.'

'Yes,' she said. 'I know you do.' But even her voice sounded distant.

He led her to their waiting carriage where the two greys drooped and the coachman sweated and the long white ribbons hung unnaturally still in the heat, and they drove to Bury through the sunbaked fields, side by side and unnaturally quiet.

The reception was nothing more than a blur of faces to the pair of them. They greeted their guests and were kissed and congratulated and supposed they were saying the right things, and they sat at the head of the table and pretended to eat in the buzz and clatter all around them, and cut the cake with due ceremony and a very wobbly knife. But it was an unnatural meal. And Caroline felt that she was the most unnatural of women.

When she'd made up her mind to marry Henry and live in

258

Richmond and give him both the prospect and the love he needed, it had never entered her mind to doubt that she could do it. But now her whole being was full of doubt, as she sat beside him with a shiny new ring on her finger and felt nothing. No excitement, no affection, not even for Nan. Nothing. I am unnatural, she thought miserably, forcing herself to smile at her guests. What will become of me?

What became of her was a change of clothing into her blue going-away gown, and another ride in the carriage, this time across Angel Square and down Northgate Street to the new station that had just been built outside the town, where she and Henry climbed into their railway carriage under a last and blinding shower of rose petals and to a chirrup of goodbyes.

And then with a strong whiff of soot and sulphur and a high-pitched screech of wheels they were off and on their way to London. Married and on their own at last. And rather to her surprise Henry stood up, let down both the carriage windows and pulled down the blinds.

'Won't people think it rather odd that the blinds are down?' she wondered.

'Let them,' he said with splendid arrogance.

'But what if someone should want to get in?'

'They can't. I've booked the carriage.'

'How could you do that?'

'I paid for all the seats, that's how,' he said, looking very pleased with himself. Actually it had been Joseph's idea, but there was no need to tell her that. Joseph had given him lots of advice in that lethargic way of his and he meant to follow most of it, if she gave him the chance. 'Nobody can disturb us, my dearest darling girl. We have the place to ourselves.'

And suddenly that peculiar, familiar, wedding excitement began to tremble in Caroline's belly. What was he going to do? He looked so intense and so handsome with his skin glowing in the half light he'd created, and those dark eyes shining, and his moustache bushier than she'd ever seen it. What was he going to do? Oh she did hope he would.

He sat beside her and put an arm about her waist and drew her towards him so that they were both still moving together as their first kiss began. And it was delicious. She wanted it to go on for ever, for that gently moving mouth of his was trawling pleasure all through her in the most wondrous way. When he stopped and seemed about to raise his head, she put her hands into the warm hair at the nape of his neck and held him, moving her own lips from side to side to continue the pleasure, and encourage him to go on. Which he did, for he needed very little encouragement. When they finally drew apart they were both flushed and breathless.

'Oh!' she said, 'I do love you after all.' He was like the Prince in the fairy tale waking Snow White from her trance with a kiss. Oh, just like the Prince in the fairy tale.

Desire was so strong in him he didn't notice what she was saying. He wanted to kiss her and kiss her and go on and on until they got to Richmond and their own home and their own bed and the final pleasure he'd waited for and needed and deferred for so long, the pleasure that would surely reward them both if he followed brother Joseph's advice. 'Um,' he said kissing her again.

By the time they reached the terminus at Shoreditch Road, they were so dishevelled that it took them several giggling minutes to make themselves presentable enough to go out into the forecourt and hire the cab that would take them across the Thames to Nine Elms to catch the train to Richmond.

It was late afternoon and the sky above their sooty city was such a dazzling white it hurt their eyes to look at it, and the streets were hot and dusty and pungent with horse manure. But neither of them cared. They sat in their trundling cab together, thigh to warm thigh and hand in tingling hand, waiting with delicious anticipation for the privacy of their next enclosed journey, and the chance to kiss again.

And so the bride came blushing into Richmond, where the groom carried her most lovingly and lingeringly over their new threshold, and they greeted all the new servants they'd hired who were standing in line in the hall ready to meet them, and Henry asked Farren, the butler, if everything was arranged as he'd requested, and was assured that it was, and then they walked arm in arm up their old oak staircase and into their newly decorated bedroom with its beautiful view over the darkening river.

There was warm water waiting in the ewers and scented soap in the dishes and fresh towels on the rails.

'We have plenty of time to wash and change,' Henry said, with his arm still about her waist. 'They are not to serve supper until ten o'clock.'

'Then you may kiss me again,' she said.

And again and again. All the time, pausing only to shed shoes and stockings, to untie a cravat and remove a waistcoat, to unhook a bodice, step out of skirt and petticoats and remove those fearful stays which were pinching most cruelly.

'Oh!' she said, flinging them across the nearest chair when the last hook and eye had been released, 'you don't know what a lovely thing it is to breathe again.'

'Come to bed,' he said, catching at her hands as she pirouetted to celebrate her freedom, 'and you shall breathe as much as you like.'

'Shall you kiss me again?' she said, allowing him to lead her.

'Oh yes, you lovely, greedy creature. But there are better ways to love you than by mere kisses.'

'Better than kisses?' she said breathlessly. It brought her heart into her throat even to consider the possibility. His shirt had fallen off one shoulder revealing a chest shadowed with soft dark hair, and below the white cloth of his dishevelled garment his legs were very long and very muscular.

'Much, much better,' he promised, tumbling backwards onto the bed with his arms held firmly about her lovely yielding waist, so that she fell with him and they rolled over and over among the covers, flesh against flesh, and giggling. 'Let me show you.'

So he did.

And it was.

Chapter 19

When the train carrying the bride and groom was finally out of sight, the wedding party left standing on the platform at Bury St Edmunds found themselves at rather a loss. Speeding a departing couple from a railway station was a new experience and quite an exciting one, but afterwards there was nothing left to do except pack up and go home themselves. All the fun and interest seemed to have left with the newly-weds.

Matilda was the first to make for her carriage, announcing her intention of taking Billy back to their house in Chequer Square at once, and confiding to Nan that he'd had more than enough excitement for one day, and the sooner they went back to their nice quiet summer routine, the healthier he would be. And once the first Easters had left most of the others followed, Annie and James to Rattlesden with their children and grand-children in a procession of carriages and a cheerful muddle, the groom's sister Jane and her family to Cumberland, school friends to cabs, college friends to horse, and the Ippark Easters to their country seat after a courtly farewell to Nan.

'I hope you will visit with us in Sussex, Aunt Nan,' Joseph said, 'now that we have made one another's acquaintance at last.'

'Aye,' Nan said, 'I will. Depend upon it. Seeing that we're related all over again, in a manner a' speaking.'

The last pair to say goodbye were Mirabelle and Edward.

'You are more than welcome to stay with us for a day or two,' Nan suggested. She and Frederick Brougham had decided to forego the capital until the weather improved.

Neither of them had any desire to be stuck in the stench of London, where, as they all knew only too well, the drains smelt, the river stank, the roads were foul with rotting horse manure, drinking water was in scant supply and evil-tasting, and the slums bred cholera. No, no, much better to stay in Bury. But now that Caroline had gone, the place was suddenly far less attractive and she recognized a real need of other young company to replace her absent favourite. If she could persuade this young woman to remain behind, it would lift the day a little. She was quite the most intelligent of her new relations, and had been telling them all about Mr Dickens' new novel, which was to be called *Dombey and Son* and sounded most promising.

'That's uncommon kind of you,' Mirabelle said. 'I'm to visit my cousin in Hertford later in the month, but a day or two here in the country air would be most refreshing.'

But Edward declined. 'No, thank 'ee kindly, Nan,' he said. 'There's work to be done. Pa may rest, but the work don't. Mirry may stay if she pleases, but I must get back.'

So Mirabelle stopped at Angel Hill and went to the theatre that evening with Nan and Frederick and Will and Euphemia, and entertained them afterwards with gently malicious gossip about the players. Her company was enlivening, just as Nan had hoped, and that was just as well, because Will and Euphemia were both quiet and cast-down. For a supposedly joyous occasion, Nan thought, this wedding was having a very odd effect upon them.

The five of them stayed on in Bury together for more than a week, visiting Annie and James at Rattlesden, and Billy and Matilda in Chequer Square, riding every morning and finally attending the Summer Ball at the Athenaeum.

But on the morning after the ball a letter arrived for Mirabelle, and when she'd read it, she told them that, dearly though she loved their company, she must soon be moving on.

'I promised my cousin in Hertford that I would visit with her this month,' she explained, 'and here's the month more than half gone and her letter forwarded on to remind me.'

Will was going back to work that morning and seemed relieved to be off on his travels again. There was to be a meeting of Chartists in Nottingham which his new editor, Mr

Forster, said was 'part of something brewing', and he was to attend it and report on it.

'Perhaps you and Mirabelle could travel part of the way together,' Nan suggested.

'I mean to take a coach across country to Ely and catch the train to Nottingham from there,' he said. 'We could keep company on the coach, I daresay, for the Hertford line runs from Ely too. I don't fancy London in this heat.'

'Quite right,' Nan approved. 'There en't no sense a-running into trouble. I mean to keep out of the place too, as much as I may. I shall travel down now and then whenever I'm needed. Frederick is a gentleman of leisure, of course, and don't need to travel anywhere.'

'Except to be with you and run my estate and keep my practice healthy,' Frederick observed wryly, 'and that don't take more than two lives and twelve months in a year.'

She grinned at that, knowing what a lot of work he put into his legal practice. 'What shall you do, Pheemy?' she said.

'I should return to London, I think,' Euphemia said. 'Perhaps I could travel down through Hertford with you, Mirabelle?' And when Mirabelle smiled her agreement, 'There is so much work to do in Jimmy's school, and with Caroline married and Matty so near to . . . '

The little hesitation was necessary because she couldn't say that Matty was pregnant, not in front of Will and Mr Brougham. That wouldn't have been proper.

'Of course,' Nan said smoothly. 'She'll be glad of your company, my dear, especially in this heat. You must persuade her to rest as much as she can. She's a deal too conscientious for her own good is our Matty.' The baby was due in September and it was no weather to be carrying in.

'She is fortunate to have such a charitable cousin to attend upon her,' Mr Brougham said in that courteous way of his. 'May you be rewarded, my dear.'

'Amen to that,' Nan said. 'But not in Heaven. I'm for rewards of a more temporal kind.'

And although they didn't know it, there was a reward of a particularly temporal kind awaiting their charitable Euphemia almost as soon as she returned to Clerkenwell.

She and Will and Mirabelle set out on their travels later that morning, with their three oddly assorted attendants, brisk Tom Thistlethwaite, limping Bessie and Mirabelle's maid, who was a dour-faced, determined old lady called Duffy. The coach journey was dusty and uneventful but the trains were very decidedly hot, even with the windows open as far as they would go.

'Luckily I have brought some eau de cologne,' Mirabelle said, when Will was gone, fishing the little phial out of her handbag. 'So refreshing on a long journey I always think.'

It cooled their wrists and temples most agreeably.

'Caroline takes cologne on a journey,' Euphemia remembered, and the memory made her aware of how much she missed her cousin. 'I wonder how she – they are.'

'Well enough, I daresay,' Mirabelle said, 'and not thinking of us, you may be sure. 'Tis a love match, is it not?'

'Yes,' Euphemia sighed, envying them despite her resolution not to do any such thing. 'It is.'

'Then they are fortunate indeed,' Mirabelle said lightly. 'Most of us mere mortals have to contend with a lesser state, do we not?'

The question was so direct it made Euphemia blush. 'Well,' she hesitated, 'I have no knowledge upon which to make such a judgement.'

''Tis my opinion, cousin Euphemia,' Mirabelle said, smiling at her with her one sound eye, 'that most gentlemen are unable to give their love in quite the undivided way that is expected of women. In this age of progress they are more concerned with building a reputation or a fortune. Now ain't that so?'

Euphemia had to admit that it probably was.

'Whilst we are expected to devote ourselves exclusively to our menfolk, and to run their households and rear their children, if we have any.'

'Yes, that is true,' Euphemia said. And she thought how willingly she would devote herself to Will if he would only give her the chance.

'Ambition, you see,' Mirabelle went on. 'That's what it is. A quality we ain't supposed to possess, if you ever heard such nonsense. Why should we be any different from our brothers?'

The raw earth of an embankment gave way to the green of

open fields and the passing flick, flick, flick of a copse of tall trees.

'I mean to extend my literary salon to journalists as well as writers this autumn,' Mirabelle said. 'An interesting breed, journalists. Perhaps I could prevail upon your cousin Will to tell us about Ireland and the potato famine.'

'I doubt it,' Euphemia said. 'He don't speak of it to anyone, not even us.' And it was true. If they wanted to know where he'd been and what he'd been doing they had to read his articles. It was curious that until Caroline's wedding she hadn't noticed how very guarded he was, but he'd been so distant with her during the last week she could hardly help being aware of it now.

'Creatures of extremes,' Mirabelle said. 'Reticence is common to one half of the profession and loquacity to the other. The reticent are the more interesting. I will see what may be done with cousin Will.'

'I doubt if you will prevail,' Euphemia felt she had to repeat her warning. 'He is a very private creature.'

'And you love him, I think,' Mirabelle said shrewdly.

It was possible to be honest with this oddly outspoken cousin. 'Yes, I do.'

'Which love ain't returned?'

'He loves me as a brother,' Euphemia temporized.

'But not in the way you would wish.'

'No, I fear not.' It felt so final to admit it like this, but there was no doubt about it, not after the chill of the last week.

'Then you'd best find an ambition,' Mirabelle said, practically. 'That's my advice. Or take a husband from the many who love you. You have refused several, have you not?'

'Yes,' Euphemia admitted, cheered by the memory. 'But I do not think they were particularly eager for acceptance.'

'How so?'

'They took their answer without argument.'

'Gentlemen,' Mirabelle said, as if that explained it. 'And the more fools they. So if it ain't to be Mr Will Easter, you'll need an ambition. Have you found one yet?'

'I have found an occupation, for I teach in the ragged school.'

'Very commendable,' Mirabelle approved. 'When love is

doubtful it is sound policy to keep oneself occupied, but I would advice you to find an ambition as well. Ambition is more demanding. Would you care for a little more cologne?'

Euphemia dabbed the cologne on her hot forehead, and as the evaporating spirit cooled her head, she wondered where Will was and if he ever thought of her when he was away from home. She decided with a sigh that he probably didn't.

Euphemia would have been surprised and gratified if she'd known how often she was in Will's thoughts during his long hot journey to Nottingham.

Caroline's marriage had had a peculiar effect upon Will Easter, and one that he hadn't expected at all.

It had all begun in church, at the moment when Uncle James had smiled at Henry and told him, 'You may now kiss the bride.'

The women in the congregation had caught their combined breath in a little suppressed sigh of satisfied romance, and the sound had made Will feel irritable and uncomfortable, so that he had to look away from them at once and find something else on which to focus his attention.

What he found was Euphemia's lovely madonna face. It was turned towards her embracing cousins and wore an expression of such melting tenderness that he was lifted with a rush of overpowering affection towards her. And to his surprise and shock he realized that it was quite the wrong sort of affection. He wanted to step forward to the altar rail and take her in his arms and kiss her, not courteously and gently as Henry was doing, but over and over again, with all the passion he was feeling so strongly. In fact, if he hadn't been twenty-eight years old and sensible, he would have imagined he had fallen in love.

It was a blessing that he was in church with a ceremony and a congregation to restrain him, otherwise he might have spoken to her there and then. Poor Pheemy. What a shock that would have been, when they'd been like brother and sister all these years. As it was, the service and the reception gave him a chance to get these new improbable feelings under control, although as he realized in the next few days, now they'd been roused they refused to disappear altogether. It made his life

267

horribly difficult. Obviously he couldn't run the risk of being alone with Euphemia, but he even felt ill at ease with her when they were in the same room and with other company about to chaperone them. Ill at ease and unshielded, somehow, open to misunderstanding and the possibility of misinterpretation. In fact if Nan hadn't had the tact to invite cousin Mirabelle to stay, life could have become quite awkward on several occasions during the last week. It was very upsetting.

So when he arrived in Nottingham and Tom Thistlethwaite packed his luggage aboard a cab saying, 'Sight better'n weddings, eh?' he was happy to agree.

'Can't be doing with all that pie-jaw,' Tom said cheerfully. 'Give me the single life, that's what I say. Love 'em and leave 'em.'

'Sworn bachelor, eh?' Will teased, climbing into the cab.

'Lord, love yer, yes,' Tom said, shutting the low door after him, 'never found a woman I could put up with fer more'n a week. A day's too much sometimes. I likes ter be up an' away. Ready fer the off are we, sir?'

Yes, Will thought, as the cab rocked them over the canal and into the town, that's about the size of it. Tom and I are the sort of men who have to be constantly on the move. Always ready for the off. If we stay in one place for too long we stifle, or start thinking foolish thoughts. And it occurred to him that his friend Jeff Jefferson was the same. We're just not the marrying kind. That's what it is. We've been bachelors too long to change now. Was it any wonder he'd felt uncomfortable at his sister's wedding?

By the time the cab racketed through the archway into the long courtyard of the Flying Horse in Cheapside he had turned his mind away from the confusion of the last week and was ready for anything. Which was just as well, for the ancient coaching inn was crowded with people, merchants and bankers, horse riders and horse traders, a quiet group of Chartists up for the meeting, and newspaper men from every paper in London.

It wasn't long before Will found three friends from Fleet Street and the Strand, and the four of them decided to dine together, drink together and pool their expenses and their findings, 'being,' as the man from the *Chronicle* said, 'I don't see much chance of a revolution with this little lot'. And certainly the Chartists in the Flying Horse were a sober crowd, speaking low, drinking little and dining frugally. In fact they took themselves off to their meeting so quietly that Will and his friends didn't see the going of them.

But the meeting was easy to find, for it was being held in the Market Square, a mere hundred yards away from the Flying Horse and it was brilliantly torch-lit.

Unfortunately the torches seemed to be the only brilliant thing about it. The first speeches were boring and predictable, and so was the first decision that was put to the vote. Chartists everywhere would collect signatures for 'a third and over-whelming petition for universal suffrage'.

But then just as Will was beginning to think that he would hear nothing new and was folding up his notebook ready to put it back in his pocket, the main speaker of the evening arrived. And the main speaker was Mr Feargus O'Connor.

He was in electrifying form. 'Yes,' he roared. 'Let us say "yes" five million times to the six points of our Charter. Let our procession fill the streets of London. Let our combined and potent voice be heard. But let us take other action, for I tell you, my friends, a petition is not enough. We must be bold in innovation, forthright in pursuit of power. And to that end, gentlemen, I tell you here and now, that I intend to stand for Parliament in this constituency. Let the sitting members look to their laurels. Tell our local worthies, Mr Hobhouse and Mr Gisbourne, that their days are numbered.'

'Now that's more like it,' Will said, taking notes as well as he could in the darkness. That was news.

And there was more to come. Their renowned speaker had taken other action too. He had founded a 'Land Society' and was proud to tell them what its objects were. 'We mean to purchase land on which we shall settle a chosen company, selected for the purpose, in order to demonstrate to the working classes of this Kingdom, firstly the value of land, as a means of making them independent of the grinding capitalists; and secondly to show them the necessity of securing the speedy enactment of the 'people's charter' which should do for them nationally, what this society proposed to do sectionally, namely, to accomplish the political and social emancipation of the enslaved and degraded working classes'. Three communes were already planned, and would soon be built, in Rickmansworth in Hertfordshire, and Snig's End in Gloucestershire, and at Minster Lovell, near Oxford. 'The next stage of the revolution has begun, my friends! It must and will progress!'

The news was greeted with the first cheers of the evening. And Will made up his mind to interview Mr O'Connor and set off through the crowd towards him at once.

Mr Feargus O'Connor was even more forthcoming in private than he'd been on the rostrum. 'The revolution is upon us,' he said. 'Write that to your readers, young man. The revolution is upon us. Let our masters beware. What cannot be won by petition and persuasion will be taken by force of arms.'

'An armed rebellion?' Will enquired.

'If necessary. Yes.'

'Does he mean it?' the *Chronicle* wondered, as the four reporters strolled back to the Flying Horse through the smoke-filled air.

'Yes,' Will said. 'I think he does.'

'Is the long-awaited English revolution about to begin at last?'

It was an exciting thought.

'If I wanted something as much as they want the vote,' Will said, trying to see the Chartists' point of view like a good journalist, 'I'm damned if I'd go around just signing petitions, especially when they've already had two of 'em ignored. Their patience must be running pretty thin, don't you think?'

'What would you do eh, Easter?' the *Chronicle* asked.

'I'd take a gun to somebody's head, I daresay, the same as they will.'

'It's lucky you've got all you want then.'

But *had* he? The words echoed in his mind all night, as he tossed and turned on an uncomfortable bed in a hot airless room under the eaves. *Had* he? He was a reporter now, but he couldn't deny the shaming knowledge that he had chosen to change jobs despite his father's death and at quite the wrong time for the rest of the family. It was a demoralizing way to have achieved what he wanted. It left him with a feeling of resentment and dissatisfaction, as though he should be striving for more and greater things, perhaps to make amends. But how could he do that, when he had no idea what they were? And then there was this peculiar change in his attitude towards Euphemia, who had done nothing at all to provoke it and certainly didn't deserve it. It hurt him to be behaving in such an irrational way. He was still tossing and still wondering when the window panes grew grey and cocks began to crow. And he was no nearer an answer.

In Bedford Square Euphemia was wakeful too.

It was very lonely in Nan's great house, even with old Bessie to fuss over her and Cook to pet her and feed her with nourishing food, and at night, on her own in the bedroom that she and Caroline had shared for nearly nine years, she missed her cousin too painfully to be able to sleep, especially with that odd, honest conversation with cousin Mirabelle still reverberating in her mind. It was quite a relief to get up in the morning and order the carriage to take her to Clerkenwell so that she could be busy with Jimmy and Matty and their various children.

They were all delighted to have her back.

'Just in the nick of time,' Matty said. 'We're to have an important visitor on Monday.'

'From the Church?' Euphemia asked, for that was where most of Jimmy's important visitors came from.

'No indeed,' Jimmy said, beaming at her. 'Not the Church, Pheemy dear. Oh no indeed. The aristocracy. We are to receive a visit from your Miss Nightingale.'

'The nursing lady?'

'The same. Ain't that an honour? She and her family are staying at the Burlington Hotel and she is making the rounds of as many ragged schools as she can find.'

'Don't she mean to nurse any more?'

'According to Canon Fielding her family won't allow it,' Matty confided. 'Which is hardly surprising when you consider what dreadful women most nurses are. Drunken harridans for the most part, I fear. But then again, he says they don't approve of anything the poor lady wants to do. In fact, between you and me, my dear, I'm not at all sure they even know about these visits. So we are all the more honoured.'

271

The news was so exciting that for the next few days Euphemia couldn't think of anything or anybody else. Not even Will and Caroline. She tried to imagine what the lady would look like, and decided that she would probably be gentle and frail and rather timid if her family disapproved of her so much, but splendidly dressed of course, because the Nightingales were extremely wealthy.

On Monday morning she took particular pains to dress herself as well and as neatly as she could, and all through the morning, while she helped Matty in the linen cupboard and the two nursemaids in the nursery, she was dreaming of the visit. But in the heat of their crowded schoolroom she was too busy to do anything but attend to her pupils, with the result that the Nightingale party had arrived and were walking through the doorway before she was aware of them. And Miss Nightingale was the very reverse of what she had expected.

For a start, although she was one of three ladies being introduced by Canon Fielding, there was no doubt of her importance. She was modestly dressed in a simple gown of violet silk trimmed with a neat collar of blonde lace, and her hair, which was thick and chestnut coloured, was simply dressed too, parted in the middle and drawn back to be hidden under an unassuming lace cap. But she had such an air about her, a quiet yet forceful authority, which was partly due to the way she walked, for she was tall and willowy and moved with a lilt, as though she were dancing, and partly to her manner of speaking, which was as quiet and musical as her walk, but mostly to her style of questioning, which was direct and knowledgeable and disconcertingly probing. Like a man's.

The very first thing she noticed was that the children had clean hands and faces. 'Do you wash them, Mrs Hopkins?' she wanted to know. And when told that they did, she enquired about the cost, writing down their answers in a little black notebook. How many bowls did they use? How much soap? Who provided them? How often were the towels washed?

'Has their cleanliness contributed to better health, would you say?'

'It has made some contribution certainly,' Jimmy told her.

'In what way?'

'We have fewer children absent with sickness and diarrhoea.'

'You feed them too, so Canon Fielding tells me, so it is possible that this may account for their improved health too.' Giving him a smile.

'We hope so.'

'What do you feed them, Reverend Hopkins? I would be interested to know.'

While Jimmy told her all he could about the soup they prepared each day and suggested that she might care to walk across to the rectory and see the preparations for herself, the children stood by their benches and watched their visitor in awed silence. And really, Euphemia thought, you couldn't blame them for she was plainly a great lady and very beautiful, with such a strong face and such intelligent grey eyes. A lady to admire and follow. If she ever decided to start her school for nurses, she thought, then I would like to be one of them.

By the time Miss Nightingale had inspected the kitchen, school was over for the day and the scholars dismissed. Matty and Euphemia walked slowly back across Clerkenwell Green hoping to see their visitor again before she left. To their delight, Jimmy had persuaded the whole party to take tea. And at last, over cucumber sandwiches and the best Chelsea tea service, Euphemia got a chance to talk to Miss Nightingale about nursing.

'You have worked here more than a year, I believe,' Miss Nightingale said, making polite conversation.

'Yes,' Euphemia said, and then greatly daring, 'but if I had my dearest wish it is another job I would be doing.'

'Indeed?' Miss Nightingale said, assessing Euphemia with those shrewd grey eyes. 'And what would that be?'

'I should like to become a nurse.'

Miss Nightingale smiled. 'It is a poor profession,' she said, 'full of drunkards and women of low repute.'

'Yes,' Euphemia said. 'I know. But if nurses were to follow Mr Chadwick's advice, and keep their patients clean and well fed, and if there were to be proper drainage and a clean water supply, in the way he advocates, then the profession might change.'

'Indeed.'

'And given the right person to lead them into healthier ways nurses might change too.'

'That is my hope and belief, Miss Callbeck.'

'If the time were to come,' Euphemia dared, 'when a different kind of woman were required to train for the nursing profession, I should like to be one of them.'

'That might well be,' Miss Nightingale said. 'You are one of the Easters, are you not?'

Euphemia admitted that she was, and was drawing breath to offer her services there and then, when Canon Fielding turned the conversation to a consideration of the cost of slates and slate pencils and the moment passed.

But when Miss Nightingale was taking her leave of her host, and his 'two able assistants' she dropped a last encouragement towards Miss Euphemia Callbeck. 'I do not forget the matter we spoke of,' she said as they shook hands. 'I will send you a pamphlet I have written upon the subject. I am very glad to have made your acquaintance.'

And then she was gone, climbing into her carriage very straight of spine and graceful. Oh, a very great lady!

That night as she lay in her lonely bedroom watching the stars, Euphemia couldn't sleep for excitement. She had taken Mirabelle's advice after all, and found an ambition and a cause. One day, somehow and somewhere, she would be a nurse, one of the new kind of nurses, putting Mr Chadwick's ideas into practice. She missed Caroline more than ever now that she had such amazing news to tell her.

Caroline and Henry were still enclosed in love and idleness. With servants to wait on them and cooks to feed them and no visitors or correspondence to concern them, they had evolved a new and luxurious pattern to their lives; nights spent making love, sleep in the cool of early morning, a ride after breakfast, lunch on the terrace where they could enjoy the occasional breeze that flickered up from the Thames, languid afternoons in the shade of the garden. Sometimes they strolled down from terrace to terrace until they reached the river, where they sat with their bare feet in the warm water and watched the coots and the swans and the bright skiffs drifting at ease, and talked of everything and nothing while they waited for evening and the welcome of their magical bed. 'Our pleasure palace,'

Henry had said on that first night. And pleasure palace it was.

The days passed without notice. They supposed they had spent a week together, but it could have been two, or three, or ten. On one particularly oppressive afternoon when the swans were asleep and the skiffs were nowhere to be seen, they took off the few clothes they felt obliged to wear for decency's sake, and went for a swim, he in his shirt and she in her chemise. Or to be more accurate he went for a swim while she lay in the shallows, near the privacy of their garden wall and let the green water ripple the heat from her body.

'You are like a water nymph,' he said, admiring her white limbs and running his fingers down the delicious curve of her spine.

'And you are my river god.' Oh, so handsome with his wet shirt clinging to his body.

He sat beside her in the shallows and bent to kiss her, tangling her damp hair in his fingers. 'Let us go back to the house.'

'Yes, yes,' she said, in a swoon of pleasure and cooling water. 'Let's.'

And so the pattern continued and the honey month passed. And neither of them saw any reason for change. Until the night of the thunder storm.

Chapter 20

It had been a most unpleasant morning, sticky and oppressive and airless. Even on the river there was no breeze at all and the heat was so excessive there was no escape from it, indoors or out. By midday Caroline and Henry had decided that the only comfortable place to be was underwater, so that was where they spent the afternoon, with two parasols propped among the pebbles at the water's edge to provide a little extra shade.

Towards two o'clock, Caroline noticed that there were two cauliflower clouds heaping in the hard blue of the sky above the river. They grew with amazing speed, erupting higher and higher into huge billowing curves of grey and white and purple.

'Aren't they beautiful,' she said, lying on her back in the shallows so that she could gaze straight up at them. 'Like an Arabian palace.'

But Henry took a more prosaic view. 'We'd better go in,' he said, and he began to dislodge the parasols. 'We're in for a storm.'

It was an understatement. The first hot drops spattered their foreheads as they scampered indoors, and minutes later the sky was riven with lightning and the rain began in earnest. It fell with such violence that it looked more like a mountain torrent than rainfall, pouring onto the garden from the great height of the clouds and pitting the grey river with so many close packed holes that it looked like a nutmeg grater. Before Henry and Caroline were dried and dressed there was a lake on the lower terrace, the roadway was a running stream and hailstones were cracking against the window. It was marvellously exciting, and it went on for hours and hours.

At six o'clock Farren the butler came into the drawing room where they were watching from the bow window, and stood before them with his spine curved into a crescent and his head drooping as though it were too heavy for his neck. Henry had known him long enough by now to recognize the stance, which was assumed whenever the man was about to carry out a complicated instruction or when he was anxious as to what his orders were going to be.

'What is it, Farren?' he said, keeping his voice perfectly still, like Joseph always did when he was dealing with a difficult servant.

'If you please, sir,' Farren said, 'the basement is full of water.' His hanging face was a picture of gloom. 'We got the wine out of the way of it, sir, and the kindling is in the kitchen, you'll be pleased to know, but we couldn't do much about the coal.' There were over four tons of coal in the cellars so that was hardly surprising. 'We thought you'd want to be informed, sir.'

'Quite right,' Henry approved. 'Do we have a pump?'

'Oh yes, sir. Johnnie's a-using of it now.'

'We'll come down and see,' Caroline said.

The butler's head lifted and his eyebrows shot up with surprise. It was not usual for the lady of the house to inspect the basement when it flooded. All his previous employers had kept well away from such emergencies. 'It is very wet, ma'am,' he warned, 'and none too clean.'

'I'll wear my boots,' she said.

It was eerie down in the cellars with clusters of yellow candles flickering light into the gloom and gangs of servants wading about in the black water like miners in a flooded cavern. The pump didn't seem to be having any effect at all, although Farren assured them that everything was under control.

'You'll need a good hot meal inside you after all this,' Caroline said. 'I'll go up and see to it directly.' And she went stomping off.

'A character,' Mr Farren said to the housekeeper, when the cellars were finally drained and the good meal had been served and eaten.

The housekeeper, who was called Mrs Benotti, was stout and stolid. 'An Easter, Mr Farren,' she said. 'All the same are the Easters. Renowned for it. Characters to a man are the Easters, Mr Farren, even if they're women.'

The next morning was quite cool, their impromptu lake had drained away and the garden was greener than they'd ever seen it.

'We will take breakfast downstairs in the breakfast room,' Henry said. The drop in temperature had renewed his energy.

It was a novelty to be up and dressed and to have their meal waiting for them on the side-board and *The Times* laid neatly beside Henry's plate. 'We are like an old married couple,' Caroline said, for the table arrangements reminded her of breakfast with Nan and Mr Brougham.

'Ask Farren to come up,' Henry said to the maid, as she set the coffee pot on its stand. 'We ought to see if there's been any more damage anywhere. It wouldn't surprise me if there'd been some windows cracked.'

But Farren reassured them. The cellars were still tacky but the water had all been pumped away, and he'd inspected every room and all the windows were intact, they had his word for it.

'Thank heavens for that, eh,' Henry said, cheerfully admiring Caroline's glossy curls as she sat in the sunshine.

'It's August now you see, sir,' Farren said. 'We always have storms in August in this part of the world.'

'August already,' Henry said. 'Fancy that!' And it occurred to him that he really ought to be getting back to work. He'd been away for nearly three weeks. Perhaps it was fitting that the heat and the honeymoon should come to an end together. 'Would you have the carriage ready for me, Farren, at half past eight, if you please.'

'Where are we going?' Caroline asked, when Farren had curved his spine into its obedient crescent and removed himself from the room.

'You may stay here in the garden, my love, and enjoy the better weather,' he said, 'but I must go back to work.'

'Quite right,' she said. 'We've been idle long enough. We will go back together.'

'There's no need for that,' he said. '*I* must work, of course, but now that we are married there is no need for you . . . '

278

'Why not?' she asked, and there was a steely quality to her voice that should have warned him.

But he was still buffered by contentment and he missed it. 'Wives don't work, my darling,' he said easily. 'Not in our level of society. They have husbands to work for them. There is no necessity for you to work now. And besides, it wouldn't be proper.'

'I worked before we were married,' she said. 'We worked together and you were quite happy about that. So I can't see any reason why I shouldn't go on working now.'

'That was different,' he said, speaking rather stiffly because he was annoyed that she was arguing with him and especially over such a trivial matter when he was so plainly in the right. 'You needed an occupation then, but you don't need one now. You've occupation enough being a wife. No, no, I will work and you will stay at home.'

'What squit!' she said, using her grandmother's trenchant word, because it made her so cross to hear him talk such nonsense.

He looked up at her angry face and realized that he had made a mistake. Surely she didn't really *want* to go to work? That would be downright unnatural. Married women never went to work. Not in these enlightened times. But she was folding her table napkin in a slow deliberate way that was rather unnerving. It was too late to retract what he'd said so he decided to be shocked by her language instead. 'Caroline! What a word to use!'

'If you think I mean to sit at home and twiddle my thumbs,' she said, ignoring the distraction, 'when there are deals to be made and publishers to persuade, then you are very much mistaken.' She put the napkin beside her plate, stood up and walked away from the table.

'Where are you going?' he asked, following her.

She paused at the door, her face hard. 'To get ready, of course. I told you. I'm coming with you.'

'It ain't up to you to say what you'll do,' he said, his voice rising in anger that she should oppose him so strongly. 'You are my wife and you'll do as I say.' And he held onto the door knob to prevent her leaving.

'I will not!' Struggling with his hands.

'You will!' Opposing her with all his strength.

'You can't tell me what I may and mayn't do, Henry Easter. I shall do as I please the same as I always have.' She was stamping her feet with anger. 'I'm an Easter, dammit.'

'And I am not?'

'Don't be foolish. Of course you are. What has that to do with it?' She was still trying to pull his hands away from the door knob.

He was too cross to answer her sensibly. Somehow or other battle had been joined and now he had to go through with it and defeat her. 'Devil take it,' he shouted at her. 'If you go on like this, I shall lock you in.'

She stopped pulling at his hands, turned and walked coolly away from him. 'Very well then,' she said. 'I shall jump out of the window.'

'From the first floor?'

'From the first floor. You see if I don't.' And really with that dark face blazing and her eyes glaring she looked capable of anything.

'You're supposed to obey me, Caroline. I'm your husband.'

'Squit!'

'Love, honour and obey! You promised.'

'Squit! Squit! Squit!' Stamping her anger at him.

'Hush!' he said. 'Do you want the servants to hear?'

'I don't care,' she shouted. 'I'll shout if I want to. Let them hear.'

There were wheels scraping the cobbles outside the window. 'Here's the carriage,' he said. 'Now look here, Caroline, I am going to ride to the station, where I mean to catch the nine o'clock to London, and I'm going on my own. I forbid you to come with me.' His face was haughty with anger.

'Hoity-toity,' she said, turning her back on him. 'Do as you please, but don't imagine you will stop me. If I can't come with you, I shall go on my own.'

His fury was so intense he was afraid he might hit her. How could she oppose him so? After all that love? When they'd been so happy? Impossible woman! There was only one thing to do, if he were to continue to behave honourably, and he did it quickly, leaving her and the room without another word.

He was trembling with fury all the way to the station. How

dare she make such a scene! How dare she defy him! It was more than he could bear. But the gentle rocking journey to Nine Elms calmed him, and by the time he arrived in the Strand he was almost himself again, back in the world of men and work where people didn't fly off into tantrums all the time.

His colleagues were full of gossip about the gale. Windows had been broken all over the City, they said, and several were missing in the Easter headquarters. But that was nothing according to Mr Jolliffe, his clerk. Seven thousand panes of glass had been smashed in the new House of Commons, and St James' Theatre had lost eight hundred, and Burlington Arcade was completely destroyed. 'Never known a storm like it, Mr Henry sir.'

It was rewarding to be able to put repairs in hand at once, and after that to deal with a daunting pile of correspondence. He worked all morning, answering one letter after another, passing those that simply needed acknowledgement across to Mr Jolliffe, and entering reported alterations to rail and coach timetables onto the chart that now covered the far wall of his office with instant and up-to-date information.

'So many changes in such a short time,' he said to Mr Jolliffe in mock complaint. 'I turn my back for five minutes and they put on ten more trains. Everything happens so quickly nowadays.'

'That's progress, so they say, Mr Henry. And all progress is to the good, now ain't it?'

'True,' Henry said, picking up the next letter.

It was from Mr Chaplin of the London Birmingham Railway with 'some news that may interest you'. A Bill was currently being passed through the Commons to enable the building of an extension to the South Eastern railway line which would run from Ashford to Canterbury. 'I shall take shares as soon as they are offered and would strongly advise you to do the same.'

Well now, that *was* news. 'Have you heard anything of this?' he asked, handing the letter across to Mr Jolliffe.

'Rumours, Mr Henry. There has been talk. Shall I circulate it?' All information about new lines was always circulated within the company.

'Yes,' Henry said vaguely, because they both knew it was always done and he had already begun to write his reply.

281

So the letter was circulated, and the first pair of hands into which it was passed by an eager and congratulatory Mr Jolliffe belonged to the new Mrs Easter, who'd been working in *her* room, catching up on *her* correspondence ever since she had arrived that morning.

She took action on it at once, sending a runner round to Mr Chaplin's office with a note to suggest that the two of them should meet in Mr Cranshaw's Tea House in the Strand some time that afternoon to discuss the matter. If a new line was to be built then Easter stalls could be incorporated into all the station designs from the very beginning, and in the most advantageous positions. It was splendid news.

The runner returned within the hour with the message that Mr Chaplin was agreeable to four o'clock and would bring his colleagues from the South Eastern with him. By twenty past five the better part of the deal had been provisionally agreed upon. She returned to the Easter headquarters in high good humour. And walked straight into Henry in the foyer.

The sight of her put him into such a muddle of emotions that he didn't know what to say to her – fury that she'd disobeyed him so blatantly; confusion because he hadn't expected to see her; desire because triumph was making her glow with the most beautiful boldness.

'I've had a marvellous afternoon,' she said, tucking her hand in the crook of his arm. 'Are you going home?'

'I was,' he said, annoyed with himself that he should want her so much when she'd behaved so badly.

'Good,' she said, smiling straight into his eyes. 'Then I will tell you all about it as we go. Is the carriage ordered?'

He was amazed at her. Had she forgotten their dreadful row? She showed no signs of remembering it.

She sat beside him all the way to Nine Elms, snuggled affectionately against his side, and told him all about her meeting with Mr Chaplin and his associates, plainly expecting him to approve of it. Which he had to do when he'd heard about it, because it was an excellent deal, and the businessman in him knew it. But even so, even so . . .

'How did you know about it?' he asked, feeling quite cross.

'Why, from the letter you circulated, of course. Had you forgotten? Mr Jolliffe brought it to me.'

Damn Mr Jolliffe, he thought. He should have had more sense. Or I should have told him to avoid her. But how could I have done that, when I had no idea she was in the building? She was attracting him so strongly he couldn't think logically. It would have been easier if her eyes weren't quite so large or quite so loving. 'Caroline,' he said, and the word was a caress.

She turned her face towards him and kissed his cheek. 'Wait till you hear what I found out about Mr Chaplin,' she said. 'He means to go into parliament, did you know that?'

'A sensible move,' he said, trying to concentrate on what she was saying.

They talked business all the way back to Richmond, where he was surprised to find their dog cart waiting for them as if they were expected, and when they reached Richmond Hill, he discovered to his further amazement that she'd ordered dinner for them before she left home that morning and seemed to have known that they would be returning together, for there was a most appetizing smell of roast duckling rising from the kitchens and Mrs Benotti was there to greet them in the hall.

'Just enough time to dress for dinner,' she said.

He stood in the hall watching her as she climbed the stairs, trailing her hand along the banister as if she were caressing it. 'Have you forgotten how we parted this morning?' he asked, and although he'd intended the question to be a rebuke, all he could hear in it was surprise.

'Oh yes,' she said easily. 'That's all forgotten. We're bound to fight now and then, ain't we, seeing who we are?'

He followed her up the stairs shaking his head at her sang froid. But it had been a terrible row, he thought. Terrible. He remembered it very clearly. And what was worse, he'd thought he'd won it.

But as he was to learn in the weeks that followed, winning and losing were not words that figured in his wife's vocabulary. And neither was obedience. She simply side-stepped all three, and did whatever she wanted to, answering for it afterwards if he queried it. The next morning she was up and dressed before he was and travelled to the Strand with him as though that was what they'd both intended, explaining that she had an appointment with Mr Longman the publisher. And it was all said and done with such ease that he couldn't find a way to oppose her.

She had such style, that was the trouble. The bull-headedness that troubled him as a husband was an advantage when it came to business. And so was her outspokenness. 'That's not very good,' she would say when a negotiation didn't go quite the way she wanted. 'I shall have to look into that and see if I can improve it a little.' And the amazing thing was that the men she dealt with allowed her to do it.

By the time Nan came back to London at the end of August, the new deal was completed and a second, for the branch line to Margate, had been begun. It was infuriating but impressive.

'We will hold a family supper to celebrate,' she said as they dressed to attend Nan's dinner party at Bedford Square. 'It's high time we began to entertain. I haven't seen Will and Euphemia for ages.'

'And after that perhaps you'll stay at home for a little while and take a rest?' he suggested.

'I might,' she said, grinning at him. 'And then again I might not. You ain't going to start all that again, surely to goodness?'

'I don't think people approve of you working,' he said.

'Who doesn't?'

'Well, Mr Maycock and Mr Jernegan for a start.' They'd both made several caustic comments about it, more or less in his hearing.

'Old fuddy-duddies,' she said, swooping across the room to kiss him. 'We don't need to worry about *them*.'

But he did worry. What she was doing was unnatural and he wished she wouldn't do it. But for the life of him he couldn't think how to stop her, now.

Nan made everything worse by praising her. 'I saw Mr Chaplin this afternoon,' she said, 'and I hear you've done wonders. You must show me the plans tomorrow.'

It was a lively evening. Mirabelle was full of information. Three new writers were about to burst upon the London scene. 'They are called Currer, Ellis and Acton Bell,' she said, 'and Mr Newby tells me they've written the most extraordinary novels. I shall invite them to my very next soirée.'

'I trust I shall be invited too,' Mr Brougham said courteously.

'Indeed sir,' Mirabelle said. 'You shall head my list. And perhaps you will persuade cousin Will to join us.'

'If he ever stops long enough to join anybody,' Nan said. Will was the one member of her family who wasn't present at her dinner. 'I en't seen hide nor hair of him since the wedding, he's been so busy gadding.'

'We read his articles, of course,' Mirabelle said. 'He seems to be following this new National Petition very closely.'

'I wonder he bothers,' Edward said, disparagingly, 'since it won't amount to anything.'

'What news do you have of Miss Nightingale, Euphemia?' Mirabelle said, deftly ignoring him.

Euphemia looked pale but she too was full of information. 'We have been corresponding,' she said with shy pride.

Caroline was delighted. 'Miss Nightingale, the nursing lady?' she asked.

'The same.'

'But my darling Pheemy, how marvellous!' Caroline said. 'Shall you meet her, do you think?'

'We have met already,' Euphemia said, exchanging smiles with Matty and Jimmy. 'In fact, she has agreed to accept me as one of her nurses as soon as she can find suitable premises for a school.'

'How marvellous!' Caroline said again. 'When will that be?'

'Not just yet, I fear,' Euphemia said. 'She has been rather ill, you see, and her family have sent her abroad for a year or so to recover. I believe she is in Italy at present. But she told me what books I am to read and I've been studying them most closely.'

'Every night, according to Bessie,' Nan said, grinning at her, 'as soon as she gets back from Clerkenwell, as if she don't work hard enough there, in all conscience.'

'We don't know what we'd do without her, do we Matty?' Jimmy said.

'No,' Matty said. 'I certainly don't.' Her pregnancy was too far advanced to hide, but she'd come to Nan's dinner party notwithstanding.

'Are you well, my dear?' Nan wanted to know.

'A little fatigued sometimes,' Matty admitted.

'She works too hard,' Jimmy said. 'That's the trouble. She's too conscientious.'

'It's a family failing,' Nan said. 'But a good one.'

After the meal while Mr Brougham, Henry, Edward and Jimmy were still at table and Nan and Mirabelle were keeping Matty company in the drawing room, Caroline and Euphemia went for a stroll in the garden, following the familiar paths, arm in arm as they'd done on so many evenings.

'Oh, I *am* so glad to see you again, my dearest,' Euphemia said. 'And looking so well and happy. You are happy, are you not?'

'Ecstatic,' Caroline said. 'Being married is . . . ' But then she hesitated, for these were private pleasures that Euphemia couldn't possibly know about.

'Full of holy joys,' Euphemia said.

What a curious thing to say, Caroline thought, but she didn't pursue it because she had something rather more important that she wanted to ask Euphemia about.

'If Miss Nightingale is to be abroad for a year or so,' she said, 'she ain't likely to start her school much before next April, is she?'

'No,' Euphemia said, smiling as if she already knew what was going to be said next.

'Have you studied midwifery in these books of yours?' Caroline said.

'Oh, my dearest girl!' Euphemia said, throwing her arms about her cousin's neck. 'When is it to be? Is it in April?'

'Would you nurse me, Pheemy? I'd rather it were you than anyone.'

'Oh yes, yes, my dearest. Does Henry know?'

'Well, not yet. I'm only just getting accustomed to the idea myself.'

'How happy he will be!'

He probably will, Caroline thought. But she knew it was equally probable that he would tell her to stay at home.

Chapter 21

Matty's baby was born two weeks later on 17 September, a daughter, and just what her parents had secretly wanted. She was christened Mary Matilda, with Caroline, Henry and Euphemia standing as her godparents, and she was doted on from the first tentative hour of her life, because she was such a good little thing and so frail.

Euphemia now spent nearly all her time in Clerkenwell Green, teaching in the afternoons and helping to care for the baby and her two brothers during the mornings and early evenings. But every Wednesday she took time off from her charges and caught a train to Richmond to visit Caroline.

Wednesday was the one day of the week that Caroline spent at home. It gave her a chance to ensure that her household was being run according to her wishes, and was a small compromise to Henry's continuing opposition to her work with the firm. He was really being ridiculously difficult about it, insisting that she stop work 'now' every time a new deal was completed, and roaring off into a row when she didn't agree with him. Of course making up again afterwards in their accommodating pleasure palace was always delightful but it made telling him about the baby absolutely impossible. September came and went, October blazed red and gold, November breathed white fog from the river, and according to Euphemia she was 'half way there', and she was certainly beginning to change shape, but she still hadn't said anything.

Nan and Mr Brougham made plans to leave London for Westmoreland as soon as the first fog choked the City. On the Wednesday before they travelled, Nan came over to Richmond for the afternoon with Euphemia, because Caroline had made such a point of inviting her that it was obvious there was something afoot. The reason became clear as soon as the three of them were settled before the fire in the drawing room and were taking tea.

'I've been thinking of ways to increase trade,' Caroline said just a little too casually as she poured the first cup. 'I can't see any reason why we shouldn't sell other travelling necessities on our stalls as well as books.'

'Have 'ee now?' Nan grinned at her. 'And what might they be, pray?'

'We could start with foot warmers and mufflers,' Caroline said, 'now that the weather is getting colder. And if they succeed we could try reading lamps and matches.'

'You have it all planned, I see,' Nan laughed at her.

'I have thought about it, yes,' Caroline admitted. Which was true enough. She'd planned it thoroughly, considering all the most likely articles that could be sold and listing the wholesalers she would contact. 'But I've gone no further, naturally. Not until I had the chance to discuss it with you.'

'Which is why I was invited here this afternoon, I daresay,' Nan said, grinning again.

'It was one reason,' Caroline admitted. 'But only one. I miss you sorely when you leave us, you know.'

'Aye,' Nan said, for that was true too, and they both knew it. 'Well then, you'd best start work on your new plan, I suppose. At the least it'll keep 'ee occupied.'

'You will have a baby to keep you occupied soon,' Euphemia said, feeling she really ought to remind them both.

'Oh, not for ages and ages,' Caroline said. Time enough to think about the baby when it was born. 'I've a deal to do before that.'

'Have you told Henry yet?' Nan wanted to know.

'No, not yet,' Caroline admitted easily. And then she changed the subject quickly, in case Nan understood her motives just a little too well. 'You see how natural it is for women to work. I declare we've been talking all afternoon about the work we do, exactly as three men would have done, now ain't we, Nan? I don't believe there's a ha'porth of difference between us in this respect.'

'Except that we breed,' Nan said.

'Yes, so we do,' Caroline admitted, 'but that don't stop us thinking.' And any woman who means to live peaceably with her husband and still keep working has to think very hard.

Fortunately on this occasion her forethought was paying handsome dividends. With Nan's permission she could start work on those new goods tomorrow, then as soon as two or three negotiations were well and truly under way and couldn't possibly be left to anybody else, she could break her news to Henry.

In the event it was Henry who broke the news to her.

They had been making love most pleasurably and were drowsing side by side in the restfulness that always followed the sharpest pleasures.

'Do you breed, sweetheart?' he asked, stroking her rounded belly with gentle finger tips.

'Yes,' she said, too well satisfied to lie or defer. 'Does that please you?'

'Does it please you?' he said, opening his eyes to look down at her.

'Of course.'

'Then it pleases me,' he said, kissed her forehead and was asleep before she could say another word.

When she woke the next morning it surprised her that it had been so easy. And she was even more surprised when he made no objection as she began to dress for her working day. It was almost as if he'd accepted at last, as if he didn't mind.

Actually he was being as cunning as she was. He'd been wondering for several days now, hoping that her thickening waistline would prove to be the sign of a pregnancy, and planning how to act if it were. He gave little thought to the child, beyond a vague assumption that it would be pleasant and proper to have an heir. It was the pregnancy that was his hope, because a pregnancy could be his salvation too. And not a minute before time.

Now that Caroline had embarked on her scheme to sell foot-warmers and such, and with Nan's connivance too, which was annoying, he knew it would be useless to argue with her to stay at home. He would wait until she'd secured supplies of all these unnecessary goods, which shouldn't take long, and then he would urge the need for rest.

It took until Christmas for the goods to be ordered, and she only stopped then because the wholesalers had closed down, and the two of them had promised to spend the holiday at Ippark with Joseph and Emmeline.

Fortunately it turned out to be a long, leisurely holiday, extending well into the new year of 1847, and taking Caroline to within three months of her confinement.

Now, Henry thought, as they travelled home to Richmond through the darkened countryside, now is the right time for her to stay at home. I shall speak of it tomorrow morning over breakfast.

It was a waste of breath.

'Rest?' she said. 'What do I need with rest? I'm as fit as a flea.'

'In your condition . . . ' he began.

But she already had her bonnet on. 'Time enough for rest when I feel fatigued,' she said. 'I'm off to the Mile End today to see about some shawls. With the spring coming ladies are bound to need shawls, don't you think?'

'But it's January,' he protested.

'Quite,' she said briskly. 'So you see there ain't a minute to lose. Have you ordered the carriage for half-past?'

She was impossible. There was no arguing with her, no living with her. As the weeks progressed and the child grew to very obvious proportions he began to worry that it would be born in the Easter headquarters. To say nothing of the fact that she was upsetting the tender susceptibilities of the regional managers.

'I can't tell her anything,' he complained to Joseph, when they met in his brother's club in Piccadilly. 'She was bad enough before the child, but I tell 'ee she's a deal worse now.'

'She'll settle,' Joseph promised, enjoying his brandy. 'They always do. A sort of nesting spirit comes on 'em all of a sudden. Always does. You'll see.'

But Henry couldn't imagine Caroline nesting. She was far too brisk and energetic.

'Well, of course she is,' his brother agreed. 'She's an Easter, dammit. Cheer up, little brother. Things'll improve when her cousin moves in. Pheemy, ain't it? A woman of sense, your Pheemy.'

The woman of sense took up residence in the middle of April, when Nan and Mr Brougham had returned to London, there was less sickness in Clerkenwell, and the lamps and shawls were selling particularly well.

For a few days Caroline was quite cheerful to superintend the hiring of nursemaids, the furnshing of the nursery and the arrangement of the lying-in room that adjoined it, for, as she confessed to her nurse, she would be jolly glad when her pregnancy was over and done with. The child was packed so tightly inside her belly that she was often very uncomfortable, even in the shapeless gowns and boxy jackets she'd had made to cover her awkwardness, but she was too restless to settle, and after a week at home, she began to prowl through the house grumbling that she felt imprisoned.

'Yes,' Euphemia sympathised, 'but it will soon be over now, my darling. How if we were to take a ride in the countryside?'

'I'd rather take a train into London,' Caroline said. And off she went, with Euphemia in anxious attendance.

Her behaviour infuriated Henry, particularly as he didn't like to check it for fear of harming the baby. And it drove Mr Jernegan and Mr Maycock into apoplexy.

'It's downright disgusting,' Mr Maycock said, spraying spittle all over the corner of Edward's desk. He and Mr Jernegan had come up to the Strand together to see if the rumours were true and they were both horrified to find that they were. 'Don't she have any sense of propriety, appearing here day after day in that condition? Mrs Easter should stop her.'.

'Mrs Easter approves, I fear,' Edward told him, wiping the spit from his desk with the duster he kept ready for such emergencies. There were times when he found Mr Maycock rather trying.

'Then her husband should.'

Edward put the duster back in its tray and shrugged his shoulders eloquently.

'When our dear Queen is enceinte,' Mr Jernegan said,

'which it has to be said is often the case, although I'm sure it is a cause for congratulation to her devoted subjects, if a trifle expensive if you follow me, when our dear Queen is enceinte you don't see even so much as a scrap of her in public places. No indeed. Not a scrap. Our dear Queen has the discretion to hide herself *away*.'

'*Courage, mon vieux*!' Edward said. 'The child will soon be delivered and so will we.'

'Amen to that, Mr Edward sir,' Mr Maycock sprayed, 'for I tell 'ee, 'tis a scandal sir. It ain't proper.'

'Ah, but what if we ain't delivered?' Mr Jernegan said. 'What then? If you want my opinion, we're being taken over, that's what's happening.' His long saturnine face glowered with righteous indignation. 'It's Mr Henry this and Mr Henry that at every blessed meeting nowadays, and if it's not Mr Henry it's Mrs Henry and that's a sight worse when you consider where she ought to be. We're being taken over by a pair of interlopers, for when all's said and done, who are they? He ain't a true member of the family, and she's a woman. We shall never be rid of him or her.'

'If the child don't do the trick,' Edward said, giving his two colleagues a knowing smile, 'then there are other ways to kill the cat. We shall get what we all desire in the end. Never fear. Meantime, we may be rid of the lady in less than a month. Think of that, Mr Jernegan. In less than a month.'

But until then they all had to wait, each with his individual hopes. And misgivings.

The child was born in the early hours of 3 May after a labour in which his mother prowled and groaned and tried to make herself comfortable in all sorts of positions, lying and sitting. She even tried a pile of cushions set on the floor because she said the bed was impossible. And she kept her maid, young Totty Jones from the ragged school, perpetually on the run, fetching hot drinks and cold sponges and more and more cushions.

During a lull in the long first stage, and after she'd sent Totty off for raspberry tea so that she wouldn't hear, she asked Euphemia how the baby was going to get out. She had wondered about it earlier but had been reluctant to broach the subject, even with her dear Pheemy. Now she was full of anxiety about it.

'Why,' Euphemia said, 'by the same route as it got in.'

Caroline was quite shocked. 'Pheemy!' she said, her grey eyes enormous above pain-flushed cheeks. 'Do you know about – that?'

'Oh yes,' Euphemia assured. 'I was brought up in India, don't forget, and in India everybody knows about it. In India, love between men and women is considered a holy thing, you see. There were statues in the temples showing it all, exactly, in every detail.'

That was so amazing it made the pain recede. 'Statues!' Caroline said. 'I can't believe it. Why, I've never even heard anyone *speak* about it. Did you see them, these statues?'

'Oh yes,' Euphemia said again, and her lovely madonna face didn't seem the least bit troubled. She was dressed in the full-length white linen apron and the white starched cap advised by Miss Nightingale, and suitably accoutred, she was taking everything that happened with a most commendable calm, even though she wasn't at all sure she would know what to do when the moment of birth actually arrived.

'What were they like?'

'They were beautiful,' Euphemia said. 'Full of joy and satisfaction.'

'Good heavens!' Caroline said. What an extraordinary thing. She would never have thought of it as holy. Full of pleasure certainly, but not holy. Holiness was for priests and saints, like Mama. And yet Mama must have done those things too, otherwise she and Will would never have been born.

But then another pain took hold and squeezed philosophy and speculation quite away. 'Oh!' she panted, clinging about Euphemia's neck, 'I shall never have another baby as long as I live. I swear it.'

Euphemia decided it was time to send the newly returned Totty to fetch the doctor.

By the time he arrived Caroline was in the throes of pains so extreme that Euphemia was quite worried beneath the calm of that professional apron. But he was comfortingly unruffled and having declared that there was no cause for alarm he sat himself by the window, opened a chink in the curtains and proceeded to watch the sky.

And in the event the child was born without any need of his help. It was a boy, as pink as poached salmon and with an amazingly wrinkled face and a cavern of a mouth and the oddest crest of dark damp hair like a coxcomb. Caroline was delighted with him and took him in her arms and kissed him over and over again and told him he was the dearest little duck, and when Euphemia suggested that it might still his cries if he were put to the breast, she fed him at once and with pleasure, smiling at Euphemia over the top of his busy black head, and ignoring the doctor completely.

By the time Henry was finally allowed into the room to inspect his offspring, she was completely recovered, and held the baby up between her hands for him to see, glowing with pleasure.

'Madam is a natural mother,' the doctor said, as he and Henry went back downstairs.

'I'm glad to hear you say so,' Henry said. It was past six o'clock and they could hear the servants clattering up and down the back stairs. A new day was beginning, and everything was as it should be.

'It ain't always the case, I'm grieved to say,' the doctor confided.

'But it is with Mrs Easter.'

'Oh indeed.'

Thank heavens for that, Henry thought. Now we can live our lives as we should, with the man of the house earning the living and the woman at home with her baby. And for the next two weeks, it seemed that he was right.

Caroline spent her days in a milky trance, either feeding the baby or cuddling him or eating enormous meals herself or held fast in a glowing sleep. Her friends and relations came to visit, bearing gifts, the child was named, Henry after his father and William after his uncle, his great-uncle and his great-grandfather, and the date for his christening was set. And they were all peacefully happy together.

And even when she was allowed up and came downstairs for her first dinner with her husband, she talked of nothing except little Harry and what a dear good boy he was, and how strong.

She was still decidedly plump after the birth, plump and easy, pink cheeked and bright eyed, and she looked so happy it was a joy to see her. Oh yes, Henry thought, a natural mother, and he loved her with the most pleasantly protective warmth because of it.

So it was all the more of a shock to him when the papers arrived for the next regional manager's meeting in June and she told him she was going to attend.

'You can't!' he said. 'I forbid it.'

'Oh come,' she rebuked, sparkling at him from the other side of the breakfast table, 'we ain't starting all that again, surely? Of course I shall attend. I've had a simply splendid idea while I've been at home with Harry, and I've talked it over with Nan and done a lot of work on it, and now I can't wait to tell everybody all about it.'

He tried to keep his temper and be reasonable. 'Tell me about it,' he urged, 'and I will present it to the committee on your behalf.'

'No fear!' she said. 'I mean to be there to see their faces when I tell 'em. That'll be half the sport.'

'And what is to become of poor Harry while you are so employed?' he wanted to know. 'You have a child now, Caroline, and you must stay at home and care for him.' And it grieved him to hear how pompous he sounded, particularly when he knew that what he was saying was right and proper.

'As if I wouldn't,' she said. 'You mustn't worry about Harry, my dearest. Harry will be looked after just the same as ever. He shan't want for anything, I can promise you. As if I would ever neglect my baby!'

'I don't see how you can say that, if you mean to go traipsing up to London to attend this meeting.'

'Why, I shall take him with me, of course,' she said, helping herself to another slice of toast from the rack.

He could feel his heart sinking in his chest. 'Oh, Caroline!' he said. 'Why must you act in this way? It ain't seemly.'

'You sound just like Papa,' she said cheerfully. 'He was always saying things weren't seemly.'

'He was probably right, poor man,' his son-in-law said with miserable fellow-feeling. And as there didn't seem to be any way of persuading her, and he couldn't shout at her when she'd just had a baby, and in any case she'd taken away all his appetite, he left the table and went upstairs to prepare for work.

All through that day, whenever he had a moment for thought, he pondered the problem she'd set him. If she went to the meeting and put her plan into operation she would go on and on with it until it was completed, no matter how hard she had to work and how often it took her out of the house. It was no use appealing to Nan because her support had already been canvassed and won, and although Euphemia would be sympathetic she would hardly be able to persuade a determined character like Caroline. It needed a man to cope with her, and now that her father was dead there was nobody else who could do it. Uncle Billy was too feeble to stand up to anybody, through no fault of his own poor man, for he couldn't help being ill, and Edward was no good either because there was something about him that you couldn't trust, and although Will understood her, he spoiled her as much as everybody else, and in any case he was rarely at home.

No, there was nothing for it, he would either have to oppose her himself or allow her to go to the meeting. And he couldn't oppose her when she was so recently confined. That would be neither fair nor proper. So the meeting it had to be, even though he knew her attendance was unwise. Perhaps the regional managers would solve the problem for him by rejecting her idea out of hand.

But of course they didn't. She presented it too well.

The managers' reports were read and accepted with some modifications, and when Nan handed the meeting over to her granddaughter, 'who has a new plan to present to 'ee, which I'm sure you'll welcome'.

They prepared to listen politely, turning their faces towards her, although Henry noticed that Mr Maycock and Mr Jernegan were frowning and Edward was wearing the blank expression that showed he was keeping his feelings under tight control. To everyone's surprise and interest she began by circulating a report of her own. When had she had that printed? Henry wondered. And by whom? No wonder she said she'd done a lot of work on this. And he had to admire her despite his annoyance.

'This is a very simple plan, gentlemen,' she said as the clerk placed the last paper in front of the last manager, 'however, in my estimation, it will increase the takings at most of our shops by something in the region of 20%. It will require extra workers of course, porters, counter hands, warehousemen. I have estimated the likely cost of such an increase. You will find the figures on the second page of my report. And as you are the lynch pins of the entire operation I have estimated a potential increase in your salaries too, as you will also see, which is likely to be somewhere in the region of 20% depending upon the sales in your area, as you would expect.'

It was masterly. Except for Mr Maycock and Mr Jernegan the regional managers were eating out of her hands even before they'd opened the report.

'What I propose,' she said, 'is that we should sell books at all our shops as well as from our railway stalls. The way forward for this company is to extend the range of the goods we sell. If you are agreeable to my suggestion we shall cease to be merely newsagents and become newsagents, stationers and book-sellers, with our signs altered accordingly.'

They were warm with excitement at the idea. Some of them were already writing surreptitious figures in the margins of the report, estimating what their salary increase would be. Even Mr Jernegan and Mr Maycock had stopped frowning and were looking interested. But it was Edward's reaction that was the most surprising.

When the buzz died down a little, he looked across to Nan to show that he would like to speak, for he was always perfectly correct on these occasions.

'May I say, cousin Caroline,' he said, 'how much I welcome and support your proposal, which seems to me quite excellent. In fact not just excellent but obvious, as are all good ideas, when once they've been thought and developed and explained, are they not? I hardly think we shall need to put this matter to the vote, for I cannot imagine anyone about this table who would see anything in it that they could possibly oppose. There might be one or two who might have, shall we say, doubts,' glancing at Mr Jernegan, 'but I think I may assure them that a plan like this should give us all the very thing we require, and probably in a shorter time than we now think possible. That being so I would like to second my cousin's proposition.'

A throaty 'Hear hear' rumbled about the table, but Nan required a vote, just the same.

It was a unanimous triumph. And the pleasure and excitement of it spilled over into Nan's customary dinner that night.

It would have been an exciting party in any case, because Will had come home that afternoon, and what was even better, intended to stay in London for 'about a month'. So for the first time since the autumn, all ten 'London Easters' were gathered about Nan's table; Billy and Matilda, Edward and Mirabelle, Jimmy and Matty, Caroline and Henry, Euphemia and Will.

He was in splendid humour and exceedingly handsome, for while he'd been travelling the country, covering Chartist meetings and following the progress of the third National Petition, he'd put on weight and grown a beard. Not a neat moustache and a carefully trimmed Spanish goatee like Henry's but a full bristling set, covering the whole of his lower jaw in thick curls of hair only slightly darker than those that covered his head. It gave him an air at once dashing and formidable, like a military man or a sea-captain.

He was full of stories, about Mr Feargus O'Connor's election as Member of Parliament for Nottingham, about the five million signatures already gathered on the National Petition, about the new potato famine in Ireland and the trade recessions in France. 'We are still in the middle of railway expansion here in England,' he said, 'but in France the navvies are being laid off.'

'So France will be your next destination,' Mr Brougham said.

'It seems likely.'

'I hope I may persuade you to be a speaker at my next literary salon if that is to be the case,' Mirabelle said. 'Our neighbour's politics are always intensely interesting to the London literati.'

'If I am back in London at the time,' he said.

'Which ain't likely, Mirry,' Edward pointed out. 'For I'm deuced if I ever knew a man with such itchy feet.'

'That is a sign of a man with a mission,' Billy said, helping himself to more wine, despite Matilda's scowl of warning. 'Always knew what he wanted, even as a lad at college.' He too had aged noticeably during the winter, but in his case the change was deterioration. His eyes were bloodshot and the skin of his cheeks threaded with purple veins.

'No,' Will said, smiling at his uncle, 'it's a deal more simple than that. I go where the work takes me. That's the truth of it.' It wasn't the entire truth, but he could hardly confess to that. He actually took as many commissions as were offered, and the further he had to travel the better, for that kept him away from home and the difficulties of the continuing attraction he felt for Euphemia. 'The men with the mission are my editors. A reporter is really little more than a camera obscura, like Mr Fox Talbot's new machine. We see the scene and we describe it. No more.'

'But when your view is printed in a newspaper and published to the world, it will surely have an effect upon its readers, will it not?' Frederick Brougham inquired.

'That is what we all hope,' Will admitted, 'but it can't be guaranteed. Scores of us wrote about the starvation in Ireland, but the poor weren't fed, even so.'

'Carrie is the one with the mission,' Nan said, smiling at her. 'We've had revolution in the firm this afternoon and accepted it unanimously what's more.'

I shall never stop her now, Henry thought, watching his wife as she glowed and smiled. She will go back into the firm and work as hard as she ever did, as though she were single, or a man. There is no stopping her. And the thought made him sigh.

Fortunately there was so much happy talk about the table that nobody noticed him. Except Euphemia. And she was sighing too.

To be dining with Will again after such a long time, and to know that she would see him frequently during the next month, was such an exquisitely tantalizing pleasure that she could hardly bear the pain of it. During the winter and spring while she'd been hard at work in Clerkenwell and looking after Caroline in Richmond she had persuaded herself that her love for him was a childish passion, over and forgotten, but the sight of him now, so handsome and self-assured, had renewed all her old feelings and magnified them a hundredfold. She loved him more than ever, only now she knew how hopeless it was. What a blessing she was still staying in Richmond with Caroline. To be living in the same house for a month would have been a torment, and plainly something she would have to avoid in the future. I will write to Miss Nightingale, she decided, for she must be returned by now, and perhaps she will be able to recommend a hospital where I could train, preferably somewhere abroad.

Fortunately Caroline solved Euphemia's problem for her the very next morning, by begging her to stay on and help with the baby while she set about ordering the books for her new venture.

'Henry will be so much more happy about it, if you do,' she said. 'He don't like me to work you know, poor darling. They could spare you for a little longer at Saffron Hill, could they not?'

They had to spare her for more than six months, for it took until the end of the year to organize the book sales to Caroline's satisfaction. But organized they were, eventually. And on the day before the December meeting the first returns to show a 20% increase in sales arrived at the Easter headquarters. She took them straight into Henry's office in triumph.

'There you are, you see,' she said, 'wasn't I right?'

'Yes,' he said, grudgingly, 'you were.'

'And Harry has taken no harm of it?'

That had to be admitted too, for he was a fine fat baby and travelled with her most contentedly, always providing Euphemia was with him too.

'So you see.'

He felt he had to warn her that her luck might not always hold, that her judgement might sometimes be faulty, that she was doing the wrong thing, dammit. But he couldn't find the words for fear of starting a too public row. 'You can't always do exactly what you want,' he said.

She gave him a rapturous and infuriating smile. 'I can't see any reason why not,' she said.

There were plenty of reasons why not, and one of them was sitting in a dark tavern in Holywell Street entertaining his 'valued friend and colleague', Mr Leonard Snipe.

Chapter 22

The Six Jolly Sea-Salt Fishermen in Holywell Street was an ugly tavern and peculiarly ill-named. It was a cramped, narrow building blackened by soot and standing at the dirtiest corner of the street between two perpetually steaming piles of rubbish and manure. Being more than a quarter of a mile from the banks of the Thames it had never served any fishermen in the whole of its existence, sea-salt or otherwise. And if by chance one had ever strayed into its musty interior he would have been hard put to it to be jolly, for the place was low-ceilinged, ill-ventilated, dark and dirty, in fact more like a dungeon than the 'place of public recreation and refreshment' that it claimed to be.

However, it suited Mr Hugh Jernegan's present purpose to perfection. None of his colleagues would have dreamed of looking for him in such a place and he and Mr Snipe, having hidden themselves in the smoke of the chimney corner among the pewter pots and the fire irons and several broken baskets full of sea-coal and flotsam, could speak as freely as their natures would allow. For what was soon to be said or hinted at was fraught with danger for both of them and it was imperative that they shouldn't be overheard.

The time had come for Mr Edward Easter to remove his troublesome cousin from the firm and make a play for his own rightful position in it, which was, of course, as managing director and eventual owner, and then, and this was far more important, to instal the first full management committee with voting rights for every member and Mr Jernegan himself as chairman. There would be no more nonsense then, no more petticoat government, no more interlopers, no more selling of disreputable newspapers like that deplorable *Northern Star*. No, no. The firm would have tone. That's what it would have. Tone. And high time too.

Mr Edward was content to let matters take what he called 'their natural course'. If you ever heard of anything so feeble!

'Ordering all those books could be the end of her,' he'd explained. 'All that work! Think of it! She'll find she's bitten off more than she can chew.'

Mr Maycock hoped so, spluttering his enthusiasm.

But Mr Jernegan meant to make sure of it. He'd always known that what they needed to frighten the lady away was a nice juicy little scandal. And on the day Mr Edward introduced him to Mr Snipe and his 'delectable publications' he knew how it could be brought about.

'It has always been my opinion,' he was saying, peering through the smoke that was billowing from the fire, 'that members of the Society for the Suppression of Vice have no conception at all of the nature of art and the artist. No conception at all.'

'None,' Mr Snipe agreed, picking the bones from the bloater that Mr Jernegan had so kindly provided for him.

'Nor of the perfectly natural desires and inclinations of mankind, which we all share to a greater or lesser degree.'

'They are most of them women, you see, sir, which don't exactly predispose them to such intelligence. More's the pity.'

'Quite,' Mr Jernegan said. 'Take *The Doors of Delight*, for example. An exquisite book. One might almost say uplifting, might one not?'

'My sentiments entirely. Would that more gentlemen could be uplifted by it. But that is not the way of things, sir, as well we know. It ain't the way of things at all. There's gauntlets to be run and prying eyes to be avoided. It ain't a book to sell by daylight.'

'But if it were,' Mr Jernegan pressed, seeing an advantage, 'you would be happy to sell it, I presume.'

'A hypothetical supposition, sir, given the state of the opposition. Mr Walker's premises were raided only last week and all his stock impounded to be burned, and a finer set of prints a gentleman couldn't hope to find anywhere in the kingdom.'

'A crying shame, sir. It grieves me to hear it.'

They devoured their bloaters for a few seconds, as the smuts blew up from the fire to settle like flakes of black snow on their heads and shoulders and all over the table, bloaters, bread and butter, porter and all. Then Mr Jernegan tried again.

'I have often wondered how many copies of a book such as *The Doors of Delight* would sell.'

'Sufficient, I daresay.'

'Ah, but that would depend upon whose definition of the word "sufficient" you employed, would it not?'

'Aye. It would.'

'I would be interested to know what number you would consider sufficient, sir.'

'Why, the number I could sell, I daresay.'

'Which would be . . . ?' Mr Jernegan prompted.

'It would vary according.'

'To . . . ?' Devil take the man! There was no need to be quite so circumspect.

'The weather,' Mr Snipe said blandly. 'The time of year. The number of gentlemen who required it.'

'And how many might that be?'

'Could be ten, could be twenty, could be none at all. There's no way of knowing.'

Information at last! 'But if there were some way of knowing, then you would welcome it, I daresay.'

Mr Snipe looked up from the mangled spine of his fish and regarded his host with a speculative eye. 'You will allow me to make so bold as to ask, sir,' he said, 'where this conversation might be leading us. Not that I would wish it to lead us anywhere you understand, but there is a certain import to it, which don't escape my notice.'

'Would it surprise you to hear that it might be leading to a possible business proposition?'

'I am not in the business of being surprised,' Mr Snipe said. 'That would hardly be to my advantage if you take my meaning. What manner of business proposition was it you had in mind, sir?'

Now it was Mr Jernegan's turn to be cagey. Sounding out the waters was one thing, setting sail in them quite another, even to catch this particular fish in this particularly fishy inn.

'Well now, as to that,' he said, looking Mr Snipe boldly in the eye so as to display his honesty, 'this is all at a most tentative stage at present, as I am sure you will understand.'

'Tentative is my middle name, sir.'

'Quite. Oh quite.'

'Howsomever, you did have some proposition in mind, I daresay, however tentative. Was it another customer, perhaps, a gentleman, shall we say, too shy to make the first advance?'

'It was too good an opening to ignore. 'Several gentlemen, I do believe.'

'In London or further afield?'

'In London to start with. Further afield later.' He had weighed anchor. Now what would happen, would happen.

'And how many gentlemen would there be, would you say?'

'To be plain with you,' Mr Jernegan said, giving his honest stare again, 'and it is always best to be plain, is it not, I believe the time is approaching when a certain bookseller and newsagent, well known to me but which I am not in a position to name as yet, as you will understand, well then, this bookseller and newsagent might be prepared to consider selling from the list of a publisher such as yourself.'

'You don't say so, sir.'

'I do.'

'Would this bookseller and newsagent, whom we would not name of course, not be afraid of the Society we were speaking of earlier, if you take my meaning?'

'With an established and discreet clientele there is less risk, is there not?'

'That is so, if the clientele are well known to the seller, not otherwise.'

'Oh, I think I could assure you on that point. The clientele would be very well known, and the sale discreet. We would not be contemplating such an arrangement were there to be any real risk attached to it, now would we? I ask you as a gentleman of sensibility.'

'You say not,' Mr Snipe admitted.

'Then I may take it, that should the bookseller and newsagent be prepared to sell some of your publications in some of their shops under the most discreet conditions, you would not be averse to the arrangement.'

'If the price were right and discretion guaranteed, it could prove to be a profitable transaction for both parties.'

'As I surmised, sir. As I surmised.' The pot-boy was lurking among the smoke clouds in case they meant to give him another order. 'Brandy to celebrate our understanding, I think, sir.'

'How long would it be before this company we spoke of required a sight of my list?' Mr Snipe asked as the pot-boy dissolved into the darker recesses.

'Some weeks,' Mr Jernegan said vaguely. 'After Christmas certainly. It ain't a thing to rush, you'll agree. And to tell 'ee true, the bookselling side of the business is only just established.'

'Aye,' Mr Snipe said. 'I have seen the present stock in the Fleet Street shop.' His face was bland in the firelight.

'Meantime I daresay you could provide me with one of your more artistic publications. *The Goddesses of Greece*, for example.'

'I could.'

'Then pray do, sir, and I will send one of our representatives to see you upon some future date.'

'Aye. There is no harm in that.'

He seemed cautious but the hook was baited. Now to enlist the help of Mr Maycock, who would be quite the most suitable representative to send, and to persuade Mr Edward to sway the December meeting.

It turned out to be far more difficult than he had imagined. For Mr Maycock was in an intransigent mood, questioning everything, and spraying like a watering can.

When Mr Jernegan told him that he'd discovered some rather interesting books that he thought the company ought to offer, and that he hoped Mr Edward would suggest their sale to Mrs Henry, he began to complain at once.

'We are all having to sell enough books as it is,' he grumbled, 'without offering her more.'

'I told you,' Edward explained patiently. 'If we overburden her, she will be forced to resign.'

'Or take on two more secretaries. That's what she'll do. That's my opinion.'

'No,' Edward insisted, using his duster, 'she won't. She likes to be her own boss and make her own decisions. You know that. So that is how we will catch her. Hoist by her own petard.'

'She ain't a mouse, dammit,' Mr Maycock grumbled. 'She's a woman grown and quite sharp enough to see through a trick.'

'Now come,' Edward said. 'We are not out to trick her, as you put it.'

'Are we not?' Mr Jernegan said, from his seat beside the window. 'Well now, I rather thought we were.'

'And what sort of trick did you imagine we were planning, Mr Jernegan?' Edward asked, speaking slowly so as to give them both time to prepare themselves for the next stage of this conversation, wherever it might take them, for he could see that Mr Jernegan was plotting something, and the knowledge excited him.

'We ain't playing tricks at all,' Mr Maycock said, 'or you may count me out of it.'

'I had been considering the possibility of a little, shall we say, scandal?' Mr Jernegan said, gazing out of the window at the wintry Strand below him.

'There is risk to scandal,' Edward said, watching both his allies carefully.

'Then let us have no part of it,' Mr Maycock said, and he left his seat beside Edward's desk and went to sit beside the fire, as if he were distancing himself from the discussion.

'If we play for high stakes,' Mr Jernegan said, 'there are bound to be risks involved, ain't that so? And I assume we play for very high stakes.'

'High enough,' Edward said, very coolly. 'Voting rights for your committee for example.'

'Voting rights for our committee with Mr Edward Easter as director of the company and myself as chairman?'

'That would seem a happy working relationship.'

'Then perhaps the time has come to talk of ways and means, Mr Edward.'

'What do you have in mind, Mr Jernegan?'

'I think it would be good sport to tease Mrs Henry into accepting one of Mr Snipe's publications,' Mr Jernegan said.

'Who's Mr Snipe?' Mr Maycock said suspiciously.

306

But Edward let out his breath in a whistle of surprise and admiration. 'Could we do it?' he asked.

'Mr Snipe is agreeable to providing the books,' Mr Jernegan said, 'which is a start, you'll allow. Now all we have to do is to persuade the committee to accept – shall we say – artistic books in addition to those we sell already, and to find some way of teasing Mrs Henry into doing what we wanted, which shouldn't be beyond the bounds of possibility. I do believe . . . '

'Who is Mr Snipe?' Mr Maycock worried.

'He's a publisher,' Mr Jernegan said, 'some of whose books contain – um – illustrations that would make some people complain sufficient to put Mrs Henry into an embarrassing position, if they knew she'd took 'em, which we could make sure they did, if you take my meaning.'

'Naked women, you mean?' Mr Maycock said, lips a-wobble.

'Artistic studies,' Mr Jernegan corrected.

'She wouldn't accept 'em,' Mr Maycock said. 'Never in a thousand years. She reads every single book. I've seen her do it. And I hope you don't imagine we could ever sell 'em, Mr Jernegan. Not naked women. There'd be the very devil of a row if we did that.'

'Oh no, no, no,' Mr Jernegan assured. 'We wouldn't sell 'em. Dear me no, Mr Maycock, there'd be no need for that. All we'd need to do is *order* 'em, once we've teased Mrs Henry into accepting 'em. In fact, sir, if it worries you, you could be the man responsible for handling the order, could he not Mr Edward? And then you would be quite sure no harm could come of it.'

That seemed an admirable plan to both his listeners, although Edward was only giving part of his attention to it because he was busy plotting how to persuade his cousin into accepting the books in the first place.

'If we were to arrange matters,' he said, thinking aloud, 'so that she had scores of new books to consider and all at once, what's more, she wouldn't be able to look at them all, let alone read them. We could urge all the others to ply her with books, too. That's how it could be done, Mr Jernegan. With sustained pressure, who knows what we might achieve. Oh, it's a capital idea. I think we should do it.' It would just serve her right for pushing herself into the firm, where she had no business to be.

'And here's the meeting tomorrow,' Mr Jernegan pointed out, 'come just at the right time for us to make a start.'

'Leave the meeting to me,' Edward said, happily confident. 'I'll sway 'em, you just see if I don't.'

It was a very easy meeting to sway, for all the members were in congratulatory humour and Nan was in a rush to have the whole thing over and done with so that she could start her long journey back to Westmoreland with Mr Brougham.

Caroline started the proceedings by serving them all champagne, 'to mark our success' and Henry had written a résumé of all the reports, 'since they all say much the same thing, with minor variations', so there was very little left for the regional managers to do except enjoy each other's company and drink their champagne. They reached 'any other business' in less than a quarter of an hour.

'Never knew a meeting go so quick,' Nan approved. 'Do we have any other business?' Expecting none.

'Well,' Edward said, catching her eye. 'There is a little matter we might like to consider.'

'Yes?'

'It has occurred to me,' he said, smiling his most charming smile, 'that we might like to extend the range of the books we sell, seeing the success we're having. At present we offer novels and poetry, and books on travel and home management, do we not?'

That seemed to be agreed.

'But no books on art or sculpture or architecture, for example.'

'Would they sell?' Nan wanted to know.

Several of her managers thought they would.

'I brought along a rather fine art book,' Edward said, following Mr Jernegan's excellent advice and placing *Goddesses of Greece* on the table before them. 'It is rather expensive at present as you will see, but with the sort of sales we could offer I'm sure the price could be adjusted.'

'It usually is,' Caroline agreed, picking up the book and glancing at the pictures.

'Do you want to propose an extension to our current list?' Nan asked, and she seemed quite happy about it.

'No,' Edward said cautiously. 'Not yet. It might not prove to be such a good idea on mature consideration. I thought we might all look for suitable books and send copies of them to Mrs Henry before the next meeting and then we could reconsider the matter in the light of what we've found.'

'You will be inundated with books,' Henry warned his wife.

But the challenge excited her, as Edward had known it would. 'Inundate all you like,' she said. 'I think it's an excellent idea.'

And so it was agreed. And to Mr Jernegan's hidden satisfaction the second hook was baited.

Now it was simply a matter of waiting for the tide, for the moment when, hard-pressed and over-worked, the foolish Mrs Henry could be persuaded to accept Mr Snipe's scurrilous material without looking at it. Mr Maycock was just the man to do it, and simple enough to be persuaded to it, but the moment would have to be carefully prepared and it would be best done at a time when her natural supporters were out of town. And of course the two most important people who ought to be removed were Mr Will Easter, who was always an unknown quantity, and Miss Euphemia Callbeck, who would be sure to help her cousin if she were there to do it. It was the most difficult problem in the whole affair, for as an employee of the firm Mr Jernegan knew he couldn't possibly influence any members of the family.

But the fates were on his side. In January Miss Nightingale wrote to Euphemia from Rome to tell her that there was now no doubt in her mind that she would found a hospital 'in the very near future' and to suggest that Euphemia should prepare herself for that future by enrolling as an assistant, 'for a month or two' at St Bartholomew's Hospital, 'where you will not learn the things you ought to do as a nurse, but will most assuredly see all those things you ought not to do, and what is more important, will discover whether or not you have the stomach for the profession.'

And in February Will was despatched to Paris to cover a

Grand Reform Banquet which was to be held there to further the cause of universal suffrage.

He went without very much enthusiasm, because reform meetings were two-a-penny these days and rarely provided anything exciting enough to make a good story, but happily enough because his old friend Jeff Jefferson was travelling with him.

'We shall be home in a day or two,' he said, as the two of them climbed aboard the train to Dover, with old Tom Thistlethwaite in attendance.

'You don't think there'll be a revolution then?' Jeff said, taking his seat. His editor had been full of speculation about the possibility of a new uprising, which was why he was being sent out.

'Over a reform meeting?' Will said. 'In these enlightened times? I doubt it. Parisians might have gone in for armed rebellion back in 1789, but they won't take that sort of action now. This is 1848.'

But as events were to prove, Paris in 1848 was a city of surprises.

Chapter 23

When Will and Jeff Jefferson arrived in Paris it was late afternoon and already growing dark, but the city seemed peaceful. The old tenements were still there like dark cliffs lowering over the cobbles, there were the usual vociferous crowds in the streets, and the gas lights in the boulevards cast their golden shells of illumination on the grand old houses and the splendid new carriages that were returning home after an afternoon's entertainment. The ladies were magnificently dressed in crinoline skirts a great deal wider than the fashion in England, and the gentlemen were plainly dandies, in silk cravats and velvet coats and plush hats in every conceivable colour. If a revolution was being planned they didn't seem to be aware of it.

However, when the three travellers reached the centre of the city, it was plain that there *was* something going on. Every café was loud with argument and the Place de la Concorde was full of prowling citizens. So they sent Tom Thistlethwaite off to prepare their lodgings, and then walked straight into the nearest argument, notebooks at the ready.

'What is happening, monsieur?' Will asked.

'You are English?' the nearest man replied. 'Arrived for the Reform Banquet?'

'Yes.'

'Then you could have saved yourself the journey. The banquet is cancelled.'

That was a surprise. 'But why?' Jeff asked.

The man shrugged. 'This is what we ask ourselves,' he said. 'It is by order of the Prefect of Police, damn him. There is to be no banquet and no demonstration neither. It is all forbidden.'

'Is it true, do you think?' Jeff asked in English as he and Will moved away from their informants.

'We'll go and find the Chartist delegation, and see what they have to say,' Will decided. 'They'll know if anyone does, and I've been invited to dine with them as soon as I can.'

They set off through the noisy streets to find their compatriots, who had taken rooms in a tenement in the Rue Montorgueil, not far from the city market of Les Halles. The concierge said they were out, dining at a small café near the old church of St Eustache. 'You will see them, messieurs,' she said. 'They are so numerous and so English.'

Which was true enough, for there were over two dozen of them and they filled the little eating house, crowded around four overloaded trestle tables and all talking at the tops of their voices. And their leader was none other than Dr Taylor from Birmingham who, despite grey hair and an ageing stoop, still sported the sort of seafaring uniform that Will remembered him wearing at the time of the Bull Ring riot all those years ago.

'Come in! Come in!' he boomed. 'I am glad to see that you London journalists are starting to arrive. Have you heard the news?'

They told him they had, and asked if it were true.

Apparently it was, and all done on the orders of Monsieur Guizot, the Prime Minister. 'Although I wouldn't want to cross 'em if I were that gentleman. The Parisians are a volatile crew and there's a rare mood hereabouts.'

'Do you think there will be a revolution?'

'Personally,' Dr Taylor said, 'I doubt it. But who can tell? There are others among us of a different opinion. My friend here, for example, who is a journalist like yourself.' And he turned on his stool to pluck at the sleeve of the gentleman who was sitting beside him. 'You think an uprising likely, do you not, sir?'

The man turned to give them his full attention. 'Aye, I do,' he said. 'Particularly now that these gentlemen have arrived from t'London newspapers.'

'How so?' Will asked, intrigued. It was flattering to think that his presence would make a difference to the situation.

'Things will be said in t' streets that should have been said at t' banquet,' the man told him, 'and all of 'em things that Monsieur Guizot would rather were left unsaid, so he'll do what he can to stop them. Bad enough that t' people of Paris will hear them, worse if they are to be spread to t' people of England. Governments are t' same t' world over, public knowledge of their actions is anathema to them.'

A rough looking man, Will thought, for he looked like a navvy, squat, stocky, and weatherbeaten, with broad shoulders, a barrel chest and scarred, hairy hands. But he knew what he was talking about and spoke with authority, so that people around the table paid attention to him, stopping their own conversations to hear what he was saying. Will was puzzled by his accent which was a hybrid unlike any he'd ever heard before, mixing the occasional clipped speech of the midlands with the burr of another broader, foreign dialect, and yet using the words of Oxford English with such ease that they were plainly natural to him. A mysterious mixture and therefore interesting.

'You work for a newspaper, I understand?' he said, probing for more information.

'Aye,' the man said. 'I started with the *Hobart Town Gazette* back in Van Diemen's Land eighteen years ago. Now I freelance, selling where I can. My last article was taken by the *National* here in Paris.'

Will had never heard of the *Hobart Town Gazette* but he recognized Van Diemen's Land as somewhere in Australia. That would account for the odd accent. 'You are one of the English delegates, I presume?'

'No sir,' he said. 'I've not seen England these twenty-two years, not since '25. I met these gentlemen by chance at the English pension. I came here from Vienna.'

This was even more interesting. 'Was there unrest in that city too? All the reports suggest it.'

'Aye. There was, sir. There's a reforming spirit all over Europe, in t' states of Italy, in t' Austrian Empire, here in France, in England, a great reforming spirit. It only needs one spark to set it all ablaze.'

'Then shall we see changes, do you think?'

'I hope so, sir, when it's been my life's work to bring 'em about.'

He's a fighter, Will thought with admiration, and certainly he was looking at the face of a fighter, strong but guarded, the shock of grizzled hair bold above a very seamed forehead but the beetling eyebrows lowered to keep his eyes in shadow until he chose to lift his head. There was a blue scar on his right cheek, most of his teeth were missing, and his nose was spread and ugly, having been broken long ago and on several occasions from the looks of it. But his eyes were surprisingly gentle and knowledgeable, large grey eyes fringed with a sweep of black eyelashes. They reminded Will of somebody else's eyes, but before he could think who it was, there was a commotion in the square outside, and the English delegation rushed out as one man to see what was happening.

It was a demonstration. But a very different one from any that Will and Jeff had ever seen before. These men weren't marching in the sober English way. They were running, in a column so wide and so closely packed that it filled the width of the street. Their arms were linked aggressively and they were bellowing the Marseillaise like a battle cry. To Will and Jeff, used to the mildness and sobriety of the Chartist demonstrations in England, they looked threatening. But their Australian friend seemed perfectly at home with such a crowd and instantly disappeared into the charge, to return some minutes later, glowing with news.

Every workshop in the city had closed down, he told them. The people had taken to the streets, to show that 'poor fool Guizot' exactly what they thought of his decree.

'Then it's an uprising?' Will asked.

'The start of one.'

It was the news they wanted and the two friends lost no time in writing it up, hurrying off to the Post Office to ensure that they caught the last post out of the city that night, ready to be sent on to London and Cambridge by the new electric telegraph from Folkestone.

'I believe,' Will wrote, surprised to be actually penning such words after all, 'that we may have witnessed the first act in a new revolution.'

By the next morning there was no doubt of it.

The great crowds were still milling about in the Place de la Concorde and filling the space before the Madeleine, but during the night the National Guard had been called out and the troops had arrived, a hundred thousand of them according to the morning papers, and there were certainly plenty standing guard ostentatiously before the public buildings. In a matter of hours, cannon had been positioned at all the road junctions between the Madeleine and the Bastille, the rich had disappeared, and the city had drawn up its battle lines.

It was a cold bleak day but the streets were warm with anger. At every corner someone was making a passionate speech and from time to time a new column of protestors arrived from the suburbs in the east, singing the Marseillaise or their new, more bloodthirsty hymn, 'Mourir pour la Patrie'.

Will and Jeff stayed beside the crowd, waiting for violence to break, but the morning passed and nothing much happened. The marchers prowled and waited, and the troops stood where they were and waited, the Marseillaise was sung, speeches were declaimed, but there was no conflict. As the afternoon wore on even the air seemed to be brooding and Will and Jeff grew bored with inaction and set off to walk up to the Madeleine to see what was happening there.

They'd barely gone a hundred yards before the crowd ahead of them began to cheer. 'Vive la Réforme! Vive la Garde Nationale!' And then everybody in the street was running, hurtling pell-mell towards the Rue Lepelletier, and Will and Jeff were caught up in the crush and ran with the rest, straining their necks to see what was happening in front of them.

There were two lines of National Guardsmen formed up across the entrance to the Rue Lepelletier, about a hundred and fifty men in all, standing at ease with their officers in the midst of them, and the people were rushing at them headlong, to fling their arms about their necks and kiss them on both cheeks in a frenzy of joy. 'Vive la Reforme! Vive la Garde Nationale!'

Will's rush came to a halt in front of a stolid guardsman with a young woman hanging about his neck. He looked sheepishly happy, pleased and embarrassed all at the same time.

'We have declared for Reform,' he said, when Will asked him what had happened. 'That is, some of us differ about

Reform, but we are agreed about Guizot! Guizot must resign!'

'We are one with the people of Paris,' his neighbour said, as another wave of rejoicing citizens bore down upon them. 'We stand for universal suffrage. One man, one vote.'

Will and Jeff were being jostled about so much that there was no chance of asking any more questions, but they had learned enough to make a story.

'Back to base,' Will said, pushing his way through the hordes.

As the two friends reached the corner where the Rue Lepelletier met the Boulevard des Italiens, they saw a column of cavalry and infantry approaching on the trot, mounted Guardsmen and cuirassiers, and behind them, infantry of the line. At the intersection they made a move as if they were going to wheel into the street, but then they saw the National Guard who were still being rapturously embraced, and they paused. There was a moment of indecision, the order was given to march on, but none of them moved, although the horses fidgeted and snorted. Then without order or warning they turned around and retreated up the Boulevard. It was an amazing victory and the cheers were prolonged and triumphant. And of course it made a perfect end to the story.

By the time both reports had been written and despatched, it was growing dark and the streets were emptying.

'I suggest we go down to Les Halles and see if we can find the Chartists,' Will said. 'They might know what will happen next.'

But there was no sign of their English friends at the Pension, and the café they'd occupied two nights before was shut and shuttered, which was hardly a surprise because most of the streets around it had been closed off by barricades, which had been rapidly put together from upended carts, heavy furniture and cobblestones, and were now being reinforced by anything the citizenry could lay their hands on. They were lit by rush torches and manned by a gang of formidable men armed with rifles and pistols. Busy among the builders was a stocky figure that looked familiar.

It was their new friend from Van Diemen's Land.

'What a day!' he said, wiping his hands on a piece of rag, as they walked towards him. 'Things are quiet enough for t' moment but we've had all sorts happening here. T' National Guard have joined the uprising, and t' students have been wi' a petition to the Chamber of Deputies asking for t' ministers to be impeached. Took it to t' office of t' *National* newspaper, so they did. I met 'em there.'

They told him about the extraordinary scene in the Boulevard des Italiens.

'Much t' same has been happening all over Paris by all accounts,' he said, 'which is t' reason for t' present calm, I shouldn't wonder. If all t' Guards have thrown in their lot with t' people, there's hope of a settlement. T' troops marched off, you say?'

'Meek as lambs,' Jeff told him.

'It's an interesting situation,' their new friend said. 'I'm for a spot of supper while t' lull continues. Would 'ee care to join me?'

'That's uncommon kind of you,' Jeff said, 'Mr – ' And then he hesitated because he couldn't remember the man's name.

'Rawson,' their friend said. 'And you are?'

'Jeff Jefferson, from the *Cambridge Chronicle*. And this is my friend Will Easter, scion of the great firm of A. Easter and Sons.'

'Well, here's a thing,' Mr Rawson said, smiling at them in amazement and pleasure. 'Not related to Mrs Harriet Easter by any chance?'

And Will suddenly realized who he must be. 'Caleb Rawson,' he said. 'Of course. W is for Weaver. You were a weaver in Norwich when I was a child in Rattlesden. Caleb Rawson. The man from Peterloo!'

'T' same.'

'How extraordinary! To meet here in Paris!' This visit was one surprise after another.

'It is that. But we were speaking of Mrs Harriet Easter.'

'Harriet Easter was my mother.'

'Was, sir?'

'She died when my sister was born.'

'I'm uncommon sorry to hear it,' Mr Rawson said, and his face suddenly looked much older, drawn and chilled.

'Where shall we dine?' Jeff asked. 'There don't seem much

317

open hereabouts, and if there's to be a battle I'd prefer to die with a full belly.'

'Behind t' battle lines and across t' river,' Mr Rawson said. 'If you'll follow me.'

They dined on the left bank of the Seine in a small café that opened its doors unwillingly but served a filling stew and a passable apple tart. Then they talked for an hour or two, sometimes about the uprising, but mostly about the Easter family in general and Harriet Easter and her bravery on the field of Peterloo in particular, which seemed a peculiar thing to be doing in a city prepared for revolution. When they finally emerged from behind the shutters, it was pitch dark and the streets were deserted.

'You'd best stay with us tonight, Caleb,' Will said. 'I'd not fancy anyone's chances of crossing the city now.' There were no street lights on the north bank and the place was unnaturally quiet.

So he stayed, since the concierge said she had plenty of rooms available, and in the morning they all had breakfast together in Will's room, wondering what had happened overnight and what the day would bring.

The news was stunning. King Louis Philippe had abdicated and the Prime Minister, the hated Monsieur Guizot, had resigned.

'Then it is all over,' Jeff said, 'and the war won without bloodshed.'

'In two days!' Will said. 'Why, we shall be home again within the week.' It was hardly credible. 'I suppose the rest of the government will resign too.'

'We will go out presently,' Caleb said, 'and see.'

The streets were still full of people, marching arm in arm with their new allies in the National Guard, drinking and singing, and in high good humour. But it took Will and his friends until early evening, when they met up with some of the Chartists, to discover anyone with any information. The government had gone to ground, Dr Taylor said, and he and several others named the Hôtel des Affaires Etrangères as the chosen bolt-hole. The three friends decided to go there and see for themselves as soon as they'd dined.

The Hôtel was surrounded by troops, some standing to

318

attention with their rifles at the ready, some lolling about with their weapons slung across their shoulders. Although they were nominally on guard, they were taking the job lightly, as though there were no real danger, and the crowd that faced them were good humoured too, laughingly taunting that the rats should be allowed to leave their sinking ship. There wasn't really much to report, and Jeff and Will were on the point of walking off to see if they could find some news elsewhere, when they heard the approaching crunch-crunch-crunch of a running column.

It was a very big demonstration, about six hundred people carrying torches and charging up the Boulevard des Capucines with their arms linked, singing as they ran. There was something peculiarly menacing about them, a heat and passion that made the milling crowd give way and the soldiers take guard with some apprehension. Within seconds they were ranged in front of the Hôtel, hard-facing the guards, panting a little from their exertions, but still singing 'Mourir pour la Patrie' at the tops of their voices, with a harsh roaring sound somewhere between a shout and a growl. And when the song ended they began to taunt with a vengeance, abusing the soldiers and calling for the deputies to be brought out 'like the scum they were' to face 'the judgement of the people'.

The alarm and excitement they engendered was palpable. But even so nobody was prepared for what was to happen next.

A young man suddenly detached himself from the marchers, and walked coolly across to the officer in command. For a second Will thought he was going to spit or hurl abuse, but instead he took a pistol from his pocket and fired it straight at the officer's head. Blood and brains sprayed into the air, the crowd roared and groaned, and the officer fell backwards with half his face blown away. It was so quick and so brutal it was almost impossible to take it in.

Retribution was even quicker. Rifles were up and aimed and firing at the crowd even before the people had gathered enough wit to scatter. Will and Jeff hurled themselves away from the line of fire like everyone else, running and shoving at the fusillade cracked among them.

They only stopped when they were completely out of breath, and by then they were at the far end of the Boulevard des Capucines and the marchers had stopped too and were beginning to regroup. Nobody knew how many had been hit, although several had seen bodies on the ground and one man said he'd seen two people fall. And nobody knew what should be done next.

Will and Jeff waited for about a quarter of an hour, afraid and edgy, but staying where they were because they didn't want to miss anything and they knew that something else was sure to happen given the high feeling that was running.

After a few minutes Caleb Rawson came walking towards them. He knew no more than they did, but he hardly had time to tell them so when they heard the tramp of an approaching crowd, and the song of death, 'Mourir pour la Patrie', being chanted in a dreadful low growl. This time the column was slow marching. They were preceded by four men carrying torches, and they were escorting an open cart completely surrounded by torch-bearers. The light was strong and theatrical. Inside the cart there were five dead bodies.

When the head of the column reached the corner of the Rue Lepelletier the song changed to a roar of fury so terrible it made Will's hair stand on the nape of his neck. 'Vengeance!' they screamed. 'Vengeance!'

'We've a revolution to report now, gentlemen,' the weaver said. 'A revolution and no mistake. This is t' spark that'll set fire to Europe. We'll none of us see England much before t' summer, take my word for it.'

The next few days seemed to prove him right, for a great deal happened and very rapidly. The next day the revolutionaries published a proclamation in a newspaper called the *Commerce*. The Chamber of Peers was suppressed and the Chamber of Deputies dissolved. The nation was now a republic and all adult citizens who had attained their majority were electors. It was they who would decide the composition of the next Chamber of Deputies, and the elections would be held on 26 April. The revolution had achieved its ends. Universal male suffrage had arrived.

At the end of the week Jeff Jefferson had to go back to England because he'd written his story and spent his allowance, but Will received a sizeable cheque from Mr Forster, and instructions to take the next train to Vienna. 'This revolution is spreading and will spread,' his editor wrote. 'Proceed to Vienna. Then follow wherever it leads.'

'I've a mind to proceed to Vienna myself,' Caleb Rawson said. 'I've good friends in that city, and there's naught for me in England now.'

'We might travel together,' Will suggested. The weaver was good company and would be a useful guide.

So the matter was agreed and the three companions went their separate ways, Jeff to the calm of Cambridge and Will and Caleb to follow the revolution.

And back in England Euphemia packed her bags ready for St Bartholomew's and her first three months as a hospital nurse.

Chapter 24

'Night duty?' Caroline said. 'Oh Pheemy, you can't work at night. It will make you ill. And besides, we shall never see you.'

'It is only for four weeks,' Euphemia said, 'and four weeks in three months is very little. If I'm to be a nurse I must work in a hospital, and if I work in a hospital I have to take my turn on night duty. You do see that, don't you?'

'Oh I see it,' Caroline agreed, 'but I don't like it. Can't you just work during the day and come back here at night?' She and Henry were dining at Bedford Square and the four of them were still sitting at table over the brandy.

'People are ill at night too, you know, Carrie.'

'Well, yes, I suppose they are. I'm being selfish, I daresay.'

'The arrangements are all made,' Nan said weighing in to help Euphemia who was beginning to look beleaguered. 'No going back now, eh Pheemy?'

'You'll be as far away as Will with his wretched revolution,' Caroline complained. 'We don't even know where he is.'

'His letter said he was going to Vienna first,' Nan told them, 'but that don't mean much the way things are going.'

'I hope he has the sense to stay well away from gunfire,' Henry said. Will's last report from Paris had been very alarming. 'It all sounds jolly dangerous to me.'

'Well, of course it's dangerous,' Caroline said. 'That's why he does it, ain't it Nan? Danger is exciting.'

'To you maybe, miss,' her grandmother said, grinning at her, 'but not to your brother. You've a deal too much daring, always did have, but he's a cautious crittur. He goes where the work takes him, and if there's danger to face, he'll face it, but he don't court it. He never has.'

'Thank heaven for that,' Henry said, teasing Caroline. 'It's as well we've one sensible member in the family.'

And got pinched by the least sensible.

It had been an excellent meal, a sort of farewell party for Euphemia who was off to St Bartholomew's Hospital in the morning. It was a sad occasion nonetheless, for it marked such a change, and for once it was a change that Caroline didn't welcome. Euphemia had lived with her at Richmond for ten months now, ever since young Harry was born. The child doted on her and was never so good as when she was cuddling him and carrying him about on her shoulder. Who would pacify him when she was gone? And especially now when there was so much work to do in the firm. The regional managers had been sending her books by the crateload, and with the March meeting rapidly approaching she soon had to make her mind up which ones to order. It was going to be very difficult.

'Come now, my workers,' Nan said. 'Time we were off to Sadler's Wells. An evening of laughter, that's what we need, before we all buckle down again in the morning. 'Tis my opinion we all work too hard, but that's in the nature of the Easters I suppose, and there en't much I can do about that. Howsomever, tonight, is for *The Merry Wives of Windsor*. Even Mr Brougham has promised to stop poring over that dratted case of his for *this* production. I have his solemn word he'll meet us in the foyer. So hassen you up.'

And she was right of course. The evening did them good, lifting Frederick from his preoccupation with a difficult case, Henry from his irritation at Caroline's continuing passion for work, Caroline from her sadness at losing Euphemia's company, and Euphemia herself from the secret apprehension that had been disturbing her dreams ever since she agreed to be a nursing assistant at St Bartholomew's. Not that she had any doubts about her ambition. It was just that tomorrow she would be walking into the unknown, out of the cosy certainties of domestic life into another world where she would be learning and entirely on her own.

*   *   *

Next morning she drove off to the hospital in a state of inner turmoil.

St Bartholomew's stood on the east side of the rough open space of Smithfield. It was a well-proportioned building of three classically graded storeys, surmounted by a balustraded parapet and topped by a tiled roof on which chimneys smoked in obedient ranks. Its principal front opened onto a quadrangle that faced the chaos of the market but since it was a building that knew how to impress and how to keep its distance, neither the drovers nor their terrified beasts, nor the eager butchers who awaited them ever dared to encroach upon its premises, venturing inside the building only when an accident or their own knives had turned them bloody. In short, it was a daunting place and just the sight of it made Euphemia's heart leap in her bosom.

She took her travelling bag, thanked the coachman and walked into the hospital, keeping her face calm even though her hands were trembling.

The entrance hall was an enclosed oaken space dominated by a magnificent staircase that wouldn't have looked out of place in a palace. The ceiling above it was ornately decorated and the stairwell consisted of two huge murals in which classical figures struck bronzed attitudes or languished palely, according to their sex.

There were several doors leading out of the hall, and although they were all shut they were helpfully labelled, 'Counting House', 'Committee Rooms', 'Admission', 'Examination', 'Discharges', so she was able to walk around them until she found the one she wanted: 'Matron' in stern black letters.

Matron turned out to be a stout woman in her forties, with a florid face and rough hands and a strong smell of onions on her breath. Her dress was a sober blue wool but she wore no apron and no cuffs and her cap, far from being the neat covering that Miss Nightingale advocated and Euphemia fully intended to wear, was a luxury of lace-edged frills.

'Miss Callbeck?' she said disapprovingly. 'Well, I suppose I must welcome you to the hospital, since that is my function, or one of my functions, but pray allow me to tell you, my dear, you are making a great mistake. A hospital is no place for a lady. Unless you're an actress or some such. You ain't an actress by any chance?'

Euphemia admitted that she wasn't.

'No,' the Matron said. 'I thought not. Ah well. You'll learn, I daresay. Follow me.' And she set off at a brisk pace out of the hall.

The oddity of the welcome cheered Euphemia as nothing else could have done. To be met with such disapproval was an encouraging sign, clear evidence that Miss Nightingale was right, that there was a battle ahead of any woman who wanted to change the system, and most important of all that the system was ripe for change. She followed the Matron's blue gown into her very first ward, squaring her shoulders for what lay ahead.

It was a dismal place, as far away from the grandeur of the hall as Saffron Hill was from Buckingham Palace. There were twenty narrow beds ranged on each side of the long room, about half of them occupied. The floorboards were poorly cleaned and there was a slatternly woman slumped in a chair in the middle of the room with her cap over her eyes, fast asleep. She woke with a start when the Matron kicked her shins in passing, but it took her a long time to get her eyes into focus and even longer to struggle to her feet.

'Where is Mrs Rumbold?' the Matron asked her sternly.

'If you please, mum, in the office, mum,' the woman said.

She was swaying where she stood and, as Euphemia noted with distaste, she smelled strongly of spirits. But that was only one unpleasant smell among several very much worse. Plainly slops weren't emptied often enough, and patients weren't properly washed. Many were lying most uncomfortably without any bed linen apart from a dirty blanket. Yes, Euphemia thought as she followed the Matron to the office at the end of the room, 'you will see what ought not to be done' right enough.

They found a tall woman arranging kidney dishes in the office. She was introduced as Mrs Rumbold, and it appeared that she was in charge of the ward.

'Miss Callbeck will be with us for three months,' the Matron said. 'She wishes to learn how to be a nurse.' And her expression showed how little she thought of that for an ambition.

Mrs Rumbold was surprised by it too. 'Are you sure that is

what you want, my dear?' she asked when the Matron had gone.

'Yes,' Euphemia said firmly. 'It is. What would you like me to do?'

'There is not much needs doing this morning,' Mrs Rumbold said, returning to the kidney dishes. 'They've had their breakfast, those who could eat it. We don't do much till the doctor's been. The other nurses have gone off to have theirs. They'll be back presently.'

'I could talk to them, perhaps.'

'I feel I should warn you, my dear, you will learn very little from such women.'

'Then perhaps I could wash some of the patients.'

'Ah!' Mrs Rumbold said. 'If only you would.'

So Euphemia took herself off to the office and unpacked her white apron and her neat starched cap, and put them on as well as she could without a mirror. Then she went off to meet her first patients. She was most upset by what she found.

The beds were allotted to children with fevers, mostly measles and scarlet fever which she could recognize, although some had rashes she'd never seen before, and two looked suspiciously like typhus. According to the books she'd studied, fever cases should be sponged down at least twice every day, and once an hour when the fever was at its worse. But most of these poor children hadn't seen soap and water since they arrived. They'd been left to sweat and suffer on their own and they were consequently very uncomfortable and very dirty, tossing about on their narrow beds and groaning in their sleep.

To make matters worse, there was no water in the ewers, and the slatternly woman was fast asleep again.

Very well, she said to herself, the porter shall get some.

But the porter wasn't prepared to do any such thing and was most affronted to be asked. 'That ain't my line a' country,' he said. 'Not water ain't. Whatcher want wiv water anyways?'

While he was protesting, the other four nurses sauntered back from their breakfast. They were a motley crew, an elderly woman with uncombed grey hair escaping untidily from beneath her cap, two younger women, equally poorly dressed and dishevelled, one dark and surly and the other fair and vacant, and a skinny girl who couldn't have been more than fourteen and looked woefully undernourished. But at least she was friendlier than her three companions and when Euphemia explained why she wanted the water, she offered to lead her down to the courtyard and help her carry it back.

They each found two pails and set off on their errand.

The child said her name was Taffy Biggs, 'daft, innit, when I'm so little', and that she 'come out the orph'nidge'. But for all her lack of weight and inches she was extremely helpful, struggling back to the ward with her two full pails, and showing Euphemia where the flannels were kept and even finding two bowls, while the rest of the nurses sat about the table in the middle of the ward playing cards with the slatternly woman.

It took Euphemia and Taffy the rest of the morning to wash just five of their patients, and at twelve o'clock they had to stop what they were doing because Mrs Rumbold suddenly came out of the office looking brisk and efficient to announce that it was doctors' rounds.

And after the doctors had walked solemnly from bed to bed prescribing leeches and aperients as they went, it was time to serve the children their mid-day meal, which was a very watery stew containing shreds of vegetable and the occasional lump of rather gristly meat. After which the nurses retired to their office to eat a bowl of the concoction themselves. It was every bit as unappetizing as it looked.

Never mind, Euphemia comforted herself, as she ate what she could of it, when we've finished here I can clean up that poor little mite in the next bed. But unfortunately for the poor little mite, Matron had other ideas. As Taffy was filling the bowl with fresh water, a porter arrived with 'a message for Miss Callbeck'. She was wanted in 'Admissions', so he said, and would she please to follow him down.

'Admissions' was a long, chill, empty space more like a corridor than a room, and as sparsely furnished as the ward. It contained a wash stand on which there was a rather dirty bowl and a ewer full of cold water, a wall cupboard where cotton wool and dressings were kept, and a row of cane chairs ranged against the wall for the patients, two of whom were slumped upon them, waiting for her.

They looked like dockers or butchers, but it was difficult to tell because they were both so bloodstained. One was supporting the other, who had a dirty cloth clutched to his forehead and was dripping blood from it onto the sawdust on the floor.

'I brung 'im 'ere, ye see,' his friend explained, 'on account of 'e was 'ere before, when 'e cut 'is 'ead on a cleaver. Show 'er the scar, Tommy. See. All dahn that side.'

It was an ugly scar but Euphemia hardly glanced at it. Her attention was drawn to the gaping wound she revealed on the man's forehead when she lifted up that blood-soaked pad. It was six inches long and spurting blood alarmingly.

She stayed calm with an effort. 'How did you come by such an injury?' she asked the man.

'Trafalgar Square,' the man said, wincing as she eased the last section of the pad away from the edge of the wound. 'The Grand Assemblage. Me an' Charlie got copped. Is it bad, miss? Was we right ter come?'

'Of course you were,' she said, wondering how she could stem that dreadful flow.

'Is it bad?'

'No,' she said, and was pleased to hear how convincing she sounded. 'It's nasty, but we'll soon have you patched up.'

He let out his breath in a great sigh of relief. So it *was* beneficial to give comfort and reassurance, as the books claimed. 'I think you might need a stitch or two. I will give you a clean dressing and then the doctor will look at you. Meantime I will clean the wound for you.'

That was an amazing idea. 'Clean it?' the man asked, squinting up at her. 'Wash it, you mean? Whatever for?'

'To help it to heal more quickly,' she said. 'Dirty wounds are more likely to turn septic.'

'Well, blow me down. I never knew that.'

She sent the porter to ask one of the doctors if he would be so kind as to attend a patient. Then she found a bowl and filled it with water from the ewer, took a little cotton wool from the cupboard, and set about her first attempt at nursing. She was very clumsy, which shamed her, and he endured stoically, which made her feel even worse, but by the time the doctor arrived, smelling strongly of cigar smoke and none too pleased to be taken from his meeting, the wound was clean.

Then four other casualties arrived, all from the same demonstration, two with head wounds, one with a broken arm and one who said his foot had been run over by a cart.

'Why, it looks like a battle,' she said, joking to cheer them. 'You have been in the wars.'

'We have that,' one man said. 'You should ha' seen it. The cops come down on us like ninepence. So you know what we done. We took up the fence round ol' Nelson's column and we set about 'em good an' proper.'

'And what was it all about?' she asked, as she examined the second gash of the afternoon.

'Why, to support the French Revolution and win the vote, to be sure. We seen the coppers off, didn't we Horace? Horace'll tell yer.'

Horace was the man with the swollen foot. 'They come back though, didn't they,' he said lugubriously. 'They come right back, more of 'em than ever. They was still scrapping when we come away.'

Sure enough, casualties continued to limp into the hospital all through the afternoon, and soon more nurses were sent for and the long narrow room was full of people. By the time her long shift ended, Euphemia was tired to the bone, her white apron crumpled and bloodstained and her feet aching as if somebody had been treading on them all afternoon. She could see why Miss Nightingale had told her to wear lightly soled shoes. And she was very glad indeed when Nan's carriage arrived to take her home to Bedford Square to the luxury of clean clothes, scented soap and lovely warm water, to a well cooked meal, which was delicious even if she did have to eat alone, and to the eventual and superlative comfort of her well cleaned bedroom.

It wasn't until she was in bed and almost asleep that she remembered Henry and Caroline and baby Henry and wondered how they'd been getting on all through this long, long day. At least, she comforted herself, it couldn't have been as difficult for them as it had been for her.

But she was quite wrong. It had been very difficult indeed.

For a start the baby had been fractious all day, grizzling to be fed at the most inappropriate times, and refusing to settle to sleep no matter what anyone tried to do to placate him. Totty made things worse by explaining that he was missing Miss Euphemia, poor little man.

'Don't start that,' Caroline said crossly. 'If you've nothing more sensible to say you'd better take him away and see if you can rock him to sleep by the fire. I've got books to read. I can't spend all day feeding babies.'

Books to read was an understatement. She'd never seen so many, piled up on her desk, and in heaps on two of her chairs, and even set down on the carpet. Cousin Edward seemed to have been bringing them in all day long.

'I know you want to make your decisions quite soon, Carrie,' he'd said when he arrived with the last lot. 'Is there anything else I can get you?'

'A bit of peace and quiet,' she said, grinning at him ruefully. 'I shan't have time to look at all these, let alone read them.'

'Then I'll leave you to it,' he said, giving her his most charming smile. 'Mustn't get in the way of business.'

'I wish young Harry thought the same,' she said, picking up a book from the nearest pile.

'If I were you,' he suggested, 'I'd check the top and bottom one in every collection and leave all the others to fend for themselves. Two should be enough to show you the quality.'

'If the worst comes to the worst,' she said, 'that might be a good idea.'

And the worst did come.

Harry was disconsolate without Euphemia. He grizzled his way through the next ten working days, stopping only when his harassed mother took time away from her decisions to hang a 'Do not disturb' notice on her door and sit behind a screen in her inner office and feed him into a better humour. The days passed far too quickly. Soon it was the day before the quarterly meeting and there were still six piles of books needing attention, the list of intended orders wasn't drawn up and just when she was at her wits' end and ready to scream at the next interruption, Mr Maycock came bumbling into her office with what he dared to call 'a last minute addition'.

'Impossible!' she said. 'There isn't time for any more. I've still all these to look at.'

His fat face fell visibly. 'Oh dear!' he said. 'I thought them quite excellent, upon my soul I did, or I wouldn't have brought 'em. You *did* say we were to show you all the books we considered suitable. It is written in the minutes. I have my copy here.'

'I have half an hour,' she told him sternly, looking at the clock.

Fortunately Edward came breezing in just at that moment. 'Now, now Mr Maycock,' he said, 'you're not plaguing our Mrs Henry at this late hour I hope?'

'Just one last selection, Mr Edward,' Mr Maycock spluttered. 'That's all. I've brought them up on Mr Jernegan's instructions. I'm sure it won't take a minute and they are truly excellent books. *Art books*, if you know what I mean. Beautifully produced.'

'I've all these . . . ' Caroline began, gesturing at the six heaps.

'I tell you what,' her cousin suggested. 'Let Mr Maycock leave his selection and if he'll pop off and hold the fort in my office, I'll stay here and help you with these. I haven't got much else to do.'

'Would you?' Caroline said with surprise. 'Oh, I'd be so grateful.' How very kind of him and she'd always thought him such a selfish young man!

'It's the least I can do,' Edward said, positively beaming at her. 'Well, cut along, Mr Maycock. You can leave all this to me.'

And he was splendidly helpful, taking the first collection onto his lap immediately, and rejecting it with equal speed. 'Not very well produced,' he said. 'Look at that binding. It would come apart in seconds.'

She agreed that the books wouldn't do.

'You try those,' he said, carrying the next pile across to her desk. 'Top and tail 'em, like I did. That's all you really need to do to get the feel of things.'

The top book he handed her was a properly written description of the Colosseum in Rome, printed on poor paper and with a nondescript illustration. She inched the last book from

331

the bottom of the pile, and it was equally poor. 'Well!' she said.

'No good?' Edward asked. 'Neither are these. I know I wouldn't buy 'em. I say Carrie, we're getting through this lot at a rate of knots.'

Three piles had been discarded already. It was quite heartening. 'Many hands make light work,' she said, reaching for the next collection. It was the pile Mr Maycock had left on her desk just a few minutes ago. *Goddesses of Greece*, she said, opening the first book. 'That looks familiar.'

It was a handsome book, full of well drawn sketches of Greek statues, and reasonably priced too.

'These might do,' Edward said, handing her a book from his pile.

It was a collection of etchings, mostly landscapes, and rather expensive. In fact, very expensive when she compared them to the Greek Goddesses.

'No,' she said, 'I think I prefer these.' And she took up the next book on Mr Maycock's pile.

'Top and tail,' Edward laughed at her, 'or we'll be here all night.' And he slid the bottom book from under the pile and handed her that instead.

It was called *Roman Goddesses* and was every bit as well produced as the first one. 'Yes,' she said, 'we'll have these.'

'Then I'll tell you what we'll do,' he said, picking up the pile at once and holding them against his chest. 'We'll let old Maycock order them for us. That will teach him to go pestering you at the last moment.'

'What about the rest?'

'These are no good,' he said, nodding his head towards the pile he'd just been examining, 'and that only leaves the three little green books on the chaise longue. Bit on the small side, but they might do.'

'Leave them with me,' she said, 'while you attend to Mr Maycock. And thank you for your help. It was very kind of you.'

'It was a pleasure,' he said.

And so Caroline made her decisions in time and was able to tell the regional managers that the new books were on order and would be on sale at the stalls on Mr Chaplin's London to

Birmingham line before the next quarterly meeting. And Nan was happy to see that Henry and Edward were as pleased about the announcement as she was.

Edward was so excited about it that as he and Mirabelle dressed for the customary dinner that night, he couldn't talk of anything else.

'The time is coming, Mirry,' he said, preening before the cheval glass, 'when your husband will be the undisputed manager of the firm. What do you think of that, eh?'

He looked so pleased with himself, his fair hair burnished by the gaslight and his eyes dark and bold above the rich blue of his evening jacket.

'You expect Caroline to stay at home now that Harry is crawling?' Mirabelle said, adjusting her pearl necklace. 'Well, it's true she won't be able to keep him in an office for very much longer, but I daresay she'll leave him at home with Totty and go on with her work just the same.'

'She should stay at home with him herself,' he said. 'It's only right and proper. A busy office is no place for a woman. Think of the mistakes she could make.'

'So far as I know,' Mirabelle said, 'she ain't made any.'

'But she might, eh? She might?'

What has he been up to? she wondered. He was far too eager for her to agree with him. Far too excited. 'And what of Henry?' she said, in her slow teasing way. 'Do you expect him to stay at home with the baby too?'

'He might find himself in a position where he would wish to resign,' he said. 'Oh Mirry! I am so near to success! And newspaper sales up for the third month in succession thanks to all this trouble in Paris.'

'I'm sure they would be most gratified to hear how useful their sacrifice has been.'

'Sacrifice?' he asked, frowning at her. 'Really Mirry, you do say the oddest things.'

'Some of them were killed, were they not?'

'Well, of course they were. You have to expect deaths in a revolution.'

'Then let us hope that nobody gets killed in London when

333

the Chartists present their petition. I'm sure poor Pheemy has dealt with enough broken heads to last her a lifetime. And it would be pleasant if we could send Will news of a well ordered English demonstration, would it not?'

But Edward wasn't the least bit interested in such things.

'The manager of the firm,' he said, smiling at his reflection. It only needed one letter of complaint, and he was quite sure it wouldn't take Mr Jernegan long to organize that.

Chapter 25

The letter arrived wrapped in a parcel like a birthday present, addressed to 'The person who is responsible for selling books at the Easter stalls on the London to Birmingham railways'. The post boy carried it cheerfully into Caroline's office one bright May morning.

'Present from a satisfied customer, I shouldn't wonder, ma'am,' he said as he set it down on the desk among all the other mail.

She opened it as soon as he'd gone, quite warmed by the thought. It was a copy of one of Easter's special cheap editions. She recognized the green cover at once.

'How odd!' she said, turning over the accompanying letter and beginning to read.

'Sir,' it said,

'I wish to draw your attention to the enclosed, I will not say "book" for that would be too kind a word for such an abhorrent publication, which I purchased from your stall on the railway station at Birmingham. I took it to be a book about art, but as you well know sir, I was sadly mistaken.

'At first I could not believe that such rubbish was being offered for sale so brazenly and hoped that it was an aberration which had turned up upon the stall by accident.

'I resolved to ascertain the truth of the matter at the earliest opportunity, and within a week visited every railway station on the Birmingham line. It was a painful and

335

a humiliating inspection. The same unmitigated rubbish encumbered the bookshelves of every bookstall I visited. The purchasers were not few and far between, but the greater their number the more melancholy the scene. Were all the buyers daily travellers? Did they daily make these precious acquisitions? If so, it was a dismal speculation to think how many journeys it would take to destroy all decency for ever.

'You should be ashamed of yourself, sir, to purvey such rubbish to the public. And if you are not, sir, then you very soon will be. My solicitor will shortly be in touch with you, for I mean to take action against you and your company for causing a public nuisance, which must not be allowed to continue.

'I am sir, your enraged customer,

M.J. Furmedge (Esq)'

Before she could understand the meaning of the words she received their anger, violently and physically, like a punch to the stomach. It made no sense to her to be sent such an angry letter, but that didn't diminish the shock. The writer's fury was obvious even from his handwriting, black and spiky, jabbing across the page as though he meant to corrode the paper. But she tried to be reasonable, thinking how extraordinary it was that something as harmless and pleasant as a book could rouse somebody to such an outburst. What did he mean by calling it a public nuisance? How could a book be a public nuisance? What could it possibly be about this one that had made him so angry? And she picked it up and held it in her hands while she recovered her balance, the familiar green cover rough under her fingers.

Then she opened it.

This time the shock was so extreme it made her feel sick. She was flooded with a sudden primitive fear, so strong that it took all the colour from her face. She could feel the blood draining away as if she'd been wounded. She wanted to scream, run away, hide, anything rather than stay where she was and see what she saw. But it had to be faced, this obscenity on the page, this revolting, ugly, unnatural nakedness. Because this was an Easter book, a book she'd chosen herself. But how could that be? She would never have chosen such a fearful thing. It wasn't possible.

She stood there, forcing herself to stay calm, as words from the letter began to filter through into her intelligence, 'solicitor', 'action', 'must not be allowed'. A court case, she thought, understanding at last. Dear God, if there is a court case, everyone will know about it. The firm could be ruined. What am I to do? I shall have to get every single copy out of the bookstalls at once. And released into movement at last, she picked up the book and the letter and ran pell-mell down the corridor to find Henry.

She was so distressed she ran straight into his room without waiting for the clerk to announce her as he ought to have done, to the astonishment of the six men from the warehouse who were standing before the wall charts, discussing something with Henry. They turned as one man at the rush of her entry, their eyes bolting with surprise.

'Caroline! My dearest! What is it?' Henry said, looking up at her wild face. 'Could you excuse us for five minutes, gentlemen? I will solve this problem for you presently. You have my word.'

They left reluctantly, being obviously and avidly interested in what had brought her into the room so precipitately. She didn't see them go because by then she was weeping.

'What is it?' Henry said again, putting his arms about her and lowering her into the armchair in his familiar loving way. 'Tell me what it is.'

She handed him the book and the letter, mutely, with the tears running down her cheeks, and he took them and read the letter where he sat. But when he opened the book she put her hands over her eyes, because she couldn't bear to see the shock she knew it would give him. The long hiss of his indrawn breath was bad enough. She listened anxiously as he stamped to his feet and paced about the room, breathing noisily and angrily.

The chill in his voice when he finally spoke to her was terrible, for she'd been expecting comfort and tenderness, not anger. 'You were responsible for this,' he said. 'How could you allow such a thing to be sold? How could you? I thought you checked every book.'

'I did,' she said, looking up at him at once, her tears dried by his coldness. 'I do. I always do.'

'Then how did this happen?'

'I don't know,' she said. 'It's all so vile I can't even think. What am I to do about it, Henry? You must tell me.' And she looked straight up at him, the expression on her face an appeal for help even stronger than her words.

But his anger was more violent than her abhorrence. He was beside himself with it, shaken by the pornographic pictures, panicked by the threat of a lawsuit, furious to be so suddenly at risk and all through no fault of his own. 'How could you have been so foolish?' he said. 'We shall all be ruined if this gets out. Ruined! I thought you had more sense.' All the good work he'd done in the last two years was to be undone in a second, the position he'd earned for himself, the status and respect he enjoyed, it would all be gone, all of it, and all because of her stupidity. 'How could you have been such a fool?' He was pacing again, full of useless, restless energy.

'Don't speak to me like that, Henry,' she said. 'It wasn't done a-purpose. You've no right to call me names. It ain't kind.'

'Kind?' he said, his voice rising with anger despite all his efforts to keep calm. 'Why should anyone be kind to you when you've been selling this filth?'

'I didn't sell it,' she said sharply, his anger firing hers, just as it always did. 'You speak as though I was standing behind every bookstall urging people to buy.'

'You ordered it, which amounts to the same thing.'

'Ordering isn't the same thing as selling,' she said, trying to be reasonable, but aware that she was being petty.

'In this case it's exactly the same,' he said. 'Don't quibble! You should be above that. It's exactly the same.'

Why are we quarrelling about a word, Caroline thought weakly, when that book is lying on the table? 'What are we to do?' she asked. She'd had a plan in her mind when she first ran into the room but his anger had shattered it so thoroughly she couldn't even remember the beginning of it.

Solving problems was beyond him in his present state. He was so angry he wanted to kick something, or punch the wall like he'd done when he was a child. 'How could you have countenanced such a thing?' he said, his mind stuck in the impossibility of it all. 'Couldn't you see how disgusting it was? Or didn't you look?'

'I did look. I look at every book. Oh, Henry, my dear, help me. I'm being punished enough.'

'Then you must have seen this one.'

'No, no, no, I didn't. I would never have bought it if I had. Surely you can see that.'

'Then you didn't look,' he said, exasperated by her lack of logic. 'Oh God, *why* didn't you look? You stupid, stupid woman.'

'Don't abuse me.' She was shouting now, fighting back.

'I've every right to abuse you,' he yelled. 'You've ruined the firm. Ruined my life! Don't you understand? This is what comes of meddling in men's affairs instead of staying at home and looking after your child like a proper mother.'

The injustice of such a charge made her catch her breath with pain. 'That has nothing to do with it. Nothing at all. How can you . . .'

Anger was pushing him further and further away from reason and control. He turned on his heel and spun away from her, shouting as he went. 'It has everything to do with it. You should never have come here in the first place. Nan was a fool to allow it. But no, you would work. You would have your own way. I've never known anyone so selfish. Self! Self! Self!' He turned to face her, his face blazing. 'That's all it ever is with you. You've never cared for anyone except yourself. Not me, or Nan, or Pheemy . . .'

'I have so!' she said, springing to her feet to face him. 'I have! Look how I love Harry! And . . .'

'Harry!' he said throwing up his hands in the most scornful gesture. 'Poor little beggar. You don't love Henry. Not as a woman should. Dragging him here like a parcel day after day, making him cry. You don't love Harry. You don't love anyone. Look how you spoke to Pheemy when she went to St Bartholomew's. "You mustn't work at night or I shall never see you." That ain't love. That's self! That's all it is. Self! Self! Self!'

The pain of understanding stabbed into her brain like a needle, as she recognized the truth of what he was saying, and rejected it in the same sharp instance, shaking with conflicting furies. 'We're not talking about love,' she said. 'We're talking about that book.'

'*I*'m talking about love!' he raged. 'Or your lack of it. That's what I'm talking about.' With the last remaining vestige of reason he knew he was saying unpardonable things that he didn't really mean, but his brain was boiling with suppressed anger and the words erupted from him, hot as lava. 'Love!' he said striking the table with his clenched fist. 'You don't know the meaning of the word.'

She walked round the table to face him, suddenly and unaccountably afraid of that heavy fist but determined not to let him see it. Her mouth was so dry she had to lick her lips before she spoke. 'I see what it is,' she said, her chin in the air. 'Your precious position is more important to you than I am.'

Now it was his turn to hear the truth and reject it. How dare she say such a thing? How dare she even know such a thing? 'Never mind my position,' he shouted. 'I'm not talking about my position. My position ain't important. This will be the ruin of the *firm*. Don't you understand? The *firm*.'

'Squit!' she shouted, sensing his inconsistency, but too shocked and angry to analyse it or understand it. 'It ain't the firm. It's you. All that nonsense about being a poet, when you're no more a poet than I am. And now you puff yourself up with this precious position of yours. I may be selfish, Henry Osmond, but you're vain. That's what you are. Vain!'

He advanced upon her, trembling so much that even his face was shaking. 'Stop it! Stop it! You ain't to say such things! I'm not the one who sold those books.'

'I didn't sell them. I ordered them.' Oh God, why were they back in this stupid argument again?

'Sell! Order!' he yelled, clenching and unclenching his fists. 'There's no difference. How many more times have I to tell you?'

'I didn't sell them!' she said, standing her ground. 'Oh, what's the use in this? I came to you for help and all you do is argue over words. I thought you'd protect me. But there's no help or kindness in you at all. You don't care. That's the truth of it. Your precious position, that's all it is. Your vanity.'

'Stop it! Stop it!' he roared at her. 'You ain't to say such things. You ain't . . . '

'I'll say what I like, dammit, I'll say . . . '

His anger exploded into action, all control shattered. He had to hit out, to throw something, anything to stop these awful words, to put an end to all this ugliness. He grabbed at her, his hands falling on her shoulders, fingers tightening, and then he was shaking her, his face distorted with passion, shaking her violently, so that her head jerked from side to side, and her stinging words blurred and became a cry, 'You – ya-aah – aagh!' And she tore herself from his hands and stepped back, her eyes blazing with such fury that he was stricken dumb by it, his anger wilting away, and he stood before her panting and trembling and anguished at what he'd done.

'How dare you!' she said, speaking with an ice-cold control he'd never heard before. 'How dare you lay hands on me! Nobody has ever laid hands on me in all my life. Nobody! And nobody ever will again, do you understand?'

Hair pins were still tinkling from her hair onto the floorboards, and the little scrabbling sound irritated him.

'You asked for it,' he said, shamefaced, but trying to defend himself. 'You drove me to it.'

'Nobody!' she said. 'Ever!'

'If you'd checked those books . . . '

'Our marriage is over,' she said coldly. 'I can't live with you now. Not after this. You understand that.'

His mind was stuck. He couldn't, wouldn't understand what she was saying. 'If you'd only . . . '

'I am leaving you, Henry,' she said. 'I hope it preys on your conscience that you drove me to leave you. If you have one.' And she picked up the book and the letter and made a dignified exit, face set, spine straight, skirts swishing angrily.

I am on my own, she thought, as she walked back to her office. I must deal with this on my own. She was yearning for Nan or Will or Euphemia. But Nan was in Bury with Mr Brougham, and Will was miles and miles away in Paris, and Euphemia was working at St Bartholomew's Hospital again. Dear Euphemia, Caroline thought, I do love her. She takes everything so calmly, and she knows so much. Look at the way she talked when Harry was being born.

341

'Look at the way she talked.' Why, of course. Euphemia had seen statues. There were statues in the temples in India showing – well – all that sort of thing. She'd said so. Perhaps there was hope. Perhaps these drawings weren't bad after all. Not to someone used to seeing such things. Euphemia would know. And Euphemia might still be at home because she didn't leave for the hospital until after ten o'clock. Before she did anything else she would test Euphemia's opinion.

Anger had stiffened her resolve as well as her spine. She knew exactly where she was going now and exactly what she was going to do, and she started doing it the moment she was back in the office. First she ordered her clerk out into the Strand to get her a cab. Then she sent a runner down to the warehouse to ask Edward if he would be so kind as to come up to her office for a moment or two. As this horrid matter was bound to affect the warehouse sooner or later, she had better tell her cousin about it too and particularly as six of his men had been in Henry's office when she ran in.

But Mr Edward had gone out 'not five minutes since', according to the runner. 'Gone like lightning he was, the minute Jack an' the others come down from Mr Henry's.'

The cab was waiting outside the main entrance, as she could see from her window.

'No matter,' she said calmly. 'I will tell him when he returns.' Then she put on her bonnet and gloves, wrapped her shawl lightly about her shoulders and went downstairs to give the cabbie his instructions. If he made good time she could reach Euphemia before she left the house.

Euphemia was tying her own bonnet when her cousin knocked on the door.

'Carrie!' she said. 'How nice to see you, my darling, but I'm just off to St Bartholomew's. Didn't you realize that?' And then after a closer look at her cousin's expression, 'Oh my dear, is anything wrong?'

'Henry shook me,' Caroline said.

'Oh my dearest! How terrible!'

'So I have left him. Harry and I will be living here from now on.'

342

'Oh, Carrie my dear! Would you like me to stay at home with you? I was just off to Barts but I could send a message.'

'No,' Caroline said at once. 'Of course not. You mustn't do any such thing. I wouldn't hear of it. No, no. I've a cab waiting at the kerb. I shan't even make you late, I promise. Put on your gloves and we can talk on the way. I need your advice.'

It was enclosed and intimate inside the cab, but even so Caroline had a moment of doubt before she took the book out of her reticule and handed it across. 'This came to me with a letter of complaint,' she said. 'The man who sent it called it a public nuisance, and when I showed it to Henry, he shouted at me and abused me and . . . Well you know what he did. I haven't shown it to anyone else. I think it's horrible, but I could be wrong because I know nothing about such things. Would you look at it please, my dearest, and tell me what you think? You are the only person I could possibly ask to do such a thing.'

Euphemia looked at the book, and although her face remained calm, she shuddered visibly. 'Oh, Carrie my dear,' she said sadly, 'this is an evil, ugly book, fit only for the flames. It ought never to have been written.'

'And never sold,' Caroline said. Her little hope of reprieve was gone. It *was* as bad as she'd thought.

'Never,' Euphemia said. 'And yet presumably it was sold, was it not?'

'Read the letter,' Caroline said, 'and I will tell you all about it.'

'What will you do?' Euphemia asked when her cousin had told her all she could. From the approaching sound of bleating sheep they knew they were close to Smithfields.

So Caroline told her that too, quickly before they stopped at the hospital gates. And Euphemia kissed her and promised she would help in any way she could. And then the rush of the day took them away from each other and Caroline told the cabbie to take her back to Bedford Square.

Once there she let herself into Nan's study and wrote two letters, very quickly and fluently.

The first was to Harry's nursemaid in Richmond, telling her to pack the baby's clothes and toys and bring him straight to Bedford Square on the very next train. Totty was to come with her and any other servants she thought necessary. 'I am to be away for a day or two,' she write. 'Totty is to bring all the linen and all our summer clothes and you are all to stay in Bedford Square until I return.'

The second was to Will.

'My dearest brother,' she wrote.

'You cannot know how unhappy I am as I write this to you. An absolutely disgusting book has found its way, I truly do not know how, onto the Easter stalls. A gentleman has bought a copy and written me an abusive letter and means to take the firm to court for causing a public nuisance.

'If you could come home, even for a day, my dear, dear Will, you would be such a comfort to me. Of course I realize that you have work to do which might make your return impossible, and if that is the case I shall not blame you or berate you if you cannot do as I ask. Nevertheless it is the thing I most desire.

Your ever-loving sister,
Carrie.
P.S. I am staying in Bedford Square.'

Then she addressed the envelopes, sending Will's letter to Vienna and marking it 'Please forward', and instructed the butler to see that they were taken to the post, and to call her another cab.

For the second time in her life she was running away from trouble, and of course she was running straight to Bury St Edmunds and Nan.

344

Chapter 26

Nan Easter had spent the afternoon in the rectory garden at
Rattlesden with her daughter Annie, her two granddaughters
Meg and Dotty and all seven of her Norfolk great-grandchildren. It had been a lovely idle afternoon, settled with
sunshine. The older children had been building themselves a
tree-house, and a fine untidy eyrie it was; the babies had slept
in the porch as plump and easy as cats; and Nan had sat in the
shade of the holm oak with Annie and watched and gossiped,
and once, it had to be admitted, drifted off into a brief cat-nap
of her own. Now she was waiting with happy anticipation for
the four o'clock tea she always took at the rectory. Meg and
Dotty had already gone indoors to supervise it.

Since her three grandchildren had taken over the day-to-day
running of the firm she had led a much less hectic life, wintering in Westmoreland with Frederick, summering in Bury, and
with plenty of time for family visits and the sort of social
occasions she enjoyed. 'And why not?' as Frederick said. 'You
have earned your laurels, my dear.'

Caroline's abrupt arrival into the garden was like a sudden
storm.

'Why, my dear child!' Nan said, sitting up at once, as the
pony cart skidded to a halt on the drive with a roar of
'Whooah!' and a spatter of gravel. 'What brings you here?
And at such speed. It must be something serious.'

Caroline jumped from the cart and ran to kiss her grandmother and Annie and to wave at the children. Her cheeks
were harshly pink, her hair uncombed and her eyes strained

and shining. Excitement or temper? Nan wondered as they kissed. Well, we shall soon know.

But Caroline waited until the cart had been led away to the stables before she said anything. Then she exploded her news upon them. 'I've left Henry,' she said, standing before them with her hands on her hips in the defiant stance they both remembered so well from her childhood.

Annie decided to take it calmly. 'Oh, what nonsense!' she said. 'Don't say such things. It ain't seemly. Come and sit here on the bench with us. We're going to take tea presently.'

Caroline stayed where she was, her crinoline settled and bulky, as if it would never sway into movement again. 'I mean it,' she said. 'We've had the most frightful row and I've left him.'

'Wives don't leave their husbands,' Annie told her implacably. 'It ain't allowed. And all lovers have tiffs. You will get over it.'

Nan reached for her walking stick and eased herself out of her chair. 'Come into the house, Carrie,' she said, 'and tell me what all this is about.' Whatever was troubling the child it was more serious than a lover's tiff. She had that goblin look about her, with her brows puckered like that and her pretty mouth drawn in. Come into the house. Annie will stay here with the children, won't you my dear?' giving her a flickering glance of warning.

'Of course,' Annie said easily, turning her attention at once to the untidy eyrie in the trees.

'Come you on, then,' Nan said, and she walked towards the porch as briskly as she could on legs grown stiff with idleness.

They could hear Meg and Dotty giggling together in the kitchen and there was plenty of coming and going between there and the dining room, but the parlour was cool and empty.

They sat in the window seat together, framed by Annie's floral curtains and with her flowering garden busy beyond them, and Caroline thought how peaceful and loving and beautiful it was in this place, and was ashamed because she was the bearer of such ugly news.

'Now,' Nan said. 'Suppose you tell me, eh?'

'I *have* left Henry,' Caroline said. 'I meant what I said. Harry and I have moved back to Bedford Square. You will accept us, won't you Nan?'

'I don't have a deal of choice seeing it's a fait accompli,' Nan said, but her eyes were smiling even though the words sounded stern.

'I had to leave him, Nan.'

'Why?'

'He shook me,' Caroline shuddered. 'He actually laid hands on me and shook me.'

Then it *was* serious. 'Tell me all about it, child. From start to finish, if you please.'

So the story was told, with surprising calm this time, and the letter was read and the foul book displayed.

'Well now,' Nan said, when she'd folded her spectacles back into their case, 'for a start we'd best get these dratted things off the stalls as quick as we can before more harm's done.' And she rang the bell and sent the answering servant off to fetch Bessie. 'Have you done anything about them?'

'Not yet,' Caroline confessed when the maid was gone. 'I was too upset. Oh Nan, Henry said we should all be ruined. Was he right?'

'It's like enough if we don't look slippy,' Nan said. 'We'll take a dish of tea here with Annie and the girls and then we'll go back to Bury and tell Mr Brougham what we're about and then we'll go to Birmingham. The sooner we start the better. There en't a minute to waste.' And as Bessie came hobbling into the room, 'Ah, Bessie my dear, we've got to be back in Bury the minute tea's over. Some wretched book's been sent to our shops by mistake and Carrie and I will have to see to it.'

So that's the explanation we are going to use, Caroline thought, and was impressed by the ease of it, and flooded with gratitude and admiration for this amazing grandmother of hers. If only Henry could have behaved like that.

Bessie tut-tutted with annoyance. 'An' all in this lovely weather too,' she said. 'What a waste! Never you mind mum, I'll see to it.'

Half an hour later they were on the road to Bury, where Mr Brougham was shown the book and told the story and asked if he would act for them should the matter come to court, and

347

agreed that he would. And then, once Bessie had packed an overnight bag, they set off for Cambridge and their first train. By midnight they were in Peterborough and their immediate plans had been laid. They would travel from station to station up and down the London Birmingham line, and all the offensive books would be gathered in, addressed to Caroline at the Strand and sent back by rail.

'Printed in Holywell Street, you see,' Nan said, examining the fly leaf. 'No publisher's name of course for fear of the police. Just Holywell Street, London. Well, that's enough. They'll be easy enough to pick out. Let's pray they en't sold too many of the dratted things.'

They were easy enough to pick out. She was right. But it took five days travel to visit every single bookstall along the line and by then it was plain that there were more than a dozen offensive books on offer and that scores of them had been sold.

'There could be more complaints, I suppose,' Caroline said fearfully, as they travelled on from Watford to Harrow.

'Aye, there could.'

'What are we going to do now, Nan? Will there be a court case do you think?'

'Take one thing at a time, my dear, same as I always do,' Nan said, rather wearily. The last five days had drained away too much of her energy and now sitting in the relative comfort of this carriage she knew it. 'There's no point a-worritin' till things happen. If there's to be a court case we shall know soon enough, I daresay. Meantime the books are withdrawn. We've done all we can.'

'You are so good to me,' Caroline said. 'Anyone else would have been angry.' It was true, but it reminded her of that awful row, and that pinched her face with distress.

'You've had enough anger to contend with for the moment,' Nan said, brusque but sympathetic.

'Yes,' Caroline said. 'I have.' But at least the relief of taking action had lifted her sense of foreboding. Nan was right. If there was to be a court case they would face it when they knew what it was to be. There was no sense in worrying about it beforehand. But her guilt persisted, and Henry's accusation resurfaced, filling her thoughts.

'Am I selfish, Nan? *Was* that why all this happened?'

'We're all selfish,' Nan said, answering carefully because she could see how important it was, 'every single one of us! 'Tis the nature of the beast. The only difference being that we don't always call it selfishness. We say we're single-minded or determined, like me, or headstrong.'

'Like me,' Caroline admitted.

'Aye, child. Like you.' At least she had the grace to see that.

'Is it a sin, Nan?'

'Some might say so.'

'Do you?' It was important to know.

'No,' Nan said. 'I don't. Not always. There's good in it as well as bad, d'you see? 'Tis the very thing that makes a good businessman. Or a good business woman. But it makes hard hearts too. There's a fine balance between pushing on for the good of the firm and everyone in it, and pushing on simply to satisfy your own desires and appetites.'

This was a new idea to Caroline and she pondered it deeply, her eyes inward looking and her forehead scored with effort, as the train rocked them onwards.

'It could have been selfish of me to work after Harry was born,' she said, but the tone in her voice showed that she didn't believe it. Yet. 'I *did* drag him about with me, poor little thing, and he didn't like it.'

'Well, that's possible,' Nan said frankly. 'Which might account for your mistake. It en't like you to be careless and that's a fact.'

The line curved suddenly, throwing them both off balance and making their bodies sway sideways in unison, and as the train continued in its new direction, the late evening sun slanted in low through the carriage window to light Nan's face like a spotlight. Such a strong, merciless beam it was, revealing old white hair and parchment skin etched with myriad lines, and those dear familiar brown eyes not brown at all but faded to olive, edged with green. *Why*, Caroline thought, she is an old lady, a very old lady. I ought to be looking after her, not expecting her to look after me, and yet here I am burdening her with all this. And for the first time since the parcel arrived she was torn with remorse for what she'd done.

'Oh Nan,' she said, leaning forward to catch the old lady's

349

hands and hold them tenderly. 'I *am* selfish. It's true. I'm being such a nuisance.'

'You en't a nuisance,' Nan said.

'I wish I'd checked all those books. If I had this to do again I'd look at every single one.'

'There's no use crying over spilt milk,' Nan said.

'No,' Caroline agreed sadly.

''Tis best to think of other things,' Nan advised.

'Yes,' Caroline said. But what other things? Were there other things? And immediately she asked them, the questions lifted another, most important thing out of her general consciousness and into her mind. 'I am carrying again,' she said. How dreadful to have forgotten *that*.

'Are you so?' Nan said, smiling at her. 'Does Henry know of it? No. I'll wager you en't told him.'

'No,' Caroline admitted. 'I haven't. And I shan't now.'

'Oh, my dear heart alive, child,' Nan said. 'You do run true to form. When is it to be?'

'January.'

'A long time yet,' Nan said. Time for the court case to be over and done with and this quarrel patched up and a good deal else besides. 'A long time yet.' And she closed her eyes on her weariness.

When the door banged shut behind Caroline's furious spine, Henry stood where he was in the middle of his office, too shocked to move or speak. His entire body was burning with emotion, sweat beading on his forehead and pouring from the palms of his hands, but his mind had stopped functioning. At one level of consciousness he knew he should take action to reduce the damage that her awful pornographic book was certainly doing, but he wasn't capable of reasoning out what to do. His workaday self was aware that there were routine decisions to be taken, and orders to be given, but these things were beyond him too. There was only the stark fact that he had laid hands on his wife and shaken her as though she were an enemy, as though he hated her, and the memory of those cold final words of hers. 'I am leaving you.'

If only he could claw the last hour back and live it all differently. He would take her in his arms and comfort her and promise to help her, not shout and rage. He would never lay hands on her. She was right. That was unforgivable. But he had done it. How *could* he have done it, when he loved her so much? How *could* he?

Mr Jolliffe was at the door with his hands full of letters to be signed, and no expression on his face. He was fussing with pens and ink, rearranging the bottles, keeping his eyes discreetly lowered. There was work to be done.

'Thank you, Jolliffe,' Henry said, automatically taking up the nearest pen.

'Message from the warehouse, Mr Henry sir,' Jolliffe said, much too calmly. 'Mr Edward's cut off to Bristol all of a sudden, and none of the Newcastle parcels have gone. Are they to be despatched as usual?'

'Yes, yes,' Henry said vaguely. 'As usual, of course. Everything is to proceed as usual.'

'You have an appointment with Mr Tubthorpe, sir,' Jolliffe reminded. 'At half past ten, sir.'

'Yes, Yes. An appointment with Mr Tubthorpe.' Life went on in its haphazard, predictable way. 'Has he arrived?'

It was a terrible day, but he got through it by taking one numb step after another, solving the problem for the six warehousemen as he'd promised, talking to Mr Tubthorpe as it was expected, doing what had to be done, with no awareness of time or action. When the carriage arrived to take him to Nine Elms station, he went with it because he couldn't think of anything else to do. He wasn't going home, of course, he was merely returning to the house where he would sleep. Home was with Caroline and little Harry and he knew with a terrible sick certainty that neither of them would be in Richmond now.

Nevertheless he kept up a bold front, explaining to the butler that Mrs Easter had urgent business to attend to and would be away for some time, and eating as much of his dinner as he could, so that no one would suspect that anything was wrong.

Farren's face was its usual polite mask. Not that Henry would have expected anything else, whatever the circumstances. But once he was below stairs again the butler's expression changed.

'They've had a bust-up this time,' he said to Mrs Benotti.

The rest of the servants were eating their dinner in the kitchen but these two, being the senior members of the staff, dined together in the housekeeper's parlour, beyond the reach of more vulgar ears.

'Didn't I tell you?' Mrs Benotti said, pouring cream over the mound of gooseberries and piecrust on her plate. 'Sending for baby like that. Oh, I knew they'd come to it sooner or later the way they will go on. You can't go hollerin' an' shoutin' all the time without coming to a bust-up sooner or later. Stands to human reason.'

'Which they ought to use now and then,' Farren said. 'Is there any more of your excellent gooseberry pie, Mrs Benotti?'

They might have been gratified to know that Henry used his reasoning powers all night long. For the second time that day his head was full of questions he couldn't answer, buzzing like bees in a bottle. Oh, where was she? And what was she doing? How was he to live without her? Would it even be possible to continue in the firm? Or would he have to start afresh in a new company and without his wife or his son? Nan would have every right to ask for his resignation. In fact it would probably be more sensible, and certainly more honourable, if he were to tender it himself, before she asked. Oh, how could he have done such a thing? If only he hadn't!

It was a relief to be able to get up in the morning and cut off to the office again. And an even greater one when a letter arrived from Nan at the end of the afternoon, with the news that all the 'abominable books' were being gathered in. The next morning the first of the packing cases arrived, addressed to 'Mrs Caroline Easter' and sent by rail from Birmingham. So at least he knew where she was and could assume that since she was with Nan she was being cared for, which was another relief. But he still had no idea what his next move ought to be.

He thought about it night after night, sitting beside his window, gazing down at the shivering expanse of a moon-silvered Thames and the ominous shadows of trees and hedge-rows. But there were no answers. Only regret.

Finally when the week-end came around and the packing cases were still arriving and there was no more news of

Caroline or Harry, he caught the overnight train to Cumberland and went to visit his sister Jane. She would probably scold him when she knew what he'd done, but he needed advice and comfort so much he was prepared to take the risk.

Jane had always been a sensible young woman, so now, even though she was surprised to see her brother unannounced and without his family, she didn't say so. He was welcomed and fed and told all the family gossip, as if there were nothing untoward. And when the children had been taken off to the schoolroom for their Saturday lessons, she suggested a walk in the grounds. Whatever it was, he would tell her sooner or later, just as he'd done when they were children together. And sure enough, once they were out of sight of the house, he began the confession she expected.

She listened quietly, walking beside him with her hand resting on the crook of his elbow and her parasol tilted so that she could watch his face. When he described how he'd shaken Caroline she caught her breath with a shudder, and when he spoke of his regret she patted his arm, but she said nothing until she was quite sure he'd finished his story. Then she sat down under the shade of the nearest lime tree.

'That fearful temper of yours,' she said. 'It was always the same. I can remember times when you struck the wall in temper and all your knuckles bled.'

'If only it had been the wall this time,' he said ruefully.

'Yes,' she agreed. 'Better bleeding knuckles than a lost wife.'

'Have I lost her, Jane?'

'We must hope not, for we love her dearly.'

'Oh Sis, she came to me for help and I shouted at her.'

'Yes.'

'What am I to do?'

'Why, court her, my dear. Court her all over again.'

'Write to her?'

'That would be a start.'

'But what if she don't answer?'

'Then you will write again.'

In the peaceful garden under the rustling shade of the lime it was possible to hope. 'Do you think she will come back to me?'

'Only if you can persuade her that you will never be cruel to her again. You have put yourself beyond the pale by such an action, you know, my dear.'

He was horribly crestfallen. 'I do know. I do. If only I hadn't.'

'It will be a long road back, I fear,' she told him honestly. 'But with time and patience and self-restraint, who knows?'

Chapter 27

The Easter family made good use of the railways that Sunday.
The newspapers were transported by rail of course, as they
always were, and the last two packing cases were sent to the
Strand from the last two bookstalls, but in addition to that, no
fewer than four members of the family were travelling to
London too, Henry from Cumberland, Edward from his
diplomatic visit to Bristol and Caroline and Nan from their
five-day labours.

It was late at night by the time the two women finally got
back to Bedford Square and Nan was too exhausted to speak.
Fortunately Euphemia was woken by the sound of their cab
drawing up at the kerb, and she came down at once to welcome
them home, and fill a warming-pan for Nan's bed with embers
from the kitchen fire, and see to it that her night-gown was
aired. Then she and Caroline eased their weary traveller out of
her clothes and sponged her face and hands with warm water
and settled her to sleep as if she were a baby.

By that time Caroline was asleep on her feet.

'Tell you 'bout it in the morning,' she muttered as she laid
her head on her old familiar pillow in her old familiar bed. 'So
glad you are here, Pheemy, my dearest.' She was asleep with
the last word hanging from her lips.

The next morning was chaotic because they both overslept
and when Caroline finally woke the first thing she wanted to do
was to rush off to the nursery to see Harry and be reunited in a
smother of hugs and kisses. And to make matters more hectic it
was Euphemia's last day at the hospital before she began a fort-

night's holiday, so there was barely time for more than a mouthful of breakfast and the briefest exchange of news before her carriage was waiting at the door.

'Tomorrow I will stay here with you, I promise,' she said as she kissed Caroline goodbye. And then she was gone in a swish of hospital skirts and an unfamiliar waft of starch and disinfectant.

Her departure left Caroline feeling curiously deflated. She'd worked so hard and travelled so far during the last five days and now the world was suddenly still and rather empty, sitting here in Nan's pink and white breakfast room, with the smell of toast and coffee all around her, and bacon and kidneys and mushrooms on the side-board behind her, and no one to talk to. And that dreadful letter and the threat of a court case still hanging over her head like a great sword waiting to fall and cut her to pieces. Without even thinking of Henry – and she couldn't bear to think of Henry, it was too painful.

'I shall go to the Strand as soon as I've had breakfast,' Nan said, stepping briskly into the room with her maid beside her. She was dressed for the day, her white hair neat under its black lace cap, a triple lace collar immaculate over her blue and black gown, that determined stick tapping the polished floorboards. 'The solicitors could have written already and the sooner we know what they intend the better. Mr Brougham will be here tomorrow and there's the accounts meeting not three days away. I've a deal to do. I will have kidneys and bacon, Jennie.'

The solicitor's letter, Caroline thought, and the words nipped at her heart and closed her throat. The letter that will bring all this out in the open so that everyone will know what a dreadful mistake I've made. 'If you don't mind,' she said, keeping her voice steady with a conscious effort, 'I will spend the day here with Harry. It would be foolish to extend our book trade with this matter hanging over our heads, don't you think?'

'Aye, I suppose it would,' Nan said kindly. 'The truth is that neither of us can do very much at present. I shall come home myself when I've seen what's what.'

The dreaded letter had arrived while they were away. It was waiting on Caroline's desk, couched in terms that were politely reasonable even though the information they imparted was every bit as bad as they'd feared. The firm of A. Easter and Sons in general and the person responsible for book sales in particular were to be sued under the Vagrancy Act of 1824 on the grounds that on the tenth day of May 1848 they had committed a public nuisance, viz offering for sale a lewd publication of gross indecency entitled *Joys in the Persian Garden*. The hearing was set for October 1848. They had the honour to be, Yr most obednt servts . . .'

Well, now we know the worst of it, Nan thought, brushing her hands against each other in that old familiar gesture of hers, so 'tis just a matter of planning our campaign. That's all. And keeping it as quiet as she could so as to protect their sales. The slightest breath of scandal always had a devastating effect on sales. She would tell Billy that afternoon when he came into the warehouse, and Henry and Edward now, but there was no need for it to go any further.

She sent one of her young runners down to the warehouse to find Mr Edward, and when the boy was gone, she walked along the corridor to Henry's office.

At various moments during the previous five days she had pondered the question of what she ought to do about Henry. His behaviour had been highly reprehensible, that was true, and certainly bad enough to warrant dismissal, but quarrels between husbands and wives were usually a private concern, and he had never raised a finger to Caroline before, and there was always the hope that they would see sense and make it up. Then again there were the undeniable facts that he was a valuable member of the firm, and the only person who could cope with John's complicated timetables, and a member of the family in his own right. All in all it was a peculiar situation. She was no nearer a decision when she stepped into his office.

He jumped to his feet at the sight of her, standing to attention like a trouper, and she was moved to see how distressed he looked. He was thinner than usual and very pale and there were mauve shadows under his eyes.

But he greeted her courteously, offering the most comfortable seat, which she accepted; suggesting coffee, which she declined.

'You had better see this,' she said, putting the solicitor's letter on the desk before him.

He read it soberly.

'The books have all been gathered in,' she said.

'Yes,' he said. 'I know. I saw the parcels and guessed what they would be. Is Caroline . . . ?'

'Caroline is still grievously upset by your behaviour.'

'You know of it?' he said and his frozen hauteur showed how painful it was to have to ask such a question.

'Of course.'

'If you wish,' he said, holding his head high and looking at her steadily, 'I will tender my resignation. You would have every right to ask for it.'

'Aye, I daresay.'

It was a hard moment for him, but he faced it squarely. 'When should I leave?' he asked.

She was touched by his correctness and that haughty vulnerable pride. 'I've no desire to see you leave at all,' she said. 'And certainly not before we've faced this trial. You're a deal too valuable.'

'But a deal too cruel to your granddaughter.'

'Whatever possessed 'ee?'

'I don't know,' he said, honestly, finding that he could talk to her about it after all. 'I was so angry I didn't think. Now I would give anything to wipe the slate clean.'

'I don't doubt it,' she said, 'only life en't that simple.' Then she turned their attention to other matters. 'Now then, Mr Brougham will be returning to Bedford Square tomorrow. I daresay he'll want to question Caroline first, and then anyone else who is involved, and after that we shall know what line the firm is to take. I will keep you informed, you have my word. It will take time, all this.'

'Yes,' he said. 'Of course. It will take time.'

And then Edward came sauntering into the room, so the conversation had to stop, which was a relief to both of them.

If Nan had been impressed by the way Henry reacted to the solicitor's letter, she was puzzled and annoyed by Edward's insouciance.

'A bad business,' he said, when he'd scanned the letter, 'but these things happen, I daresay. We shall have to consider some way of avoiding such mistakes in future, shall we not?' What do you mean to do about it?'

'Mr Brougham will act for us.'

'Act for us?'

'In the court case.'

'But it won't come to court, surely?' he said. This wasn't what he expected at all.

'Yes,' Nan said, 'it will.' She was aware that Henry was standing behind her stiff-spined with anger and grinding his teeth so fiercely she could hear them where she sat, and really it was no wonder. Had this fool boy not read the letter? 'Meantime we will keep this in the family.'

'Oh, of course,' he said, recovering himself. 'Is there anything else, Nan dear? I was in section 3 you know, in the middle of taking stock. I ought to be getting back.'

'Well, only one other thing,' she told him, feeling he should know it all. 'You'll be glad to know all the books have been gathered in.'

'What books?'

'Why, all the others.'

Now he was shocked and showed it. 'You mean there were others?'

'Yes. Of course there were.'

'On sale?'

'On every bookstall from here to Birmingham. It took your cousin and me five whole days to root them all out.'

'But I don't understand it,' he said. 'I mean, I thought it was just one book.'

'If only it were,' she said, annoyed by his lack of understanding. Then, as he was fidgeting to leave, 'Oh, cut on back to the warehouse, do. I will keep you informed.' He might be a bit of a fool, but at least he was eager to get back to work.

She would have been very annoyed if she'd known that he didn't go anywhere near the warehouse when he left her. He sent a runner down instead with a message to his workmen that he would be away for an hour or two and that they were to go to the stalls section to pack foot warmers and reading lamps till he returned. Then he left the building through the side door and caught a cab to Mr Jernegan's office, above the Easter shop in Regent Street.

'An unexpected pleasure, Mr Edward,' Mr Jernegan said. 'You have just caught me too. What timing. I've been out all morning. Can I offer you a glass of something?'

'What's all this about a court case?' Edward said, his eyes bolting.

'Ah yes. One of Mr Snipe's books, I believe. Mrs Henry hasn't been seen in the Strand since the letter arrived, so they tell me. You must be very pleased.'

'They were on sale,' Edward said. 'On sale, Mr Jernegan. At every bookstall from here to Birmingham. Who put them on sale, Mr Jernegan?'

Mr Jernegan's answer was silky smooth. 'Why, you did, Mr Edward sir.'

'I did! I did!' Edward roared in disbelief. 'How can you say such a thing? I gave you strict instructions that they were never to reach the bookstalls. You were to arrange for someone to write in and complain, that was all.'

'And someone has. You should be very happy, Mr Edward sir. Your plot, if we may make so bold as to describe it so, and I think we may make so bold, your plot has been a great success.'

'Success!' Edward shouted. 'There'll be a scandal when this comes to trial. The firm could be ruined.' This wasn't what he'd intended at all. 'What the devil were you playing at?'

'I was simply obeying your instructions, Mr Edward sir, as I shall be sure to tell anyone who asks me. It ain't for the likes of me to suggest action, no indeed, and nobody would expect it. I'm merely an employee of the firm. A man who takes orders from his superiors, if you take my meaning.'

'Mr Maycock was in this too. He'll know what really happened.'

'Maycock is a catchpaw and a fool,' Mr Jernegan said, savouring his brandy. 'He did his part when he ordered the consignment in the first place, according to your instructions, Mr Edward sir, as I'm sure you'll remember. I think you'll find, sir, that Mr Maycock knows very little and will say less.'

'Good God, sir, this is hideous,' Edward said.

'It is what you wanted, Mr Edward sir.'

'Call me a cab,' Edward ordered. The shock was making him feel quite sick. 'I must go home at once. This is hideous. Hideous. You won't get away with it.'

'There is nothing to get away with, as you put it,' Mr Jernegan said. 'But I will arrange for a cab since that is what you want. I always obey orders, Mr Edward sir.'

Actually he arranged for two cabs. The one that arrived first took Mr Easter for a brief stop in the Strand and then on to his home, the other, which came ten minutes later, took Mr Jernegan to the offices of the *Daily Record*. If there was going to be a difference of opinion, then the sooner he told his version of the story the better.

Despite her worries Caroline was almost happy that afternoon. She and Totty and the nursemaid took Harry out for a drive in the countryside, over Primrose Hill and past Kilburn Wells all the way to the pretty little village of Willesden Green. The sun was pleasantly warm, the sky a most delicious blue and the prospect marvellously rural. The fields were yellow with corn, and there were strawberries and cream for sale at a little thatched cottage at the crossroads. It was all a little unreal, but enjoyable just the same.

When they got home Euphemia was back from the hospital and wearing a pretty tea gown instead of that awful starchy uniform, and there was plenty of time to sit in the garden and talk. Euphemia was full of sympathy and said all the things her cousin needed to hear. And what with the sunshine and the sense of being supported Caroline was soon feeling far more like herself again, so that when Nan arrived home with the solicitor's letter, she took it calmly, ordered fresh tea and said it was no more than she had expected.

Her calm was short-lived.

As Nan was drinking the fresh tea, the butler arrived in the garden with a letter for Miss Caroline and an evening newspaper on his silver tray.

'Beg pardon, ma'am,' he said to Nan, 'but the housekeeper thought you ought to see this.'

While Caroline opened her letter, Nan took the paper and spread it out on the tablecloth in front of her. 'What is it,

Morris?' she asked. ' ''Strikes in Paris.'' That en't Mr William's work, surely? Not in the *Evening Record*. 'Tis the wrong paper.'

'No, ma'am,' Morris said, 'begging your pardon. It's the article alongside. About Easter's, ma'am. We thought you ought to know.'

' ''Easter's to be sued over sale of lewd book'',' Nan read calmly, as Caroline and Euphemia caught their breath a little too audibly. 'Ah, I see. Yes, Morris, you were right to show me. Thank Mrs Brown for me, if 'ee will. There was another matter, was there not?'

'Yes, ma'am. Miss Caroline's letter.'

'Ah, I see. Thank you.'

When the butler was back in the house and out of earshot, Caroline and Euphemia rushed to read the paper. 'We were going to keep it in the family,' Caroline said. 'How could they possibly know about it?'

'Quite,' Nan said grimly. 'You en't spoke of it to anyone, I know that. And apart from us and Mr Brougham the only other people I've told are Billy and Edward and Henry.'

'Is it in any of the other newspapers?' Euphemia wondered.

'If it en't,' Nan said, 'it soon will be.'

'But who could have told them?' Caroline worried.

'Billy never would,' Nan said. 'And for all his faults I don't think Henry would either.'

'No,' Caroline agreed. 'He wouldn't. The firm is too important to him. He told me that in this letter.'

'Was it from Henry then?' Nan asked, glancing at it.

'Yes,' Caroline said sadly, looking down at the closely written page. 'He wants to apologize to me.'

'Oh, I'm sure he means it,' Euphemia urged. 'You will give him a hearing, won't you my darling? Oh, I know he behaved quite dreadfully but we all make mistakes.'

'I don't know what I shall do,' Caroline said. 'It all seems so distant in the light of the trial and this article and everything. I truly don't know. I shall have to wait until the case is over and done with before I can even think about it.'

'Shall you answer his letter?' Euphemia said. 'Oh, do that at least. I'm sure he didn't mean to be cruel. It was done in haste.'

'But it was done,' Caroline said. 'And all the words in the world can't alter that.'

'I shall have a few words to say to Edward in the morning,' Nan said grimly.

But Edward had other plans.

Chapter 28

Mirabelle was in her drawing room supervising the arrangements for the poetic salon that was to be held there that evening. It was her custom to choose a different colour scheme for every occasion so as to surprise her guests and bring a little excitement to the discreet blue and green of the decor. Tonight's colours were magenta, rose-pink, gold and white, and therefore involved not only the most elaborate flower arrangements, which she was attending to herself, but also a change of curtains, a display of silver and considerable re-arrangement of the furniture. She and the housekeeper and six of her servants were all hard at work on the transformation when Edward came panting into the room.

She could see at once from his flushed forehead and over-bright eyes that something serious was amiss, so she extricated herself from her chores as quickly and gracefully as she could and led them upstairs to their bedroom before he could reveal too much to the servants' sharpening ears.

'What is it, my dear?' she said, when the door was shut on the possibility of being overheard.

'We are going to the Continent,' he said dramatically, 'for a holiday. What do you think of that? I've seen Papa. It's all planned.' His agitation was now very marked indeed, his hands trembling and a nerve pulsing beside his left eye.

'An admirable plan,' she said. 'When is this to be?'

'Why, today!' he said, half demanding, half pleading. 'Tonight.'

'Now come, Edward,' she said, sitting down in her easy

chair beside the window and averting her poor eye from his gaze. 'That is impossible, as well you know. I have a salon tonight. It is all arranged.'

'You can cancel it, can't you?' he said, and now his voice sounded petulant.

'I have over fifty guests invited,' she said gently. 'It would be neither proper nor kind to disappoint them.'

'But it is proper and kind to disappoint me.'

'Not at all,' she said glancing at him. 'Had you mentioned this earlier I would have been more than happy to comply, but as things stand it cannot be.'

'And if I insist?' he said, scowling at her, blue eyes strained and unblinking.

'You may insist all you please,' she said, 'but I must be here for the salon. A holiday, however pleasant, cannot be allowed to take precedence over one's duty.'

'You have a duty to me.'

'Certainly.'

'Then pray do as I say. Obey me.'

'Now come, my dear,' she said, turning her head to face him fully, 'this is a worthless argument, for you know very well that I cannot obey you. We are not free agents in this matter, however much we may wish to be.'

His frustration and fear exploded into anger. 'You do not love me!' he shouted. 'I see it all now. I mean nothing to you. This wretched salon is more important to you than I am.'

'Maintain a sense of proportion, Edward, I beg you,' she said, endeavouring to indicate with a backward glance from her good eye that the servants would hear him if he went on shouting.

But he had lost his balance completely. There was no stopping him. 'The world is all awry,' he said. 'Women work where they've no business to be. Can you wonder mistakes are made? What else would you expect? Women should stay at home and look after their husbands. That's what women should do. There's hardly a woman alive nowadays who knows how to behave. And wives disobey their husbands, as well you know. And a poor state the world is in when that happens. It's against the teaching of the church! Against nature! And then there are underlings with no sense of their place in society.

365

Underlings don't know how to behave either. They won't do as they're told. They take it into their heads to act without instructions! I ask you! Underlings! It's all wrong! How can anyone survive in such a world? Is it any wonder I need a holiday? I should go away at once, before I suffer a brain fever. It's enough to send me straight into a brain fever, it is indeed. How would you like that? But no! No! I see it all. You wouldn't care. I could fall dead at your feet and you wouldn't care. You haven't an ounce of love in your body or you would come away with me now. Where are you going?'

For Mirabelle was walking across the bedroom towards his private cabinet. 'Mirabelle?'

She was choosing a key from the bunch that hung from the chatelaine at her waist, fitting that key into the lock of his secret cupboard. His secret cupboard! The cupboard where he kept his fantasies. The cupboard she wasn't supposed to know anything about. Dear God!

'You are in a panic, my dear,' she said calmly, 'or you would not speak so wildly of other people's faults when your own are so glaring. Or do you imagine I know nothing of them? Now then, is your sudden decision anything to do with these, I wonder?'

His precious collection was being thrown across the bed out into the terrible light of unforgiving day. His precious, private, candle-light collection. *The Jolly Companion, The Man of Pleasure, The Garden of Delights.* Books written by men, published by men, read by men. Books that no woman should ever, ever see. What was she thinking of?

'How dare you!' he shouted. 'How dare you do this? These things are secret.'

'I have known about them for as long as you have been reading them,' she said coolly. 'And if I am not mistaken these are the sort of books that Easter's are accused of selling, if we are to believe the *Evening Record*.'

'Don't speak of it!' he yelled. 'Do you hear? This is unbearable.'

'It is the time to speak of it,' Mirabelle said implacably. 'More than the time to speak of it.'

'But it's a secret!' he shouted, beside himself with rage and fear. 'How did you know?'

'It is impossible to keep secrets,' she said. 'You should have learned that by now. There is always someone who knows. Now come, my dear, would it not be better to tell me what it is that frightens you so?'

He closed his face against her, and his ears. 'I am going to the Continent,' he said. 'Now. This very minute. As you do not appear to possess sufficient loyalty to accompany me I shall go alone.' He would go to Paris, that was what he'd do, and find cousin Will.

'You may run as far as you please, Edward,' she said, 'but the truth will out notwithstanding.'

But he was already packing, hauling a suitcase from the cupboard and throwing clothes into it with abandon. I cannot stop him or help him, she thought. He must endure this on his own. And there was a poetic justice about the thought because he'd read those hideous books on his own. So she went back to preparing her salon.

Cousin Will and Caleb Rawson had been back in Paris for nearly ten days, and Caroline's letter, having followed her brother from city to city all across Europe had finally caught up with him. The envelope had been readdressed so often it was really rather impressive, but the contents irritated him.

'A book!' Will said, passing the letter across the table to Caleb. 'What a fuss to make over a book! Dearly though I love her, Caleb, I really think she'll have to manage this on her own.'

'Aye,' Caleb agreed. 'We've more to do here than think on books.'

There had been continual trouble in Paris ever since the end of May, when the new government called out the troops to prevent a strike, and the Attorney General and the Advocate General both resigned over it. The first democratically elected government had been a horrible disappointment, for although the revolutionaries in Paris had elected equally revolutionary deputies, to everyone's surprise the new voters in the country-side had returned all the old guard, the very men who'd been opposing universal suffrage all their lives and who had no intention of allowing any further changes. Consequently the new Chamber found it almost impossible to govern. Money was scarce, food was expensive, and unemployment was worse than ever. And now the National Guard was on stand-by; there were troops all over the city and the barricades were going up again in the Place de la Bastille and across the Rue St Denis and the Rue St Martin just as they had been in February. It was no time to be thinking of going home.

'I will answer her tonight,' Will said, putting the much scrawled envelope into his writing desk. Meantime there were other more important things to attend to. He gave Tom instructions to keep all the servants within doors once the marketing was done, and then he and Caleb set out for the barricades in St Antoine.

It was a beautiful summer's day. The sky over the boulevards was as blue as a thrush's egg and the air was balmly. Quite the wrong sort of weather for a battle, but there was no doubt at all that a battle would begin sooner or later. The rich families had already fled and their fashionable streets were empty of everything except stray cats and sparrows; most shop windows were shuttered with iron; there were no omnibuses and very few cabs; and troops were on guard at every bridge and every public building. The smell of fear was everywhere, potent and alarming and rank as river water.

When they reached St Antoine they saw that the new barricade at the Rue St Martin was over ten feet high and still growing. It was a solidly built wall, buttressed by torn-up cobble-stones and constructed around four carts set on their sides to provide protected firing positions, and it would have been impossible to scale without the ladder that their revolutionary friends swung over the side for them. The men of St Antoine had obviously been hard at work all night, and not surprisingly some of them were snatching a few hours' uncomfortable sleep among the rubble, but there were still gangs digging a trench in the roadway in front of their fortification, and according to their leader, a solid-looking factory hand called Jean-Jacques, there were others inside the buildings on either side of the road breaking gaps through the walls between the cellars so as to provide an underground escape route from house to house.

'We are miners, Monsieur,' he said. 'Engineers for the Revolution. Come and see.'

And certainly the men they found wielding pickaxes down in the dark and dirt of the cellars looked very much like miners, stripped to the waist and streaked with sweat and coaldust.

They were glad to stop work for a moment or two and answer Will's questions, and they seemed very well informed, telling their two visitors exactly where all the newly arrived troops were to be found: 'Two squadrons of cavalry in front of the National Assembly, messieurs; a squadron of dragoons bivouacked before the Hôtel de Ville, with several companies of the line, we cannot be sure how many for they still arrive; a battalion stationed in the courtyard of the Prefecture of Police, as you would expect.' They'd even heard a rumour that there were infantry men billeted in the hall of the National Assembly itself.

As Jean-Jacques said, 'The preparations are formidable, messieurs.'

'Then you expect to see action today?' Will asked.

'No monsieur, not today. The troops still arrive and there is more cavalry to come. The ramps are still down in the Gare du Nord.'

'When do you think it will be?'

'Soon, monsieur. Very soon.'

'In that case,' Will said to Caleb as they walked away from the barricade, 'I'll write this up straight away.' There was a café just around the corner. He could go there.

Caleb had an article to deliver to the offices of the *Citizen*. 'I shall be back in an hour,' he said.

Caleb arrived with a newspaper tucked under his arm and his face signalling news even before he'd walked into the café and sat down at Will's table.

'Read that,' he said, pushing the paper across to his friend. It was Mr Jernegan's story. 'Easter's to be sued for sale of lewd book.'

'Oh God!' Will said. 'Poor Carrie. Then it is serious. No wonder she wrote to me. What am I to do, Caleb? I ought to go home. Could I travel to London and be back before they start fighting, do you think?'

'I doubt it.'

'I ought to go back, you know. She is my responsibility. Always has been.'

'She has a husband, I think.'

That was true, Will thought, but the postscript on her letter had made him wonder whether they were still living together. 'Yes,' he said, agreeing because this wasn't a doubt to be discussed with a stranger. 'But I still feel responsible. I've looked after her ever since she was a little girl you see, Mama having died.'

'If you like,' Caleb offered suddenly, 'I could travel for you.'

'Would you, Caleb? That's extremely kind of you.'

'I've been ten years on t' road back to England,' the weaver said wryly. 'High time I crossed t' Channel, I should say.'

'But don't you want to stay here and see the battle?'

'I've seen too many battles in my time,' Caleb said. 'And most of them ended in defeat for t' poor. I used to relish battles when I were young. Nowadays . . . ' He shrugged. 'Besides which,' and he paused as though what he was about to say pained him, 'I was unkind to your mother once, I'm sorry to say. I've regretted it since, when it was too late. Now here's a chance to make amends.'

'I can't imagine you being unkind to anyone,' Will said. 'And I'm sure you can't have been particularly unkind to Mama or I should have noticed it.' What an odd creature this man was. He seemed to have forgotten that Mama was a lady. As if a weaver could be unkind to a lady.

'Happen,' Caleb said vaguely. There was a group of men walking up the road towards the barricade, all of them bristling with guns. No, he really didn't want to see another blood-letting.

'If you could just call in on her,' Will said, 'and explain what is happening here. Tell her I will come home as soon as ever I can. I will pay your fare, of course.'

'Nay lad, you'll do no such thing,' the weaver said with great pride. 'I pay my own way in the world. Always do, always have done.'

So as Edward was crossing the Channel in one direction, Caleb Rawson was crossing it in the other, going home to England at last after an absence of twenty-three years and not at all in the way he'd planned. He'd hoped to return to friends and colleagues, to pick up his old life and work for the cause, to see his Harriet again, and now none of those things were possible, for his friends were scattered, the cause was cold, and Harriet was dead. If he hadn't been a resolutely cheerful man it could have been a sad home-coming. As it was, he found himself lodgings, had a good night's sleep and a hearty breakfast, and set off to Bedford Square to help Will's sister. 'Call in at breakfast time,' Will had advised, 'then you'll be sure to catch 'em before they all go rushing off to work.'

Caroline and Euphemia and Nan were still at table when the butler announced his arrival. 'A person in the hall says he's come to see you. From Paris, so he says, with a message from Mr Will.' His expression showed his disbelief and disapproval.

'Ask him if he wouldn't mind waiting for a few minutes,' Nan instructed. 'Then show him to the parlour. We will join him there presently.'

'I'm in no mood for visitors,' Caroline said, which was plain from the goblin expression on her face. 'Not this morning with all these dreadful things in the papers.' The scandal was spreading alarmingly and the popular papers had all written scathing articles that morning.

'It en't his fault, poor man, whoever he is,' Nan said, as she led them out of the breakfast room. 'And if he's come from Will he ought to be welcomed.'

But that didn't protect him from the sharp edge of her granddaughter's tongue.

He was standing beside the parlour window looking out at the square, but he turned as soon as he heard Nan's hand on the door and walked towards them eagerly. 'Mrs Easter ma'am, your servant. Caleb Rawson. We met many years ago in Rattlesden.'

The sight of him gave Nan a palpable shock. My heart alive, she thought, the weaver. Harriet's weaver. After all these years. It was like greeting a man come back from the dead. But worse, for this man brought a secret with him, and it was a secret that could hurt them all, even more terribly than this affair of the pornographic books. My dear heart alive! What a thing to happen. But she kept calm and introduced Euphemia and Caroline as though this were an ordinary social call.

'You have a message from Will, I believe,' she said when they were all seated in the customary circle in the middle of the room.

'He said to tell you he'll return as soon as he can,' the weaver told them. 'There's a deal going on in Paris at present or he'd have come home sooner.'

'Aye,' Nan said, 'we've read of it.'

'Is he well?' Euphemia asked, and was relieved to be told that he was.

Caroline set her face and said nothing. She knew her brother had work to do in Paris and that she'd told him herself that she would understand if he couldn't return, but she felt deserted, even so.

'Are you still a weaver, Mr Rawson?' Nan asked.

'No, ma'am. I'm a reporter, like your grandson. Before that I've been a sail-maker, infantryman, seaman, meat-porter, jack of all trades.'

'The last I heard you were on your way to Australia.'

'Van Diemen's Land, ma'am. For seven years.'

Is he going to admit that he was transported? Nan wondered. Why, that would be foolhardy. Especially with Caroline in her present mood. And she decided to stop him before he could run such a risk. 'Tell us about the situation in Paris,' she said. 'Is it as bad as the papers say?'

So he told them as briefly as he could, and found that he was talking to Mr Easter and Euphemia, because Caroline was patently bored by what he had to say.

Then there was an awkward pause, while they looked at one another for some indication as to how the conversation should proceed. And Nan, gazing at the stocky figure seated before her, suddenly remembered how he used to look, when his hair was thick and dark, just like Caroline's, and his young face wore the same glowering goblin look she'd just seen at her own breakfast table, that short brow flushed and wrinkled, those fine grey eyes blazing fury. My heart alive, she thought, they *are* alike.

'I knew your mother,' Caleb was saying to Caroline, 'many years ago.'

It was a mistake. He should have addressed her as Miss

Caroline, not with such directness. She was instantly and massively offended. 'Then you have the advantage of me, sir,' she said icily, 'for I did not.' Then she rose and made it quite clear that she intended to leave. 'If you will excuse me, Grandmother, I have work to attend to.'

'I hope we shall meet again,' Caleb said, rising too and holding out his hand.

'So I see,' she said, ignoring the proffered handshake and turning her body away from him so abruptly that her skirts gave a snake-hiss of anger.

'I must leave too, I fear,' Euphemia said gently, trying to make amends. And she shook his hands warmly and then fled, afraid of the strength of emotion this odd visitor of theirs had managed to rouse.

'You must forgive them, Mr Rawson,' Nan said to cover any possible embarrassment. 'We have rather pressing matters to attend to today.'

'Aye, I know,' he said. 'I read of it in t' Paris papers. Happen I can help you.'

She gave his offer thought, watching him shrewdly. It seemed genuine, and as she remembered, he wasn't a man to flatter or say things he didn't mean. Besides, if he knew the truth about Caroline's parentage it would be natural that he would want to help her. 'The firm is to be taken to court for selling a lewd book,' she said.

'Aye,' he said, imperturbably, 'I thought t' were summat of t' sort.'

'There is worse,' she said, deciding to confide in him, for heaven only knew they needed allies. 'News of it was given to the *Evening Record* and this morning the story is in all the popular papers, so somebody in the firm has been deliberately telling tales.'

'Do you know who it might be, ma'am?'

'Not yet.'

'Then look to see who would benefit from it. That's my advice.'

It was sound advice and they both understood it.

'I will visit again if I may,' he said. 'Meantime I'll see what gossip I can gather, being a reporter if you take my meaning. The *Evening Record*, you said.'

'I always try to be at home at four o'clock,' she said. 'Old ladies like their tea, you see, Mr Rawson.'

'So do returning exiles, ma'am,' he said. 'And this one will return to you as soon as I've any news. Be sure of it.'

Chapter 29

'Now then, my dear,' Frederick Brougham said to Caroline, as she and Nan settled themselves in his chambers in Lincoln's Inn the following afternoon. 'Let us see if we may discover some of the facts concerning this business. Firstly I must tell you both that Mr Furmedge is bringing his action in conjunction with the Society for the Suppression of Vice. Consequently we are facing a crown prosecution in the law courts. But that is what we expected, is it not? So we need not take any further distress from the knowledge.'

Caroline was surprised to be feeling so little emotion of any kind. After the misery of seeing her mistake blazoned in the popular press she was now unexpectedly calm. What would happen, would happen. It was simply a matter of waiting and enduring.

'However,' Mr Brougham was saying, 'if we could discover the name and whereabouts of the publisher of these hideous books, then the involvement of the Society could prove to our advantage. Their lawyer has given me to understand that they would prefer to take action against the publisher rather than the distributor. Mr Furmedge takes a different view, I believe, but as the Society is paying the costs, I imagine their view would prevail. That being so I propose to make it part of our objective to discover the publisher. Which is the point at which I shall begin this morning.'

The hideous books lay in a pile on his desk, looking remarkably ordinary in their plain green covers. 'You say that you cannot remember ordering these books,' he said to Caroline.

'No.'

'Nor seeing them before the book in question was delivered to you with Mr Furmedge's letter?'

'If I had seen them before I should certainly have remembered, I can assure you.'

'Quite. However, in a court of law these things have to be proven beyond a doubt, so could I ask you if you would examine them again.'

'All of them?'

'Indeed yes. Perhaps you could start by considering the titles. Are any of the titles familiar to you?'

She picked up the first book from the pile and read the title, but it meant nothing. 'No,' she said. But to her surprise the fourth title *was* familiar. '*Goddesses of Greece*,' she said. 'Why yes. I remember this. I looked at this one.'

He turned to give her his full attention. 'Do you remember when this was?'

'Oh yes,' she said. In that odd passionless state of hers she remembered it clearly. 'It was the last afternoon before the regional meeting. I was in a rush. Edward was helping me and he said,' (Oh how well she remembered it!) ' "Top and tail them".'

'By which he meant . . . ?' Frederick prompted.

'Look at the top book on the pile and then the bottom one and ignore the rest.'

'Ah!' Nan said. 'So that was how it happened.'

'Mr Maycock brought in another pile at the last moment and Edward said he should do the work of ordering them to make amends for being a nuisance.'

'We progress,' Mr Brougham said, nodding his white head. 'Did he order them? Can you remember?'

'He must have done.'

'Then we need to interview this man,' Frederick said to Nan. 'It might be possible to shift the onus of responsibility upon his shoulders if that is where it belongs.'

'The firm is being taken to court too, is it not?' Caroline said. 'I would have to represent the firm.'

'Unless we were able to name the publisher,' Frederick said. 'If the Society were in a position to take action against the publisher they might well see their way to dropping one or other of the charges against the company.'

'Then the sooner we see that wretch Maycock, the better,' Nan said. 'I'll send a messenger for him the minute I get back to the Strand. Is there anything else?'

'Not for the present,' Frederick said, smiling at her. 'If I hear anything more during the day I will tell you of it at dinner.'

But there was something else, and it had already arrived in the building. The two women were on their feet and ready to leave, Nan buttoning her gloves and Caroline automatically tying her bonnet, when a clerk shadowed into the room and bent to mutter a message into Frederick's ear.

'Here's your Mr Rawson arrived, my dear,' Frederick said, 'with information that concerns us all, or so it would appear.'

So they stayed to see what it was.

Mr Rawson was rather out of breath and his grizzled hair was standing on end like a badly used brush, but his triumph was obvious and warming. He grinned at them so widely that they could see every single one of his remaining teeth.

'I've come hot-foot from t' *Daily Record*,' he said. 'Your informant is unveiled, Mrs Easter ma'am. He gave no name to t' reporter but t' man says he'd remember well enough and he gave me a fair description. But then, when I went down to t' lobby and made a few inquiries there, one of t' hall porters knew him by sight. 'Tis a feller called Jernegan, so he says, and he works at Easter's in Regent Street.'

'Would the hall porter swear to all this?' Mr Brougham asked.

'Aye, he would.'

'Then this is splendid news, Mr Rawson. Perfectly splendid. You see what strides we make, Caroline.'

'Mr Jernegan,' Nan said grimly. 'Well now, that don't surprise me at all, for the man's a wretch. Always has been. You've done well, Mr Rawson. We're beholden to 'ee.'

'Happy to be of service,' the weaver said, beaming at them.

'Mr Jernegan shall answer to us as well as Mr Maycock,' Nan said grimly. 'They shall come here together.'

So it was arranged. And Mr Rawson was asked to attend too 'for identification purposes'.

'Now,' Nan said, 'perhaps we shall get to the bottom of it.'

But that was easier said than done.

* * *

Mr Maycock was so anxious he spluttered like a candle in a breeze but he was adamant that he couldn't remember suggesting those particular books to Mrs Henry. Such books were abhorrent to him, he said. He would never have suggested that such books be offered for sale. Never. And having taken a stand right at the very beginning of his interview, he maintained it to the end. He couldn't remember ordering the books either, although when pressed he admitted that he might have signed an order slip for them, 'under somebody else's instructions'. But that was as far as Mr Brougham could push him. He couldn't remember somebody else giving him such instructions, so naturally he couldn't name the somebody else, whoever it was. He couldn't remember visiting the publisher, whoever he was either.

'In short, sir,' Mr Brougham said, 'what you are asking me to believe is that you cannot remember anything at all.'

'No sir,' Mr Maycock said stoutly, 'my memory serves me very ill indeed.'

'Or very well,' Nan suggested with heavy sarcasm.

'There is little to be gained by further questioning at this stage,' Frederick said to Nan.

Mr Maycock was allowed to cough towards the door. But just when his hand was on the door knob, Mr Brougham spoke again, and this time with theatrical clarity, addressing his words to Nan. 'Perhaps, Mrs Easter, it would be fairer to Mr Maycock were we to tell him that we know of certain transactions in Holywell Street.'

'I see no reason to divulge any information to Mr Maycock,' Nan said, acting her part without any theatricality at all. 'He would only forget it.'

Mr Maycock seemed glued to the door knob, his neck strained with the effort of listening.

'Even so . . . ' Mr Brougham said. 'Mr Maycock, would you spare us a few more moments of your time?'

'Sir,' Mr Maycock said obediently, turning from the door to face them.

'Were we to be shown certain – shall we say papers – upon which your signature was set, and which indicated that an order for certain books had been made in your name and under your signature, then that would alter your conception of this business somewhat, I daresay? It might even, shall we say, jog your memory?'

'If you have such papers, sir,' Mr Maycock spluttered, 'I should see them, sir.'

'There is nothing in law which requires that to be done, Mr Maycock. Should the matter come to court, which it very well may, and you were asked to give evidence, which again you very well could be, then of course, you would see the document in question and be asked to testify whether the signature upon it were yours or no.'

'Meantime it en't nobody's business but ours,' Nan said tartly. 'You may go, Mr Maycock. We don't need to detain you.'

Mr Maycock's face was visibly torn with indecision, his flabby lips swinging from side to side as he scowled, his mutton-chop whiskers shifting and trembling, his eyes blinking, while Nan and Frederick and Caleb stared at him implacably and Caroline watched as though she were at a play. Finally he gave a gulp like a frog, gathered himself and leapt out through the door, opening it so clumsily that he hit his shins.

'Now,' Frederick said calmly, ringing for his clerk, 'we will take coffee. That will refresh us and give our two gentlemen adequate time to stew in their own juice.'

Caroline was impressed despite her apathy. 'Why, it's like a play,' she said.

'Yes, my dear,' Frederick agreed. 'The law and the theatre have a deal in common.' And as his clerk came into the room, 'Coffee now, Mr Mellors, if you please. And are the gentlemen together?'

'Yes sir. In the waiting room, sir. How long should they be left?'

'Give them twenty minutes,' Frederick said. 'That should be ample for our purposes, I think. Then show Mr Jernegan up, if you please.'

Mr Jernegan was sullen with apprehension, his long saturnine face brooding darkly and his spine poker-stiff. He sat down without a word, glancing apprehensively at Nan and Caroline.

Now it was Caleb Rawson's turn to join the drama, answering Mr Brougham's opening question with the assurance that, yes, this was the gentleman who had been seen in the offices of the *Daily Record*.

'And known by name I believe you said, Mr Rawson?'

'Yes indeed, sir. Known by name. No doubt of it.'

'Perhaps you would care to comment?' Mr Brougham suggested courteously to Mr Jernegan.

'I was in the newspaper office, yes sir. I admit it,' that gentleman said. 'But under orders, sir. Under orders. I would not have undertaken such a mission without orders.'

'From whom, sir?' Nan said. 'If you wish us to believe you, you must name the man.'

'It won't be agreeable to you, Mrs Easter,' Mr Jernegan said, looking sideways at her with an expression that was both calculating and smug.

'Devil take it, Mr Jernegan, none of this is agreeable to me. Name the man.'

'It was your grandson, Mrs Easter. It was Mr Edward Easter.'

The news came as no real surprise to Nan Easter. She had suspected it in a vague uncomfortable way for some time, and the certainty had hardened when she'd heard about his precipitate holiday. 'As I imagined,' she said. 'You tell me nothing I don't know.'

Her reaction was a disappointment to Mr Jernegan but he persevered. 'It was his idea that we should show Mrs Henry the books we considered suitable.'

'And you considered these books suitable?' Mr Brougham asked.

'No sir, I did not. I never laid eyes on them. I know nothing about them.'

'But you knew about the court case that you reported to the *Daily Record*?'

'I knew something of it, sir.'

'Something?'

'Yes, sir. I knew what Mr Edward told me about it.'

'And what did Mr Edward tell you about it?'

That was a poser and required thought. 'He told me that – um – questionable books had been sold and that Mrs Henry had received a letter of complaint about them.'

'And?'

'And he sent me to the paper, sir.'

'So,' Frederick continued, 'we are to assume that Mr Edward wanted this story to be printed by the *Daily Record*?'

'I'm sure I couldn't answer for Mr Edward's intentions, sir.'

'Could you not?'

'It ain't for the likes of me to question the purposes of our employers,' Mr Jernegan said, retreating behind formality. 'Oh no, sir, that wouldn't do at all, as I am sure you appreciate. Orders are given, you understand, and we carry them out.'

'As Mr Maycock did when he went to Holywell Street, to the premises of Mr – er,' searching through the papers on his desk.

'Exactly the same, sir, yes.'

'He was obeying instructions?'

'Yes.'

'Even though he knew this man was a publisher with a reputation for – what was your term? – questionable books?'

That was another difficult question, requiring another prolonged pause. 'I'm sure I couldn't say. You would have to ask Mr Maycock.'

'It did not occur to either of you that what you were doing would bring disrepute to the firm?'

'That was not our intention, sir.'

'Then why do it?' Nan said.

Truculent silence.

'Come now, Mr Jernegan, I want an answer.'

'I couldn't say, ma'am. I couldn't speak for Mr Maycock. Nor Mr Edward neither.'

'Howsomever,' Mr Brougham said mildly, 'we may safely assume that you had reasons for your own actions.'

'I suppose so.'

'Then tell us what they were,' Nan insisted.

Mr Jernegan looked her full in the eye without speaking for several long seconds while he tried to judge whether it would be more to his advantage to speak than to keep silent. When he spoke it was with a boldness so harsh that it grated their ears. 'We did it, Mrs Easter, so that everybody would see that a commercial firm is no place for a young lady.'

'Indeed?' Nan said icily.

He realized his mistake and floundered, trying to justify himself. 'Not meaning any disrespect to you, ma'am. Only about books you see, ma'am. To choose books, ma'am. Books should be chosen by men. Books ain't a woman's business.'

'I doubt if the Misses Bronte would agree with you,' Frederick said dryly, 'nor Mrs Gaskell.'

'They may write 'em,' Mr Jernegan went on, spurred by Nan's glare. 'That's true enough. I mean to say I can't deny that. But they shouldn't choose 'em, now should they? In all conscience they shouldn't choose 'em. Being there are books written that no lady ever sees nor ever should see. It don't make sense to let a lady choose. Well, I mean to say, if these books had been chosen by a man none of this would have happened, now would it?'

'If my memory serves me aright,' Frederick said, 'they *were* chosen by a man. By Mr Edward Easter, is that not so? Or did you choose them? Is that it?'

'No, sir. I did not.'

'Or Mr Maycock, possibly?'

'No sir,' Mr Jernegan said frantically. 'It was Mr Edward, sir. You have my word.'

Nan jumped to her feet as if there were springs under her shoes. 'Get out! You loathsome object!' she yelled at him. 'Get right on out. Take a week's pay, you and Maycock both, and leave my employ this minute. And if you've any sense at all in that hideous head of yours, which I very much doubt, you'll get as far away from me as you can, for if I ever see hide or hair of you again I won't be answerable for the consequences.'

Her rage was so terrible that he ran from the room, eyes bolting, without waiting for Mr Brougham to dismiss him or stopping to close the door behind him.

'Good riddance to bad rubbish!' Nan said, dusting her hands of him. 'To plot against you, my dear. I never heard the equal of it.' Then she remembered that Frederick had been in the middle of an interrogation, and grimaced an apology at him. 'Oh Frederick, my dear, were there more questions you wanted to ask?'

'No,' he said mildly. 'We shall glean no more from that

quarter. I doubt whether he knows the name of our publisher, and if he does he won't divulge it now.'

'Never you mind, my dear,' Nan said to Caroline, fiercely protective. 'We'll find him, never you mind.'

But Caroline sat stunned by the impact of what she'd just heard. They hate me, she thought, understanding what had been said because she'd been able to receive it with so little emotion. Even my own cousin hates me. It didn't make sense. What did I ever do to him that he should hate me? They'd never liked one another very much, because he was so spoilt and because he'd always been so superior, especially when she was little, but she'd never hated him. She'd never wanted to shame him in front of everybody, or trick him, or plot against him. Why, it was hideous. Like a nightmare. Family shouldn't behave like that.

'I think it might be sensible for us all to go home,' Caleb said quietly to Nan. He'd been watching Caroline's pale face all through both interviews, noticing how still she was and how silent, and he was torn with pity for her, pity and paternal concern.

'Yes,' Nan said, glancing at that pale face herself. 'Time we were getting back.'

'If you'll allow me, ma'am,' Caleb said to Nan, offering his help instinctively, 'I will find this publisher for you.'

'Could you?' Nan said.

'I don't know,' he had to admit, 'but I'll do my darnedest. We have an address if not a name.'

'We have a street,' Mr Brougham corrected. 'And a street full of such questionable publishers and other activities that are a great deal worse. It will be a Herculean task.'

'I will do my best,' Caleb said, smiling at that poor pale face. 'If Mrs Easter will dress me like a merchant, I'll see what a merchant can discover.'

'I'll do better than that, Mr Rawson,' Nan said warmly. 'If you are to work for us in this manner, I shall take you onto the Easter payroll.' And when he opened his mouth to protest, 'Now come, if I accept your services I shall be depriving you of the time you need to earn a living at your chosen trade, en't that so? Very well then, since that would prey upon my conscience, you must humour me and accept my wage.'

383

So it was agreed, and the weaver was persuaded to accompany the two women back to Bedford Square, so that he could be fitted out with suitable clothes.

'My heart alive!' Nan said, as the carriage trotted northwards along the Tottenham Court Road. 'This has been a morning and no mistake.'

'If only it would all end here,' Caroline said sadly. But as all three of them knew, their difficulties had only just begun. 'You are very kind to help us, Mr Rawson. I am glad Will sent you here.'

'Happy to be of service,' Caleb said. And he was. For the first time in his life he was working to help an individual rather than a cause, but the reward was the same. Nay better. 'After all t' good work your mother did for t' poor, it's t' least I can do.'

'You knew my mother well, did you not, Mr Rawson?'

'Aye. I did.'

'Was she a saint?'

'No,' he said, surprised by the question, 'she wasn't a saint. We're none of us saints. She was a very good woman.' And for a brief and uncomfortably vivid moment he remembered her, lying mutely in his arms on that one rushed fearful occasion when he'd made love to her, taking her as carelessly as he'd taken all the other women in those far-off, selfish days, more shame to him. And he regretted it now as he'd regretted it during his convict days. 'A kind, loving woman.'

'Do you think she would be ashamed of me, Mr Rawson?'

His answer was so forthright it lifted her spirits. 'Ashamed of you? Facing all this much wi' such courage? I should just think not. Why, she'd be proud of thee, lass.'

This time the familiarity of his speech was comforting. And so was the sight of that rough honest face of his. 'I have a picture of you at my cousin's house in Clerkenwell, Mr Rawson,' she said. 'My mother drew it as an illustration in a little primer she made to teach Will to read. W is for weaver. One day when all this is over, I will show it to you.'

'I shall be honoured,' he said.

But all this was not over.

*　　*　　*

The next morning the newspapers were dominated by reports that another revolution had broken out in Paris. But in lesser columns below the main story they also gave the date of Easter's impending court case. And the *Daily Record* added the information that two of Easter's managers had been summarily dismissed. 'On the grounds that there is no smoke without fire,' the article said, 'we venture to suggest that many of the rumours currently circulating in London could well be true.'

'Deuce take it,' Nan said. 'Why don't they leave us alone? That won't help trade.'

It didn't help Billy Easter either, for he could hardly avoid the gossip in the Easter warehouse, and it didn't take much intelligence to work out that his son must have been the Easter involved with Mr Maycock and Mr Jernegan, because the only other candidate besides Nan and himself was Henry and he was distraught at what had happened. And *he* hadn't run away.

Matilda had been furious about that ever since she came home from Mirabelle's salon.

'What were you thinking of to allow him to go on this silly holiday?' she demanded. 'You might have known how bad it would look. And he should have known better than to leave you here at the unhealthiest time of the year. What was the matter with him?'

But he forbore to tell her, because it was plain from her distress that she already knew.

'I shall have you took ill again,' she complained. 'Oh, it's too bad! It really is!'

'I won't work too hard, I promise, Tilda,' he said, trying to reassure her. 'Trade is always slack in the summer.'

But it fell off alarmingly during the next two weeks. Soon Easter's were hardly selling any books at all.

'Is there anything I can do?' Caroline worried when she'd persuaded Nan to show her the sales figures.

'No,' her grandmother said. 'There's nothing any of us can do, except wait, and waiting en't in my nature.'

'Nor in mine until now,' Caroline said. And now she couldn't think of anything else to do except wait.

'If only Mr Rawson could find this awful publisher,' Euphemia said. 'What a difference that would make!'

'Mr Rawson has a job on if he's to do that,' Nan said

grimly. 'Oh, he'll do his best, I don't doubt, but we should be fools to hold out much hope of his success.'

But unknown to all of them Mr Rawson had an ally.

Mirabelle's salon had not been a success. Nearly half her guests failed to appear and those who did had plainly already heard rumours for they were just a little too solicitous as to her husband's whereabouts, and took her careful answers about 'a much-needed holiday' with patent disbelief.

Then two days later *The Times* printed a discreet reference to the affair, and her good friend Mrs Abernethy called with the news that Mr Maycock and Mr Jernegan had been given notice. So she knew it was time for her to take action. As soon as Mrs Abernethy had gone, she put on her bonnet and went to visit Mr Brougham.

He received her guardedly, which was only to be expected, and told her nothing more than she already knew. But she persevered with her mission.

'If my reading of this situation is correct, Mr Brougham,' she said, 'it would not surprise me to hear that you are endeavouring to find the man who published the books.'

Mr Brougham admitted the truth of her assumption. And waited.

'I think I may know the gentleman's name,' Mirabelle said, 'and I suspect that I have in my possession a printed list of the books he sells, or sold, as the case may be.'

'I will not ask you how you came by it, Mirabelle my dear,' Mr Brougham said, when she'd taken the paper from her reticule and laid it upon the desk before him, 'but you will allow me to tell you how very much I admire your courage in this matter, and your loyalty to Mrs Easter.'

'I can depend on your discretion, Mr Brougham.'

'Of course.'

'Edward is not a bad man,' she said, as she closed her reticule. 'Ambition is his downfall. He needs to feel important. As we all do, do we not?'

'To a greater or lesser degree. Do you wish me to convey any of this information to Mrs Easter? Without naming my source, of course.'

'No sir, not yet. I would rather wait a little until we know where Edward is and what he intends to do.'

'You think he will write?'

'I hope so.'

'And return?'

'That too, Mr Brougham. In time. I am sure of it.'

Chapter 30

When Edward disembarked at Boulogne he was still so enmeshed in panic that he couldn't think of anything except his frantic need to get away as fast and as far as he could from the horrors that had suddenly risen about him like wraiths from a graveyard. He didn't notice that the train to Paris was two thirds empty and he gave no thought at all to the reported revolution. In fact, as he approached the city and the cannons began to fire down upon it from the great hill of Montmartre, he assumed it was merely thunder rumbling overhead, and ignored it.

Once he was in the station, it was obvious, even to him, that there was something going on. There were no cabs, no omnibuses and very few porters, only troops and their horses and their supply wagons. Now and a little late he began to think that it might have been a mistake to come to this city, and he made up his mind that he would spend one night there with cousin Will and then press on again as soon as he could.

But finding his cousin was another difficulty he hadn't anticipated. The concierge at the address on Will's letter said she hadn't seen Monsieur Eastaire since February, and sent him next door. Next door suggested that he try round the block, and round the block offered him four or five other apartments in the vicinity and told him that Madame Morisot's was the most likely.

It didn't look likely to Edward, being disappointingly scruffy, and horribly full of people. But to his relief the concierge assured him that Monsieur Eastaire *did* live there, and when he reached the second floor, which was pungent with the most appetizing smell of stew, and knocked at the door, which was clearly labelled 'W Easter', somebody came running to open it.

His welcome was another surprise. The doorman turned out to be Tom Thistlethwaite, and in such an agitated state that he actually spoke first without being spoken to. 'Oh, Mr Edward sir, what a blessing you're here! I been worried out 'a me wits.'

Edward decided to ignore his social gaffe because the man was plainly upset. 'What is it, Tom?' he said. 'Where is Mr Will?'

'That's just it,' Tom said. 'I don't know. I ain't seen hide nor hair of him since yesterday morning. I'm worried out a' me wits. Anything could've happened.'

It was necessary to take over. 'Do you know where he was going?'

'He was off to them barricades, that's where,' Tom said, scowling his anxious disapproval. 'In the faubourg, right plumb in the line a' fire from all them cannons on Montmartre.'

Right plumb in the line of fire, Edward thought. That didn't sound very healthy. But he shrugged the thought away because there was a job to be done and he'd undertaken to do it now, and being an Easter there was no turning back. Not yet anyway. 'Have you looked for him?' he asked.

'I was to stay here,' Tom said. 'He give me strict orders.'

'Very well,' Edward said decisively, 'now I am countermanding them. Get your hat and coat and we will go and find him.' The stew would have to wait until they all returned, even though his stomach was rumbling for it. With any luck it shouldn't take them long.

'Lead on,' he said to Tom, when they were out in the street. 'The sooner we go, the sooner we shall get back.'

'We got to get over the river first, Mr Edward sir,' Tom said. 'The faubourg's in the east by Les Halles.'

They headed for the Seine, through streets emptied of people and full of rubbish, piles of ash and heaps of stinking nightsoil that had obviously been left to accumulate for weeks. It was alarmingly quiet out in the open like this, but as they neared the quaysides they could hear the sound of wheels being driven roughly over cobbles and men shouting orders, and at that they quickened their pace, for at least company would be preferable to this sinister emptiness.

The quayside was thronged with people. There were soldiers keeping all the bridges to the Ile de la Cité completely empty except for the Pont Neuf and that was crowded with carts and carriages all trying to cross the river on their one available route. If we are to get across too, Edward thought, we shall have to fight against all that traffic as well as the guards.

Two high-sided carts had stopped beside the pavement where he stood. Both of them were full of elderly men and women wrapped in blankets and obviously ill.

'What is happening?' Edward asked the driver.

'We clear the hospitals, monsieur. We vacate our beds for the wounded. There is to be an attack.'

'Do you know when?' The cart was on its way again. They were moving apart. 'Tell us quickly for the love of God.'

'Tonight, monsieur.'

'If we are stopped,' Edward said to Tom, 'we are working for the hospital. Come on.'

But they weren't stopped. There were so many people pushing and shoving and arguing on that narrow bridge that two more were hardly noticed. When they got past the island to the north side of the river it was necessary to follow the carts for some considerable distance before they dared set off on their own again because everybody seemed to be moving in the same direction away from the bridges and the troops were watching with nervously sharp eyes and rifles at the ready.

At last they were in empty streets again and heading east. And now they passed the signs of a recent battle, walls pitted by shot; pools of blood still congealing damply on the cobbles or smeared in long, tell-tale trails where the dead or injured had been dragged away; dead mules and horses lying in ungainly heaps, some already beginning to bloat and smelling most vilely. And above it all hung drifting shrouds of smoke, grey yellow and sulphurous, and the sharp, bitter smell of gunpowder.

'Is it much further?' Edward asked. They were approaching a crossroads and he was feeling horribly vulnerable. There was no way of knowing what might be lurking round the corner.

Tom didn't have time to reply for at that moment there was an explosion no more than a hundred yards ahead of them. The noise of it swelled in their ears as the blast threw them to the ground. For a brief second, Edward was aware that the air was full of bricks and fragments of stone, and that people were screaming, and then there was a second explosion further off and he scrambled to his feet and hurled himself at the nearest doorway for shelter. He and Tom were tugging at the door together, and so was a scruffy urchin who had flown in behind them like a bat into a cave.

It was the urchin who opened the door. 'Follow me,' it said and immediately shot off through the hall, trailing stink behind it, into a dark corridor, through a plain deal door and down a rickety staircase into the cellar. They could still hear the bombardment, but at a distance. The sound of their own laboured breathing was louder.

The urchin had found a candle and was scratching for flame in a tinder box, muttering with impatience. The wick caught light, flickered and then bloomed into a fat golden tulip in the foetid darkness. And they saw that she was a girl, tousle-haired, layered in rags, with a pistol in her belt, but decidedly female. 'Voilà!' she said. 'Where do you wish to go?'

'Can we go anywhere?' Edward asked her, speaking in French because English would plainly have been wasted on her. 'We are in somebody's cellar, is that not so?'

'The houses are empty, citoyen,' the child said. 'From here we may run through the cellars wherever we please. All that is needed is a master key.' And she touched the key suspended round her neck and hid it underneath her rags.

'Could you take us to the barricades?'

'Which barricade?'

But neither of them knew. 'I search for my cousin,' Edward explained. 'An Englishman called Mr Easter.'

The girl's face erupted into smiles. 'Monsieur Eastaire,' she said. 'Monsieur Guillaume Eastaire. I know him. A good citizen. Follow me.'

They followed as well as they could in the darkness, climbing through narrow gaps in the walls and stumbling over coals, while the noise of gunfire rumbled overhead, until after about a quarter of an hour, lamplights suddenly flickered in the darkness ahead of them and the girl began to run.

'Come back!' Edward called in panic. 'Don't leave us, I pray you!'

Voices were talking rapidly in a French so quick and slurred he couldn't understand it.

'She's led us into a trap,' he whispered to Tom. 'Get ready to run for it.'

But before either of them could run anywhere, Will's face loomed at them from behind the blue-edged corona of an approaching lantern. He was filthy dirty and his beard was untrimmed but it was decidedly Will.

'Who's there?' he said in French.

'It's me,' Edward answered in English. 'Edward.'

'Good God! What are you doing here?'

'I came to find you and . . . '

'And Tom too,' Will said, speaking roughly and quickly. 'Thank the Lord for that. We need all the water we can get, as quick as you can. That last one fractured a main, and there are so many wounded. Take these buckets. I'll get more. Marie will lead you. Hurry!'

'Just a moment,' Edward said. 'We didn't come here for that . . . '

But the buckets had been thrust into Tom's hands and Will was already gone.

'Well, just for a little while then,' Edward said. It was infra dig to allow himself to be put upon like this but what else could he do?

He and Tom worked obediently for the next two hours, struggling from cellar to cellar until they came to an empty house where the pump was still working and then labouring back again with those awkward buckets slopping, and up to an ill-lit kitchen where the stone flags were strewn with the injured bodies of men and women, some of them so young as to be almost children. Their uninjured companions wandered amongst them, doing what they could to staunch the endless flow of blood and offering the precious water.

'So many wounded,' Edward said to Will after his seventh or eighth sortie.

'They've been fighting hand to hand,' Will explained. 'For the barricade. Most of them were cut by bayonets.'

'Dreadful,' Edward said. 'When are you coming back to your apartment?'

'Come upstairs, and I will show you why I cannot answer you,' Will said, picking up a candle and walking from the kitchen.

Edward wasn't really sure that he wanted to go upstairs, but by now he was too tired to argue. So he followed, up eight flights of stairs and into an empty room on the fourth floor. It had obviously once been a bedroom for it still contained the broken frame of a four-poster, but now it was being used as a look-out post. In the light from their candle he could see that the mattress was propped up against the window, and crouched against their make-shift defence were two children, a boy and a girl, keeping watch, rifles in hand.

'How does it go?' Will asked in French.

'Badly,' the boy said.

'Have you taken sides with these people?' Edward whispered in English. 'I thought reporters were supposed to be impartial.'

'So did I once,' Will said, snuffing the candle. 'But this is a war. You can't stand on the sidelines in a war, Edward. You have to take sides. Look out of the window and you'll see what I mean.'

They joined the two children behind the mattress and peered down into the moonlit battle that was going on below them.

Tall though it was, the barricade had been breached, its cobble-stones scattered about the street, and its flag post snapped in two. Now some of the defenders were struggling to mend it, hauling furniture into the gap, and bringing cart-loads of fresh cobbles from further along the street, their straining backs grimed and urgent. But there were too few of them for such a task and they worked under a continuing fusillade. He could hear bullets whistling overhead and pinging against the walls, and beyond the barricade red and orange fires spat into the darkness. And as his eyes grew accustomed to the moonlight he realized that they were too few because so many of their companions were dead. There were bodies everywhere, grey with death and dust, lying in black pools of blood, their limbs spreadeagled where they fell, their faces still grimacing in anguish. Some of them were hideously wounded, with gaping holes in their heads, or stumps of dark red meat where their arms should have been. One man had half his head blown completely away. The bile rose into Edward's throat at the sight of him. Why on earth had he come to such a place?

Yet very few of the insurgents were fighting back. He could see four men lying among the cobbles training their pistols on the opposing army, but they didn't fire.

'Why don't they fire?'

'We have little ammunition now,' Will said. 'Every bullet must count. They will wait until the next attack.'

'Will there be another attack? Now?'

'It is likely.'

'And the dead?'

'The dead will wait too. There is no time for the dead in the middle of a battle. Only for the living and the wounded. When it's quiet we'll get the wounded out and back into the suburb.'

'But if they have run out of ammunition would it not be better to surrender?'

'The French army don't take prisoners, you see,' Will said bitterly. 'I think they've been given orders to kill every insurgent they can find. It's a massacre. There is nothing for it but to fight on to the bitter end.'

'They kill us like flies, monsieur,' the boy said, speaking in French but as though he had understood what they were saying. 'We are dead men, all of us.' And yet he spoke with a sombre pride that Edward found moving despite his own fear of the place and his abhorrence of the carnage below him.

'I will stay tonight and help you to get the wounded out,' he said. It was the only thing he could do in the circumstances. He would stay here until this awful business was over and *then* he'd move on.

The killing went on for days. There seemed no end to it. Under cover of darkness they put the wounded on carts and dragged them back to their hovels in St Antoine. They filled water tanks when they could, using the cellars as underground roadways, and from time to time somebody cooked a watery stew and dividing it equally, in the manner of communards, brought tin plates of it to anyone who was hungry. And the killing went on.

At last, after an interminable time, an attack was launched on their barricade that was so ferocious that the remaining defenders took to their heels and fled through the cellars, taking their walking wounded and Will and Tom and Edward with them.

'Is it over?' Edward gasped as he followed Will through the darkness.

'I couldn't say.'

'Where are they going?'

'To other barricades, to the country.'

'And you?'

'To my apartment, if I can.'

They emerged into total darkness in a narrow alley between two rows of tall, unlit, decaying tenements. There was no time or energy for leave-taking. People were scrambling off in both directions. If they were to get away, this darkness was their only hope.

'South,' Will said, 'and don't run. Running looks bad. If we are stopped, leave the talking to me.'

Every other street was guarded by troops. They were stopped three times, but their interrogators seemed satisfied with Will's explanation that he was a reporter looking for a story.

'Write that the revolution is over for good and all,' one officer said, peering at them in the light of his lantern. 'Tell your readers that. We have had a blood-letting here in France and revolution is dead.'

It was an enormous relief to be back in the apartment, almost as if they'd all escaped home to England. The servants had gone, of course, and there was no food in the house but there were beds to sleep in and no sound of gunfire.

'Sleep tonight,' Will said. 'Food tomorrow.' And he dropped across his bed and fell asleep at once, still fully dressed.

Edward and Tom took off his boots and removed as many of his filthy clothes as they could without lifting him and then they took themselves off to bed. It was past midnight and they were tired to the bone.

Tomorrow, Edward promised himself as he drifted off, I will have a bath and a meal and then I will catch the next train out of this city no matter where it's going. Enough is enough.

But Fate had other plans for him.

In the early hours of the morning he was woken by an unfamiliar sound, a rhythmic, insistent rattling, like something being shaken. He got up at once and lit a candle and went to see what it was, opening the shutters first to peer out anxiously into the empty street. Then he realized that the noise was coming from his cousin's room.

Will was lying on his back with his mouth fallen open and the whole of his body visibly shaking. The noise that had woken Edward was the sound of bedsprings creaking and teeth chattering. Good God! What now?'

'Wake up!' he said, shaking Will's juddering shoulder. 'What's the matter with you?'

But his cousin only opened his eyes for a weary second and gave a long terrible groan. 'Feel so bad,' he said. His forehead was burning and his skin clammy with fever.

Oh God! Edward thought. What am I supposed to do? And he remembered Mirabelle who was always so calm and efficient when anyone was ill and for a few panicking seconds ached to have her beside him. But he was on his own now. There was no one else to take responsibility.

'I'll get a doctor,' he decided. Tom was in the doorway rubbing the sleep out of his eyes. 'Get a doctor, Tom, as quick as you can.'

It took a very long time to find one, most of them having been commandeered to serve as surgeons to the army. The sun rose and Will groaned from the bed to use the chamber, falling back upon the covers afterwards totally exhausted. From then on Edward spent his time emptying one chamber pot after another, with growing nausea and alarm. By noon his cousin was passing blood and was in such extreme pain that he couldn't talk. His cheeks were flushed with fever, but the rest of his face was like sweating putty and his tongue had a yellow coating.

But at long stinking last Tom returned with a doctor, an elderly man who spent more than a quarter of an hour negotiating his fee before he would walk into the bedroom to examine his patient.

'He has dysentery,' he said. 'The bloody flux. There are cases all over Paris.'

'What is to be done?' Edward said. Dysentery was serious. People died of it. 'You can cure him, can you not?'

But the doctor wouldn't commit himself as to the possibility of a cure. 'I will give him castor oil to purge the bowel and tincture of opium to relieve the griping,' he said. 'Keep him in bed, keep him warm. Give him plain boiled water to drink. Not pump water. Pump water is lethal. The fever should subside in a day or two. If he becomes delirious send for me again.'

He was delirious all night, and raving, about some woman in Ireland, 'starving to death and the warehouses full of corn', about his mother, 'she won't die, will she, Papa? Say she won't die', about Caroline, 'she wrote to me, you know. She was worried . . . about something. I can't remember. Should have gone back to help her, my poor Carrie.'

It was a gruelling night. Edward sat beside him and listened to his ravings and sponged the sweat from his forehead and supported him when he had to stagger from the bed to use the chamber yet again. At daybreak they both fell into a troubled sleep and neither of them woke till mid-day, when Will groaned to the chamber again.

'Are you better?' Edward asked when he'd helped him back into bed again.

'A little, I think,' Will said. 'The pain ain't quite so strong.'

'Could you fancy anything to eat?'

'God no!'

'You won't mind if I get Tom to cook me some breakfast?'

'No, no. You go. I mustn't keep you.'

'I'll be back directly,' Edward promised. 'Call if you need me.'

As he ate Tom's rough bread and cheese breakfast, he remembered his plans, and grimaced to think how thoroughly they'd been wrecked. Not that it mattered. After the horrors of the barricades and the terror of death and now this new ordeal of an illness that could so easily kill, the need for flight was a thing of the past, and the great sin he'd fled reduced to nothing more terrible than a trivial mistake. Only one thing was important to him now, and that was to nurse cousin Will back to health. This was a family matter. The trial was simply a distant irrelevance.

In London on the other hand it was an approaching ordeal.

Chapter 31

In the dark streets around the Seven Dials in Soho, Caleb Rawson was hard at work, even though the task he had set himself was growing more difficult and uncomfortable by the day. For a start he was ill at ease in his merchant's clothes because he knew they didn't suit his ugliness at all. But worse than that, oh a deal worse, was the abhorrence he felt for the man he'd set himself to find. Pornography was an obscenity to him, a denigration of all the precious qualities in women that he'd learned to value and admire during his seven years as a convict and his long trek home to England. Nevertheless he was determined to hunt his quarry down no matter how much time and energy it took. He owed it to Harriet Easter, and he owed it to her daughter.

Ever since he'd first met Harriet's daughter he'd felt peculiarly responsible for her, admiring her passion for life and pitying her present misery, almost as though she were a child of his own. Which for all he knew she might very well be. His affair with her mother had been almost exactly nine months before she'd been born, and although they'd only made love once, he knew such things were possible. Sometimes he caught himself looking at her and seeing reflections of his own face, dark, low of brow, grey eyed, and far too similiar for mere coincidence. And then he would yearn to be able to acknowledge her and claim her for his own and be loved by her. But on other occasions he would scold himself for such ridiculous fancies, and remind himself that he was an ex-convict wandering the world, and that she was an Easter and granddaughter to the great Nan, and very unlikely to prove to be anything else. But Easter or no she needed his help, poor young woman, if she was to come through this trial without serious harm.

There was very little time left now, for the case was a mere six weeks away and he was no nearer to tracing this man they wanted than he'd been on the day he started. He'd established that he was no longer operating from Holywell Street, for although none of the publishers there would admit to any knowledge of him, the third man he'd visited had been talkative enough to let drop that several of his colleagues had left the street quite recently.

'Rumours of a police raid, you see, sir,' he said. 'As if the police ain't got better things to do.' And to Caleb's hidden satisfaction he actually admitted that he knew where 'one or two' of them had gone. It took a lot of persuasion and several sovereigns before he would part with addresses or 'whereabouts', but Caleb's persistence was finally rewarded. Since then he'd been checking these new addresses, methodically, one after the other, but without success.

Tonight's destination was the fifth on the list and the nearer he got to it the less promising it looked. The Seven Dials was the dark centre to seven narrow alleys renowned for their poverty and violence. Rubbish lay piled beside every doorway, beggars huddled against every wall, the smell of filth and decay clogged the very air he tried to breathe. It was a noxious place and hardly the sort of neighbourhood for a gentleman, even one seeking the most secret of pleasures.

Number 27 St Martin's Lane was a grimy terrace shared by six people plying for trade of one sort or another, with a reluctant lantern above the front door to illuminate the little cards on which their names were printed, each one set beside its own individual doorbell, Mrs Dalrymple, milliner and gentlemen's assistante, Mr Grange, furniture restorer and cleaner, Mademoiselle Fifi, who didn't specify her line of business at all. And there amongst them was Mr Leonard Snipe, publisher.

Found at last! Caleb thought as he pressed the appropriate bell. And although he had long since decided that he didn't believe in anything so unlikely as a God, he found himself offering up a prayer as he waited for Mr Leonard Snipe to open the door. Let some good come of all this at last, he urged. Let this evil man be punished instead of my innocent girl.

The door opened and a very ordinary man stood before him, an ordinary middle-aged man, of middling height, and middling appearance, dressed plainly in a servant's brown suit, three colourless waistcoats, and unobtrusive buff linen. 'Yes, sir,' he said, standing inside the shadow cast by the half-opened door.

'Mr Snipe?'

'Well now,' Mr Snipe said, 'I'm sure I couldn't say, sir. That would depend.'

To be given such a devious reply after such an aggravating search was irritating, but Caleb kept his temper and spoke smoothly. 'Now that's a pity, for I've business to do with Mr Snipe, and business worth a mint of money what's more.'

The mention of money encouraged Mr Snipe. 'If I could just say who is calling, sir?'

'Why, you know better than that, man,' Caleb said, giving vent to a little of his honest scorn. 'In matters like this we must all use discretion, ain't that so? It don't do to go shouting names.'

'Indeed,' Mr Snipe agreed. His face was still expressionless, but there was an alertness about the way he held his head that showed he was listening attentively.

'I act on behalf of two very powerful families,' Caleb said with perfect truth. 'Uncommon powerful families, if you take my meaning, sir. T' sort of people who couldn't possibly trade direct, not in t' present climate of opinion, I tell 'ee straight.'

Mr Snipe seemed to understand that too. 'A matter of business, was it?' he asked.

'Books,' Caleb said shortly. 'Books for *connoisseurs*, if you take my meaning.' That was the word that had unlocked doors in Holywell Street.

'Ah!' Mr Snipe said thoughtfully, but he didn't invite Caleb into the premises and he didn't say anything else.

'You were particularly recommended by a friend of mine.'

'Indeed?'

'He assured me you could provide me with some of the books upon this list.' He pulled the paper out of his pocket and handed it across into the shadow.

Mr Snipe examined the list closely, holding it towards the candle.

'Excellent publications,' he said, 'but costly.'

'Money is no object,' Caleb said, and pulling his wallet out of his trouser pocket, he opened it briefly so that the man could see the bank notes packed inside. That was another trick that had brought results in Holywell Street.

It brought results here too. At last Mr Snipe stood aside and asked his visitor if he would care to enter.

It was a long entrance, up four flights of stairs following the eerie shadows of the candle, and into a small cramped room overlooking the street. There was a truckle bed in one corner and a table under the window, but apart from that the room was furnished with packing cases, which seemed to be doing duty as chairs, book shelves, washstand, clothes-horse and even candle holders.

'I'm in a bit of a pickle, as you see, sir,' Mr Snipe said, 'on account of a rather precipitous move occasioned by the police, which won't surprise you given the present climate of opinion. Did you wish to purchase any of these books?'

'My brief is to buy the most expensive one and examine all the others,' Caleb said as casually as he could. 'Do you have copies of all of them?'

Mr Snipe consulted the list again.

'Two of these are out of print,' Mr Snipe said, 'but I could show you some of the others.'

This is our man, Caleb thought, his heart constricting. But he kept calm.

'All of 'em, if you please,' he said. 'I'm not empowered to buy unless I see them all.'

Mr Snipe sighed and considered, gazing at his list. Then he agreed. 'If you would be so kind as to sit down here, sir, I will get them for you.'

Here was on the only chair in the room and a mighty uncomfortable one, but Caleb sat on it with what patience he could muster while Mr Snipe unpacked boxes and removed books and muttered to himself.

And finally there they all were, all the books on the list except two. If this man didn't publish them, he certainly sold them. It was evidence enough.

'I have a summons here for you, Mr Snipe,' Caleb said, producing his second and more powerful document. ''You will see t' matter to which it pertains, when you read it.'

Mr Snipe's face changed colour and shape in an instant, like a placid dog baring his teeth to snarl. 'Devil take 'ee, sir!' he said. 'What a trick to play! Dammit all, ain't a man to earn an honest living? I took you for a man of discernment.'

'And found a man of honour.'

'Honour!' the pornographer growled. 'Don't talk to me of honour. There ain't no such thing in the world. This is a calumny. I shall fight it, dammit. I don't take this sort of thing. I'll have you know I have powerful friends.'

But Caleb was already out of the door. Rail all you like, he thought, it'll make no odds now.

On the way back to his lodgings in the Strand, he called in at Bow Street police station to warn the sergeant on duty that there was a pornographer on his patch who had been served a summons and ought to be watched in case he made a bolt for it. Then he asked for pen and ink, and leaning against the sergeant's counter, he wrote two short letters, one to Nan and the other to Mr Brougham and folded them, with great satisfaction, into the envelopes he'd been carrying about with him all this time for just that purpose. Then he took a cab to Bedford Square to deliver them, even though he knew the house would be dark and asleep. Which it was. Then and at last he went home to his well-earned rest. From now on, things would improve for Miss Caroline Easter. They had reached the turning point.

Over in Paris a turning point of another kind had very definitely been reached. After weeks of illness Will was on the mend at last. The doctor pronounced himself well pleased, although he warned that the flux could return and that the patient should be treated with great tenderness for several months yet.

'Could I travel?' Will wanted to know.

'By easy stages,' the doctor said. 'And if you are careful not to overtire yourself. Yes, it might be possible.'

'Tomorrow,' Will said to Tom and Edward when the doctor was gone. 'We will travel tomorrow. I can't wait to be back with Nan and Carrie and . . . If I can get home I shall be completely well again, straight away. You'll see.'

'Which means I got ter pack I suppose?' Tom teased.

And I've got to face the music, Edward thought, for he could hardly leave old Tom Thistlethwaite to escort Will back to London on his own. It took two of them to support him when his legs gave way, as they often did, even now. No, no, poor old Will was in far too weak a state to travel alone. But oddly, after so many difficulties it was possible to consider this return and to accept it too, if not with equanimity, then at least with resignation. He knew now that he should never have run away in the first place, and that he would have to go back sooner or later. Will's illness had simply made it sooner, that was all.

And perhaps in a way, the sooner the better.

It was a nightmare journey, for on top of everything else Will was sea-sick and by the time they got to Dover, he was too weak to stand and had to be carried ashore in a chair.

It quite frightened Edward to see how ill he looked, propped in the corner seat of their first class carriage with his eyes shut and his cheeks greeny grey. 'Soon be home, old thing,' he said, trying to be encouraging.

'Be better presently,' Will muttered. 'It'll pass.'

'I'll get you a newspaper,' Edward offered. 'Catch up on the news, eh?' That might take his mind off things. And he shot off to the Easter stall.

It was ominously empty, with very few newspapers on display and no books at all.

'You are sold out of books I see,' he said conversationally to the young man behind the counter.

'No sir,' was the rueful reply. 'Books don't sell these days. All sent back, books is.'

'Dear me,' Edward said. 'That can't be good for trade.'

'No sir, it ain't. Trade's bad an' that's a fact. All on account of some court case or other, so they do say.'

And that is all on account of me, Edward thought miserably as he took his paper back to the train. There was no way he could avoid the knowledge.

In Bedford Square, Nan and Caroline and Euphemia were taking tea in the garden with Mirabelle. It was a warm afternoon early in September and the garden was lush with sunshine, the lawn speckled with pink-edged daisies and the shrubbery banked high with the great yellow and white blooms of the chrysanthemums. The four women were sitting on the terrace in the shade of the magnolia tree and Euphemia was nursing Harry on her lap and feeding him with sponge cake. Consequently they were both spattered with crumbs and had gathered a chirruping chorus of sparrows and finches to peck and flutter beside their feet.

In such a peaceful place it was hard to imagine that the Easter case was a mere three weeks away. And yet Mr Brougham was out that very afternoon, visiting the Society for the Suppression of Vice to hear what they had decided to do about the two Easter prosecutions now that Mr Snipe was under arrest and awaiting trial. And Mr Rawson had gone with him, just in case they needed his evidence to bring Mr Snipe to court.

'I do admire Mr Rawson,' Euphemia said. 'Any man who is prepared to stand up in court and name an evil demands our total respect, wouldn't you say so? Put your little cakey on the plate, Harry my darling.'

'He's a curious man,' Caroline said, 'but I think he's brave. He don't seem to worry at all about appearing at a trial.' She couldn't even think about it without feeling sick with worry.

'Perhaps the Easter case won't come to court now,' Mirabelle said.

'Oh, I do hope not,' Euphemia said, setting down her cup and saucer and smoothing Harry's crumbs from her skirt. 'Well now, my lovey, have you eaten that nice cake all up? I shall have to get you another one, shan't I?'

'If he eats any more he'll go off bang,' Nan said.

The butler arrived with two letters on a tray.

One was addressed to Nan in Mr Brougham's beautiful

405

copperplate and had been sent by hand, the other had come through the post, and was addressed to Euphemia.

'Is it about the case?' Caroline asked, as her grandmother opened the envelope and set her glasses on her nose ready to read.

'Aye, I daresay,' Nan said distantly, reading as she spoke.

'What does it say?'

Mirabelle got up and removed Harry from Euphemia's lap so that she could open her letter too. It was so quiet in the garden that they could hear the traffic passing on the other side of the house. She covered her skirts with a table napkin and sat the baby firmly in the middle of it before she gave him back his sponge cake. And he waited patiently, holding out his fat hands. 'There now, my dear,' she said quietly. 'Ain't you the best boy to be so good when your mama is so worried.'

Nan rustled the paper to her lap and took off her glasses. 'We've only one count to face now, my dear,' she said to Caroline. 'They mean to drop the charges against you and merely sue the firm.'

'Thank heavens for that!' Mirabelle said with feeling.

But Caroline's face was still taut. 'Then I shall appear for the firm,' she said.

'That en't necessary,' Nan said. 'Not now. Thanks to Mr Rawson.'

'*Somebody* will have to appear.'

'Yes, I daresay.'

'Then who is it to be?'

'We can think of that later,' Nan said vaguely.

'No, Nan dear, we can't. If we think of it later it will be you, and I can't allow that. I was responsible for selling the books on the stalls, so I must be answerable in court.'

'But . . . ' Nan said.

'No buts,' Caroline said lovingly. 'I'm prepared for it now, so I shall do it. I can't have you standing up in court to answer for my sins. Fair's fair.'

I must intervene, Mirabelle thought, so as to give Nan a chance to accept. If they go on talking she will fight on to no purpose. 'Do you have good news too, Euphemia?' she said.

'I think it rather depends on how you look at it,' Euphemia said, setting her own letter down on the table.

406

'What is it, Pheemy?' Caroline asked.

'Well,' Euphemia said, smiling round at them all. 'Actually, it's from Miss Nightingale. She has offered me a job.'

Caroline felt her heart sink. It was a sensation that was much too familiar these days. But she smiled at Euphemia and gave her an encouraging answer, for she had to try to be unselfish, indeed she did, after all the trouble she'd caused. 'But how splendid,' she said. 'What sort of job?'

'It appears that she has been offered a hospital of her own at last,' Euphemia said. 'It is in Harley Street, a hospital for governesses. She has offered me a position there.'

Caroline's heart sank even further. 'You will take it, of course,' she said, trying hard to be cheerful. 'When do you start?'

'In two weeks' time, I fear,' Euphemia said anxiously.

'In two weeks?' Now that *was* alarming. It would mean standing the trial without Pheemy to comfort her.

'I would live here, of course,' Euphemia said. 'We could talk about – everything, every evening.' Her lovely brown eyes were lustrous with distress. 'But if you . . .'

'You must take it,' Caroline said quickly. 'Of course you must, after waiting for it all this time. Why, you mustn't even think of refusing. Now tell us all about it.'

But if there was any more to tell none of them ever heard it, because at that moment one of the parlour maids came hurtling out into the garden with her cap askew and her face red with alarm. 'If you please, ma'am,' she said to Nan, 'Mr Will's come home ma'am, an' he's in the hall, bein' ever so ill, and could somebody come please.'

All four women were on their feet in an instant, Caroline and Euphemia running full-tilt into the house, their crinolines swinging violently, Mirabelle, held back by the weight of the baby, following more sedately with Nan.

To Caroline's anxious eyes the hall was littered with luggage and full of people, the butler actually wringing his hands, which was a thing she'd never seen before, housemaids watching with their mouths open, cousin Edward – what was *he* doing there? – looking anxious and dishevelled with his expensive blue jacket covered in filth, Tom Thistlethwaite kneeling on the tiled floor with one arm under Will's back, and Will himself, dear, dear Will, slumped against the banisters at the foot of the stairs, pale as putty, with his eyes closed and two red fever spots as round as pennies on his cheeks, groaning.

'What have you done to him?' she said fiercely to Edward.

'He's had dysentery, Miss Caroline,' Tom answered. 'He's been bad fer weeks. We thought he was better.'

'The doctor said he was well enough to travel,' Edward said, trying to defend himself.

'You could have killed him,' Caroline blazed at them. 'What were you thinking of to make him travel in such a state?'

'He took bad on the journey, miss,' Tom said.

And Will opened his eyes and looked up at them. 'Carrie?' he said. 'Pheemy?'

Then everything else was forgotten, the trial, Caleb's assistance, Mr Brougham's letter, Miss Nightingale's offer, Edward's treachery, Tom's folly in bringing him home so ill, everything. There was only Will, lying on the floor groaning in pain, only Will and her great affection for him.

She dropped to her knees in a swish of sinking cotton and took her brother's poor damp head into her lap. But Euphemia was more practical.

'Go to the kitchen,' she said to the nearest housemaid, 'and tell them to prepare as much hot water as they can. They're to fill the stone hot-water bottles and bring them up to Mr Will's bed first, and after that all the jugs and ewers they can find. I shall need fresh towels, but I will get them myself on the way upstairs. Send Totty up to us at once and Mary-Anne and Bessie if you can find her, but don't wake her if she's sleeping. Harry must be kept right out of the way,' she explained to Caroline. 'We don't want him to take the infection. Now perhaps,' she said to Edward, 'you and Tom could help him upstairs to bed. The sooner he's lying down and in the warm the better.'

By the time Nan and Mirabelle arrived in the hall she had everything under control.

So quiet and efficient, Nan thought, watching her. Why, she's a splendid nurse. No wonder that Miss Nightingale has offered her a job.

But Mirabelle only had eyes for Edward, struggling up the stairs with his cousin's limp arm draped about his neck.

'Mirry,' he said. 'I . . . ' And then he saw Nan, standing small and straight with those white hands gnarled across the head of her walking stick, looking at him with those sharp eyes of hers. 'Nan. I must tell you . . . '

'There en't time for any of that now,' she said sharply. 'You do as Euphemia says and get your cousin up to bed. I'll deal with you later.'

Chapter 32

Once Will had been put to bed, Edward went straight home with Mirabelle, partly because he couldn't think of anything else to do and partly because he couldn't bring himself to face Nan's wrath, not then, not just then, not until he'd had a rest and a chance to wash. It was an uncomfortable journey, because she didn't say a word to him all the way and only looked at him once, and then with her bad eye, so that he couldn't guess what she was thinking. But he'd come home to face the music and if her disapproval was part of it, so be it.

To his surprise the moment they were home and the front door closed behind them, she was full of the most practical concern, fussing over him in exactly the same way as Caroline and Euphemia had fussed over Will. His valet was sent for, hot water was provided for him, clean clothes laid out on their bed, and while he washed and shaved, she went down to the kitchen to ensure that cook provided what she called 'the best possible meal'.

'You must be hungry after all your travels,' she said. And although he was afraid he wouldn't have the stomach for any dinner, he surprised himself by the strength of his appetite.

When the meal was over she escorted him to her private parlour and poured him some of her best brandy. It was almost as if he were an honoured guest instead of a returning delinquent.

'Now,' she said, when he was settled, 'you must tell me everything that has been happening to you since you left here.'

It took until eleven o'clock, because the story of the slaughter

410

on the Paris barricades led backwards by inevitable degrees to his attempt to force Caroline from the firm.

'It seems so ugly now,' he confessed, standing beside the empty fireplace and gazing intently at the embroidered flowers on the firescreen because he couldn't bear to look anywhere else. 'Cruel and petty. You cannot know how much I wish it undone.'

'Yes,' she said seriously, 'I do know. It is clear on your face, my dear.'

'Has the case come to court yet?' he asked, still concentrating on the flowers.

'It is to be in October,' she said. She told him all she knew, including the fact that Caroline had left her home in Richmond and gone to live with Nan in Bedford Square.

'Because of the scandal,' he said, and the words were more statement than question.

'The scandal is partly the cause,' Mirabelle said, diplomatically. 'She suffers grievously on account of it, for she means to face it out and take responsibility for it in court.'

'I intended her to take responsibility for ordering the book,' he said. 'That was my plan, I admit, but I never meant it to end up in court. Oh Mirry, what am I to do?'

She got up and stood beside him, slipping her hand into the crook of his elbow. 'I would advise you to tell your parents everything you've just told me,' she said.

He knew it had to be done, but the thought of it made him wince.

'And Nan of course. You must tell Nan.'

That was even worse, but he agreed to do it. Somehow it was possible to agree, standing here with her hand soft in the crook of his arm and her face grown warm and handsome with affection, and the remembered smell of her flesh rousing the most unexpected and curious tenderness.

'Time for bed, I think,' she said. 'We will go up together.'

He could hardly believe his ears. 'Am I to sleep with you?' he asked.

'Why ever not, my dear?'

'Because of what I have done,' he said. 'Because of . . .'

'Let us concern ourselves with the positive side from now on,' she said, looking at him sideways with her good eye, a very straight look, and, if he hadn't known such a thing was quite impossible, a loving one. 'You have witnessed a revolution and nursed your cousin through a fever and brought him home to his family, safe if not entirely sound. Now it is time for bed.'

'You speak as though you would welcome me there.' Did he want to be welcomed there? Yes, he did. Surprising though it seemed, he did.

'Of course.' And again that loving look.

'As though you might love me,' he said, greatly daring. Would she answer that too?

'I have always loved you,' she said. 'Always.' Ever since that first moment when she'd seen him standing beside the fireplace at the Merryweather ball, so young and handsome. 'And I still do. More than ever now. Because I am the only one who *will* love you through the months that lie ahead of us.'

'You never told me so before,' he said, amazed and flattered and realizing how very much this woman meant to him, and how much he wanted to be loved by her.

'I could not have told you before,' she said. 'It would not have been fitting. You might have been annoyed to hear it, or you might have mocked me for weakness, and think how badly we should have fared then.'

The old arrogant Edward would have been affronted to hear such things said, the new Edward, changed by suffering and the terror of battle, accepted it as the truth. 'Yes,' he said, 'I might well have done such a thing. I would not do it now, Mirabelle.'

'No,' she said. 'I know that.'

It was the most tender homecoming. Afterwards he lay beside her in their moonlit room, amazed and satisfied. 'I love you, Mirry,' he said. It was a drowsy statement of fact.

She touched his cheek with her finger tips. 'Did I not tell 'ee we should grow to love one another?' she said.

'Yes,' he said, closing his eyes. 'And so we do.'

The next morning he went to visit his mother and father.

Despite his misgivings, his second confession was shamefully easy, partly because he'd accepted his culpability now that he'd spoken to Mirry, and partly because his parents both

412

went out of their way to make excuses for him, his father in anguished confusion, and his mother with a doting tenderness that increased his guilt most painfully.

'You will go back to the warehouse, won't 'ee my dear?' Matilda asked when his confession was over. 'There is such a lot of work.'

'If Nan will have me, Mama.'

'Of course she'll have you,' Matilda assured. 'With your father in no fit state to carry the burdens, who else would she turn to?'

'Are you worse, Papa?' Edward asked with concern.

'It's the heat, dear boy,' Billy said, wiping his forehead with a handkerchief. 'Deuced hot today. Always feel worse in the heat.'

'Then you must stay at home and leave the work to me,' Edward said.

'Did I not tell 'ee the boy would see us right?' Matilda said triumphantly. 'You'll go straight there this minute, won't you Edward?'

Edward had been dreading this return and hoping to delay it, but he could hardly refuse when they'd been so forgiving. There was nothing for it but to take the carriage to the Strand, which he did, feeling horribly uncomfortable, and wondering what on earth he would say when he met up with Nan or Caroline. How could he possibly face up to Caroline?

But the Fates were on his side. The men in the warehouse accepted his return without comment, as if his 'holiday' had been prearranged and expected. And according to Mr Jolliffe, Nan and Henry were both expected to be out of the building all day, and Caroline never came into it, 'on account of that awful court case hanging over her head, poor lady'.

So it was an ordinary working day after all and by the end of it he felt as if he'd never been away.

In Bedford Square, Euphemia had spent the last twenty-four hours attending to Will. She'd put him to bed with hot water bottles on either side of him 'to ease the pain in his poor stomach' and a draw-sheet under him 'just in case', and while they were waiting for the doctor to arrive, she'd washed him limb by limb in the way Miss Nightingale advised for bed-ridden patients, but with Tom to clean his private parts, for although she would have cleaned him all over willingly and seen no shame in it at all, it was necessary to avoid any embarrassment he might feel when he recovered. And then, when the doctor had visited and prescribed tincture of opium and laudanum, and administered a particularly horrible saline aperient, she'd sat by her patient's bed until he fell into a sticky sleep at a little after midnight.

Then and only then, she crept from the room to write a letter to Miss Nightingale. Honoured though she was to receive her kind invitation, she wrote, she was unfortunately not in a position to accept it. Her cousin had returned home from France seriously ill with the dysentery and so her nursing skills were needed at home.

Whatever her decision might have been before his return there was no question where her duty lay now. Her darling was home and ill and needed her. That was enough.

She sat up with him all night, because by three o'clock he was running a fever and so delirious he didn't know who she was. And in the early morning when his temperature dropped, as she was hoping and expecting, the griping pains returned, and needed two doses of laudanum and the application of towels wrung out in boiling water before they would ease at all.

The doctor called again at ten o'clock and commended her nursing and said his patient was in better shape than he'd been the previous evening. But he added that it would be a long, difficult business to restore him to health.

'I am a great nuisance to you,' Will said when the medical man was gone.

'You are not to say such things,' she told him, speaking surprisingly firmly for his gentle Euphemia. 'You have given me a chance to practise my skills.'

'Oh Pheemy,' he said, as he drifted off to sleep again, 'I *am* glad to be home with you.' Everything would be all right now he was home with Pheemy.

She was certainly an excellent nurse, sitting with him until he slept, soothing away his pain with hot water bottles and hot towels, dosing him with tincture of opium, according to the doctor's instructions, and preparing special invalid food to tempt him to eat again, for he was painfully thin. She served him calf's foot jellies, and albumen water, and little pots of beef tea, and arrowroot cooked smooth and creamy, and individual sago puddings flavoured with vanilla. And gradually day by day she watched him improve. And gradually day by day he told her all about the revolution, horrors and deaths and all, because it filled his head with its enormity and even though it wasn't a fit subject for an ordinary woman, it was different with Euphemia.

'I can talk to you about anything, Pheemy,' he said. 'Ain't that quite the most extraordinary thing? Don't you think so? Absolutely anything. You were the only one I could confide in when Papa died. The only one. I told you things then that I couldn't even tell Nan. And now here I am telling you all this. If it is too painful you must stop me.'

It was often very painful to her, but she didn't stop him, for she could see how necessary it was to talk, almost as if the words were helping him to make sense of the events.

'When I first started work for Mr Dickens,' he said, 'I thought how good it was to stand apart from the things I was reporting. I didn't want to be involved at all, even though I could see how admirable involvement was, because Mr Dickens threw himself into everything, heart and soul, and we all admired him tremendously. But now see how I've changed. If they'd given me a gun I think I would have fought for the revolution come the finish, I was so caught up in it. They had right on their side, Pheemy. It wasn't just the vote, you see. They wanted work and food for their children and a roof over their heads. The sort of things we Easters take for granted. And the government was denying them even that. And when they rose in protest they were killed like flies.' The memory of it in his present state of weakness brought him close to tears, so that he had to turn his head away from her to give himself a chance to recover.

Euphemia stood up and walked to the window, where she stood tactfully looking down at the sunlit garden. 'I suppose we all change as we grow older,' she said. And she thought how much her light-hearted Caroline had changed since the scandal.

'Not you,' Will said. 'You don't change, Pheemy. Heaven be praised for it. You are just the same as always, just the same as I remembered you all the time I was in Paris.'

'Did you?' she said, looking back at him, smitten by a sudden and quite unreasonable hope.

'Oh yes,' he said. 'Every single day. You were my lifeline then. As you are now.'

But then the doctor arrived most inopportunely and the conversation had to stop.

On the fifth day she allowed him to get up and sit by the window in the sunshine, and on the tenth when Nan and Caroline were in Lincoln's Inn discussing the case with Frederick Brougham, she got Tom to help him to dress and to cut his hair and trim his beard, and then she took him down to the garden and let him sit in the shade of the magnolia and enjoy the fresh air for half an hour.

'Now that's better,' she said, smiling at him. 'You've got some of your colour back. You look more like yourself.'

'I don't know what I would have done without you, Pheemy,' he said. 'You've been a brick.'

And that is how he really thinks of me, Euphemia thought sadly. A brick. Not a woman to love and marry. And yet she loved him more than ever, with a new protective yearning that was so acute it was painful. 'I shall cook you a little coddled egg for dinner tonight,' she said professionally. 'I think you are ready for it.'

'Then I think I am ready to be told about this court case,' he said, 'which you have been keeping from me, haven't you Pheemy?'

'On doctor's instructions,' she admitted. 'He said I was to say nothing until you were strong enough to withstand it.'

'As I am now,' he said.

So she told him everything he wanted to know, from the perfidious conduct of Mr Jernegan and Mr Maycock and how marvellous it was when Nan dismissed them, to Mr Rawson's devoted detective work in Seven Dials – what a blessing you sent him to us – and finally to Caroline's long separation from Henry.

'She's been here ever since,' she said, 'and she won't answer his letters or even let us talk about him.'

416

'Poor Carrie!' he said. 'Can nothing be done? Oh, I know it was a dreadful thing to lay hands on her like that, but we all make mistakes, Pheemy, and they loved one another so dearly. Couldn't we ask him to visit?'

'No,' Euphemia said quickly. 'No, no. Indeed we couldn't. Not until this awful trial is over. She says she can't think of anything until that and we must respect her wishes. If we were to invite him here now it would make matters worse.'

'I wish I could see her,' her brother said. 'An hour or two now and then wouldn't hurt, surely?'

'She shall visit as soon as the doctor declares you fit enough for company,' Euphemia promised. 'You wouldn't want to pass on your infection, I'm sure.'

'No,' he admitted. 'That is true. You are right, Pheemy.'

'A little patience,' she said, smiling at him. 'That's all.'

'That's not my strong suit,' he said, 'but I will do my best.'

Over in the Strand Henry was doing his best to wait in patience too and finding it equally difficult.

He would have liked to send Caroline one more letter, but he didn't do it, for fear of being ignored again. He would have liked to visit her and see little Harry, but he didn't do that either, for fear of being rebuffed or upsetting her. In fact, he couldn't think of any action he could take without running the risk of upsetting her. So he took refuge in work.

There were now so many railways operating in Great Britain, that it was an opportune time to transfer all Easter's trade from the stage-coaches, which were few and far between and often unreliable, to the trains, which were fast and frequent and dependable. It gave him something to keep him occupied while he waited for the outcome of the court case and the bustle of activity it caused in his office was comforting after the isolation of his life in Richmond.

Edward came to his office to see him not long after his return, and tried to tell him how sorry he was for the trouble he'd caused – as if that would do any good! – but he froze him out so thoroughly that he didn't make a second visit. And although Nan looked in nearly every day, they only discussed business. So despite work, it was a lonely life. And a very difficult one.

It was difficult for Edward too, although like Henry he was kept extremely busy in the warehouse. His father had worked very slowly while he'd been away. It was really quite alarming to realize how slowly. He'd let a lot of matters slide, which now had to be attended to before they all got into a muddle. And to make matters worse all the autumn stock was arriving early for some reason. Soon he was working longer hours than anybody else in the building, and all without knowing whether his job was secure or not, because Nan hadn't spoken to him and he hadn't plucked up sufficient courage to speak to her.

In the end he decided he would have to go to Bedford Square. If Nan were in he would see her, and if not he would talk to Caroline, if she would agree to see him, and if he got the chance he would offer to take her place in court. He'd been thinking about it for a long time and it seemed an honourable way to try and make amends. And if neither of them would see him, he could always cut along and find out how Will was, for although news of him filtered through to the warehouse, it wasn't the same as seeing him.

It was a disastrous visit.

Nan was on her way out and very brusque, cutting into everything he tried to say, quick as a whip.

'Everything in order in the warehouse?'

'Yes, I think so. The autumn stock . . . '

'Good.'

'I am so very sorry for all the trouble I've . . . '

'So I should think. Still, no use crying over spilt milk. What's done is done.'

'If I could make amends I would be . . . '

'Tush, lad. What could you do? You're back at work, en't you? Let that be enough.'

'Am I to stay in the firm, Nan?'

'Can't see any reason why not,' the old lady said. 'Being it's a family firm and you're family, no matter what you've done. There's the carriage. Are you going up to see Will?'

'I had hoped I might see Caroline.'

'Can't guarantee it,' she said as she brisked out of the door. For an old lady she moved with extraordinary speed, that

418

ebony stick fairly clicking over the floorboards. 'She's out in the garden with Will and Euphemia and it's the first time they've been allowed together since Will took ill. Ring and see.'

When he'd rung the bell and sent the parlour maid on her errand, his nerve failed him. I'll wait five minutes, he thought, and then I'll go. She won't want to see me. She won't come in.

But she did, gliding into the room so quietly that she was standing in front of him before he heard her approach.

'Yes,' she said. She'd been of two minds whether to see him or not. In fact if it hadn't been for Euphemia's urging she'd have sent him away unseen. It had been so pleasant sitting in the autumn sunshine with Will at last, and they'd been talking so happily together, just like old times, so it annoyed her to see this obnoxious cousin of theirs, particularly as he looked well-fed and confident and full of himself. He's caused all this trouble with those foul books of his, she thought, and he dares to come here as if nothing were the matter.

He was upset to see how much she had changed. There was a hard, watchful quality about her that hadn't been there before, and although her body seemed fatter, her cheeks were haggard.

'I came to apologize to you, Caroline,' he said, speaking quickly before he lost his courage altogether under that unforgiving stare.

'So I should think,' she said.

'I had not intended all this,' he said.

'It's a great pity you intended anything, to my way of thinking.'

'Yes. It is.'

'Well, you've apologized now,' she said ungraciously. 'Is that all you want?'

'No,' he said. 'I want to make amends.'

'You can't.'

He played his trump card, hopeful that this at least would provoke a good response. 'I would like to take your place and represent the firm in court.'

It wasn't a trump at all. She was furious. 'If that ain't just like you, Edward Easter,' she said. 'You may like all you please but you shan't do it. I never heard such presumption in all my born days. Here I've been preparing and preparing every day for months and you come bowling in here bright as a button and think you can take over.' It had cost her so much to accept this responsibility, she was so ready for it now, tight as a spring with dread and daring. 'How dare you do such a thing? How dare you!'

'I meant to help you,' he stammered.

'Well, you don't help me. You don't help me at all. You're nothing but an unmitigated nuisance. And you don't understand a thing. If I stepped down now, you wouldn't be the one to fill the breach, it would be Nan. Our poor dear Nan. And let me tell you she is far too old and frail to be asked to do such a thing. Oh, go away! It makes me feel sick to see you. It was all your fault in the first place, you and those two revolting cronies of yours. Go away.' All her loathing for him was rising in her, choking her like tears. How could he be so foul?

He ran from the room. It was cowardly and childish but he couldn't help it. And as soon as the front door closed behind him, she ran too, straight out into the garden and into the safety of Euphemia's arms, sobbing as she ran.

'I should never have seen him, Pheemy,' she said. 'He was so foul you'd never believe.'

It took them a long time to calm her and dry her tears and agree with her that Edward was a brute and had no right to visit.

'Just as I'd prepared myself for it,' she said, 'he comes bowling in, telling me he's going to take over. How can he be so insensitive? It's going to be bad enough, Pheemy, without him making it worse.'

'Bathe your eyes, my dearest,' Euphemia said. 'It will soon be over. It is only two weeks away now, think of that.'

'Will it?' Caroline said bleakly.

'Yes,' Euphemia promised. 'It will. Everything will be different, you'll see. Won't it, Will?'

'I promise,' Will said.

In fact Will Easter did more than make promises. Despite Pheemy's insistence that they should leave well alone until after the trial, he decided to take action. At the end of the week when he was allowed out of the house at last, he went to visit his cousins in Clerkenwell.

They were delighted to see him and when he told them he had a plan for bringing Caroline and Henry together again they listened with undivided attention.

'It all depends on you in the first instance,' he explained. 'If you would invite Henry here for supper, on the first day of the trial perhaps, I could come round later in the evening and tell all three of you what had happened, just as though everything were back to normal, d'you see. And after that we could offer other invitations, a celebratory dinner when the case is over for example, with lots of people there and plenty of good food and wine and so forth and Caroline and Henry both among the guests. We can't let them go on and on not seeing one another. It's ridiculous. What do you think?'

Matty thought it was a wonderful idea.

'To play Cupid,' she said, her scarred face shining. 'What could be better? Oh, you are quite right, Will. They should be brought together again.' It would make amends for her brother's dreadful behaviour, running off like that just at the moment when the firm needed him most.

'Do you really think we ought to meddle?'. Jimmy said, cautiously. 'It *is* a matter between husband and wife, when all's said and done.'

But his wife overruled him. 'Of course we should,' she said. 'Tell us how we are to go about it, Will. We will invite him here on the first day of the trial, of course. What else would you like us to do?'

So Henry received his invitation and accepted it gratefully. And Will's plot was laid. And the case of Easter versus Furmedge was a mere three days away.

421

Chapter 33

On the night before the court case Caroline Easter couldn't sleep at all. She lay in her white bed, hot and uncomfortable and fidgeting, while the house slept all around her. She listened to Euphemia's soft breathing and the crack and creak of the cooling stairs and the occasional muffled thud of soot falling in the chimney, and the more she strained after the rest she needed, the more it eluded her. Finally she got up, easing herself carefully from the bed so as not to wake Euphemia, and went to open a window, so that she could cool herself while she looked down into the garden in the middle of the square.

It had been warm and dry over the last few days and the pavements were so thick with dust that now, in the moonlight, they looked as though they were covered with sand. The plane trees were dusty too and from time to time, when a slight breeze caught them, they rustled like tissue paper.

She was doomed, Caroline thought miserably as she leant out of the window. By the end of that day she would be named and known for a 'purveyor of filth', just as that awful man described her in his letter. She would never live it down. Even if the judge found for the firm she would still be tarred with it. Purveyor of filth. It was a horrid thing. And there was no escaping it. There in the clarity of moonlight, looking down on the uncompromising emptiness of the square, there was no escaping the truth of anything. How was she to endure it?

And as if in answer to her questions the baby moved for the first time. It was such a little tentative wriggle that had she not been standing so still she might have missed it. But there was no mistaking it. There it was again, flicker, flicker, flicker, but stronger now, and more like a pulse than a wriggle. A reminder that life went on, that there was always hope, that she carried both within her, even in a moment as bleak as this.

She stood at the window for a long time enjoying the sensation of this new life she carried, rejoicing in it, despite her anxieties. Even if the judgement went against her, even if she never saw Henry again – would she ever see him again? – there was always this life, this new precious life. When she finally climbed back into her bed, she slept almost at once.

The next morning Euphemia brought her breakfast upstairs, as though she were a bride. She was touched to be so tenderly treated and kissed her cousin most lovingly to thank her. But it was doomsday come at last even so.

And such a peculiar day. The breeze that had stirred the plane trees during the night had become a gale by daybreak, hurling the dust into the air in choking grey-brown clouds. The sun rose slowly through the murk that morning, and the sun was red as blood. It made Caroline shudder to see it. It was a horrid day for a horrid deed.

The journey to the law courts was unpleasant too, even though Nan and Will and Euphemia were all with her. There was dust everywhere, kicked up by the horses' hooves, swirled into the air by the carriage wheels, blown high by the gale, coating their shoes, dirtying their gloves, settling visibly on hats and jackets, clogging the very air they tried to breathe. By the time they reached Temple Bar, Caroline even had grains of it under her tongue.

Dust hung in the air inside the Law Courts too, suspended in sunbeams, powdering the legal volumes on the clerk's desk, speckling the legal ink in all those legal inkwells, settling silently on all those antique black robes and play-acting wigs.

'This dust!' she complained to Mr Brougham, trying to sneeze without drawing attention to herself.

'The Courts are dusty by definition, my dear,' Mr Brougham said, trying to make light of it with a joke. 'We call it the obfuscation of the law.'

Jokes were lost on Caroline that morning. She had her mind set on one thing and one thing only. The sooner their case began, the sooner it would be over.

But as she was slowly to discover during a long bewildering morning, the law took its course in a tortuous way. She expected to be tried, found guilty and fined within an hour, but instead of that she sat on a very hard seat beside Mr Brougham while various lawyers talked interminably and boringly about the Vagrancy Act of 1824, quoting cases and verdicts from the intervening years. None of it made any sense to her at all.

By the time the court adjourned for lunch her head was dizzy with bewilderment, and nothing had happened. Or at least nothing that she'd noticed.

In fact her husband had been in the court all morning, watching her quietly from the public gallery, but as she'd sat, equally quietly, watching Mr Brougham and the Counsel for the Prosecution, she hadn't seen him.

It upset him to see how gaunt she looked, sitting below him in the well of the court in her decorous blue dress and that neat lace cap, and he loved her quite desperately because she was being so courageous and pig-headed and stubborn and altogether admirable. Like everyone else in the Easter headquarters, he'd heard how Edward had offered to take her place in this court and how firmly and finally she'd rebuffed him. Old Billy Easter had told Mr Jolliffe about it, thus making certain that the story was given the widest circulation, for it showed both his son and his niece in the best possible light. And Henry had recognized the truth of it at once. It was so like her, his dear determined Carrie, so exactly like her. Oh, how passionately he was waiting for this trial to end! Perhaps then he could visit her, and tell her how very sorry he was and how very much he loved her, and pet her perhaps, and praise her, and put all this long separation behind them. Now that he'd seen her again he was torn with love for her. Somehow or other he must earn her forgiveness. It was true she'd ignored all his letters, but when this case was over . . .

There was a stir in the court as Mr Brougham's junior rose to leave ahead of him and Caroline stood up too, to make way for the man. With an exquisite shock of surprise and delight, Henry realized that she was pregnant. The dear girl! Oh, she must accept him back. Surely!

The judge was making a pronouncement: ' . . . perfectly

proper for the case to proceed.' Mr Brougham and Mr Prosecution were bowing.

'As Your Lordship pleases.'

'I suggest we adjourn for lunch.'

It was necessary for Henry to get out of the building quickly or he and Caroline might meet on the stairs or in some other inappropriate place, and he couldn't have borne that. He would return that afternoon, he promised himself as he sped off through the dust of the Strand, and he would see the end of it. But there was so much work waiting for him in his office that he didn't finish it all until nearly seven o'clock. Never mind, he thought, as he left the office to drive to Clerkenwell. He would attend again in the morning. And meantime there was Matty's dinner to enjoy, which was a sign that things were getting better.

The case resumed that afternoon at quite a different tempo. Within minutes of her arrival in court the charge had been read and Caroline had been called to the witness box to be asked whether she represented the company and how she intended to plead. She declared that she was guilty because that was what Mr Brougham had advised her to say, and because she felt guilty, oh indeed she did, very, very guilty, standing there in that awful court with the judge glaring down upon her.

Then the Prosecuting Counsel rose to make a fiery speech in which he denounced the firm of A. Easter and Sons for 'tampering with the morals of our society and allowing the twin evils of literary turpitude and creeping obscenity to fly loose and corrupt the unstained innocence of our young'. She noticed that Uncle Billy was so incensed by all this that his face turned puce and Aunt Matilda had to put a plump hand on his arm to restrain him.

But then it was Mr Brougham's turn as he rose to plead mitigating circumstances.

'Firstly,' he said, 'I feel that I should tell the court that as soon as the evil nature of these books was known to the firm, copies were instantly withdrawn from all shops and bookstalls.'

'Instantly, you say, Mr Brougham?' the judge enquired.

'Within five days, m'lud.'

'Five days. Yes I see,' the judge said, making a note of it.

'I should also point out that A. Easter and Sons have put all available resources at the disposal of Mr Furmedge and the Society for the Suppression of Vice, to ensure that the person responsible for publishing the said volumes should be apprehended by the police and his entire stock impounded, which, as I daresay your Lordship is aware, has already been done. There is, I am reliably informed, a case pending.'

'Indeed,' the judge said, noting that too. 'I was not aware, but I'm uncommon pleased to hear it.'

'Moreover . . .'

'Is there a moreover?' the judge said, sounding surprised. 'Ah well, proceed, if you please, Mr Brougham.'

'Moreover,' Mr Brougham said again, 'I understand that the two persons responsible for suggesting the initial purchase of the said books to my client, Mrs Caroline Easter, have now left the employ of the company.'

Somebody was on his feet in the public gallery, shouting at the top of his voice. 'That is a lie, sir. A monstrous lie!'

All heads swivelled towards him and Caroline saw that it was Mr Jernegan who was shouting and that Mr Maycock was climbing onto the seat beside him waving his arms in the air and shouting too. 'Monstrous! We are victims, sir! Innocent victims!'

'Clear the gallery!' the judge said with splendid calm. 'I will not have unruly behaviour in my courtroom.'

But damage had been done. There were several recognizable reporters in the public gallery, and as the ushers arrived to march the two protestors away, they got up and followed the struggling party out.

The Easter family shot anxious messages from eye to eye, Caroline to Nan, Nan to Billy, Matilda to Edward, Will to Caroline.

'Leave it to me,' Billy said to his wife. 'I'll attend to 'em.' And he eased himself out of his chair and left the courtroom as quickly as he could.

Mr Jernegan was holding forth to a group of reporters, all of whom were writing eagerly, while Mr Maycock stood beside them nodding agreement.

'We were all *asked* to recommend books. Who asked us? Mr

426

Edward Easter. Mr Billy Easter's son. You saw Mr Billy in court. He is known to you, I believe. Well, Edward was the fair young man sitting beside him. We were *totally innocent* of any misdemeanour. As I say . . . '

Billy waded into their midst. 'Now write this down,' he said to the reporters. 'I've heard enough from the mouth of this gentleman to sue for defamation of character. Have you got that?'

'Hold on!' one reporter said. 'Do you mean it ain't true?'

'Pack of lies from start to finish,' Billy said trenchantly, speaking loudly to cover what Mr Jernegan was saying.

'You see how we are treated! You see! Mr Maycock will confirm . . . '

But Mr Maycock was already walking away.

'Mr Maycock will confirm nothing,' Billy said scornfully. 'Mr Maycock knows the truth of it, don't 'ee Mr Maycock?'

Mr Maycock's plump shoulders were disappearing through the far doors.

'I wonder that you're all out here when the truth of the matter is being told inside the court,' Billy said.

The heat in the lobby was making him pant. But they were moving off, thank the Lord; the danger of scandal was passing. Now if he could just get shot of that damned Jernegan feller.

'Don't you want to hear my story?' Mr Jernegan called after their departing backs.

'Of course they don't,' Billy said to him. 'Be off with 'ee, sir! Ain't you done enough damage for one lifetime? Be off or I'll not be answerable for the consequences.'

'Oh yes!' Jernegan mocked. 'It's all swagger and bully out here but you've had to plead guilty in there, you and your precious firm, and that's what counts. That's what people will remember. Well, I hope you're all ruined, so I do. Letting women run a firm. It's downright unnatural.'

'If I had a horsewhip, sir,' Billy said, purple in the face with fury, 'I would use it on you, sir, here and now, so I would.' He could see the ushers moving towards him. Perhaps it was just as well, because he was feeling too ill to deal with this wretched man on his own. I should have brought Edward with me, he thought. And then a wave of nausea made him stagger, and a second wave of weakness and breathlessness took the strength from his legs, and he knew he was falling, into heat and red light and a sudden terrible pain across his chest.

By the time the ushers reached him he was unconscious.

'What are we to do?' they asked one another. 'His Lordship won't like his case disturbed twice in one afternoon.'

But somebody would have to come out and attend to the poor gentleman, judge or no.

'We'll get a note to Mr Brougham, discreet like,' the Court Usher decided. 'He'll know what to do.'

Mr Brougham's speech was over, and the judge was giving his verdict when the Usher crept back into the court.

'I have considered all the mitigating circumstances mentioned by learned counsel . . .'

'Give this note to the lady in red silk,' Mr Brougham whispered, writing his message quickly.

' . . . However, I am duty bound to say that given the serious nature of the charge, even instant action of the kind described is not sufficient . . .'

Matilda got up, moving so quickly that the swish of her skirt was as loud as a handclap. She sent a quick glance of appeal to Edward and was gone.

' . . . It is no excuse to claim ignorance of the quality of these books. Their quality should have been known. It is the responsibility of a bookseller to know exactly what it is he is offering for sale . . .'

Edward was on his feet, following his mother.

'There's a deal too much unnecessary traffic in this court this afternoon,' the judge said. 'Do any further members of the Easter family wish to leave my presence before I proceed to judgement?'

I would, Caroline thought, staring at him boldly, if only I could. The nearer his judgement came, the more frightened she felt, her heart banging against her ribs and her hands shaking and her mouth so dry that she had to keep licking her lips to be able to swallow. Now I know what the poor bears felt like in the old days, tied to the stake and waiting for the mastiffs to tear them to bits. Hurry up, she willed the judge, say it, get it over with. You've drawn this out quite long enough. She wasn't a bit surprised that Edward and his mother had made a

428

run for it. At least I've stayed the course, she thought proudly. I didn't run.

'I find for the plaintives,' the judge boomed, looking down at the remaining Easters. 'I find the firm of A. Easter and Sons guilty as charged, consequently the firm of A. Easter and Sons through their representative, Mrs Caroline Easter, is fined £1,000 which will I trust persuade it to exercise more care and discretion in the future.'

A thousand pounds, Caroline thought. It's a fortune. We shall all be ruined. And it's all my fault. I caused it. I meant to increase our trade, make Papa proud of me, help the firm, take the burdens away from Nan. And now instead I burden her with this. How could I have done such a thing?

She stood up, shakily, aware that her belly was trembling, and that Euphemia was still holding her hand. Everybody in the court was talking, standing, walking. The place seethed with movement. Dust was leaping into the air from every gown, brown choking dust, hurtling towards her to choke her to death, brown as mastiffs. She couldn't breathe, couldn't breathe, couldn't . . .

Will and Euphemia caught her as she fell, and Nan and Frederick who were discussing the payment of the fine with the Clerk of the Court turned to see her slumped across her brother's arm. Before they could push through the crowd, Caleb Rawson was leaping to help her, springing over the benches as though they were hurdles, his grizzled hair bouncing with every step, quick and urgent and to Nan's observant gaze peculiarly graceful. Where had he come from? She'd had no idea he was in the court.

Caroline was groaning as he reached her and Will and Euphemia were struggling to support her sudden weight, Will aware of his present miserable weakness, Euphemia loosening her cousin's bodice and chafing her hands but knowing that there was no way she could lift her without help. They were both grateful when the weaver scooped her up in his arms and carried her out into the gangway as though she were a baby. 'Put tha little arm about my neck, lass. Aye, that's it, I've got thee. Tha's safe wi' me.'

Nan and Frederick were beside him.

'First Billy and now Caroline,' Frederick said.

'Billy?' Nan asked.

'He was taken ill in the lobby. That was why Matilda left the court.'

'Was he bad?'

'A fainting fit, so the usher told me.'

'We will attend to Carrie first,' Nan decided. 'I will find out about Billy later. Home if you please, Mr Rawson.'

'I must return to Chambers, my dear,' Frederick said.

But she hardly noticed him go.

Caroline was still groaning in and out of consciousness when they reached Bedford Square and Caleb carried her into the house. Although Euphemia tried to assure them she would be better once she was out of her heavy clothes and brought to bed, Nan sent for the doctor.

'I don't like the looks of her at all,' she said. 'Better safe than sorry to my way of thinking.'

Dr Owen arrived within the hour and was taken straight upstairs to see his patient for by then she was running a high temperature and muttering with nightmare.

'How wise you were to send for me, dear lady,' he said to Nan. 'Your granddaughter is suffering from brain fever, I fear. We must take action at once. There is not a moment to lose.'

'What is to be done?' Nan said, much alarmed by the news.

'You must send for a barber,' the doctor told her. 'All that hair must come off for a start, and then I will bleed her. That should bring some relief. I brought my cups, just in case. Fortunately I never travel without them.' He was a great believer in the value of bleeding.

'I will cut her hair,' Euphemia offered. She would be more gentle than a barber.

So the treatment was begun, with Euphemia in nursing attendance, and Nan and Will and Caleb waiting in the parlour to hear the outcome, and the servants gathered in the kitchen subdued and eager for news.

The only person in the house who didn't know what was happening was Caroline herself, and for her, nightmare and reality were so horribly entwined that she had no idea where

430

she was or what she was doing. She was tied to a stake inside a circle of fire with a red sun burning her and mastiffs howling towards her, fangs dripping. Or was it Edward holding that horrid book under her nose, saying 'top and tail 'em'? What did he mean? The mastiffs had seized her by the arm. She was being torn limb from limb. She could see locks of her hair lying on the counterpane. Who was tearing out her hair? The mastiffs were running wildly about her with dark hair trailing from their mouths like weed.

'Don't let them pull off my arms!' she begged.

Euphemia's gentle face gradually grew into focus before her, saying, 'Hush, my dearest. It's all right. I'm only cutting your hair, that's all.'

But somebody was hurting her arm. It was Mr Jernegan, stabbing at her with a knife, shouting 'Monstrous lie. Let her be fined a thousand pounds.' There was blood all over the sheet, pumping out of her arm into a horrid little china cup. 'Oh Pheemy!' she moaned. 'I feel so bad. So bad. Am I going to die?'

And Euphemia's face returned, speaking softly as though she were a long way away. 'It will soon be over, my dearest, soon.'

'I don't want to die,' Caroline said, as the mastiffs sprang upon her again, knocking her backwards, falling and falling. Oh, where to? Where to? Not into death. I won't fall into death. Whatever else, I won't fall into death. Pheemy, where are you? But she couldn't see her cousin because the blackness was sweeping her away.

'We have done our best,' the doctor said to Nan when he was shown down to the parlour at last.

'My dear heart alive!' Nan said in horror. 'She en't dead, is she?'

'No, ma'am. No indeed. We are in time. But she is much weakened. Brain fever is a most serious condition. I will return tomorrow to purge her, ma'am, with your permission. Meantime she is to be kept completely quiet. No excitement of any kind. Excitement would be fatal, you understand.'

'May we go up and see her?' Will asked.

'You may peep in upon her now that she is asleep,' the doctor allowed. 'But just this once, mind. I daresay she will

431

sleep a great deal. Brain fever patients often do. When she is awake she is to see no one except Miss Callbeck, who has undertaken to nurse her. No one at all. Not even you, ma'am, otherwise I will not be answerable for the consequences. She is in a most serious condition.'

'I will do as you say,' Nan promised. 'We're beholden to 'ee, sir.'

As soon as he'd gone she and Will and Caleb tip-toed upstairs to see if Caroline was sound enough asleep for them to see her, and Euphemia let them in, one at a time. They were all profoundly shocked by the sight of her, for she had changed so much in such a short time. She was deathly pale and unnaturally still and shorn of her hair she looked pitiably young and frail.

'I cannot bear to see her so,' Will said when he and Nan were back in the parlour again.

'Henry must be told of it,' Nan said, thinking aloud. No matter what their quarrel, he ought to know. 'I've a mind to send Tom down to Richmond tonight.'

'He won't be there,' Will said, suddenly remembering the plans he'd made for the evening. 'He's dining with Matty and Jimmy. I was supposed to be joining them later. I'd clean forgot.'

'Is it any wonder?' Nan said grimly. 'Never mind, I will tell him first thing tomorrow.'

'No,' Will said. It would be heartless to keep him in the dark so long. 'He ought to know now, Nan. After all he *is* her husband. I'll cut across to Clerkenwell to see him. In any case, they'll all be wondering where I am. I should have sent a message long before this.'

'Make it a round trip while you're about it,' Nan said, remembering things too. 'Your Uncle Billy was took ill this afternoon as well as Carrie, and I en't sent to enquire after *him* yet.'

'We've had too much else to think about,' Will said. 'I'll call in on my way back from Clerkenwell Green.'

The wind had dropped at last and the sky was streaked with sunset colours as the carriage took Will to Clerkenwell. If it hadn't been for his anxiety he could have enjoyed the journey, for the city was at its best in autumn, and Clerkenwell Green could have been in a village in the heart of the country with its sheep resting under the yellowing chestnut tree and people gossiping beside the columns of the Sessions House.

But there were no lights in Matty's dining room and the house seemed ominously quiet.

'Oh, Mr Will sir,' the parlour maid said when she opened the door. 'They ain't here, sir. All gone off ter Torrington Square so they 'ave, more'n an hour since, on account a' Miss Matty's Pa being so ill. Mortal bad, so Mr Edward said when he come.'

'Thank you Ellen,' Will said, taking refuge in politeness because alarm was gripping his heart for the second time that day. 'Did Mr Henry pay a call?'

'He come not ten minutes after they was gone. Didn't stay though, not after I told him about Miss Matty's Pa.'

'Do you know where he went?' Will asked. One of the sheep was bleating, and he wished it wouldn't, for the sound was too ordinary and peaceful for such a dreadful day.

'Couldn't say sir, I'm sure. Have I ter give 'em a message?'

'No, thank you Ellen, I'm off to Torrington Square myself directly, so I daresay I shall see them before you do.'

But what would he find when he got there?

In Bedford Square Nan was still sitting wearily in her parlour when Caleb came downstairs to say goodbye.

'We're much beholden to 'ee, Mr Rawson,' she said. 'You've been a true friend to us today and no mistake.'

'I could have done no other, Mrs Easter,' Caleb said, and there was a breathless quality about his voice that made her look up at him sharply. Why, the man was trembling with excitement, bristling with it. 'Not now. Not after tonight. Not now I've seen her shorn t' way she is.'

'She will recover,' Nan said, misunderstanding his emotion and feeling she ought to comfort him.

'Oh aye. I know that,' he said. 'She's a fighter. It's not that.'

'Then what is it?'

'Why, she's my daughter, Mrs Easter. I've thought it all along, but now I'm sure. Wi' her head shaved, she's t' spit and image of the face I saw in a mirror once back in t' convict days. She's my daughter.' Then he caught his breath and stopped, looking suddenly shamefaced, as he realized that what he'd just said was an insult to this lady and her family, a slur on her dead daughter-in-law; the worst possible thing to say and at the worst possible time.

But she surprised him. 'Yes,' she said calmly. 'She is.' She'd always known this moment would arrive sooner or later, ever since he first walked into the house.

'You know it?' he said when he could find his voice.

'Oh yes. I have always known it. Sit down, Mr Rawson, pray do. I don't want another collapse on my hands today.'

He sat obediently and gratefully, wondering how she knew and how many others knew too.

'Harriet kept a diary,' she said, looking straight at him, shrewd and level-headed and truthful in the gilded light of the sunset. 'When she was a-dying she gave it to me to burn, to protect her husband from what it contained, you see, poor child. I read it before I put it in the fire, and I've kept the secret of it to this day.'

He was lost in shame at his own actions and admiration for hers. She was a very great lady, this Nan Easter.

'What are we to do?' he asked.

'Nothing,' she said, giving him that straight look of hers again. 'She's been bred an Easter no matter what her parentage may or may not have been, and mighty proud to be one, I can tell 'ee. And she's married an Easter, and bred an Easter of her own, and is like to breed another if she survives the fever. There en't a thing you can do for her now, Mr Rawson, beyond what you've done for her today.'

'I would not have told her any of this, ma'am,' he said humbly. 'That would have been a slur on her mother's good name. I make no claim upon her. It was just t' shock of t' resemblance made me speak, and now I'm sorry for it. You have my word.'

'She is very like you, Mr Rawson,' Nan said. 'She has your courage, I think, and your generosity. Let us pray she has your strength too, to pull her through this illness. And now, you

434

must forgive me if I ask you to leave. I'm an old lady and I'm tired to the bone. We will speak of this again on some other occasion.'

'Yes,' he said, rising to go as she rang the bell. 'It has been a terrible day. I'm only sorry to have made it worse by speaking out of turn. A terrible day.'

'It has,' she said, 'but it's nearly over now, thank heavens.'

'Once Mr Will is home,' she said to her maid when the weaver was gone, 'we will have a little light supper and get to bed. Cold meats and such. Will you tell Cook? And you'd better light the lamps in here. It's grown quite dark.'

But dark or not the day wasn't finished yet.

Nan was dozing in her chair when she heard the carriage return, and Will's voice in the hall talking to someone. Another young man? Surely he hadn't brought somebody home, she thought irritably. Not at a time like this. It wasn't like Will to be so thoughtless.

But then they both came striding into her parlour and she saw that the visitor was Henry and she thought she understood.

'Henry, my dear,' she said. 'I don't know whether you'll be able to see her, you know. We en't allowed in, except when she's asleep.' And what if she were to wake and see him? What a shock that would be.

'Yes,' he said. 'I know that. Will has explained, but I had to come.'

She realized that they were both looking strained and uncomfortable. 'What is it?' she said.

'It's Uncle Billy, I'm afraid,' Will said and his handsome face was pinched with distress.

She knew, instinctively, before he told her. 'He is ill?' she said.

'Very ill, Nan. Very very ill.'

'Is he like to die, Will? Tell me the truth, my dear.'

'I am so sorry to have to tell you this,' Will said, kneeling before her and taking her hands in his, 'but I cannot soften it. There is no way to soften it.'

'He is dead,' she said flatly.

'Yes. When he was taken ill in the court, it was an apoplexy.

435

He died in the carriage on the way home. Matilda and Edward were with him.'

'Poor Matilda,' she said. Then her face creased and she began to cry, terrible pent-up tears that she'd carried all through the day. 'Oh, how are we to bear it? It is too much.'

Henry was beside her in one movement, sitting with his arms about her and her poor white head on his shoulder. 'There my dear, brave, darling Nan,' he said. 'There my dear!' And she leant on his shoulder and cried like a child, with the tears running off her nose onto his shirt, and Will still kneeling at her feet, stroking her hand.

'You are such good boys,' she said when the worst of the crying was over. 'I don't know what I should do without you. You ought to be going up to see how Caroline is, Henry my dear, and I'm keeping you. And making such a mess of your shirt. Oh dear.'

'The shirt will wash,' Henry told her, 'and I shall see Carrie eventually. Shan't I? When she's better.'

'Go now, my dear,' Nan said, kissing him, for his anxiety was too touching not to be answered. 'Will will stay here with me.'

So he went, and because Caroline was sound asleep, Euphemia allowed him into the room 'for half a minute' and he stood close enough to his darling to have touched her if only he'd been allowed to. Even in the lamplight he could see how hot and ill she was, and that poor cropped head made him yearn with pity for her. We are more apart than ever, he thought, for now we may not even look at one another. How cruel life is.

'She *will* recover, won't she Pheemy?' he whispered, when the two of them had retreated to the door.

'Yes,' Euphemia whispered back. 'She will. I promise.'

And as she sounded so sure, and seemed strong enough to accept even more bad news, he told her about Uncle Billy.

'Carrie mustn't know of it,' she said. 'That's the important thing. I shan't wear mourning. Nan will understand.'

'Yes. Poor Nan.'

'What a fearful day this has been.'

'Yes,' Henry said. But it had brought him within a hand's breath of his darling again, even if they weren't allowed to

436

speak, and she *would* recover, Pheemy said so. Even in the midst of distress, there was hope in that.

They all had a long way to go before Caroline was well. And the biggest obstacle to her recovery, as Euphemia began to suspect after a week of his ministrations, was Nan's trusted doctor.

He came to the house every morning either to bleed his patient or to purge her, and sometimes he did both and departed very well pleased with himself. His visits left poor Caroline so weak and distressed that Euphemia became more and more alarmed each day. On the morning of Billy's funeral, when Caroline had been bled *and* purged she was so ill she couldn't speak. At that point Euphemia decided that something would have to be done to stop the torture.

She would speak to Will as soon as he got back from the service.

Chapter 34

Billy's funeral was a very big affair. He was buried in London in the church where he'd worshipped every Sunday of his working life, and so beside every single member of the family, except Caroline and Euphemia, colleagues came from all over the City to pay their last respects.

Even old Bessie Thistlethwaite travelled down from Bury to say goodbye to her dear boy and to weep with everyone else in that crowded church.

'Such a dear, good boy he always was,' she said to Matilda afterwards. 'I couldn't ha' loved him more if he'd been my own. No disrespect to you, Tom dear.'

'None taken,' Tom told her, giving her a hug.

Both women were being supported by their sons that day, and both were glad of it, for Bessie was tottery after her long journey and Matilda was so stunned with grief that, as she told her guests over and over again, she could never have endured it if it hadn't been for Edward and Mirabelle.

The two of them had taken charge of the funeral and stayed with Matilda through every weeping minute since Billy died, supporting her most affectionately and practically, Mirabelle because she was genuinely fond of her outspoken mother-in-law, and Edward because he was riven with guilt at the thought that his father's death was ultimately his fault.

'Whatever else we may think of Edward,' Will said to Henry as they left the church, 'he's certainly redeemed himself today.'

But Henry was more concerned about Caroline. 'Would it

be in order for me to come back to Bedford Square with you?' he wondered. 'Just to see how she is.'

It cheered Will to be able to give his permission. 'Of course,' he said. 'Quite in order and perfectly understandable. After all, you've called every other day.' And never seen her once, thanks to Dr Owen.

But this call was different.

As soon as they were in the hall, Euphemia came skimming down the stairs to meet them, her face so strained with anxiety that they both said the same thing with one voice.

'What is it? What's the matter?'

'We must get her away from Dr Owen,' Euphemia said without greeting or preamble. 'He's doing her no good. I've felt it ever since he began to treat her and now I'm sure of it. She grows weaker with every treatment instead of improving. And today . . .'

'Is she worse?' Henry asked, catching her anxiety.

'Yes, oh yes,' Euphemia said. 'When he bled her this morning it made her shake with weakness, and I know that can't be right. It can't, can it? And now she's in such a state she don't open her eyes or speak a word. Oh, what are we to do?'

But Henry was already taking action, leaping up the stairs two at a time, his long legs incisive as scissors.

Caroline was propped against the pillows in her darkened room, her shorn head damp and her eyes closed, but she opened them wearily when she heard his approach and managed to whisper his name. 'Henry?'

He was beside the bed in one stride, and gathering her poor limp body into his arms. 'My dearest girl!' he said. 'My dearest, dearest girl, what have they been doing to you?'

'I - feel - so ill,' she struggled. Was this Henry holding her? Or was she dreaming? But she was breathing in the familiar scent of his skin, leaning her head against the remembered warmth of his chest. Henry. Come to see her at last. Her own dear Henry. She had a vague puzzled memory that he had hurt her once, that she had run away from him, but now there was only relief to see him, relief to know that he would protect her. 'Don't - let him - bleed me again,' she said.

He was all instinct, all affection, knowing exactly what

action to take, and ready to take it. 'You shall come home,' he promised. 'You shall never be bled again. My own dear darling, I can't bear to see you so.'

She was weeping with weakness and relief, her sobs muffled against his jacket, aware that Pheemy was standing beside them with Will worrying behind her.

'I'm going – home,' she said between sobs, as Henry kissed her hair and stroked her spine with the most delicate affection. 'Going home.'

This wasn't quite what Euphemia had intended, if she'd intended anything, and in her present state of worried confusion she wasn't even sure of that. 'What will Nan say?' she worried. 'She's not supposed to have any excitement.'

'Tom can ride on ahead and tell Mrs Benotti,' Henry said, organizing the removal as if Euphemia hadn't spoken, 'can't he, Will? We'll travel in my carriage and pad the seat with pillows and blankets, and put hot bricks at her feet. I promise she won't take cold, Pheemy. Totty can follow on with Harry and the luggage.'

'I'll see to it,' Will said, soft-footing out of the room at once.

'You will come with us, won't you Pheemy?' Henry said, still cradling his darling. 'You'll go on nursing her?'

Was there any doubt? 'Of course, of course,' Euphemia said. 'But Nan might not think it wise. Are you sure you are doing the right thing?'

Now that Caroline was in his arms Henry was sure of everything. 'Yes,' he said. 'I am. And Nan will agree. You'll see.'

She had agreed already, for Will had met her in the hall and told her what was happening and what Henry planned to do.

'My heart alive!' she said. 'He do move fast, our Henry. He's a proper Easter. Was she truly happy to see him?'

'Yes,' Will said. 'She wept, but she was happy. You could see that.'

'In that case, we will do as he suggests. Personally, I think she should be kept quiet and calm and mend by degrees because I couldn't bear to lose her. Not after my Billy. But as he's here and they're together again and she's withstood the shock of that, then I suppose the sooner she travels the better. They're husband and wife, when all's said and done, and they ought to be together. It en't for me to say what's to be done.

Pheemy shall go with 'em of course, so she'll be in good hands, and I'll send Bessie too, just in case. You and I can follow along with young Harry.'

Tom Thistlethwaite was sent to ride on ahead of them all, and the carriages were told to return and the servants were given their orders. Half an hour later, Henry carried his darling gently downstairs and tucked her tenderly among the blankets in his closed carriage.

'You will send for a doctor first thing,' Nan instructed as he was climbing in after Euphemia and Bessie.

'We have a most sensible practitioner just around the corner,' he said seriously. 'She'll be well looked after.'

'And treated gently?'

He understood her. 'No one will ever lay a hand on her ever again,' he promised. 'You have my word.'

'I'm uncommon pleased to hear it,' Nan approved. 'Drive carefully.'

The coachman drove very slowly and very carefully, but the journey exhausted Caroline despite his efforts, and when they reached Richmond Hill and Henry carried her into the house, she groaned when he lifted her, because her back and her arms were so sore.

'Hold her gently, do,' Bessie scolded, struggling out of the carriage with a blanket ready to cover her darling against the autumn air.

'Not – his – fault,' Caroline panted, limp with weakness but defending him at once and trying not to wince. Oh, if only she could lie down again, anywhere, even on the floor. She felt so ill.

Her old bed was feather soft and as snug as Mrs Benotti's two warming pans could make it, and the house was peaceful and familiar and comforting, even though the bedroom was dark with the curtains drawn against the fever. 'So – good – to be – home,' she said. 'Where's – my Harry?'

'He followed us,' Euphemia assured her. 'In Nan's carriage with Will and Totty. He's home too.'

'Ah!' Caroline sighed with exhausted satisfaction, and slept at once.

Henry's sensible practitioner arrived forty minutes later.

Dr Brambling was one of those doctors who can make a

patient feel better simply by walking into the room. He was a tall, awkward, avuncular man, with a shock of perpetually untidy grey hair, a bush of a beard, and a craggy face. Everything about him was larger than life, from his booming voice to his size twelve feet, but his size and awkwardness were deceptive. His hands might look clumsy but they were actually extremely tender and skilled.

Now he ran them softly over Caroline's aching spine, and along the ridges of scar tissue in her arms where Dr Owen had applied his ferocious cups, and made murmuring noises of encouragement to her.

'You *have* been poorly, my dear. Yes, indeed. I can see that. Very very poorly. Is that tender? Yes, yes. I can see it is. Well now, we must build you up again, mustn't we? Can't have you tumbling down, eh? Leave that to London Bridge.'

The childish joke was oddly comforting. It was what he always said to Harry when the poor little thing had a fever.

'Now tell me,' he said, in his nice gossipy way, 'what brought this about, eh? When did you fall ill?'

So they told him, because he was the sort of man it was easy to confide in. Euphemia began with an abridged version of the court case and Caroline's collapse and from there they both went on to describe her illness and the terrible weakness she suffered when she was bled and purged, and he listened quietly, patting his patient's hands from time to time, until the tale was told.

'Well now, Mrs Easter,' he said. 'I don't think you need to be bled any more, my dear, nor purged either. What you need is fresh air, nourishing food and plenty of rest, as advocated by the good Miss Nightingale. And I think we could dispense with darkened rooms. If you are strong enough to withstand a journey, a little sunlight will do nothing but good, eh?'

And certainly drawing the curtains and letting in the daylight transformed the room and made them all feel infinitely better.

'That's an improvement, upon me life,' the doctor said. 'Now I can see you. Would you just put out your tongue for me, my dear?'

'Keep her in bed,' he said to Will and Euphemia when his examination was over and they were downstairs in the front parlour. 'Tempt her to eat. Let her sleep when she will. Sleep is a great healer. I will call back tomorrow evening and see how she is, but I feel fairly certain she will soon be on the mend. There is only one other piece of advice I should like to offer.'

Will looked a query at him.

'I think it would be helpful to hire another nurse to assist Miss Callbeck. If it were not ungallant,' he said to Euphemia, 'I should say you look as weary as your patient, my dear, and we can't have that, now can we? You need to rest too from time to time, you know, to keep up your strength.'

It was such excellent advice that they took it as soon as he'd left the house, for after working for six months in London hospitals Euphemia knew exactly where to find a good nurse. And the girl she wrote to was Taffy Biggs, care of St Bartholomew's.

That evening Henry took a tray full of small tempting dishes up to the bedroom and began the gentle task of coaxing his darling to eat. He sat beside her on the bed and fed her with a spoon, one small mouthful at a time, as if she were a child. And with every spoonful he stroked her hair and kissed her cheek and told her how very very much he loved her.

'Just a little bit more of this nice tender chicken,' he urged. 'Or a spoonful of the sauce, eh? You could swallow that, couldn't you my dearest?'

She did her best, even though the effort exhausted her.

Finally when she'd eaten all she could, he put the tray aside, took up her hairbrush and brushed her poor shorn head.

She thanked him wearily, her face very pale in the gaslight.

'I would do anything to make you well,' he said. 'Anything. I love you so much.'

'Yes,' she said. 'I can see.'

'I am so very sorry I shook you,' he said. 'If I could undo it . . .'

She put her fingers on her lips to stop him. She remembered their row, but distantly, as though it had happened to someone else. It was unimportant now. 'Hush,' she said. 'There is no need.'

'There is,' he said, with anguished repentance. 'There is. If

443

you are ever to love me again,' – and oh how much he hoped she would love him again! – 'you must know how much I regret . . . '

Her fingers pressed his words away again. 'I do love you,' she said. 'Hush! Hush! I do.'

'Oh my dearest!' he said, catching her tender fingers and kissing them most lovingly. 'I will never ever . . . '

This time she put up her mouth and stopped his anguish softly with a kiss. 'I am home,' she said, gazing her love straight into his eyes. 'It is enough.'

That night Henry slept in the blue room, next door to the nursery and a mere two doors away from his darling. Or to be more accurate, Henry passed the night in the blue room and for an hour or two actually lay in the bed and dozed, but he was far too happy to do anything so mundane as to sleep. She was home. They were together. The nightmare was over.

Caroline slept soundly all night long too, without nightmare or fever. And the next morning she sat up and ate an egg for breakfast. And although she dozed for most of the day, by the evening she was well enough to eat nearly everything on her invalid tray. When Dr Brambling put his head round the door at eleven o'clock to see how she was, she smiled at him happily.

'A great improvement,' he said. 'If you go on like this, my dear, we shall soon have you up and about.'

'I suppose I couldn't see my Harry just for a little while, could I?' she asked.

'Rest for another two days,' he decreed, 'eat well, sleep well, and then we'll see. A lot can happen in two days.'

And a lot did. Will decided he was sufficiently recovered to go back to work. Trade figures were sent to Nan which were so unexpectedly good that she was quite cheered by them, particularly as so much of the managerial work was being done by deputies. And Taffy Biggs arrived.

She was still underweight and very short, about the same height as Nan, but she was so cheerful that Bessie and Mrs Benotti said it did them all good to have her in the house. She was an endless source of gossip, which made her popular below stairs, and her arrival certainly gave Euphemia a chance to rest, for they took it in turns to sit up through the night and watch over Caroline in case her fever returned.

On the fifth day, when there had been no sign of fever, Dr Brambling pronounced himself so well pleased that he saw no reason why Harry shouldn't come and see his mother that very afternoon.

So after his mid-day rest, the little boy was carried into the bedroom. He was rather shy to start with, because they'd been kept apart for ten days, and ten days is a very long time when you're only eighteen months old, but within ten minutes he was climbing across the bed to be cuddled, and within half an hour the two of them were eating cakes, taking it in turns to feed one another, with much stickiness and frequent kisses.

That evening Caroline ate the largest meal she'd had since she took the fever. Far from making her ill, the visit had plainly made her well, just as Henry and Euphemia and the good doctor had hoped. From then on she got better by the hour.

And then it was the middle of November and a letter arrived for Nan from Frederick Brougham in Westmoreland. It was an appeal.

'The snows have begun, my dear, and soon we shall be snowed in here, and travel will be impossible. If Caroline is well enough, how dearly I should like to see you. Your last letter sounded a deal more sanguine. Might I hope for a visit?'

'Of course,' Euphemia said, when Nan visited Richmond to see if Caroline really was well enough to leave. 'You go, Nan dear. She's convalescing now. Taffy and I will look after her.'

'Not too much excitement mind,' Nan warned. 'If I'm not back before Christmas, see that she's kept quiet then.'

'I promise.'

'Then I think I might go.'

'Yes, do. A few weeks in the fells would do you good.'

Bessie had other ideas. 'You're never going a-journeying at this time of year!' she said. 'With the snow coming on and all. What next?'

Nan laughed at her. 'A journey en't hardship to me, Bessie. Not after all the travelling I've done in my lifetime.'

445

But Bessie was firm about it. 'If you're going jauncing off all that way,' she said, 'I'm going with you.'

Nan was touched by her loyalty. 'It's a long journey, Bessie,' she warned.

'All the more reason.'

'I could be away for months.'

'Then it'll be months,' Bessie said, setting her lips in the fiercest expression she could manage. 'You ain't jauncing all that way up there on your own, because I won't have it. Somebody's got to look out for you, make no bones about it.'

'And who'll look out for you, pray?'

'I don't need no one to look out fer me,' Bessie said stubbornly. 'I ain't so old as all that even if I have lost most a' me teeth.' And then, as she saw the expression gathering on Nan's face, 'Very well then, Tom shall come with us, if Mr Will don't mind. How would that suit?'

The two of them went back to Bedford Square to see what Will would say, and although he was due to travel to Cambridge to report on a jewel robbery, he joked that he was old enough to manage without Tom for once, providing he could find another servant to make his tea and clean his clothes.

So Nan was persuaded to have company on her long journey north – and was glad of it.

Will's trip to Cambridge was boring without Tom. And to make matters worse Jeff Jefferson was out of town on an assignment of his own. Normally Will would have stayed in the city for as long as he could so as to enjoy his old friend's company. Now he travelled back to London after two days. There was little to report about the robbery. The thieves had broken in through a skylight and made off with nearly a thousand pounds' worth of rings and necklaces and the jeweller was in tears, but as a story it was very small beer.

'Pack up,' he said to his new quiet servant, when the report was written. 'We will catch the four o'clock.'

But being back in a virtually empty house was unsettling. There had been so much coming and going in Bedford Square during the past few months, with Nan and Mr Brougham busy over the trial and Carrie and Pheemy always at home, and always talking. Now its unusual emptiness made him feel deserted. He missed them all quite painfully.

He would take in his report first thing in the morning, he decided as he went to bed, and then he would go down to Richmond and see how they were.

It was very cold beside the Thames the next morning and as he walked out of Richmond station the sky was blue-grey with rain clouds and a north-east wind had begun to blow. It punched him down the Quadrant towards the green, lengthening his stride and making his coat tails fly forward before him. Its force lifted his spirits and filled him with energy. He marched into the Square, using his umbrella as a walking stick and whistling happily.

And coming out of the apothecary's on the corner there was Euphemia, her russet hair blown by the wind, clutching her bonnet to her head with one hand and holding a small dangling package in the other. He'd been dreaming of her all night and thinking of her all the way down in the train, looking forward to the moment when he would see her again, and there she was.

'Pheemy!' he called, running towards her. 'Pheemy!'

She looked up in surprise, and then smiled her lovely welcoming smile, standing as still as she could in the wind until he caught up with her. She'd been to buy some zinc and castor oil cream for little Harry, she said.

'All on your own?'

'It's only a step,' she said, smiling again, 'and now I have company.'

They walked past the shops together and she told him how much better Caroline was, and thought how handsome he looked, striding along beside her with that thick beard bristling and his eyes so blue and loving. And he said he was glad to hear it and told her the story of the robbery, admiring her lovely madonna face and thinking how well her blue mantle suited her.

They'd only gone a few yards when a sleety rain began to fall, needling against their faces. Will put up the umbrella at once and held it before them. But they were too far apart for both of them to be protected by it, and presently she noticed that his shoulder was getting wet.

'Oh Will,' she said. 'It's all coming in on you.'

'Only one thing for it,' he said hopefully. 'You will have to hold my arm and walk as close to me as you can.'

And to his delight, she did. And blissful it was, for he was so warm and protective, her dear, dear Will, striding along with the umbrella held up like a shield between them and the rest of the world. If only he could love me, she thought, yearningly. What a blessing that would be! But he doesn't even think of it, I fear.

If I wanted to, he was thinking, I could lean my head down and kiss her under this umbrella, and nobody would know. There was hardly anybody about and the few people they saw were walking quickly, heads down against the sleet, taking no notice of anything or anybody. I could kiss her if I wanted to. And he *did* want to. Very very much. But he couldn't do it, of course, because she thought of him as a brother. She always had. And he wouldn't want to upset her.

'You'll be able to come home to Bedford Square soon, won't you,' he hoped. 'It's jolly empty there without you all, I can tell you.'

The thought brought her up against reality with a palpable shock, dissolving her happy mood in an instant. It would be unbearable to live in the same house without Nan to keep the balance between them. Why, they would be virtually on their own together. It couldn't be done. Indeed it couldn't. 'Oh, no,' she said. 'No.' And she gave a little involuntary sigh that was almost a shudder.

The unexpectedness of that little sound disturbed him. And so did her anguished expression, and the fact that she controlled it so quickly. 'But you said that Carrie was better,' he prompted, searching for an explanation, wanting her to continue.

Her face was calm again. 'She is. Oh yes, she is.'

'Then if that is the case, you will soon be home.' Oh, please say you will. I miss you so much. Should he tell her that? Perhaps not.

'No,' she said again, wondering how she could explain this

to him without hurting his feelings. 'I couldn't live in the same house with you, not unchaperoned, not with Nan away. It wouldn't be proper.'

'You've never thought it improper before.'

'It might be considered so now,' she said, walking on doggedly with her face averted.

'How could it possibly be improper?' he asked, wondering whether he could tease her away from this odd distress of hers, wondering whether he wanted to tease her away from it, wondering what it meant, as an equally odd and unexpected doubt flickered into his mind. 'We've always lived together so happily, Pheemy, like brother and sister.'

The harmless, hackneyed phrase destroyed her control. 'Brother and sister!' she said and suddenly there was a scornful wildness about her that made his heart leap with a new, amazing hope. 'Always that! Brother and sister! Brother and sister! Brother and sister! But we're *not* brother and sister, Will. We never were and we never will be.' She knew she was saying things that should never be said, revealing more than she had any right to do, but the knowledge only increased her wildness.

'I thought it pleased you to be like a sister to me,' he said, and was instantly alarmed to think how trite and foolish the words sounded. He cast about for something else to say, and couldn't think of anything because this new hope was depriving him of the power of thought.

'It did,' she said passionately. 'Oh, it did. It's just that now . . .'

'Now?'

She'd already said far more than she should have done. It was necessary to retreat, even though he was looking at her so lovingly she was almost tempted to continue. 'It wouldn't be proper,' she said.

He realized that she was avoiding his eyes. And now hope leapt towards certainty. 'Pheemy, my dear, dear Pheemy,' he said, standing still and putting his free hand on her shoulder so that she would turn and face him again. 'Is it because . . .' Are you telling me . . . ?'

She couldn't meet his eyes, she couldn't think, she couldn't speak, she could scarcely breathe. To have loved him for so

449

long and to be here, now, so near to saying all the things she wanted to say was more than she could bear.

He held the umbrella carefully above her head, and tried to be reasonable despite the mill race of emotion that was propelling him on. 'There are all manner of situations,' he said, 'when it is quite proper for a man and a woman to live together under the same roof.' And then, giving her his teasing smile, 'Even when they are *not* brother and sister.'

'But none that apply to us,' she said huskily.

'Perhaps,' he said, greatly daring, 'we should ask ourselves whether . . . '

The tenderness in his voice was too encouraging to be ignored. She looked her question straight into his eyes, her voice tremulous. 'Whether?' she asked.

'I used to think that love was bound to lead to loss,' he said, feeling that he ought to explain.

'Yes.' Oh, how hope fluttered in her bosom, like a caged bird beating its wings against the bars.

'I always vowed I would never love anyone . . . Never allow myself . . . '

'Yes, you did.' Oh, what was he going to say next? Would it be . . . ? Oh Will, my dear, dear Will, go on, go on. She was filled with such longing that her throat ached with it.

'I was wrong, Pheemy. You've always known that, haven't you? There is a risk in loving, that's true.' And how well he understood that now when he was risking so much to be speaking to her in this way. 'But there is so much to gain. So much . . . '

'So much,' she said, and her voice was barely more than a whisper.

'I have something to tell you,' he said, trying to be formal even though his senses were blazing. 'Something I should have told you long ago, only I wasn't sure you would want to hear it. Something so important . . . '

Her face was changing, softening, glowing as though it was being lit by sunshine, even though the wind was lifting their umbrella like a sail and they could hear the sleet pattering down upon them as sharp as shingle. 'Will?' she said, and there was such hope in the word. Hope and trust and affection. 'Oh my dear, my dear, my dear.'

There was no need for a formal proposal now, but he made one just the same. 'I love you, Pheemy,' he said. 'I want to marry you.'

She closed her eyes in the joy of the moment, lifting her face, her lips spreading in a tremulous smile. And he bent beneath the umbrella and kissed her at last, gently, because there was still enough reason in him to remember that they were out in the street, but with passion enough to say everything else that needed to be said.

Afterwards they had no idea how long they talked nor what time it took them to stroll the last few hundred yards to Richmond Hill. They didn't notice how wildly the wind was blowing them along nor how wet their feet were getting.

Caroline did, of course. 'Pheemy, dearest!' she said, when her two wind-tattered relations were ushered into her parlour. 'Just look at your boots! Where have you been?'

'Will and I are going to get married,' Euphemia said breathlessly, as though that explained it all. Which it did.

Caroline gave a squeal of pleasure and threw herself at her cousin, kissing her over and over before she flung her arms about her brother's neck. 'Oh, how marvellous! How marvellous! And about time too.' Then she rushed to the door to yell for Henry. 'Henry! Henry! Come down, do! Will and Pheemy are getting married.'

'Is this before or after lunch?' Henry called to them over the banisters.

'Lunch!' Caroline said. 'I must tell Cook we're one extra. We'll have champagne.'

The meal was a babble of happy talk. Cook came upstairs to add her congratulations and apologize because the food was so plain. 'I'd ha' done you proud if I'd known,' she said.

But Caroline assured her that none of them had known and anyway they couldn't have enjoyed her food any more, 'not if you'd served us peacock pie and caviare'.

'Which in your present state,' Henry said happily, 'would probably have made you sick.'

'Oh, ain't this fine,' she said, when Cook had departed, mollified and smiling. 'When will you marry?'

451

They answered her together, Will saying 'Tomorrow' and Euphemia 'After your baby is born'. And that made them all laugh.

'Tomorrow would be best,' Will said. He was full of confidence, glowingly sure of himself.

'No, no,' Euphemia laughed. 'We must wait a little. Until Nan has come home at least.'

'Should we write and tell her?' Henry wondered.

But they decided not to. 'Let it be our secret for a little while longer,' Euphemia said. 'Until you are quite well, my darling, and the baby is born.'

'I am quite well now,' Caroline said. 'And the baby will be born in less than eight weeks. Taffy says so. Where are you going to live? Oh, I'm so happy for you. So happy.'

Chapter 35

It was so peaceful in Penrith, cocooned in snow and completely blocked off from the worries and miseries of the outside world. And Frederick was so touchingly pleased to see them, stooping out into the snow-covered courtyard to help his dear Nan from the carriage when it had slithered to a halt, and settling her into the warmest chimney corner with a tumbler of 'good old-fashioned brandy and hot water' to thaw her, and arranging for rooms to be opened and aired for Bessie and Tom, unremittingly hospitable.

He fed her well too, for the house was well-stocked against the winter, hams hanging from the kitchen chimney and the oatmeal tubs filled to the brim, cheese and butter, sugars and spices, tea, coffee and chocolate in abundance.

'Everything we need to hand,' he said to Nan, as the lamps were being lit that evening. 'I mean to be snug this season.'

It was good to be back with him again, cosy as bears in their high warm bed, talking over all the events of the past year, and agreeing that they were through the worst of it.

'Caroline improves,' he said, as he finally blew out the candle, 'trade will pick up in the spring and tomorrow we will visit my cousins.'

'Yes,' she said, settling to sleep. He was right. Life was returning to normal.

The days that followed were quiet and easy. They visited the cousins, travelling in a horse-drawn sledge like Russians, because the snow was too thick for any other form of transport; and they went to church by sledge too and sang carols lustily;

and when fresh snow began to fall they sat by the fire in Frederick's panelled parlour and watched as the fat flakes curtained the window and felt glad to be inside in the warm. And the next morning when they woke to find that the terraced steps before the drawing room had been transformed into a sloping snowbank, and that the garden rose above them like a white hill, they were both quite pleased to think that the winter was increasing their isolation in this northern retreat of theirs. If they couldn't walk on the fells they could walk through the house. It was plenty big enough for the limited exercise they needed, and besides, it was warm.

There were so many quiet pleasures to savour, strong Scottish beef and sweet Westmoreland water, oatcakes hot from the griddle and porridge thick enough to cut. And every morning when Frederick was in his dressing room being shaved, Bessie came hobbling in to be lady's maid to her dear Nan, brushing her white hair most tenderly and easing her into her clothes and gossiping about the old days all the while. Oh, they were pleasant easy days, and they passed with amazing speed.

Nan was quite surprised to come down one morning to find the servants decking the panelled hall with boughs of yew and holly.

'Is Christmas come around so soon?' she said, fingering the red berries.

'It has,' Frederick said happily. 'Mr Mackay is to fetch the goose this afternoon.'

A fine fat goose it was and made good eating.

'Caroline is forbidden Christmas this year, poor child,' Nan said, remembering with pity.

'Only for this year, my dear. Next year, when she is quite well, she will enjoy it again, and with her whole life before her, which is more than may be said of you and I.'

'Does that distress 'ee, Frederick my dear?'

'When I have lived so long and so well and with such a companion? Fie upon you! How could you ask such a thing?'

'Aye,' she said, 'we've had a fine life together you and I.'

'And with more to come,' he told her, his long face pale in the firelight. Now that he was old his nose looked longer and sharper and his chin more angular, but his eyes were as tender

454

and teasing as ever. 'I have a little gift for you. Would you like it now?'

'Yes, yes, yes,' she said. 'At once, now, this very minute.'

It was a cameo brooch set with seed pearls, a lovely thing that had to be pinned to her dress immediately.

'Dear Frederick,' she said. 'What style you have. There en't another man living with such style. And now I've a present for you, my dear.'

'Indeed?' he teased. 'I see no parcel anywhere. And I assure you I have looked for it most assiduously.'

'I had Tom hide it behind the settee,' she said triumphantly, 'where you couldn't stoop to look.'

The only trouble was that she couldn't stoop to pull it out again, and neither of them were strong enough to lift the settee away from the wall. In the end they had to fish the package from its hiding place with her walking stick and a lot of giggling.

But it was worth the effort, for it was a thick woollen dressing gown to keep him warm in the mornings while he was being washed and shaved. Both of them were delighted by it, he because it was good to be petted by this extraordinary woman, she because she had made certain he wouldn't catch cold. His pallor in the early morning was often quite alarming.

The Christmas festivities continued. There were services and parties and even a ball at the cousins' house in the fells, which both of them enjoyed very much, even though they danced very little. And then there was Hogmanay and Tom Thistlethwaite was much in demand for first-footing, being dark haired and a stranger to the neighbourhood.

On the first day of the new year Nan and Frederick went for a drive in their horse-drawn sledge. The landscape was magical, the river Eamont steel grey between its white banks, crows tumbling black against a pearl-white sky and the snow-covered fells glistening in the pale sunlight.

'It is so peaceful here,' she said. 'I wish I could stay longer.'

'Then do so, my dear.'

'Caroline's baby is due this month,' she said. 'I must travel in a day or so.'

'Stay another week,' he urged. 'The days are long here without you.'

'My heart alive!' she said, charmed to be asked so romantically. 'That en't an invitation to refuse, upon my life.'

So they spent another week together in their snow-bound fastness. And a very cold week, for the temperature dropped lower every night, so that by morning the bedroom windows were covered with frost-ferns, layered upon the panes in such thickly intricate patterns that it was ten o'clock before the heat from the fires could clear them.

Nan and Frederick came down to breakfast later and later, preferring the warmth of their bed to the chill of the dining room. And one morning Frederick even decided that he would go back to bed for a little nap after he'd been washed and shaved.

'Quite right,' Nan approved. 'You can breakfast later.' He was paper-pale. The rest and warmth would do him good.

She tucked him under the eiderdown, still in his new dressing gown, and kissed him before she went downstairs. 'I'll be back presently,' she promised.

It was warmer than she expected before the dining room fire, so she and Bessie took their breakfast in the chimney corner.

'I've left him sleeping,' Nan said. 'I shan't go up for an hour or two.'

'Let him sleep his sleep out,' Bessie agreed, nodding her head sagely. 'Much the best way.'

So they gossiped on.

When the hall clock struck ten Nan felt it was really time he got up. 'There won't be any morning left if he goes on at this rate,' she said, as she left the chimney corner.

It was very quiet in the bedroom. She could hear the coals clicking in the grate, and the soft plop of snow falling from the branches in the garden beyond the window. But Frederick wasn't making a sound. She couldn't even hear him breathing. He must be awake, she thought, walking across the room towards the bed. But no. His eyes were still closed. Very tightly closed. My heart alive, she thought, he's in a deep sleep. And for a few seconds as she walked the last few feet she wondered whether she ought to wake him. But then she reached the bed and her hand touched his fingers, and she knew that no one would ever wake Frederick Brougham again. For her lover was dead, his face already grey and vacated, with that ancient emptiness that cannot be misinterpreted.

'Oh Frederick,' she said. 'To leave me so, my dear, without a word of good-bye.' Then she sat on the edge of the bed beside him and began to cry.

Downstairs in the kitchen Bessie was busy helping Cook to prepare the evening meal, while the scullery maids scoured some of the breakfast pots and Tom helped the butler to polish the silver. Time went on but nobody rang for Mr Brougham's breakfast and finally Bessie got worried by such a long silence and said she really thought she ought to go up and see what was what.

She found Nan still sitting on the bed and still weeping, her poor old face puffed with tears.

'Oh Bessie my dear, you see how it is,' she said thickly.

Bessie saw how it was in a glance and decided to get her mistress out of it as quickly as she could. 'Now you come down-stairs, my lovey,' she said, speaking as though Nan were a child. 'Your old hands are like ice. You jest come down with ol' Bessie. That's the style.'

'I ought to stay with him,' Nan tried.

'No you oughtn't,' Bessie said, leading her away. 'You can't help him now, poor gentleman. You've give him a good life, my dear, and he's had a nice peaceful death. You can't do more fer a man than that.'

So Nan allowed herself to be led down to the parlour, where Bessie sat by the fire and wrapped her in a blanket and gave her a dose of laudanum to ease the first pain of loss. Then she sent Tom across the fell to tell the cousins.

Two of them came straight back with him, to commiserate with Nan and, as the older one explained, 'to take the weight of this sad business from your shoulders, Mrs Easter, ma'am. You've enough to do grieving, without arranging funerals and such.'

'And just as well,' Bessie said to Cook, when the two men had gone down to Penrith to see the undertaker and the vicar. 'She's had enough to contend with, poor lady.'

'They mean to keep the house on for when Miss Penelope marries,' Cook confided. 'Your missus won't want to visit, I daresay, not without the master, poor soul. Fancy the poor man dying like that.'

''E went peaceful,' Bessie said. 'That's the main thing. There's others ain't so lucky.'

'Aye,' Cook agreed. 'That's the one comfort. Would *she* could see it so.'

But Nan had a lot of grief to cry out before she could accept that the gentleness of Frederick's death was something to be thankful for.

'We are the only ones left,' she said to Bessie on the morning of the funeral. 'First John and then Billy and now my dear old Frederick.' The coffin was being carried from the house, strewn with Christmas holly, its dark green leaves and bright berries bold against the white background of the snow. 'Now it's only us.'

'And Will and Euphemia,' Bessie said, 'and Annie and James and all their children, and Matty and Jimmy and their little ones, and Caroline and Henry and little Harry, and a new baby coming.'

'Yes,' Nan said, drying her eyes. 'A new baby coming. We must go back to London as soon as everything is settled here. I wonder how she is, poor girl.'

'Going on lovely, I shouldn't wonder,' Bessie said. 'But she'll be all the better for seeing you.'

'We might travel tomorrow,' Nan said, 'if the weather holds. There is nothing to keep us here once this is over.'

'There's the carriage come,' Bessie said. 'We'd better go down. Take my arm, Mrs Easter dear. That's it. Easy does it. I've got yer.'

Chapter 36

'It's a boy,' Dr Brambling said. 'Bravo, my dear. A lovely baby.'

'Give him to me. Give him to me,' Caroline said hungrily, holding out her arms for her new-born. 'Oh, he's lovely! Lovely! Ain't he a pet, Pheemy?'

'He's beautiful,' Euphemia said, admiring him from the foot of the bed. She was sweating and tired after the long effort of labour but this birth was a triumph. Despite the trial and her long illness, Caroline had been delivered easily. 'And born on a Sunday too, when his dear Papa is here to see him.'

'The child that is born on the Sabbath day, is bonny and blithe and good and gay,' Caroline quoted, nuzzling the baby's dark head, 'and so you will be, won't you my pet?'

'Born in time for breakfast,' Taffy said. 'Look at him rootin' around fer it all-a-ready, bless him.'

'Is it breakfast time?' Caroline said. 'I'm jolly hungry.'

'It is seven o'clock, my dear,' Dr Brambling told her, 'and you shall have whatever you fancy as soon as you've fed milord. What shall you call him? Have you decided?'

'Oh yes,' Caroline said, as the infant began to suckle. 'We decided ages ago.' It was all of three weeks. 'He's to be John Joseph, after his grandfathers.'

John Joseph was a contented baby. He fed till he slept and then lay pale and peaceful in his father's arms, blowing milk bubbles from his little red mouth to the amazement of his brother, who had been brought in for five minutes to see him, and was now using his newest word over and over again. 'Baby! Baby! Baby!'

Three days later Annie came down to visit, bringing Meg and her three youngest children with her, all of them full of eagerness to see the new arrival. Annie said he was an absolute duck and allowed all three children to cuddle him. Then they all came trouping downstairs to take tea in the parlour before their long journey back to Rattlesden, Annie and Meg and the children, and Will and Euphemia and Henry, rosy with delight at his new son. And Harry took tea with them too, delighting them all with his new word, which he was saying at every opportunity, now that he'd found out he would be applauded for using it.

In their relief and happiness, the tea party steadily became riotous. First the children joined Harry in a chant, 'Baby, baby, baby'. Then hands were clapped in rhythm. Finally the tea table was pushed to the side of the room, tea-things and all, and the chant became a round dance, 'Baby, baby, we've got a baby', with all five children and all five adults leaping and prancing among the potted plants, skirts tipping and coat-tails flying.

They were making such a noise, they didn't hear Nan's arrival. She was inside the parlour and laughing at them before they realized she'd arrived. But then they rushed towards her all talking at once, a-babble with news, and totally ignoring Bessie who was making hideous faces at them to implore them to stop.

'My heart alive,' the old lady said, when she'd managed to make sense of their bedlam. 'What a home-coming! Is Carrie well? Tell me that?'

'She blooms,' Henry said. 'She is absolutely beautiful.'

'Then I'd best go up and see her.'

'All this fuss,' Bessie said quite crossly, 'and you ain't looked to see your grandmother's in mourning, never the one of you.'

She'd been in mourning when she went away, so they'd thought nothing of it. Now they realized they might have been too quick with their news and Will and Henry were rather shamefaced.

Nan told them quickly. 'Frederick died in his sleep, my dears. That's what Bessie means. But you mustn't feel sad, for he wouldn't have wanted that at all. He valued your laughter,

460

you know. He always said you were so full of life. And now bless me, if there en't a new life arrived to welcome me home. And what could be nicer, Bessie? A new life and Pheemy and Will getting married. It's just the sort of news I needed.'

And despite Bessie's scowl, it was. To see her Carrie looking so well, with that pretty baby in the cradle beside her, lifted her spirits as nothing else could have done.

'What plans we must make now,' she said, sitting on the edge of the bed. 'When do they mean to marry?'

'In May,' Caroline said. 'They've found a house here in Richmond, just up the hill, so we're to be neighbours. Ain't that a fine thing? It's all being decorated, and Will says it looks quite dreadful just at present but it will be very grand when it's finished.'

'May,' Nan approved. 'An excellent month.'

'But we've got the christening first,' Caroline said, stroking the baby's head.

'So we have. And what could be nicer?'

John Joseph Easter was christened in Richmond parish church, on a bright brisk afternoon at the beginning of February. He was warmly wrapped in a fur-lined cloak and wore a cap of white swan's down on his tender head, and he slept peacefully through the entire ceremony, only grunting a little when the water was sprinkled on his denuded scalp. Afterwards when the procession of carriages returned to Richmond Hill to a lavish meal purportedly held in his honour, he slept all through that too.

It was a happy party, the first happy occasion in the Easter family since those terrible days in October, and so Easters gathered from every part of the kingdom to attend it, from Bury and Rattlesden, Ippark and Cumberland, Bedford Square and Clerkenwell Green. Mr Rawson was invited too, because Nan said she thought it would be a good way of showing that they appreciated the help he'd given them when Caroline was so ill.

He certainly seemed very content at their party, sitting with Nan and Annie, although Henry protested that he never took his eyes from Caroline, 'not once in the whole afternoon'.

461

'That is because she is so pretty,' Euphemia said, watching her as she stood among her guests with her new baby in her arms.

And it was true. She did look well, with her cheeks flushed and rounded, and her hair grown long enough to dress in ringlets again.

'Pretty enough to eat,' her brother said.

Nevertheless Henry was not amused to see her being given so much attention by a man who, for all his help, was only a weaver when all was said and done. And he was jolly pleased when Mr Rawson came to say goodbye and told them both that this would be the last occasion he would see them.

'Is it, Mr Rawson?' Caroline said. 'I am sorry to hear you say so.'

'I'm off to America,' the weaver said. 'To seek my fortunes. I always meant to travel there, and here's t' chance come, neat and handy, thanks to your grandmother.'

So they wished him well, and on a sudden impulse Caroline kissed him goodbye. 'I shall always be grateful to you, Mr Rawson,' she said.

'Aye, lass,' he said huskily. 'And I to thee.'

Then he turned on his heel and was gone so quickly they were quite surprised.

'What a peculiar thing, to rush off like that,' Henry said.

But there wasn't time for speculation, for there were other happy guests to attend to and a wedding to talk about.

'I shall see you in May,' Caroline said, over and over again as she said goodbye to the rest of her departing guests. 'It will be such an occasion. I can't wait.'

And a great day it was, sparkling with champagne and sunshine. This time the guests who returned to the reception at Henry's fine house on the hill were able to stroll through the gardens after the meal, walking lazily about in the sunlight so that the lawns bubbled with swirling gowns and lace-edged parasols, and Euphemia, watching from her vantage point on the top terrace, told her dear Will that it looked as though the whole garden was growing gigantic daisies.

'Are you happy, my dearest one?' Will asked unnecessarily.

He was rewarded by having his arm squeezed. To be married to her darling at last, and settled in a fine house here in Richmond, and a mere two hundred yards away from Caroline and Henry, what more could she possibly want?

'Oh Will, look!' she said. 'Caroline is paddling.'

And so she was, standing at the water's edge with her crinoline lifted above her ankles, as happy as a child in the water, and quite herself again, with Henry admiring her from the bankside, and little Harry hopping beside her, and all her nephews and nieces splashing round about her.

'Oh Will, my dear,' Euphemia said, 'this is the best day of my life.'

A better one was to follow a little under a year later when she and Caroline discovered to their great joy that they were both expecting babies in December.

'What good fortune,' Caroline said, 'to be carrying together. Think how we can help each other.'

'And our children will be company for each other,' Euphemia said, 'just as we are.' Even the pervasive nausea of early pregnancy was bearable now.

'We will visit one another every day,' Caroline said.

That made Euphemia laugh. 'We already do,' she said, for now that they lived so close to one another they were rarely apart, particularly when Will was away from home working on a story.

'Well then, we'll visit *twice* every day,' her cousin said, happily undeterred by such unnecessary logic.

Two weeks later the papers were full of news that made rather a nonsense of their plans, although it delighted Nan and Henry.

Ever since the previous summer, Queen Victoria's husband, Prince Albert, had been trying to organize a 'Great Exhibition of the Works of Industry of all Nations', which he wanted to hold in London 'to lift the spirits of the people and demonstrate all the good which progress brings'. He'd run into all kinds of difficulties because the site he'd chosen for his exhibition hall was the great open expanse of Hyde Park, which was unfortunately already covered with a large number of 'beautiful and long-established trees', none of which, so his opponents said, could possibly be cut down to make way for the sort of temporary structure he proposed.

Now, after nearly twelve months' wrangling, a solution had been found, by a gardener of all people, a certain Mr Paxton who built greenhouses and conservatories for the Duke of Devonshire. He proposed to house the exhibition in an enormous glasshouse, which could be erected round the trees and filled with plants and fountains. The newspapers were already calling it 'The Crystal Palace'.

'A glorious idea,' Nan said when she presided over the meeting of her regional managers that June. 'And splendid for trade. Just think of all the books that will be written about this! To say nothing of leaflets and programmes and I don't know what all. I shall write to Prince Albert to put the Easter newsagents at his disposal for whatever publicity he requires.'

'I think we could do better than that,' Edward said. 'I think we should take a stall at the exhibition, next door to the printing machines, for example, and put our new warehouse machinery on display. I would be happy to organize it, if you are all agreeable.'

'An excellent idea, my dear,' Nan said. 'Your offer is accepted.'

'Thank you,' he said, glad to be so warmly praised. It was the perfect opportunity to make amends, just as Mirabelle had said when she pointed it out to him. Whatever stupidities he might have committed once, he was careful to avoid all folly now.

From then on every member of the family was hard at work. Newspaper sales trebled and bookstalls doubled in size as the foundations were dug for the 'wonder of the age' and the amazing cast iron pillars were hoisted into position. And at Henry's invitation Caroline was hard at work too.

As more and more books about the exhibition began to be published, it soon became apparent that Easter's would need somebody to supervise their ordering and delivery. And who better than Caroline?

'I can think of plenty of people,' Caroline said. 'I shan't be any good at all, not after that trial.' And yet the offer was very tempting.

'The trial is over and forgotten,' Henry said. 'Why, it is two years now. I guarantee there won't be a single publisher who will even remember it.' And if they do, he thought, they'll be too busy with the exhibition to say anything.

'But I am pregnant, Henry,' she said, 'and I have Harry and John to look after.'

'Just until October,' he pleaded. 'To help me out, eh?'

'Well,' she said, laughing, 'I never thought to hear you say such things.'

'Then you will do it?'

'If you insist. After all, I *did* promise to obey you.'

In the event Caroline worked until the beginning of November, and after that she took the order books home with her and worked on from her pretty sitting room overlooking the river. Neither she nor Easter's had ever had so much to do.

She was still checking orders on the December afternoon when her third labour began, and although she sent Totty down to Euphemia's house at once to call Taffy Biggs, who'd been installed there for the last two months ready to assist them both, she went on working until her bed was made up and the pains were squeezing hard, one after the other.

The baby was a girl, with very pale skin, an angelic face, and the slightest down of silvery fair hair. They called her Harriet Jane and Henry said the name suited her to a T.

'A perfect choice,' Nan said, when she came to visit the following afternoon, 'for she's just like your mother. Imagine that.'

Caroline couldn't imagine anything nicer. 'I wonder what Pheemy will have?' she said, cuddling all three of her children about her. 'Have you been to see how she is? Taffy went down to see her this morning and she's not back yet so I'm beginning to wonder.'

She didn't have to wonder long, for Euphemia's baby was born that evening, exactly twenty-four hours after his cousin, a lusty red-headed boy, called William Henry.

'I've got so many great-grandchildren I can't count 'em,' Nan said, when the two babies were christened.

'And these two have arrived just in time for the Great Exhibition,' Annie said. 'What a year it's going to be!'

It was also the year of Nan's eightieth birthday, and that was something the family couldn't allow to pass without celebration. At Christmas time Caroline and Euphemia and Henry and Will met together to plan the occasion.

'Let's keep it an absolute secret,' Caroline said, her face full of mischief. 'We'll invite everybody down here and not tell her a word about it, and then we'll tease her down for a birthday tea, as if it isn't going to be anything special, and we'll surprise her with a party.'

'Are we to invite Edward and Mirabelle?' Will wondered.

There was no doubt about it now. 'Of course,' Caroline said.

So the plans were made and the cake ordered and the invitations sent. And Nan was so busy preparing for the Great Exhibition she didn't notice what they were about.

The Crystal Palace opened as planned on the 1 May 1851, on a day of fluttering showers and bright royal sunshine and to an audience of more than half a million people. Naturally enough Nan made sure that her entire family had prestigious seats for the opening ceremony, so they travelled to the Park in a procession.

Harry was so excited by the crush and noise in the streets that day that if his father hadn't held onto him he would have tumbled out of the carriage. And when they reached the park, the sight they saw there lifted them all into a state of amazement and excitement that was every bit as strong as the child's.

The great glass palace stretched out before them as far as the eye could see, every pane flashing diamond fires into the summer air. The flags of the nations flicked and fluttered on tall posts set all along the dazzling length of it, and the great semi-circular curve of its central transept rose miraculously against the warm sky. It was quite stunningly beautiful set among the trees, like something out of an Arabian fairy tale, and it was drawing crowds towards it in bright human streams.

The park was packed with people. There were bare-foot urchins perched in the trees like untidy flocks of sparrows, some of them standing on the branches for an even better view. Below them the visitors were arriving in their thousands, all in their Sunday best and all in a state of rapturous excitement; city clerks all long legs and battered hats; pretty girls bonneted and beribboned; boys on hobby horses and boys with hoops; little girls important in wide skirts and frilled pantaloons; babes in arms with round lollipop faces, all eyes and mouths. Mingling among them were hordes of street traders offering every provision that anyone could possibly desire; gingerbread and fatty cakes, brandy balls, pigs' trotters, and bottles of ginger beer by the truck load. Coster-women carried round wicker sieves piled with oranges, while their menfolk offered trays full of newly cut ham sandwiches. And there were cheapjacks by the score selling 'silver' medals of the Crystal Palace.

'Are we to have a fatty cake, Papa?' Harry wanted to know, as he was lifted down from his father's carriage.

'Presently,' Henry said. 'If you're a good boy. First we are going inside the palace.'

'Really truly?'

'Really truly. Hold on to Mama's hand.'

Nan was already at the door, tickets in hand, with all Matty's children hopping about her. It took the commission-aire several minutes to count them all, but at last he was satisfied and they were allowed into the building.

The dazzle of sunlight inside that vast greenhouse was so extraordinary it took their breath away. The air shone with leaping rainbows and every corner was rich with colour. The great elms were still growing under the glass, just as Mr Paxton had promised they would be, fresh and beautiful and very much alive in their new spring greenery, their topmost branches spanned by the great shining curve of the transept. Huge tapestries embroidered in scarlet and pink and gold hung from the tops of the galleries all around them, and below them the floors were covered with rose pink carpet and every stall was draped with scarlet curtains. There were white statues gleaming at every corner and right in the middle of the building was a magical fountain made entirely of crystal where the tumbling water was as white as snow and burbled and sang as it fell.

Nan had made certain of good seats right at the front of the upper gallery and immediately above the crystal fountain where they would have a perfect view of the arrival of the Queen and Prince Albert, and could watch the court assemble while they waited. And a dazzling court it was, arriving in a multicoloured procession, gentlemen-at-arms in golden helmets and cuirasses; beef-eaters in red suits and black velvet caps; aldermen in scarlet gowns and councilmen in blue ones; archbishops in white lawn sleeves and purple gowns; Egyptians in red fezes; turks in turbans; heralds in splendid blue tabards emblazoned with gold lions. In modest black amongst all that colour, the old Duke of Wellington stood out with his silver hair and his crooked back. It took the best part of an hour for all these peacock people to assemble, but at last they were all in place and everyone was still and the Easter party could see the flash of bright liveries passing the windows of the northern entrance.

The glass palace echoed and re-echoed to the braying of trumpets and the Queen and Prince Albert and their two eldest children were walking straight towards them along their own immaculate stretch of scarlet carpet. Prince Albert was in a Field Marshal's uniform, the little Prince of Wales was in a land dress, the Princess Royal in white lace with a wreath of roses in her hair and the Queen, looking unexpectedly tiny amongst so many people, wore a gorgeous pink satin gown with a diamond tiara in her fair hair. The trumpets were drowned by cheers as every single person in the palace rose to their feet ready to sing the national anthem, and Henry Willis's grand organ cleared its throat ready to play the opening notes.

'There now, what do 'ee think of that?' Nan asked her great-grandchildren.

'Magnificent,' Everard Hopkins said, speaking for them all because he was the eldest and the others were rather overwhelmed.

And magnificent it was.

After the opening ceremony they walked round the exhibition to see all the marvels that had been gathered there, steam turbines and railway engines to thrill the boys; elephants and tigers to delight the girls; halls full of exotic cloth; a gallery of stained glass windows; and rows and rows of curiosities; a bookcase as long as a train; and a looking glass thirty feet tall; and a bed like a cross between a theatre and a Gothic cathedral. In fact, there were so many extraordinary things on display that they didn't manage to see more than a quarter of them, but Nan promised that they would all come back again another day.

'And again and again?' Harry wanted to know.

'And again and again and again.'

They went back three times before the month was out, and the third occasion was on Nan's eightieth birthday.

'An excellent idea,' Caroline said, when Euphemia suggested it at one of Nan's dinner parties. 'We could all come back to Richmond afterwards and have a birthday tea.'

So it was arranged. Nan and Will and Euphemia would take all seven children for an afternoon at the exhibition and then they would all come home by train for Nan's birthday tea.

'And I must say a pot of tea won't come amiss,' Nan said when their train pulled in at Richmond station. 'And here's Tom come to meet us. How very nice. I hope you en't been a-waiting long, Tom.'

'I'd ha' waited a long time for a day like this, mum,' he said. 'Eighty years! My eye!'

And he went on saying 'My Eye!' all the way back to Richmond Hill to the children's giggling amusement.

The house was very quiet, which was a surprise, and the hall was empty, which Nan found rather disappointing because Caroline and Henry were usually waiting there to greet her whenever she arrived, and it seemed odd that they would have forgotten on her eightieth birthday.

'Where are they?' she asked the parlour maid.

But the parlour maid looked at Euphemia as though she wasn't sure what to say. Stupid girl!

'I expect they're in the ballroom,' Euphemia said, taking Everard by the hand and walking up the stairs.

'Tosh!' Nan said. 'They wouldn't be in the ballroom. The dining room, that's where they'll be.' But the dining room was empty, although the table was beautifully set and for a lot of company as far as she could see.

'What are they playing at?' she grumbled to Will as she followed him to the ballroom. 'They're not in there either. You'd hear them if they were.'

But Will had flung open the double doors with a flourish. And the ballroom was full of people, all most beautifully dressed, and all absolutely quiet. For a second she couldn't think what they were all doing there but then the band struck up the opening notes of a song and they all began to sing it. 'Happy birthday to you! Happy birthday to you!' And she knew what a splendid surprise had been prepared for her and stepped forward into the room to receive it, with Harry and little Johnnie leading her by the hand.

The entire Easter family was in the room, Annie and James, fairly beaming at her, and Dotty and her husband and all their children, and Meg and that nice farmer and all theirs. And there was Matilda with Edward and Mirabelle. 'Matilda my dear, I'm so glad to see you here. How's your poor back?' And Henry's brother Sir Joseph, looking comfortable and portly and kissing her so warmly. And his nice wife. What was her name? And Matty and Jimmy, trying to greet their children and kiss her all at the same time. And dear Caroline, holding onto Henry's arm and smiling and smiling at the complete success of her surprise. Oh, it was going to be a wonderful party!

They had tea on the terrace and Nan cut her birthday cake with a little help from Harry. After that they all trouped back into the ballroom and the band played country dances until the children were exhausted.

'How many of them are there?' Nan asked Annie, as the little slippered feet danced and skipped before them.

'Dotty has six now, including the baby,' Annie said, totting them up. 'And there's Meg's seven and Matty's five, and Caroline's three and little William Henry. That's twenty-two, Mama. Twenty-two great-grandchildren.'

'Such a family!' Nan said, quite surprised by the size of it.

'Meg's two oldest boys want to join the firm, you know,' Annie said.

470

'What could be better?' Nan said. 'What *could* be better? Are they old enough to dine with us?'

It appeared that they were and Dotty's oldest daughter with them.

'How they grow up!' Nan said. 'Twenty-two great-grand-children! Imagine that.'

It was a magnificent meal. Nan sat at the centre of the table with Will on one side and Caroline on the other and enjoyed every minute of every dish, especially the first strawberries of the season.

As the sun went down and the servants arrived to light the gas, Henry rose to make a graceful little speech of congratulation.

'At first,' he said, 'I had thought I might compose an ode in honour of this occasion. But I learnt long ago that poetry is not my forte, and anyway I couldn't think of a rhyme for Easter. Then I thought I might tell you all the history of the Easter Empire. But Caroline pointed out that some of you might like to get to bed before seven o'clock tomorrow morning. And anyway, most of you know it already. So I decided that there really wasn't anything that could be said, so perhaps you would accept this little birthday present in lieu, Nan dear. It comes from all of us with our love and gratitude for everything you've done for us over the years.'

It was a very small package and not weighty, so she undid it very carefully. Inside, in a jeweller's case padded with white satin, was a lady's fob watch. It was made of gold and ringed with pearls and the enamelled centre consisted of a single word picked out in blues and greens and purples: 'EASTER'S'. She pinned it to her dress at once.

'Speech!' her family said, applauding and cheering. 'You must make a speech.'

'It's the perfect gift,' she told them. 'I can't think of anything more fitting. "Easter's." How dear you are to think of it.'

'It was Caroline's doing,' Will said. 'She planned it and had it made.'

'I might ha' guessed,' Nan said, patting Caroline's hand. Then she returned to her speech. 'Well now, my dears,' she said. 'You've solved a little problem for me, so you have.' And she looked round the table at them, her old eyes sparkling. 'Ever since Billy's death I've been wondering what the firm ought to be called these days, A. Easter and Sons being inappropriate. Now see. Here's the answer. Caroline's answer. Easter's. We will call it Easter's, like everybody else does. What could be more fitting?'

It was a popular decision, as all their faces showed.

'Now, as I've told 'ee one thing about the firm, I suppose I might as well tell 'ee another. I've been giving a great deal of thought as to what should happen to it when I'm dead and gone.' And even though they groaned, she persisted. 'Can't last for ever, my dears. I've made old enough bones as it is. No, no, my time will come. And when it does I'd like to think the firm was in good hands. So I've made a decision and a will. As from this summer, Easter's will be run by a management committee of eight, all with equal voting rights. It's always been plain and obvious who the eight should be. Henry and Caroline, of course, because they work for the firm, and Edward, for the same reason, with Mirabelle to aid and support him – who better? – and Will and Euphemia, now that Euphemia is an Easter, and Jimmy and Matty for their good sense and compassion. All the London Easters in fact. What do 'ee think to that?'

They approved, clapping their assent and all talking at once, and Nan was glad she'd made her speech sitting down or she'd have had to stand a long time waiting for them to listen again.

But Caroline was on her feet now, holding a piece of paper in her hand. Was she going to make a speech too?

No. She handed the paper across the table to her grandmother, and everybody was attentive, listening for what she was going to say.

'This letter came for you this afternoon,' she told Nan, 'just after you left for Hyde Park. We thought you would like to read it at your party. It's from Buckingham Palace.'

'My heart alive!' Nan said, opening the envelope.

It was an invitation to Mrs Nan Easter to attend a presentation at Windsor Castle in September, with two or three other members of her family, on which occasion Her Majesty Queen Victoria would be pleased to award her with the Prince Albert

Exhibition Medal as a mark of Her Majesty's appreciation for Mrs Easter's distinguished service to the Great Exhibition.

'My dear heart alive!' she said again.

'An honour, upon me life,' Sir Joseph said. 'And richly deserved.'

'Who will you take with you?' Annie asked, leaning across the table towards her mother.

'Why, my three lieutenants, of course,' Nan said. 'Caroline and Henry and Edward. My three lieutenants.'

Chapter 37

The presentation of the Exhibition Medals took place on one of those balmy days when summer and autumn interchange and the world is unexpectedly blessed with the best of both seasons, a warm, richly coloured day, the sky a high clear dome of midsummer blue above the green Surrey fields, and the trees a glory of red and orange and gold.

'Royal weather,' Caroline said as she and Nan and Henry and Edward climbed into her carriage for the short journey from her house to Richmond station. 'And no more than you deserve, my dear, dear Nan.' They all looked very grand in their prescribed finery, the two men in morning dress and the women in splendid silk gowns, Nan's powder-blue and black and adorned with Frederick's cameo brooch and her new Easter fob watch, Caroline's dove-grey and pink, set off by Henry's splendid gift of pearls. She was glowing with animation, her cheeks flushed and those grey eyes sparkling in the strong sunshine. 'Oh, I can't wait to get there!'

'Enjoy the journey first, my darling,' Henry advised, waving to their servants who had gathered on the garden path to see them go. 'Have you got everything you need?' She was so excited she was sure to leave something behind. 'Handkerchief? Smelling salts?'

'Yes, yes,' she smiled at him. 'Everything. You and Nan and my three dear babies and all our family. What more could I possibly want?'

'Then I suppose we may drive on,' Henry said to the coachman.

474

'I don't mind a-comin' back if Mrs Henry *does* forget something,' the coachman confided cheerfully. 'After all, it ain't every day a' the week you sees the Queen, God bless her.'

They went bowling off along Richmond Hill, with the sun warm on their shoulders and the luscious valley of the Thames spreading peacefully below them.

The train was waiting for them in the station, with the station master in excited attendance ready to hand the ladies aboard and add 'my own felicitations to this happy day, ma'am. Which I mean to say you got the weather for it.'

'We have indeed,' Nan said, settling the width of her skirt into the limited space of the corner seat. 'We had it laid on special.'

They were warmed by sunshine all the way to Windsor and the three younger members of the family got steadily more excited as the royal town drew nearer.

'There are so many people travelling today,' Caroline said as they passed yet another crowded train. 'How wise we were to sell books on railway stations.'

'Travel is the passion of the age,' Henry said. 'Pretty soon it will be as easy to travel to Egypt or China, say, as it is to take a train to London.'

'If that's true,' his wife said, 'then perhaps Easter's should be negotiating for bookstalls on continental stations'

And although both men laughed at the idea, Nan took it seriously. 'Why not?' she said. 'A capital notion.'

But then their engine was swaying along the line curving into Windsor itself and there was the castle looming above them, turrets and battlements stone-massive and the royal standard fluttering from its flag-pole like a tethered bird.

By now the sense of occasion seemed to have affected the engine, for it stopped with a flourish of whistles and then spent several seconds screeching like a parrot and emitting huge clouds of white steam into the red and gold girders of the high roof, in a dramatic demonstration of its power. There were porters everywhere, assisting the honoured travellers out of their carriages and into the cabs that would carry them at exorbitant expense the few yards uphill to the palace. The forecourt was full of arrivals, all of them expensively dressed and many of them more than a little anxious. There was no doubt that it was a state occasion.

I have come a long way to be part of such a crowd, Nan thought, as her cab drove them through the stone archway into the courtyard of the palace. 'When I was young,' she said to her three young lieutenants, 'I saw the old French king having his head chopped off. And now the English Queen is a-going to give me a medal.'

'Did you really?' Henry said, impressed by the revelation. 'Were you actually there?'

'Right in the front row,' she said, her old eyes looking inwards at the memory. ''Twas a mortal cold day, I remember. The people danced. And sang. You never heard such singing. And now I'm here.'

'That's progress, Nan,' Edward said. 'What could be better?'

The cab had drawn up before an entrance hung about with flags. 'I saw her grandfather bathing in the sea once,' Nan said. 'The poor old mad King George. Naked as a babe new-born so he was, poor man, and shivering fit to crack his teeth.' How the memories came crowding. 'And her uncle, the Prince Regent, driving about town with his mistress, fat as pigs the pair of 'em. I could tell 'ee some tales about this royal family.'

'I hope to goodness she won't go saying things like that when the medal is presented,' Henry said quietly to Caroline as the old lady was eased out of the cab. 'I had forgotten how unpredictable she is.'

'Never fear,' Caroline said, gathering her skirts delicately together before she stepped out too. 'An indiscretion of that magnitude would be bad for business, and she's far too good a business woman to make such a mistake.'

They followed their grandmother into the palace, through staterooms hung with ancient portraits and windows draped with ancient curtains, in a long subdued procession until they reached an anteroom where they were greeted by half a dozen uniformed flunkeys and asked with silken deference if they would be so good as to wait.

'There's Mr Chaplin,' Nan said, nodding a greeting across

the room, 'and Mr Cubitt, the builder feller. Why, we're all in trade.'

'And what could be more appropriate,' Edward said, 'when the exhibition was laid on to show "the words of industry of all nations"?'

It had been such a splendid summer carnival they'd almost forgotten its origins. 'Well, Easter's is industrious enough, in all conscience,' Nan said, leaning on her stick. 'Especially now with trade picking up so well.'

The procession was on the move again, shuffling slowly through a pair of gilded doors at the other end of the long room, where two more flunkeys were directing people to right and left. They passed a blazing fire, enjoying the wafted heat; conversation reduced from a buzz to a murmur and finally faded away altogether; the skirts of the ladies hissed in rhythm as they glided forward. There was something hypnotic about their progress, something soothing and somnambulent, as if they were no longer part of the world.

It was no surprise to any of them that they emerged into a room of such dazzling splendour that the sight of it made them blink. They were lotus-eaters, dreaming towards magnificence. It was only to be expected.

Two enormous gold chandeliers bore crowns of blazing white candles above their heads, and beneath them, the room was so ornately gilded that it seemed a shimmer of solid gold from one end to the other. There was a throne set at one end, surrounded by a gilded arch and backed by a curtain a-dazzle with gold thread, and a gold-frogged military band at the other, sitting patiently on a gilded plinth, their instruments polished to a gleam. The portraits were gilt-framed, the chairs held out golden arms, and above it all the ceiling was so heavily encrusted with gold that it looked more like a warrior's armour than decorated plaster. An overwhelming room.

The assembled guests shuffled and shifted and were discreetly rearranged by two gently perambulating officials, and then suddenly the doors at the throne end of the room were swung open and there were the Queen and Prince Albert, he tall and formal in his dark morning dress, she in the full glory of the pink and silver gown she'd worn to open the exhibition, diamonds and all.

She made a short speech in a high clear voice, welcoming her guests and thanking them 'each and every one for the sterling service you have done to ensure the success of the Great Exhibition'. Then, while the orchestra played martial airs, she walked along the lines distributing her medals.

Henry and Edward smiled encouragement at Nan and one another, and Caroline tried to wait with suitable patience. They had come so far, she was thinking, all of them, by hard work and endurance and never being infra dig, and now here they were, two men and two women, *two women*, successful in a business world where women weren't supposed to venture, waiting to be honoured by the Queen. She had always said anything was possible, and now after everything, after the trial and brain fever and Uncle Billy's death and everything, she was being proved right. By the time the Queen walked towards them and it was the moment to drop the deep curtsey she'd been practising, she was breathless with the thrill of the occasion.

But Nan was calm, as if she'd been meeting royalty every day of her life, standing very straight and very still, with her gnarled hands resting on the ebony head of her stick, every inch the grand lady.

'Mrs Easter,' the Queen said, swaying gracefully towards her, 'you gave us so much assistance in your stalls and your shops. We could not have spread the word without you, I believe. They tell me that you were the founder of the firm.'

'Yes, Ma'am. I was.' And all so long ago. Nearly sixty years. Walking the streets of Mayfair with her little cart.

'You must be very proud,' the Queen said.

Until that moment it hadn't occurred to Nan to be proud of the firm she'd founded. It was simply a fact of her life, that was all, the firm and the family, the reason for being alive. But, 'Yes, Ma'am,' she said. 'I suppose I am.'

'Quite,' the Queen said. 'So you should be.' And then, as she turned to her equerry to pick Nan's medal from its cushion, she added something that made all four Easters catch their breath, it was so unexpected. 'I believe we have something in common, Mrs Easter, you and I.'

Nan stood still while the medal was pinned to her bodice.

The pause was necessary because she wasn't quite sure what she ought to say. But at last, she ventured, 'Indeed, Ma'am?'

'Yes,' the Queen said, giving the old lady a smile of quite melting sweetness now that the little ceremony was over. 'We have both founded an empire, have we not?'

All Futura Books are available at your bookshop or
newsagent, or can be ordered from the following address:
Futura Books, Cash Sales Department,
P.O. Box 11, Falmouth, Cornwall TR10 9EN.

Please send cheque or postal order (no currency), and
allow 60p for postage and packing for the first book
plus 25p for the second book and 15p for each additional
book ordered up to a maximum charge of £1.90 in U.K.

B.F.P.O. customers please allow 60p for
the first book, 25p for the second book plus 15p per
copy for the next 7 books, thereafter 9p per book

Overseas customers, including Eire, please allow £1.25
for postage and packing for the first book, 75p for the
second book and 28p for each subsequent title ordered.